LONE EAGLE

www.**books**at**transworld**.co.uk/daniellesteel

Also by Danielle Steel

* Published outside the UK under the title PASSION'S PROMISE

Danielle Steel

Lone Eagle

BANTAM PRESS

LONDON • NEW YORK • TORONTO • SYDNEY • AUCKLAND

TRANSWORLD PUBLISHERS
61–63 Uxbridge Road, London W5 5SA
a division of The Random House Group Ltd

RANDOM HOUSE AUSTRALIA (PTY) LTD
20 Alfred Street, Milsons Point, Sydney
New South Wales 2061, Australia

RANDOM HOUSE NEW ZEALAND LTD
18 Poland Road, Glenfield, Auckland 10, New Zealand

RANDOM HOUSE SOUTH AFRICA (PTY) LTD
Endulini, 5a Jubilee Road, Parktown 2193, South Africa

Published 2001 by Bantam Press
a division of Transworld Publishers

A catalogue record for this book is available from the British Library.
ISBNs 0593 046994 (cased)
0593 047001 (tpb)

Printed in Great Britain
by Mackays of Chatham plc, Chatham, Kent

1 3 5 7 9 10 8 6 4 2

To my beloved children,
Beatrix, Trevor, Todd, Nick,
Samantha, Victoria, Vanessa,
Maxx and Zara,
You are the most wonderful
people on earth,
and the best I know,
and I love you with all my heart.

Mom

a thousand years,
a thousand fears,
a thousand tears
we shed
for each other,
like moth
to flame,
a deadly game,
lost children
looking
for their mother,
and when hearts sing,
the music brings
magic
like no other,
the winter cold,
no hands to hold,
the summer
brief
and sunny,
and in the mornings,
pressed
close to you,
cherished moments,
tender, loving,
funny,
we danced,
we laughed,
we flew,
we grew,
we dared,
we cared
more than any soul
could know
or reason,

the light so bright,
the fit so right
for a hundred
precious
seasons,
the moth,
the flame,
the dance
the same,
then broken wings
and treasured
things
in pieces
all around us,
the dream
the only one
i long for,
here or there,
our souls
laid bare,
a million years
from now,
my heart
will
ever
hold you.

LONE EAGLE

PROLOGUE
December 1974

THE CALL CAME when she least expected it, on a snowy December afternoon, almost exactly thirty-four years after they met. Thirty-four years. Extraordinary years. She had spent exactly two-thirds of her lifetime with him. Kate was fifty-one years old, and Joe was sixty-three. And in spite of everything he had accomplished, Joe still seemed and looked young to her. There was a vibrancy to him, an energy, a driving force. He was like a shooting star, trapped in the body and soul of one man, always pushing forward, skyrocketing toward unseen goals. He had vision and brilliance and excitement like no one else. She had seen it from the moment they met. Had always known it. She hadn't always understood it, but from the first, without even knowing who he was, she had known he was different and important and special, and very, very rare.

Kate had felt him in her bones. Over the years, he had become part of her soul. He was not always the most comfortable part of her, or even of himself, but he was a major part of her, and had been for a long time.

There had been clashes over the years, and explosions, peaks and valleys, mountaintops, sunrises and sunsets, and peaceful times. He had been Everest to her. The Ultimate. The place she had always wanted to reach. From the very beginning, he had been her dream. He had been Heaven and Hell, and once in a while purgatory somewhere in between. He was a genius, and a man of extremes.

They gave meaning to each other's lives, and color and depth, and had frightened each other profoundly at times. Peace and acceptance and love had come with age and time. The lessons they had learned had been hard won and hard earned.

They had each been the other's greatest challenge, embodied each other's worst fears. And in the end, they had healed each other. In time, they fit together like two pieces of one puzzle, with no sharp edges and no seams.

In the thirty-four years they had shared, they had found something that few people ever do. It had been tumultuous and exhilarating, and the noise had been deafening at times, but they both knew that it was infinitely rare. It had been a magical dance for thirty-four years, whose steps had not been easy for either of them to learn.

Joe was different from other people, he saw what others could not, and had little need to live among other men. He was happier, in fact, when he kept to himself. And around him, he had created an extraordinary world. He was a visionary who had created an industry, an empire. He had expanded the world. And in doing so, he had stretched horizons beyond what anyone had imagined would be there. He was driven to build, to break barriers, to constantly go farther than he had before.

Joe was in California when the call came that night, and had been there for weeks. He was due back in two more days. Kate wasn't worried about him, she never worried about him anymore. He left and he returned. Like the seasons or the sun. Wherever he was, she knew that he was never far from her. All that mattered to Joe, other than Kate, were his planes. They were, and always had been, an integral part of him. He needed them, and what they meant to him, in some ways more than he needed her. She knew that, and accepted it. Like his soul or his eyes, she had come to love his planes as part of him. It was all part of the miraculous mosaic that was Joe.

She was writing in a journal that day, content in the silence of the peaceful house, as the world outside lay blanketed by fresh snow. It was already dark when the call came at six o'clock, and she was startled by how late it was. When she glanced at her watch at the sound of the phone, she smiled, knowing it would be Joe. She looked much the same as she always had, as she pushed back a lock of dark red hair, and reached for the phone. She knew she would be met instantly by the deep velvet of the familiar voice, anxious to tell her about his day.

"Hello?" she said, anticipating his voice, as she noticed how hard it was still snowing outside. It was a perfect winter wonderland, and would make for a lovely Christmas when the children came home. Both had jobs and lives and people they cared about, of their own. Her world revolved almost entirely now around Joe. It was Joe who lived at the center of her soul.

"Mrs. Allbright?" The voice was not Joe's. She felt disappointed for a moment, but only because she had expected to hear him. He would call eventually. He always did. There was a strange, long pause, almost as though the vaguely familiar voice on the other end expected her to know why he had called. He was a new assistant but Kate had spoken to him before. "I'm calling from Mr. Allbright's office," he said, and then paused again, and without knowing why, she had an odd feeling that Joe had wanted him to call. It was as though she could sense Joe standing beside her in the room, and yet she could not imagine why this man had called her, and not Joe. "I . . . I'm sorry. There's been an accident." At the sound of his words, her entire body went cold, as though she had suddenly been put out naked in the snow.

She knew before he said the words. An accident . . . there's been an accident . . . an accident . . . it was a litany she had once spent a lifetime waiting for, and then forgotten, because Joe had had so many charmed lives. He was indestructible, infallible, invincible, immortal. He had told her when they met that he had a hundred lives, and had only used up ninety-nine. There always seemed to be one more.

"He flew to Albuquerque this afternoon," the voice said, and suddenly all Kate could hear in the room was the sound of a clock ticking. She realized breathlessly that it was the same sound she had heard more than forty years before when her mother came to tell her about her father. It was the sound of time running out, the feeling of falling through space into a bottomless abyss, and she knew she could not ever let herself go back to that place again. Joe would not let this happen to her. "He was testing a new design." The voice went on, sounding like a boy to her suddenly. Why wasn't it Joe on the line? For the first time in years, she felt the hands of terror claw at her. "There was an explosion," he said in a voice so soft she couldn't bear to hear it. The word hit her like a bomb.

"No . . . I . . . there couldn't have been . . . there can't be . . ." She choked on her words, and then froze. She knew the rest before he could say it to her. He no longer had to tell her. She knew what had happened as she could sense the walls of her safe, protected world falling around her. "Don't tell me." They both sat there for a long moment, terrified into silence, as tears filled her eyes. He had volunteered to call her. No one else could bring themselves to pick up the phone.

"They crashed over the desert," he said simply, as Kate closed her eyes and sat there, listening. It hadn't happened. It wasn't happening. He wouldn't do this to her. And yet she had always known it could happen. But neither of them had ever really believed it would. He was too young for this to happen to him. And she was far too young to be his widow. And yet there had been so many others like her in his life, wives of pilots who lost their men testing his planes. Joe had always gone to visit them. And now this boy was calling her, this child, how could he possibly know what Joe had been to her, or she to him? How could he even know who or what Joe was? All he knew was the man who had built the empire. The legend he had been. There was so much more to Joe that he would never know. She had spent half a lifetime learning who Joe was.

"Did someone check the wreckage?" she asked in a voice that trembled beyond her control. Surely, if they did, they would find him, and he would be laughing at them, dust himself off, and call to tell her what had happened. Nothing could ever touch Joe.

The young man on the phone did not want to say that there had been a midair explosion that had lit up the sky like a volcano. Another pilot flying well above him said it had looked like Hiroshima. There was nothing left of Joe but his name.

"We're sure, Mrs. Allbright . . . I'm so sorry. Is there anything I can do for you? Is there anyone there with you?"

She paused, unable to form words. All she wanted to say was that Joe was there with her, and always would be. She knew that nothing and no one could take him from her.

"Someone from the office will call you later, about the . . . uh . . . arrangements," the voice said awkwardly, and all Kate could do was nod. And without another word, she hung up. There was nothing left to say to him, nothing she had to say, or could. She stared out at the snow, seeing Joe. It was as though he were standing right in front of her, just as he had always been. She could still see him the way he had looked the night they met, so long ago.

She could feel panic wash over her, and knew she had to be strong now for him, she had to be the person she had become because of him. He would expect that of her. She could not allow herself to fall into the darkness again, or give in to the terror that loving him had healed. She closed her eyes and said his name softly in the familiar room they had shared.

"Joe . . . don't go . . . I need you . . . ," she whispered as tears rolled down her cheeks.

"I'm right here, Kate. I'm not going anywhere. You know that." The voice was strong and quiet, and so real that she knew she had heard him. He would not leave her. He was doing what he had to do, where he had to be, where he wanted to be, in his own skies somewhere. As he was meant to be. Just as he had been in all her years of loving him. Powerful. Invincible. And free.

Nothing could change that now. No explosion could claim him from her. He was bigger than that. Too big to die. She had to free him once again, to do what he was destined to do. It was to be her final act of courage, and his.

A life without Joe was unimaginable, unthinkable. As she looked out into the night, she could see him slowly walking away from her. And then he turned to smile at her. He was the same man he had always been. The same man she had loved for so long. Just as he was.

The house filled with an immeasurable silence, as Kate sat long into the night, thinking of him. Outside, the snow continued to fall as her mind drifted back to the night they had met. She had been seventeen, and he had been young and powerful and dazzling. It had been an unforgettable moment that had changed her life, as she looked at him, and the dance began.

1

KATE JAMISON SAW JOE for the first time at a debutante ball in December of 1940, three days before Christmas. She and her parents had come to New York for the week from Boston, to do some Christmas shopping, visit friends, and attend the ball. Kate was actually a friend of the debutante's younger sister. At seventeen it was unusual for girls to be included, but Kate had dazzled everyone for so long, and was so mature for her age, that their hosts had found it an easy decision to include her.

Kate's friend had been jubilant, as had she. It was the most beautiful party she'd ever been to, and the room, when she walked in on her father's arm, had been filled with extraordinary people. Heads of state were there, important political figures, dowagers and matrons, and enough handsome young men to flesh out an army. Every important name in New York society was in attendance, and several from Philadelphia and Boston. There were seven hundred people chatting in the elegant reception rooms and an exquisite mirrored ballroom, and the gardens had been tented. There were hundreds of liveried waiters serving them, a band in both the ballroom and the tent outside. There were beautiful women and handsome men, extraordinary jewels and gowns, and the gentlemen were wearing white tie. The guest of honor was a pretty girl, she was small and blond and she was wearing a dress made for her by Schiaparelli. This was the moment she had looked forward to for her entire lifetime; she was being officially presented to society for the first time. She looked like a porcelain doll as she stood on the reception line with her parents, and a crier announced each guest's name as they entered in their evening gowns and tails.

As the Jamisons came through the line, Kate kissed her friend and thanked her for inviting her. It was the first ball of its kind she had been to, and for an instant the two young women looked like a Degas portrait of two ballerinas, as they stood in subtle contrast to each other. The debutante was small and fair, with gently rounded curves, while Kate's looks were more striking. She was tall and slim, with dark reddish auburn hair that hung smoothly to her shoulders. She had creamy skin, enormous dark blue eyes, and a perfect figure. And while the debutante was restrained and serene, greeting each guest, there was an electricity and energy that seemed to emanate from Kate. As she was introduced to the guests by her parents, she met their eyes squarely, and dazzled them with her smile. There was something about the way she looked, and even the shape of her mouth that suggested she was about to say something funny, something important, something that you would want to hear, and remember. Everything about Kate promised excitement, as though her own youth was so exuberant that she had to share it with you.

There was something mesmerizing about Kate, always had been, as though she came from a different place and was destined for greatness. There was nothing ordinary about Kate, she stood out in every crowd, not only for her looks, but for her wit and charm. At home, she had always been full of mischief and wild plans, and as an only child she had kept her parents amused and entertained. She had been born to them late in life, after twenty years of marriage, and when she was a baby, her father liked to say that she had been well worth waiting for, and her mother readily agreed. They adored her. In her earliest years, she had been the center of their world.

Kate's early years were easy and free. Born into wealth, as a small child she had known nothing but comfort and ease. Her father, John Barrett, had been the scion of an illustrious Boston family, and he had married Elizabeth Palmer, whose fortune was even larger than his own. Their families had been immensely pleased with the match. Kate's father had been well known in banking circles, for his good judgment and wise investments. And then the crash came in '29, and swept away Kate's father and thousands like him on a tidal wave of destruction, despair, and loss. Fortunately, Elizabeth's family had felt it unwise to let the pair commingle their fortunes. There had been no children between them for a long time, and Elizabeth's own family continued to handle most of her financial affairs. Miraculously, she was relatively untouched by the crash.

John Barrett lost his entire fortune, and only a very small part of hers. Elizabeth had done everything she could to reassure him, and to help him get on his feet again. But the disgrace he felt ate away at his very foundations. Three of his most important clients and best friends shot themselves within months of losing their fortunes, and it took another two years for John to give way to despair himself. Kate scarcely saw him during those two years. He had closeted himself in an upstairs bedroom, seldom saw anyone, and rarely went out. The bank his family had established, and which he had run for nearly twenty years, closed within two months of the crash. He became inaccessible, removed, reclusive, and the only thing that ever cheered him was the sight of Kate, who was only six then, wandering into his rooms, bringing him a piece of candy or a drawing she had made for him. As though sensing the maze he was lost in, she instinctively tried to lure him out again, to no avail. Eventually, even she found his door locked to her, and in time her mother forbade her to go upstairs. Elizabeth didn't want her to see her father, drunk, disheveled, unshaven, often sleeping the days away. It was a sight that would have terrified her, and broke her mother's heart.

John Barrett took his life almost two years after the crash, in September 1931. He was the only surviving member of his family at the time, and left behind him only his widow and one child. Elizabeth's fortune was still intact then, she was one of the few lucky ones in her world whose life had been relatively unaffected by the crash, until she lost John.

Kate still remembered the exact moment when her mother had told her. She had been sitting in the nursery drinking a cup of hot chocolate, holding her favorite doll, and when she saw her mother walk into the room, she knew something terrible had happened. All she could see were her mother's eyes, and all she could hear was the suddenly-too-loud ticking of the nursery clock. Her mother didn't cry when she told her, she told her quietly and simply that Kate's father had gone to Heaven to live with God. She said that he had been very sad in the past two years, and he would be happy now with God. As her mother said the words, Kate felt as though her entire world had collapsed on top of her. She could barely breathe, as the cocoa spilled from her hands, and she dropped her doll. She knew that from that moment on, her life would never be the same again.

Kate stood solemnly at her father's funeral, and she heard nothing. All she could remember then was that her father had left them because he had been too sad. Other people's words swirled around her afterward . . . heartbroken . . . never recovered . . . shot himself . . . lost several fortunes . . . good thing he hadn't handled Elizabeth's money as well. . . . Outwardly, nothing changed for them after that, they lived in the same house, saw the same people. Kate still went to the same school, and within days after his death, she started third grade.

She felt as though she were in a daze for months afterward. The man she had so trusted and loved and looked up to, and who had so clearly adored her, had left them, without warning or explanation or any reason that Kate could fathom. All she knew and could understand was that he was gone, and in all the profound ways that truly mattered, her life was forever changed. A major piece of her world had disappeared. And her mother was so distraught for the first few months that she all but disappeared from Kate's life. Kate felt as though she had lost two parents, not just one.

Elizabeth settled what was left of John's estate with their close friend and banker Clarke Jamison. Like Elizabeth, his fortune and investments had survived the crash. He was quiet and kind and solid. His own wife had died years before of tuberculosis, he had no children of his own, and had never remarried. But within nine months of John Barrett's death, he asked Elizabeth to marry him. They were married fourteen months after John's death, in a small, private ceremony that included only themselves, the minister, and Kate, who watched with wide, solemn eyes. She was nine at the time.

Over the years, it had proven to be a wise decision. Although she wouldn't have admitted it publicly, out of respect for her late husband, Elizabeth was even happier with Clarke than she had been with John. They were well suited, shared similar interests, and Clarke was not only a good husband to her, but a wonderful father to Kate. Clarke adored Kate, and she him. He worshiped her, protected her, and although they never talked about him, he spent all the ensuing years trying to make up to her for the father she had lost. Clarke was quiet and solid and loving, and took pleasure in the spirit of joy and mischief that eventually rekindled in Kate. And after discussing it with both Elizabeth and Kate, he adopted her when she was ten. At first, Kate had worried that it would be disrespectful to her father, but she confessed to Clarke the morning of the adoption that it was what she wanted most in the world. Her father had slipped quietly out of her life at the moment his own troubles began, when she was six. Clarke provided all the emotional stability Kate had needed after her father's death. There was nothing he denied her, and he was always there for her in every imaginable way.

Eventually, all her friends seemed to forget he wasn't her father, and in time, so did Kate. She thought of her own father quietly sometimes, in rare, solemn moments, but he seemed so far away now that she scarcely remembered him. All she remembered now, when she allowed herself to, was the sense of terror and abandonment she had felt when he died. But she seldom, if ever, allowed herself to think of it. The door to that part of her was closed, and she preferred it that way.

It wasn't Kate's nature to dwell on the past, or cling to sadness. She was the sort of person who always seemed to be propelled toward joy, and created it for others wherever she went. The sound of her laughter, and spark of excitement in her eyes, created an aura of joy wherever she went, much to Clarke's delight. They never spoke of the fact that Clarke had adopted her. It was a closed chapter in Kate's life, and she would have been shocked if anyone had spoken of it to her. Clarke's fathering of her over the past nine years since her father's death, had become part of her so seamlessly that she no longer even thought about it. He was truly her father now in heart and soul, not only in her mind, but his own. In every possible way, she had long since become his child.

Clarke Jamison was a much-admired banker in Boston. He came from a respectable family, had gone to Harvard, and was more than content with his life. He had always been happy that he'd married Elizabeth and adopted Kate. In all the ways that mattered to him, and to them, his life was a success. And certainly in the eyes of the world as well. Kate's mother Elizabeth was a happy woman. She had everything she wanted in life, a husband she loved, and a daughter she adored. Kate had appeared in her parents' lives, just after Elizabeth's fortieth birthday. It had been the greatest joy of her life. All her hopes rested on Kate, she wanted everything wonderful for her. And despite Kate's energy and exuberant personality, Elizabeth had seen to it that she had both impeccable manners and astounding poise. And once she had married Clarke, after the trauma of John's suicide, Elizabeth and Clarke had treated Kate like a small adult. They shared their lives with her, and traveled extensively abroad. They always took her along.

At seventeen, Kate had been to Europe with them every summer, and they had taken her to Singapore and Hong Kong with them the year before. She had been exposed to far more than most girls her age, and as she glided among the guests seeming more like an adult than a young girl, she was enormously composed. It was something one noticed instantly about her. One knew immediately that Kate was not only happy, but totally at ease in her own skin. She could speak to anyone, go anywhere, do almost anything. Nothing daunted or frightened Kate. She was excited by life, and it showed.

The gown Kate was wearing to the debutante ball in New York had been ordered for her from Paris the previous spring. It was entirely different from the gowns the other girls were wearing. Most of them were wearing ball gowns in pastel or bright colors. No one else had worn white, of course, in deference to the guest of honor. And they all looked lovely. But Kate looked more than that, she was elegant and striking. Even at seventeen, everything about her said she was a woman and not a girl. Not in an offensive way, but she seemed to exude a kind of quiet sophistication. There were no frills, no big skirt, no ruffles or flounces. The ice blue satin gown was cut on the bias, and seemed to ripple over her like water, it was almost a second skin, and the straps that held it to her shoulders were barely stronger than threads. It showed off her perfect figure, and the aquamarine and diamond earrings she wore were her mother's and had been her grandmother's before her. They sparkled as they danced in and out of her long dark red hair. She wore almost no makeup, just a little powder. Her dress was the color of an icy winter sky, and her skin had the color and softness of the palest creamy rose. Her lips were bright red and caught your eye as she constantly laughed and smiled.

Her father was teasing her as they left the reception line, and she was laughing with him, with a graceful white-gloved hand tucked into his arm. Her mother was right behind them and seemed to stop every five seconds to chat with friends. Within a few minutes, Kate had spotted the sister of the debutante who had invited her to the party, standing amidst a group of young people, and Kate abandoned her father to meet them. They promised to meet up again in the ballroom later, and Clarke Jamison watched his daughter with pride, as she approached the group of handsome young people, and unbeknownst to Kate, all heads turned. She was a stunning girl. Within seconds, he could see them all laughing and talking, and all the boys looking bowled over by her. Wherever she was, whatever she did, he never worried about Kate. Everyone loved her, and was instantly drawn to her. What Elizabeth wanted for Kate was to find a suitable young man and get married, in the next few years.

Elizabeth had been happy with Clarke for nearly ten years and wanted the same fate for her daughter. But Clarke had been insistent. He wanted Kate to get an education first, and it had been easy to convince her. She was too bright not to take advantage of that fact, although he didn't expect her to work once she got out of school. But he thought she should have every possible advantage, and was sure it would serve her well. She had been applying to colleges all that winter, and would go to college the following year, when she would be eighteen. She was excited about it, and had applied to Wellesley, Radcliffe, Vassar, Barnard, and a handful of others that appealed less to her. And because of her father's history at Harvard, Radcliffe was her first choice. In every possible way, her father was proud of her.

Kate drifted with the others from the reception rooms to the ballroom. She chatted with the young girls she knew, and was introduced to dozens of young men. She seemed perfectly at ease talking to either women or men, and there seemed to be a score of the latter trailing behind her every step of the way. They found her stories amusing, her style exciting, and when the dancing started, they cut in on each other constantly. She never seemed to finish a dance with the same man she had started out with. It was a glittering evening, and she was having great fun. And as always, the attention she got didn't go to her head. She enjoyed it but was very self-contained.

Kate was standing at the buffet when she first saw him, she had been chatting with a young woman who had started Wellesley that year and was telling her all about it. She had been listening intently, when she looked up and found herself staring at him. She didn't know why, but there was something mesmerizing about him. He was noticeably tall, had broad shoulders, sandy blond hair, and a chiseled face. And he was considerably older than the boys who had been dancing attendance on her. She suspected he was in his late twenties as she stopped listening to the girl from Wellesley entirely, and watched Joe Allbright with fascination as he put two lamb chops on a plate. He was wearing white tie like the other men, and he looked strikingly handsome, but there was something uncomfortable about the way he looked, and everything about him suggested that he would rather have been somewhere else. As she watched him make his way along the buffet, he seemed almost awkward, like a giant bird whose wings had unexpectedly been clipped, and all he wanted was to fly away.

He was only inches from her finally, as he held a half-full plate, and he sensed her watching him. Looking down at her from his great height, with a serious air, their eyes met. He stopped moving for a minute, as they watched each other, and when she smiled at him, he almost forgot he was holding the plate. He had never seen anyone like her, as beautiful or as vibrant. There was something fascinating about her, like standing next to something very bright at very close range, or looking into a very bright light. Within seconds, he had to look away. He lowered his eyes, but he didn't move away from her. He found he couldn't move at all, he was riveted to where he stood, and in an instant he looked at her again.

"That doesn't seem like enough dinner for a man your size," she said, smiling at him. She wasn't shy, and he liked that. He had found it difficult to speak to people ever since he'd been a boy. And as an adult, he was a man of few words.

"I had dinner before I came," he explained. He had stayed away from the caviar table, had avoided the vast variety of oysters that had been brought in for the occasion, and had been satisfied with the two lamb chops, a roll and butter, and a few shrimp. It was enough for him. And she could see even in his tailcoat that he was very slim. It didn't fit him as perfectly as it should have, and she suspected correctly that it had been borrowed for the occasion. It was an article of clothing he had never needed in his wardrobe, and he did not expect to wear it again. He had borrowed it from a friend. He had done his best to get out of coming by saying that he didn't have a set of tails. And then had felt obligated to come when his friend had gotten them for him. But with the exception of his brief encounter with Kate, he would have given almost anything not to be there.

"You don't look very happy to be here," she said only loud enough for him to hear. She said it with a gentle smile and a sympathetic air, and he grinned, admiring her.

"How did you guess?"

"You looked like you wanted to hide your plate somewhere and run away. Do you hate parties?" she asked, chatting with him easily, as the girl from Wellesley got distracted by someone else and drifted away.

They seemed to be standing alone in the midst of hundreds of people eddying all around them, and they were oblivious to everyone else.

"Yes, I do. Or I think I do. I've never been to one like this." He had to admit, he was impressed.

"Neither have I," she said honestly, but in her case it was not due to preference or lack of opportunity, but to age. But there was no way Joe could have known. She looked so relaxed and was so mature that if someone had asked, he would have guessed her to be somewhere in her early twenties and closer to his age. "It's pretty, isn't it?" she said, glancing around and then back at him. And he smiled, it was, but he hadn't thought of it that way. All he had been thinking of since he arrived was how many people were there, how hot and crowded it was, and how many other things he would have preferred doing. And now, looking at her, he wasn't as sure the party was the total waste of time he had deemed it to be at first.

"It is pretty," he said, as she noticed the color of his eyes. They were the same as hers, they were a dark almost sapphire blue. "And so are you," he said unexpectedly. There was something so direct about the compliment he had paid her, and the way he looked, that it meant more to her than all the elegant words of the dozens of young men who had been paying court to her. And although visibly ten years younger, they were far more socially adept than he. "You have beautiful eyes," he said, fascinated by them. They were so clear and so open and so alive, and so brave. She looked as though she were afraid of nothing. They had that in common, but in very different ways. If anything, this evening was one of the few things that had frightened him. He would rather have risked his life, which he did often, than tackle a group like this. He had been there for less than an hour when he met her, and the party had already worn thin for him, and he was hoping to leave soon. He was waiting for his friend to tell him they could leave.

"Thank you. I'm Kate Jamison." She introduced herself, as he shifted his plate to the other hand, and extended his right hand to her.

"Joe Allbright. Do you want some food?" He was direct and clear, and spare in what he said. He only said what he felt he needed to. He had never been one for flowery words. And she had not yet taken a plate at the buffet. As she nodded, he handed one to her. She took very little, some vegetables, and a small piece of chicken. She wasn't hungry, she'd been too excited all night to eat. Without saying a word, he carried her plate for her, and they walked to one of the tables where the others were dining, and found two seats. They sat down in silence, and as he picked up his fork, he looked at her, wondering why she had befriended him. Whatever the reason, it had improved his evening immeasurably. And hers.

"Do you know a lot of the people here?" he asked, without glancing at them, only at her. She was picking at her food, as she smiled at him.

"Some. My parents know more than I do," she explained, surprised by how uncomfortable she felt with him. It was unusual for her, but it felt as though everything she said counted, and as if he were listening to every inflection in her voice. Being with him didn't have the light, easy feeling that she had with other men. There was something startlingly intense about him. With Joe, it was as though all the frills and subterfuge were stripped away, and what you were left with was very real.

"Are your parents here tonight?" He seemed interested as he ate one of the shrimp.

"Yes. Somewhere. I haven't seen them in hours." And she knew she wouldn't for several more. Her mother had a way of settling into corners with a few close friends, and whiling away the evening, without even dancing. And Kate's father always stayed close to her. "We came down from Boston for the party," she offered to further the conversation, and he nodded.

"Is that where you live?" he asked, eyeing her carefully. There was something about her that mesmerized him. He wasn't sure if it was the way she spoke, or the way she looked at him. She looked calm and intelligent, and interested in what he was saying. He wasn't comfortable with people paying such close attention to him. And beyond her obvious intelligence and poise, she was exquisite looking. He loved just looking at her.

"Yes. Are you from New York?" she asked, abandoning her chicken. She wasn't hungry, the evening was too exciting to be bothered with eating. She'd rather talk to him.

"Originally, no. I'm from Minnesota. I've been living here for the past year. But I've lived all over the place. New Jersey. Chicago. I spent two years in Germany. I'm going out to California after the first of the year. I go wherever there's an airstrip." He seemed to expect her to understand that, and she looked at him with increased interest.

"Do you fly?" For the first time, he looked genuinely amused by her question, and he seemed to relax visibly as he answered her.

"I guess you could say that. Have you ever been up in a plane, Kate?" It was the first time he had said her name, and she liked the way it sounded. He made it seem personal, and she was pleased that he had remembered. He looked like the sort of man who would forget names with very little effort, and anything else that didn't hold his interest. But he was fascinated by her and had noticed everything about her even before they met.

"We flew to California last year, to take the ship to Hong Kong. Usually, we travel by train, or ship."

"It sounds like you've done some traveling. What took you to Hong Kong?"

"I went with my parents. We went to Hong Kong and Singapore, but up till then we'd just gone to Europe." Her mother had seen to it that she spoke Italian and French, and a smattering of German. Her parents thought it would be useful for her. Her father could easily imagine her married to a diplomat. She would have been the perfect ambassador's wife, and unconsciously he was grooming her for it. "Are you a pilot?" she asked, with wide eyes, which betrayed her youth for once. And he smiled again.

"Yes, I am."

"For an airline?" She thought him both mysterious and interesting, and watched as he unwound his long limbs, and sat back in his chair for a moment. He was like no one else she had ever met, and she wanted to know more about him. He had none of the obvious polish of the boys she knew, and at the same time there was something enormously worldly about him. And for all his shyness, she could sense a deep sense of confidence about him, as though he knew he could take care of himself anywhere, at any time, in any circumstance. There was an underlying innate sophistication about him, and she could easily imagine him flying an airplane. To her, it seemed very romantic and powerful.

"No, I don't fly for an airline," he explained. "I test planes, and design them, for high speed and endurance." It was more complicated than that, but it was all he needed to tell her.

"Have you ever met Charles Lindbergh?" she asked with interest. Joe didn't tell her he was wearing his tails, and had come to the party with him, although his mentor had been reluctant to come too. Anne was at home, caring for a sick baby. Joe had lost Charles in the crowd at the beginning of the party. Joe suspected he had gone to hide himself away somewhere. Charles hated parties and crowds, but had promised Anne he would go. And in her absence, had invited Joe for moral support.

"I have. We've done some work together. We did some flying in Germany while I was there." He was why Joe was in New York now, and had arranged for Joe's work in California. Charles Lindbergh was his mentor and friend. They had met on an airstrip in Illinois years before, it was at the height of Lindbergh's fame, and Joe had been just a kid then. But in flying circles now, Joe was nearly as well known as Charles. He just wasn't as well known to the public or as openly acclaimed. But Joe had been breaking records consistently in recent years, and some flying buffs thought that Joe was an even better pilot. Lindbergh had said it himself once, it had been the high point of Joe's life until that moment, and even since then. The two men had great admiration for each other, and were friends.

"He must be a very interesting man . . . and I hear she's very nice too. That was such an awful thing that happened to their baby."

"They have a number of other children," Joe said, wanting to dispel the potential emotion of the moment, but Kate was startled by the comment. To her, that didn't seem as though it would make a difference. She couldn't imagine the horror it must have been for them. She had been nine years old when it happened, and she still remembered her mother crying at the news and explaining it to her. It had sounded terrifying to Kate, and still did, and she felt very sorry for them. To her, the agony of it seemed to outweigh even his accomplishments, and it intrigued her that this man actually knew them.

"He must be an amazing man," Kate said simply and Joe nodded. There was nothing he could add to the adulation the world had for Lindbergh, and as far as Joe was concerned, he deserved it. "What do you think of the war in Europe?" Kate asked Joe then, and he grew pensive. They both knew that the draft had been voted in by Congress nearly two months before, and the implications of that could not be ignored.

"Dangerous. I think it will get out of hand if it doesn't end soon. And I think we're going to be in it before we know it." The Blitz had begun in August with nightly bombing raids over England. The RAF had been bombing Germany since July. He had been to England to consult on the speed and efficacy of their planes, and he knew how vital their air force was going to be to their survival. Thousands of civilians had already died. But Kate was quick to disagree with him, which intrigued him. She was definitely a woman with her own opinions, and a strong mind.

"President Roosevelt says we're not going to get involved," she said firmly. She believed him, as did her parents.

"With the draft already in place, do you believe that? Don't believe everything you read. I don't think we'll have a choice sooner or later." He had thought of volunteering for the RAF, but the work he was doing with Charles was more important for the future of American aviation, particularly if the U.S. got into the war. He thought it was vital for him to be home now, and Charles had agreed with him when they discussed it. It was why Joe was going to California. Lindbergh was afraid that England could not hold out against the Germans, and he and Joe wanted to do all they could to prepare the U.S. to help if they entered the war, although Lindbergh was violently opposed to the U.S. joining the war.

"I hope you're wrong," she said softly. If he wasn't, it meant that all the handsome young men standing around the room would be in grave danger. The entire world, as they knew it, would be profoundly challenged, and ultimately changed. "Do you really think we'll enter the war?" she asked, looking worried, forgetting their surroundings for an instant, and thinking of far more serious matters. The war had already spread in Europe to a frightening degree.

"Yes, I do, Kate." She loved the way he looked at her when he said her name. There were a great many things she liked about him.

"I hope you're wrong," she said quietly.

"So do I."

And then, she did something she had never done before, but she felt comfortable with him. "Would you like to go into the ballroom and dance?" She felt suddenly as though she had found a friend, but Joe looked uncomfortable at the suggestion, and stared down at his plate, before glancing back at her. He was not in his element here.

"I don't know how," he said, looking slightly embarrassed, and much to his relief, she didn't laugh at him, but she looked surprised.

"You don't? I'll teach you. It's pretty easy, you just shuffle around and look like you're having a good time." Dancing with her, that part at least would be simple, but not the rest.

"I think I'd better not. I'd probably step on your feet." He glanced down and saw that she was wearing delicate pale blue satin evening shoes. "I should probably let you go back to your friends." He hadn't spent as long talking to anyone in years, and surely not a girl her age, although he still had no idea that she was only seventeen.

"Am I boring you?" she asked bluntly, with a look of concern. She felt as if he was dismissing her, and she wondered if she had offended him by asking him to dance.

"Hell, no," he said laughing, and then looked even more embarrassed by what he'd said. He was far more used to airplane hangars than to ballrooms, but all things considered, he was actually having a good time. And no one was more surprised than he. "You're anything but boring. I just thought you might like to dance with someone who can dance." He and Charles had that in common too. Charles also didn't dance.

"I've already danced a lot this evening." It was nearly midnight, she hadn't gone to the buffet until then. "What do you like to do in your spare time?"

"Fly," he said with a shy smile. It was easy being with her, and talking about airplanes was all he knew how to do. "What about you?"

"I like to read, and travel, and play tennis. And in the winter, I ski. I play golf with my father, but I'm not very good at it. And I used to love to skate when I was a little kid. I would have played hockey, but my mother had a fit and wouldn't let me."

"That was smart of her, you'd have wound up with no teeth." Clearly, from her dazzling smile, he could see that she hadn't played hockey. "Do you drive?" he asked, as he sat back in his chair. For a crazy moment, he was wondering if she'd like to learn how to fly. But Kate smiled.

"I got my license last year when I turned sixteen, but my father doesn't like me to use the car. He taught me at Cape Cod in the summer. There's no traffic and it's easier there." Joe nodded but looked startled by what she'd said.

"How old are you?" He had been sure that she was in her mid-twenties. She looked so grown-up, and she was so at ease with him.

"Seventeen. I'll be eighteen in a few months. How old did you think I was?" She was flattered that he looked so surprised.

"I don't know . . . maybe twenty-three . . . twenty-five. They shouldn't let kids your age out in dresses like that. You're going to confuse some old man like me." He didn't look old to her, especially when he looked shy and awkward and boyish, which he often did. Every few minutes, he would look ill at ease for an instant, and look away, and then he'd recover himself and look her in the eye again. She liked his shyness. It was an interesting counterpoint to his flying expertise, and suggested humility.

"How old are you, Joe?"

"Twenty-nine. Nearly thirty. I've been flying since I was sixteen. I was wondering if you'd like to fly with me sometime. But I guess your parents might not like it."

"My mother wouldn't. But my father would think it was fun. He talks about Lindbergh all the time."

"Maybe I could teach you to fly someday." As he said it, his eyes were filled with dreams. He had never taught a girl to fly before, although he knew plenty of female pilots, he and Amelia Earhart had been old friends before she disappeared three years before, and he had flown with Charles's friend Edna Gardner Whyte several times, Joe thought her nearly as impressive as Charles. She had won her first daredevil solo race seven years before, and was training military pilots. She was very fond of Joe.

"Do you ever come to Boston?" Kate asked hopefully, looking suddenly young again, as he smiled. There was something exciting and feminine and youthful about her, and at the same time, he found her remarkably poised.

"Once in a while. I have friends on the Cape. I stayed with them last year. But I'll be in California for the next few months. I could give you a call when I get back. Maybe your father would like to come with us too."

"He'd love that," she said warmly. To Kate, it sounded like a fine idea. All she could think of now was how they would sell it to her mother. But who knew if he'd really call her. Probably not.

"Do you go to school?" he asked with a curious expression, and she nodded. He had stopped his formal education at twenty, and the rest of his education he had gotten in planes, once Lindbergh took him under his wing.

"I'm going to college in the fall," Kate said quietly.

"Do you know where?"

"I'm waiting to hear. I want to go to Radcliffe, my father went to Harvard. I'd go there too, if I could. But Radcliffe is close enough. My mother wants me to go to Vassar, which is where she went. I've applied there too. But I don't like it quite as much. I think I'd rather stay in Boston anyway. Or maybe Barnard here in New York. I like New York too. Do you?" Her eyes were wide as she asked him, and he was touched.

"I'm not so sure. I'm kind of a small-town guy," but as he said it, she wasn't sure she agreed. It was where his roots were, but something about him suggested that he had outgrown small-town living more than he knew. He had become part of a much larger world, he just hadn't realized it himself yet, but she did.

They were still chatting about the virtues of Boston and New York when her father wandered over and she introduced him to Joe.

"I'm afraid I've been monopolizing your daughter," Joe said, looking anxious. He was afraid Clarke Jamison was going to be annoyed with him because of her age, but it had been so easy talking to her. They had been sitting together for nearly two hours, when her father appeared.

"I can't say that I blame you," her father said pleasantly. "She's good company. I wondered where she was, but I can see she's been in good hands." He thought Joe seemed intelligent and polite, and when he heard his name, he was undeniably surprised. Clarke knew from what he'd read of him in the papers that he was a flying ace of considerable note, and wondered how he had happened on Kate, and if she knew who he was. Next to Lindbergh, he was one of the best, although less famous than he, but not by much. Clarke knew he had won cross-country flying races in Dutch Kindelberger's famous P-51 Mustang.

"Joe offered to take us flying sometime. Do you think Mom would have a fit?"

"In a word, yes," her father laughed, "but maybe I can talk her into it." And then he turned to Joe, "That's very kind of you to offer, Mr. Allbright. I'm a great admirer of yours, that was quite a record you broke recently."

Joe looked embarrassed at Clarke Jamison's praise, but pleased that he had known. Unlike Charles, Joe succeeded in avoiding the limelight whenever he could, but it was getting harder than ever after his recent feats.

"It was a great flight. I tried to get Charles to come along, but he was busy in Washington with the National Advisory Committee for Aeronautics."

Clarke nodded, impressed, and a lively discussion ensued about war developments in Europe, as Kate's mother joined them. She said it was getting late, and she wanted to go home. And a moment later, Clarke introduced Joe to his wife. He seemed shy, but very polite. And it was obvious that they were all ready to leave. Without a moment's hesitation, as they wandered toward the door, Clarke handed Joe his card. "Call us if you ever come to Boston," he said hospitably, and Joe thanked him. "We'll see if we can take you up on your offer, or if nothing else, I will." And with that, he gave Joe a wink, and the younger man laughed, as Kate smiled. Her father seemed to like Joe a lot. A moment later, Joe shook hands with her father, and said he was going to see if he could find Charles. He knew his mentor didn't like parties any better than he did, he was probably hiding somewhere, and it was hard to find anyone in the crowd. There were still at least five hundred people there, wandering between the house and the heated tent outside. And then, after saying goodnight to her mother, Joe turned to Kate.

"I enjoyed having dinner with you," he said with eyes that bored into hers. They were like deep blue glowing coals. "I hope to see you again sometime." He sounded as though he meant it, and she smiled. Of all the people she had met that night, he was the only one who had impressed her, by quite a lot. There was something very rare and remarkable about him, and she knew by the end of the evening that she had met an extraordinary man.

"Good luck in California," she said softly, wondering if their paths would ever cross again. She was not at all sure he would call. He didn't seem like the type. He had his own world, his own passion, considerable success in his field, and it was unlikely that he would pursue a seventeen-year-old girl. In fact, she was almost certain, just from talking to him, that he would not.

"Thank you, Kate," he answered. "I hope you get into Radcliffe. I'm sure you will. They'll be lucky to have you, whether your father went to Harvard or not." He shook her hand then, and this time it was Kate who lowered her eyes under the intensity of his gaze. It was as though he were examining her in every detail, to carve her into his memory. It was an odd feeling, but as he did it, she felt irresistibly drawn to him by a force that was impossible to resist.

"Thank you," she whispered. And then, with a small awkward bow in her direction, he turned, and disappeared into the crowd to look for Charles.

"He's a remarkable man," Clarke said admiringly, as they slowly made their way out, and retrieved their coats at the door. "Do the two of you know who he is?" He then proceeded to fill Kate and her mother in on his exceptional feats, and the records he had broken in the past few years. Clarke seemed to know them all.

As they got in the car, Kate stared out the window, thinking of the time she had spent talking to him. The records he had broken had meant nothing to her although she admired him for it, and realized that he was important and accomplished in the rarefied atmosphere in which he lived. But it was the very essence of him that drew her to him. His power, his strength, his gentleness, even his awkwardness had touched her in a way no one else ever had. She knew at that very moment, without question, that he had taken some part of her with him, and what was troubling her as she looked out the window, was that she had no idea if she'd ever see him again.

2

AFTER THE GLITTERING debutante ball at Christmas, as Kate had suspected, she didn't hear from Joe Allbright. Despite the card her father had given him, he didn't call. She read about him, and made a point of looking for news of him, and she saw his name in the newspapers, and even newsreels of him when he won races from time to time. He had broken several records in California, and had won acclaim for the latest plane he'd designed with the help of Dutch Kindelberger and John Leland Atwood. She knew now that Joe's flying was legendary, but he was off in his own world, far from hers, and had undoubtedly forgotten her.

He seemed entirely part of another life, light-years from hers. And she was certain now that she would never see him again. For the rest of her life, she would read about him, and remember the hours she'd spent talking to him one night when she was a young girl.

In April, she was accepted at Radcliffe, and her parents were ecstatic, as was she. The war was not going well in Europe, and they talked about it constantly. Her father still insisted that Roosevelt would not allow the United States to get involved, but nonetheless, accounts of what was happening were disturbing, and two of the young men she knew had gone to England and joined the RAF. The Axis had begun a counteroffensive in North Africa, and General Rommel was relentlessly winning battles with the Afrikakorps. In Europe, Germany had invaded Yugoslavia and Greece, and Italy had declared war on Yugoslavia. And in London, there were as many as two thousand people being killed per day in Luftwaffe raids.

As a result of the war, they could no longer go to Europe in the summer, so for the second year, they spent their entire summer on Cape Cod instead. They had a house there, and Kate had always enjoyed it. She was particularly excited this summer, as she was going to college in the fall. And her mother was grateful that she wouldn't be going far away. Cambridge was just across the river, and Kate and her mother got everything ready before they left for the Cape, where they were planning to stay until Labor Day. And Clarke was going to come up on the weekends, as he always did.

It was a summer of tennis and parties, and long walks on the beach with friends. Kate swam in the ocean every day, and met a very nice boy who was going to Dartmouth in the fall, and another who was going into his junior year at Yale. They were all healthy young people, with bright minds and good values. And a large group of them played everything from golf to croquet and badminton on the beach, and more often than not the boys played touch football while the girls watched. It was a long, easy summer, and the only dark shadows were provided by the news from Europe, which was more worrisome every day.

The Germans had taken Crete, and there was heavy fighting in North Africa and the Middle East. The British and Italians were fighting air battles over Malta. And in late June, the Germans had invaded Russia, and taken them completely by surprise. And a month later, Japan had penetrated into Indochina. It was a summer of fierce battles, and bad news from all over the world.

When Kate wasn't thinking about the war, she was thinking about going to Radcliffe. It was only days away, and she was even more excited than she let on. A lot of her friends from high school had opted not to go to college. She was more the exception than the norm. Two of her friends had gotten married after graduation, and three more had announced their engagement that summer. At eighteen, she already felt like an old maid. In a year, most of them would have babies, and even more of her friends would be married. But she agreed with her father, she wanted to go to college, although she hadn't decided what to major in yet.

If the world had been different, she would have liked to study law. But it was too great a sacrifice to make. She knew that if she chose a law career, it was unlikely that she would ever be able to marry. It was a choice one had to make, and law as a career was not a woman's world. She was going to study something like literature or history, with a minor in Italian or French. If nothing else, she could always teach one day. But other than law, there were no careers that particularly fascinated her. And both her parents assumed that she would get married when she finished school. College would just be something interesting for her to do while she waited for the right man.

Joe's name came up after she met him, once or twice in the ensuing months, not as a prospect for her, but for something new or important he'd achieved. Her father took even greater interest in him now that he'd met him, and reminded Kate of him more than once. But she needed no prompting, she had never forgotten him, nor heard from him either. He was just a very interesting person she'd met, and eventually her fascination with him began to pale. Her other pursuits, like college and her friends, were far more real.

It was the last weekend of the summer, the Labor Day weekend, when she and her parents went to a party they attended every year, usually after they returned from their summer trip. It was a barbecue given by their neighbors in Cape Cod. Everyone in the area went, there were children and old people, and families, and their hosts built an enormous bonfire on the beach. She was standing in a group of her co-horts, toasting marshmallows and hot dogs, when she took a step back from the flames, and backed into someone she hadn't seen. She turned to apologize for stepping on their feet, although she knew it couldn't have hurt much. She was wearing shorts and bare feet. And as she looked up at her victim, she saw in amazement that it was Joe Allbright. And as soon as she saw him, she just stared at him and couldn't speak, as she clutched her stick of flaming marshmallows and he grinned.

"You'd better watch that, before you set someone on fire."

"What are you doing here?"

"Waiting for a marshmallow," he said, "yours look a little over-cooked." They were turning to ash on the stick, as she stared at him, unable to believe he was standing there. He looked happy to see her, and in khaki pants and a sweater, he looked like a kid. And his feet were bare too.

"When did you come back from California?" she asked, feeling an instant rapport with him again. It was as though they were old friends, and both of them seemed suddenly oblivious to the people they were with. She had been in a group of young people, and he had driven up to the Cape with an old friend.

"I didn't come back from California," he smiled at her, obviously pleased that they'd met. "I'm still out there, I guess I will be for the rest of the year. I'm just here for a few days. I was going to call your father on Tuesday, and make good on my offer. Are you in school?"

"I start next week." She could hardly keep her mind on his words. He looked tanned and handsome, his hair had gotten blonder, and she could see how powerful his shoulders were in his sweater instead of the borrowed tails. He was even better looking than she remembered, and she felt suddenly tongue-tied with him, which was most unlike her.

And to her, he still looked like a giant earthbound bird, with his long arms, and his slightly nervous shuffling. But he seemed far more comfortable now with her. He had thought of her often, and this was a far easier setting for him. And as he chatted with her, she was still holding her burned stick with the marshmallows, which were not only burned now, but cold. With a gentle gesture, he took the stick from her, and tossed it into the fire.

"Have you eaten yet?" he asked, taking control of the situation.

"Just marshmallows," she said with a shy smile, as he stood near her, and his hand inadvertently brushed hers.

"Before dinner? Shame on you. How about a hot dog?" She nodded, and he reached for a stick, and took two hot dogs off a tray and put them on the stick. And then held them in the fire. "So what have you been up to since last Christmas?" he asked with interest.

"I graduated. I got into Radcliffe. That's about it." She knew everything he'd been doing, or the records he'd broken at least. She'd read about him in the papers, and her father talked about him a lot.

"That's good. I knew you'd get into Radcliffe. I'm proud of you," he said, and she blushed. But fortunately it was already dark as they stood on the beach, in the fine white sand that was cool on their feet.

He seemed more confident to her than he had eight months before. Or maybe that was just because they had already met. What she didn't know was that he had thought of her so often, that they were already friends in his mind. He had a way of running scenes and situations and people through his head, like a film, until they became familiar to him.

"Have you been driving?" he asked with a grin.

"My father says I'm a terrible driver, but I think I'm actually pretty good. I'm better than my mother. She smashes up the car all the time," Kate said, smiling back at him.

"Maybe you're ready for flying lessons then. We'll have to see about that when I come east again. I'm moving back to New Jersey at the end of the year, to consult on a project with Charles Lindbergh. But I have to finish up in California first." She didn't know why, but she was thrilled to hear that he was coming back to the East. And she knew that was foolish, there was no reason to think that he'd see her. He was a thirty-year-old man, and enormously successful in his own field. She was just a college girl, and not even that yet. This time, knowing who he was, she was even more impressed than she had been the first time. And it was she who felt shy. Joe was much more comfortable than he had been at the party where they first met. "When do you start school, Kate?" he asked, almost as though she were his little sister. Although, like Kate, he was an only child. They had that in common. Both his parents had died when he was a baby. He had been brought up by cousins of his mother's, whom he readily admitted he hadn't liked, and he felt hadn't liked him.

"This week. I have to move in on Tuesday," she said in answer to his question.

"That's very exciting," he said, as he handed her a hot dog.

"Not as exciting as what you've been doing. I've been keeping up with you in the papers." He smiled at her as she said it, flattered that she had even remembered him. They had each thought of the other often, but it would have been awkward to admit. "My dad is your biggest fan." Joe still remembered how interested he had been in Joe when he met him, and knew quite a lot about him. Unlike Kate, who had just thought him a nice person, and had had no idea what a hero he was.

They finished their hot dogs, and sat down on a log to drink coffee and eat ice cream. It was being served in cones, and Kate was dripping hers all over, while Joe sat back and watched her as he sipped his coffee. He loved looking at her, she was so beautiful and so young and so full of energy and life. She was like a beautiful young Thoroughbred gamboling and prancing, and tossing her mane of dark red hair over her shoulders. Never in his early life had he ever suspected he would know someone like her. The women he had known over the years had been so much plainer and more subdued. She was like a bright shining star in the heavens, and he couldn't take his eyes off her, for fear he'd lose sight of her.

"Do you want to go for a walk?" he asked finally, when she'd cleaned up the mess from her ice cream. She nodded as she smiled at him.

They walked quietly down the beach for a while, with a nearly full moon shining brightly on the water. They could see everything on the beach, and they walked side by side, comfortably close together, silent for a time.

After a while, he looked up at the sky, and then down at her, and smiled. "I love flying on nights like this. I think you'd like it too. It's like being close to God for a little while, it's so peaceful." He was sharing with her what mattered most to him. He had thought of her once or twice when he flew night flights, and couldn't help musing how nice it would have been to have her with him. And then he told himself he was crazy. She was just a kid, and if he ever saw her again, she probably wouldn't even remember him. But she had, and they felt like old friends. It seemed like a gift of destiny that they had met again. And in spite of what he'd told her, he hadn't been at all sure that he'd have the courage to call her father, and had been leaning against it. Meeting her at the barbecue had solved the problem for him.

"What made you fall in love with flying?" she asked him as they began to walk more slowly. It was a beautiful warm night, and the sand felt like satin under their feet.

"I don't know . . . I always loved airplanes, even when I was a little kid. Maybe I wanted to run away . . . or get so high above the world no one could touch me."

"What were you running away from?" she asked softly.

"People. Bad things that had happened, and feeling bad about them." He had never known his parents, and the cousins who had taken him in when they died had been hard on him. There was no love lost between them. They had always made him feel like an interloper. And by the time he was sixteen, he had left them. He would have left sooner if he could. "I've always liked being alone. And I like machines. All the little bits and pieces that make them work, and the details of engineering. Flying is like magic, it puts all those things together, and the next thing you know, you're in Heaven, way up in the sky."

"You make it sound wonderful," she said, as they stopped and sat down on the sand. They had gone a considerable distance, and they were tired.

"It is wonderful, Kate. It's everything I ever wanted to be and do when I grew up. I can't believe they pay me to do it now."

"That's because you're obviously very good at it." He hung his head for a moment, in humility, and she was touched by what she saw and sensed in him.

"One day, I'd like you to fly with me. I won't scare you, I promise."

"You don't scare me," she said calmly. He was sitting very close to her, and it frightened him more than it did Kate. What frightened him most were his own feelings. He was intrigued by her. And just being next to her drew him like a magnet. He was twelve years older than she, she was from a wealthy family, one of considerable stature, and she was going to Radcliffe.

He didn't belong in her world, and he knew it. But it wasn't her world that drew him to her, it was who she was, and how at ease he felt with her. He had never known any woman like her. Not even the ones his own age. In all his years, he had dated a number of women, most of them the ones who hung around airstrips, or girls he met through other pilots, usually their sisters. But he'd never had anything in common with any of them. There had only been one woman he had seriously cared about, and she had married someone else, because she said, she was lonely all the time, he had no time to spend with her. He couldn't imagine Kate being lonely, she was too full of life and too self-sufficient, it was that which attracted him to her. Even at eighteen, she was a whole person. From what he could see, there were no pieces missing, no needs he was expected to fill and couldn't, no expectations or reproaches. She just was who she was, and was on her own path, like a comet, and all he wanted was to catch her as she flew by.

She told him then about wishing she could go to law school, but having to give up the dream, because it wasn't a suitable career for a woman.

"That's silly," he responded. "If that's what you want, why don't you do it?"

"My parents don't want me to. They want me to go to school, but then they expect me to get married." She sounded disappointed. It seemed so boring to her.

"Why can't you do both? Be a lawyer and get married?" It sounded sensible to him, but she only shook her head, as her hair swirled around her, like a dark red curtain. It added to the sensual quality about her, which he had been fervently resisting. He had done a good job of it, she didn't even sense that he was attracted to her. She just thought he was being friendly and kind.

"Can you imagine a man who would let his wife practice law? Anyone I'd marry would want me to stay home, and have children." It was just the way things were, and they both knew it.

"Is there someone you want to marry, Kate?" he asked, with more than a little interest. Maybe she'd met someone since Christmas, or had known him before. He didn't know that much about her.

"No," she said simply, "there isn't."

"Then why worry about it? Why not do what you want till you meet the right man? It's like worrying about a job you don't even have yet. Maybe you'd meet a nice guy in law school." And then he turned to her with a question. Their legs were barely touching as they stretched them out before them, but he didn't try to hold her hand, or put an arm around her. "Is getting married that important?" He hadn't even come close to it, at thirty. And she was just eighteen. She seemed to have a lifetime ahead of her for marriage and babies. It was odd to hear her talk of it, like a career path she had chosen, rather than an inevitable outcome of what she felt for someone. He wondered if that was the way her parents saw it. It was certainly not uncommon. But unlike most women, who seemed more clandestine to him, she was so open about it.

"I guess marriage is important," she answered thoughtfully, "everyone says it is. And I suppose it will be to me one day. I just can't imagine it right now. I'm not in a hurry. I'm glad I'm going to college first." It was a reprieve for her, from her mother's plans for her. "I won't even have to think about it for four years, and by then who knows what will happen."

"You could run away and join the circus," he said, pretending to be helpful, and she laughed at him, lay back on the soft sand, and rested her head on one arm flung behind her. He had never seen anyone as beautiful, as he looked at her in the moonlight. He had to remind himself of how old he was, and that she was just a child. But she didn't look like one as she lay there, she was very much a woman. He looked away from her for a long moment, to regain his composure. Kate didn't have the remotest inkling of what was in his mind.

"I think I'd like being in the circus," she said to the back of his head, as he observed the night sky. "When I was a little girl, I thought the costumes were terrific. And the horses. I always loved the horses. The lions and tigers scared me."

"They scared me too. I only saw the circus once, in Minneapolis. I thought it was too noisy. And I hated the clowns, I didn't think they were funny." It was so like him that it made her smile. She could imagine him as a serious little boy, overwhelmed by all the action. And the clowns had always seemed too obvious to her too. She preferred greater subtlety, as did he. As different as they were, they had a number of things in common. And always, just under the surface, that irresistible magnetic pull.

"I never liked the smells at the circus, but I think it would be fun to live with all those people. There would always be someone to talk to." He laughed as she said it, and turned to look at her. It seemed so typical of the little he knew of her to like the people. It was one of the many things that drew him to her, her ease with people. He had never had that gift, and admired it in her. But to her it was natural and instinctive, an integral part of her.

"I can't think of anything worse. That's why I like flying so much. No one I have to talk to, as long as I stay in the air and off the ground. On the ground, someone always wants to tell me something, or have me tell them. It's exhausting." There was actually a look of pain in his eyes as he said it. There were times when conversation was actually painful to him. He wondered if that trait was peculiar to pilots. He had taken several long flights with Charles, when they had literally not said a word to each other, and were comfortable with it. They had only spoken, finally, once they had landed and opened the door to the cockpit. It had been a perfect flight for both of them. But Joe couldn't imagine Kate sitting in silence for eight hours. "I find people very draining. They expect so much of you. They misunderstand what you say, they take your words and twist them. Somehow, they always make things complicated instead of simple." It was an interesting insight into him.

"Is that how you like things, Joe?" she asked gently. "Quiet and simple?" He nodded in answer. He hated complications. And he knew that was what most people thrived on, but not he.

"I like things simple too," she said, pondering what he had just explained to her. "But I'm not so sure about quiet. I like talking and people, and music . . . and noise sometimes. I hated my parents' house at times when I was a kid, because it was so quiet. They were older and pretty sedate, and I had no one to talk to. And it was as though they always expected me to be a grown-up, just shorter. I wanted to be a kid, and get dirty and make noise and break things and mess up my hair. Nothing was ever messy at our house. It was always so perfect. That's a lot to live up to." He couldn't even imagine it. He had lived in utter chaos in his cousins' house, where everything was constantly a mess, the house was always dirty, and their kids were never cared for. When they were little they cried constantly, and when they were older, they argued, and were always loud. He hadn't been happy till he left. They were always telling him what was wrong with him, how much trouble he was, and threatening to send him to other cousins. He hadn't gotten attached to anyone, he had always been too afraid that they'd send him away anyway, so there was no point caring too much about them. And he had been that way ever since, with other men, and even with women, especially with women. He was happiest when he kept to himself.

"You have the life that everyone thinks they want, Kate. The trouble is they don't really know what it would be like if they had it. In some ways, I imagine it could be oppressive." She had painted a picture of rigidity and perfection. But it was also a safe environment provided for her by people who loved her, and she knew that. But she was looking forward to going to college and getting away from them. She was ready. "What would you do if you had kids? What would be different?" It was an interesting question, and made her think for a minute.

"I think I'd love them a lot, and let them be who they are, not who I wanted them to be. I wouldn't want them to be me, just themselves. And I'd let them do more of what they wanted. Like you. If they wanted to fly, I'd let them. I wouldn't worry about how dangerous it is, or how crazy, or tell them it's inappropriate, and they had to do what I expected. I don't think parents should have the right to do that, to force people into molds just because it's what they did." Clearly, she was longing for freedom. It was what he had wanted all his life too. There were no fetters strong enough to bind him. He would have broken any chain, any bond, anything that held him. He not only wanted, but *needed* his freedom, for his survival. It was something he knew he would never give up, for anyone, or anything.

"Maybe it was easier for me, not having parents." He told her then about his parents dying in a car wreck when he was six months old, and going to live with his cousins.

"Were they nice to you?" she asked, looking sad for him. It didn't sound like a happy story, and it hadn't been.

"Not really. They used me to do the chores, and baby-sit for their kids. I was just another mouth to feed. And when the Depression hit, they were glad to see me leave. It made things easier for them. They never had any money." And she had never known anything but luxury and security and comfort. The Depression hadn't touched her family financially, or her mother at least. Kate had never known anything but a safe, entirely protected existence. She couldn't even begin to imagine what Joe's life had been like. For him, flying meant freedom. She had never had that, or even longed for it. All she wanted was just a little more leeway than they gave her. She didn't have the same need for freedom he did.

"Do you want to have kids one day?" she asked him, wondering how that fit into the scheme of things for him, or if it was unimportant. He was old enough to have at least thought about it.

"I don't know. I never give it much thought, if any. Maybe not. I don't think I'd be much of a father. I'd never be there, I'm too busy flying. And kids need a father. I'd probably be happier if I didn't have kids. If I did, I'd always be thinking about what I didn't do for them, and feel bad about it."

"Do you want to be married?" She was fascinated by him, she had never known anyone even remotely like him, or as honest. They had that in common. They spoke their minds and their hearts, with no fear of what other people would think of them. It was rare for him to open up, as he did with her, but he had nothing to hide and nothing to apologize for to her. He had left no debris in his wake, and had never hurt anyone, that he knew of. Even the one girl he had cared about, who had left him, hadn't done so in anger. She had left when she realized that he simply could not be there for her. There were other things that were more important to him, but he had never hidden that from her.

"I've never known a woman who could fit into what I was doing, without being unhappy about it. I think flying is kind of a solitary life, for most people. I'm not sure how Charles manages being married, but he's not home much. I guess Anne keeps busy with her children. She's a great woman," and had suffered so unbelievably. Kate's heart still went out to her. "Maybe if I found someone like her," Joe smiled at Kate, they were friends now, "but that's not likely. She's one in a million. I don't know, I don't think I've ever thought I was cut out for marriage. You have to do what you want in life, and be who you are. You can't force yourself to be someone you're not. It doesn't work. That's when people get hurt. Badly. I won't do that to anyone, or to myself. I need to do what I'm doing and be who I am." Listening to him made her think she should go to law school. But she knew how upset her parents would be. He was on his own in the world, and always had been. He had no one to answer to, or to please, but himself. Her life was entirely different. She carried the burdens of all her parents' hopes and dreams on her shoulders, and she would never have done anything to hurt or disappoint them. She couldn't do that to them. Particularly not after what her father had done to them.

They sat together in silence for a while longer, just relaxing and enjoying each other's company, and thinking of what they had said to each other. It was all so honest, and open. There was no artifice and no pretense, and as different as they were, and their lives had been, they

44

were powerfully attracted to each other. They were like the opposite sides of the same coin.

Joe was the first to speak, as he turned to look at her again, lying peacefully on the sand, staring up at the moon. He hadn't dared to lie down beside her, for fear of what it would make him feel for her. It was better to keep a little distance between them. It was the first time he had ever felt that, but her pull was as strong as the tides, and he knew it, as he sat close to her.

"I guess we should go back. I don't want your parents to get worried, or send the police after me. They probably think you've been kidnapped." She nodded, and sat up slowly. She hadn't told anyone where she was going, or with whom, but she knew that several people had seen her leave. She wasn't sure if they'd recognized Joe leaving with her, but she had offered no explanations, and hadn't bothered to go and find her parents to tell them. She'd been afraid that her father would want to come with them, not out of any distrust of Joe, but because he liked him so much.

Joe gave her a hand and helped her to her feet, and they walked back quietly toward the bonfire they could still see far, far down the beach. She was surprised at how far they had walked, but it had been easy beside him. And halfway there, she slipped a hand into his arm, and he pressed his arm closer to his side, and smiled down at her. She would have made a great friend, except that, much to his chagrin, he wanted more than that from her. But he wasn't going to let that happen and give in to his feelings. He was in no position to do that. And in his eyes, she deserved better than he had to give. With all her ease and beauty, she seemed far out of his reach.

It took them half an hour to get back to the party, and they were both surprised to find that no one had missed them, or even noticed they were gone.

"I guess we could have stayed longer," Kate said, smiling at him, as he handed her a mug of coffee, and helped himself to a glass of wine. He very rarely drank, because he was always flying. But he knew he wouldn't be that night.

Joe knew he couldn't have kept her away from the party any longer. He was not sure he trusted himself with her. What he felt for her was too powerful and too confusing, and he was almost relieved when her parents came to find her, because they were leaving. Clarke Jamison was delighted to see Joe.

"What a pleasant surprise, Mr. Allbright. When did you come back from California?"

"Yesterday," Joe smiled, after shaking hands with Kate's parents. "I'm just here for a few days. I was going to call you."

"I wish you would. I'm still hoping to catch a ride with you one of these days. Maybe next time you're here."

"That's a promise," Joe assured him. He thought they were very nice people. They left Kate alone with him for a few minutes, to say good-bye, and went to thank their hosts, who were old friends. And then Joe turned to her, with an odd expression. There was something he wanted to ask her, he'd been thinking about it all evening. He wasn't sure if it was appropriate, or if she'd have time once she started Radcliffe. But he had decided to ask her anyway, he had already told himself that it would be safe for both of them, which was something of a delusion. But above all things, he didn't want to mislead her, or tempt himself more than he could tolerate. He was grateful now for the distance between them, physically at least. "Kate," he suddenly looked shy again, and she saw it. "What would you think about writing to me from time to time? I'd love to hear from you."

"Would you?" she asked, looking surprised. After all he'd said about not getting married and not having kids, she knew he wasn't pursuing her. She was almost sure now that all he wanted from her was friend-

46

ship. In some ways, that felt safe to her, in others, she was disappointed. She was very attracted to him. And he had said nothing to indicate that he reciprocated those feelings. Just from talking to him, Kate had guessed that Joe was a master at concealing what he felt.

"I'd like to hear about what you're doing," he said benignly, which was a cover for the unrest she caused in him. But he knew enough not to show it, at least not to her. "I'll tell you all about my test flights in California, if that's not too boring."

"I'd love it." And from the sound of it, she could pass the letters on to her father. He'd enjoy them too.

Joe scribbled his address on a piece of paper, and handed it to her. "I'm not much of a writer, but I'll do my best. I'd like to keep in touch, and hear how school is going." Joe hoped he sounded, if anything, more like an old friend, or an uncle, anything but a suitor or a potential husband. He had been extremely honest with her, or so she thought. But there were some things he had failed to mention to her, like how drawn he felt to her, and how much he feared that. If he let himself, he might lose himself to her, and the one thing he knew was that he would never let that happen. If he could channel their feelings into friendship, there would be no risk and no danger for either of them. But whatever happened, he knew he didn't want to lose her. This time, he wanted to stay in touch with her.

"You have my father's card with our address at home. And as soon as I know it, I'll send you my address at Radcliffe."

"Write to me as soon as you have it." That meant he would be hearing from her as soon as he got back to California, which was exactly what he wanted. He hadn't even left her yet, and he was already hungry for more of her. It was a terrifying situation, but one he couldn't seem to keep away from. He was pulled toward her like a light in the darkness, a warm place he wanted to be near.

"Have a safe trip back," she said, hesitating for the merest instant, as their eyes met and held and volumes were said without words, which was all Joe had wanted. He could never find the right words anyway.

A few minutes later, she walked over the dunes to meet her parents, and disappeared from sight as he watched her go. She stopped at the top, and waved at him, as he waved back. Her last sight of him was standing tall, his eyes fixed on hers, with a serious expression. And after she was gone, he walked slowly down the beach again alone.

3

THE FIRST WEEKS AT SCHOOL were frantic for Kate. She had books to buy, and classes to attend, professors to meet, an advisor to work out her schedule with, and a house full of girls to get acquainted with. It was a huge adjustment for her, but within days, she knew she loved it. She didn't even bother to go home on the weekends, much to her mother's dismay. But at least, she tried to make an effort to call them from time to time.

She'd been at school for three weeks before she finally wrote to Joe. It wasn't that she hadn't had time before that, but she had wanted to wait until she had some interesting tales to tell him. And by the time she sat down at her desk, on a Sunday afternoon, she had plenty of stories about school. She told him about the other girls, her professors, her classes, the food. She had never been as happy in her life as she was at Radcliffe. It was her first taste of freedom, and she was loving it.

She didn't tell him about the Harvard boys she'd met the week before, it seemed inappropriate, and was not something she wanted to share with him. There was one, a junior, Andy Scott, whom she liked very much, but he paled in comparison to Joe, who had become her standard of perfection for all men. No one else was as tall or as handsome, or as strong, or as interesting, or as accomplished, or as exciting. He was a tough act to compare anyone to, and Andy looked like water to wine, when she compared him to Joe Allbright. But he was fun to be with, and he was captain of the Harvard swimming team, which impressed the other freshman girls.

Instead, she told Joe everything she was doing, and how happy she was there. Her letter, when he received it, was excited and exuberant and ebullient, all the things he loved most about her. And he sat down immediately when he got the letter, and answered her, telling her about his latest designs, and his latest victory over a previously insoluble problem. He told her of his most recent test flights. But he avoided telling her of a boy who had died the day before, in a test flight over Nevada. He had been scheduled to do the flight himself, but had reassigned it so he could attend a meeting. It was Joe who had had to call the boy's wife, and he was still feeling depressed about it. But he kept his letter to her light and filled with as much news and excitement as he could muster. And when he finished it, he was frustrated with himself. His letter seemed so dull in comparison to hers, his gift with words so much less facile. But he sent the letter to her anyway, and wondered how long it would take her to answer.

She got his letter exactly ten days after she had sent hers, and sat down to write to him over the weekend. She turned down a date with Andy Scott, so she could stay in her room and write Joe a long, newsy letter, and all of her roommates told her she was crazy. But her heart was already engaged by the flyer in California. She didn't tell them who he was, or even much about him. She just said he was a friend, and told Andy that she had a headache. And nothing in her letter indicated that she had anything but feelings of friendship for him. She said nothing to give herself away, and she painted a number of amusing portraits for him, with clever words. He sat at his desk laughing out loud when he read her letter. Her description of college life was hilarious. She had a knack for seeing, and describing, the most outrageous elements of almost every situation. And he loved hearing from her.

Their letters went back and forth through the fall, and grew more serious as the war continued to worsen in Europe. They exchanged opinions and concerns, and she respected his views on the situation. He continued to believe that America would enter the war at any moment, and he was thinking of going to England again, to consult with the RAF. He said Charles had gone to Washington, and to meet with Henry Ford, who shared his point of view about the war. And then he attempted, at least, to amuse her as she did him. He was beginning to spend his days anticipating her letters, and anxious for them to come.

It was two months later, the Tuesday before the Thanksgiving weekend, when she got a phone call in the house she lived in on campus, and assumed it was her parents. She was going home the next day, and her mother probably wanted to know what time to expect her. They were having guests for Thanksgiving, and it was going to be a busy weekend. She had seen Andy for a quick cup of coffee the day before, and he had told her he was going home to New York over Thanksgiving but would call her from there. She had had dinner with him once or twice over the past two months, but it hadn't gone anywhere. She was far too intrigued with her exchange of letters with Joe, to be interested in a college junior. Joe was far more exciting than any man she'd ever met.

"Hello?" she said, expecting to hear her mother's voice, and was startled to hear Joe on a remarkably clear connection from California. The girl who had taken the call had spoken to the operator, but she hadn't bothered to tell Kate that the call was long distance and not from her mother. It was the first time he had ever called. "What a surprise!" she said, blushing intensely, but fortunately he couldn't see it. "Happy Thanksgiving, Joe."

"The same to you, Kate. How's everything at school?" He made reference to some outrageous story she had told him, and they both laughed. But she was surprised by how nervous she felt speaking to him. Something about their letters had made them both more vulnerable, and unwittingly more open to each other, and it was odd now talking to him.

"Everything's fine. I'm going home tomorrow. Actually, I thought you were my mother. I'm going to be home all weekend." She had already written that to him, but it was something to say in the silence on the line.

"I know." At his end, he was as nervous as she was. He felt like a kid again, in spite of all his efforts to appear confident with her. "I was calling to see if you'd like to have dinner." He held his breath while he waited for her answer.

"Dinner?" She sounded suddenly off balance, ". . . Where? . . . when? . . . are you coming in from California?" She felt breathless as she asked.

"I'm already here actually. This trip came up at the last minute. Charles is in town, and I needed some advice from him. I'm having dinner with him tonight, and I could come up from New York sometime this weekend." In truth, he could have waited for his mentor's advice, but he had wanted an excuse to come east, and had conveniently found it. He told himself it didn't mean anything, he was just coming to see a friend, and if she was too busy to see him, he would go back to California. But he hadn't asked her before he'd come east, because he thought it might be more compelling if he was already there when he called. It had been a clever ploy, and an effective one, but in truth he didn't really need it. She would have been thrilled to see him, and tried to keep her voice steady and unaffected as she answered.

"When do you want to come? I'd love to see you." It was the voice of a friend, not of a woman who revered him. They were both playing their parts well, though not without a certain degree of challenge. This was new to him, and to her too. She had never had a grown man pursue her, and he had never before had these terrifyingly unfamiliar feelings for anyone.

"I can come up anytime you want," he said, sounding free and easy, and she thought about it for a minute. She wasn't sure if it was the right thing to do, or how her mother would feel about it, but she thought her father might be pleased, so she decided to risk it.

"Would you like to join us for Thanksgiving?" She held her breath after she asked him, and there was a brief pause at the other end. He sounded as surprised by her invitation as she had been to hear from him.

"Are you sure that would be all right with your parents?" He didn't want to intrude on them, or cause a problem. But he had no plans to be with the Lindberghs or anyone else for Thanksgiving. He was used to spending it alone.

"I'm sure," she said bravely, praying her mother wouldn't be too angry. But they had other guests, and even though he was shy, Joe would be an interesting addition to the dinner. "Would that work for you?"

"I'd like that very much. I could fly up on Thursday morning. What time do you eat dinner?"

She knew that guests had been invited for five in the afternoon, and they would be eating dinner at seven. "The other guests are coming at five, but you can come earlier if you need to." She didn't want him to have to hang around the airport all afternoon, waiting to come for dinner.

"Five will be perfect," he said serenely. He would have come at six in the morning if she'd told him to. He didn't know why, but he was anxious to see her. After years of emotional solitude, he was deaf, dumb, and blind to his own feelings. "Is it very formal?" he suddenly asked nervously. He didn't want to appear in a suit if everyone else would be wearing a tuxedo. And if he needed one, he would have to borrow one from Charles, and send it back to him.

"No, my father usually wears a dark suit, but he's pretty stuffy. You can wear whatever you've brought with you."

"Great, I'll wear my flight suit," he teased her, and she laughed.

"I'd like to see that," she said, and meant it.

"Maybe we can arrange for a short flight for you and your father this weekend."

"Just don't tell my mother. She'll choke on her turkey, and make you leave halfway through dinner."

"I won't say a word. See you on Thursday." He sounded remarkably relaxed as she said goodbye to him, but as they both hung up the phone, they each found that their palms were sweating. She still had to tell her mother he was coming for dinner.

She broached the subject gingerly the following afternoon when she got home, and found her mother checking the china in the kitchen. She was well known for the beautiful table she set, and her elaborate flower arrangements. And she was distracted when Kate first walked into the kitchen, trying to assess her mother's mood.

"Hi, Mom. Need a hand?" Her mother looked over her shoulder in surprise. Kate was always the first to escape when she thought her mother needed help in the kitchen. She always said that domestic duties bored her, and they were demeaning.

"Did you flunk out of school?" her mother said with a look of amusement. "You must have done something really awful if you're offering to help me count china. How bad is it?"

"Couldn't it be that I'm just more mature now that I'm in college?" Kate said with an imperious look, and her mother pretended to think about it for an instant.

"That's possible, but very unlikely. You've only been there for three months, Kate. I think maturity starts to happen junior year, and doesn't come full-blown until you're a senior."

"Great. Are you telling me that after I graduate, I'll actually *want* to count china?"

"Absolutely. Particularly if you're doing it for your husband," her mother said firmly.

"Mom . . . okay, okay. I did something in the spirit of what you always tell me Thanksgiving is about." Kate looked innocent as she faced her mother.

"You killed a turkey?"

"No, I invited a homeless friend for dinner. Not homeless, but family-less." It sounded reasonable to both of them the way she said it.

"That's sweet, darling. One of the girls in your house at Radcliffe?"

"A friend from California," she hedged, trying to soften up her mother before she told her.

"It's perfectly understandable she can't go home. Of course you can invite her. We have eighteen people coming here for dinner, and there's plenty of room at the table."

"Thanks, Mom," Kate said looking relieved, at least they had room for him. "By the way, it's not a girl." Kate held her breath and waited.

"It's a boy?" Her mother looked startled.

"Sort of."

"From Harvard?" Her mother looked genuinely pleased. She loved the idea of Kate dating a boy from Harvard, and it was the first she'd heard of it. And only three months into the school year.

"He's not from Harvard," Kate dove into the icy water, "it's Joe Allbright."

There was a long pause as her mother looked at her with eyes full of questions. "The pilot? How did you happen to hear from him?"

"He called me out of the blue yesterday. He's visiting the Lindberghs, and he had nothing to do on Thanksgiving."

"Isn't it a little odd that he would call you?" Her mother looked suspicious.

"Maybe." She didn't tell her about the letters, it was hard enough to explain why she had invited him for Thanksgiving. She wasn't even sure why herself, but she had. And now she had to find some plausible reason to explain it.

"Has he called you before?"

"No, he hasn't," she was able to say honestly. Her mother didn't ask if he'd ever written to her. "I think he just likes Dad, and maybe he's lonely. I don't think he has any family. I don't know why he called, Mom, but when he said he had no plans for Thanksgiving, I felt sorry for him. I didn't think you and Dad would mind. It's kind of the spirit of Thanksgiving," she said blithely, and helped herself to a carrot from the icebox. But her mother wasn't entirely taken in, she knew her better, although she'd never seen her daughter look quite like that. But at fifty-eight, she hadn't entirely forgotten what it felt like to be wooed by an older man when you were young, or to be smitten. But something about Joe Allbright worried her. He was so remote and so aloof, and at the same time so intense. He was the kind of man who, if he turned his full attention on you, could be overwhelming. And even if Kate didn't understand that, because she had no experience with it, her mother did, and that was precisely why she was worried about him.

"I don't mind if he comes to dinner," Elizabeth Jamison said honestly, "but I mind very much if he's pursuing you, Kate. He's a lot older than you are, and not the sort of person I think you should fall in love with." How did one decide those things, who to fall in love with, and who not? And how could one control it? But Kate only nodded at her mother.

"I'm not in love with him, Mom. He's just coming to eat turkey."

"Sometimes that's how those things start, by being friends and becoming too familiar," her mother warned her.

"He lives in California," Kate said blandly.

"I'll admit, that makes me feel better. All right, I'll tell your father. And I hate to say it, but he'll be delighted. But I swear, if he offers to take your father up in some dangerous plane with him, I'll put arsenic in his stuffing. And you can tell him I said so."

"Thanks, Mom," she beamed at her mother, and wandered nonchalantly out of the kitchen.

"I thought you were going to help me!" her mother called after her just before the kitchen door closed.

"I have a paper due on Monday, I'd better get started on it!" she shouted back, but her mother wasn't fooled. The look in Kate's eyes after her mother had said Joe could come to dinner absolutely terrified her. She had had that look in her own eyes only once, when a friend of her father's had secretly courted her and broken her heart, but fortunately her parents had discovered it and intervened before anything too awful had happened. And she had met Kate's father only weeks later. But now she was worried about Kate and Joe Allbright. She spoke to Clarke about it quietly in their bedroom later that evening. She told him about Joe coming to Thanksgiving dinner, but he didn't share her fears about him.

"He's just coming to dinner, Elizabeth. He's an interesting man. He's not foolish enough to run after a girl of eighteen. He's a handsome guy, he could have any woman he wanted."

"I think you're being naïve," she said wisely. "She's a beautiful girl, and I think she's fascinated by him. He's a very romantic figure. Half the women in this country would be happy to run after Charles Lindbergh, and I'm sure some of them have tried. Joe has the same kind of mystique and charm. All that aloofness and his being a pilot make him seem like a romantic figure to a young girl."

"Are you afraid that Kate is running after him?" Her father looked startled. She had a good head on her shoulders, and her mother wasn't giving her credit for it.

"Possibly. Actually, I'm far more concerned that he may be running after her. Why did he call her at school, and not you at the office?"

"All right, I'll grant you, she's a lot prettier than I am. But she's a sensible girl, and he appears to be a gentleman."

"What if they fall in love with each other?"

"Worse things could happen. He's not married. He's respectable. In fact, very much so. He has a job. And no, he's not a banker in Boston. But that could happen, you know. She may meet a man who isn't a doctor or a lawyer or a banker. She could meet an Oriental or an Indian prince, or even a Frenchman or worse yet, a German, at Harvard, and she could wind up living halfway around the world. But we can't keep her locked up at home forever. And if Joe Allbright turns out to be the one, if he makes her happy and is good to her, I can live with it. He's a good man, Elizabeth, and I honestly don't think that's going to happen."

"What if he dies in a plane crash and leaves her widowed with a house full of babies?" her mother said, sounding panicked, and he smiled.

"What if she marries a boy who works at the bank and he gets run over by a streetcar . . . worse yet, what if he treats her badly, or she marries him just to please us. I'd rather she marry someone who really loves her," he said to his wife calmly, but she looked even more upset.

"Do you think he's in love with her?" she asked in hushed tones.

"No, I don't. I think he's probably a lonely guy with nowhere to go for Thanksgiving, and knowing our daughter, she felt sorry for him. I don't think either of them is in love with the other."

"That's what Kate said, that she felt sorry for him."

"See? Mark my words," he said, putting his arms around her. "You're worrying for nothing. She's a good girl, with a soft heart, just like her mother." Elizabeth sighed, and tried to tell herself Clarke was right, but the next day, when Joe appeared, Kate did not look sorry for him.

She looked vivacious and beautiful and excited to see him. And Joe looked dazed as he followed Kate into the dining room and sat down beside her. And as Clarke drew him out during dinner and urged him to talk about his planes, Kate sat watching him, looking awestruck. Elizabeth looked anything but reassured as she saw the looks of ease and admiration that passed between them, and she very definitely had the impression that they knew each other better than either of them was admitting. They seemed unusually comfortable with each other as they chatted side by side.

The letters had created an aura of ease between them that was impossible to conceal from her parents, and Kate didn't try. It was obvious that she and Joe were friends, and equally so that they were attracted to each other. But Elizabeth also had to admit, to herself at least, that he was intelligent, well mannered, and charming, and he treated Kate with kindness and respect. But there was something about him that frightened her mother. There was something cold about him, and withdrawn, and almost frightened, as though he had been wounded at some point in his life, and some part of him was badly hurt. In some ways, no matter how friendly he was, he seemed just out of reach.

And when Joe spoke of flying, it was with such passion, that Elizabeth couldn't help wondering if his love for flying was something any woman could compete with. She was willing to believe he was a good man, but not necessarily the right one for Kate. Liz didn't think Joe had the makings of a good husband. His life was full of danger and risk, which wasn't what she wanted for Kate. She wanted her to have a comfortable, happy life, with a man who wanted to do nothing more dangerous than step outside the house to pick up the morning paper. Elizabeth had protected Kate all her life, from danger, from harm, from illness, from pain, but the one thing she couldn't protect her from, she feared now, was heartbreak. Kate had had more than enough of that when her father died. And Elizabeth knew that if Joe and Kate fell in love, there was no way she could protect her daughter. He was far too alluring, and far too exciting. Even his reticence was appealing, it made one want to reach out and help him over the walls he had built around himself. And she could see Kate do it at dinner. She was making every effort to put him at ease and draw him out.

Kate wanted to make him comfortable, and help him feel at home. She didn't even know she was doing it. And as Elizabeth watched them, she knew the worst had already happened. More than Kate herself even knew, her mother sensed correctly that Kate already loved him. What Liz was not sure of was what Joe felt for her. Attraction certainly, and a kind of magnetic pull that he was having trouble resisting, but what lay beyond that, no one knew, not even Joe at this point. Elizabeth felt certain that whatever he felt for Kate, he was trying to resist, but without success.

And as they left the dinner table, her husband whispered to her reassuringly, as he put an arm around her shoulders. "You see, they're just friends . . . I told you . . ." Clearly, he didn't see what she did.

"What makes you think so?" she said sadly.

"Look at them, they're talking like old friends. He treats her like a child most of the time. He teases her like a little sister."

"I think they're in love with each other," she said, as they hung back for a moment from the others. They had had a nice group of friends to dinner, and Joe had been a valuable addition. It wasn't his dinner table conversation that concerned her, but his intentions about Kate.

"You're an incurable romantic, my love," Clarke said, and then kissed her.

"No, I'm not unfortunately," she said sensibly. "I think I'm being a cynic, or maybe just a realist. I don't want him to hurt her, and he could. Very badly. I don't want that to happen to her."

"Neither do I. Joe wouldn't do that to her. He's a gentleman."

"I'm not so sure of that, and he's a man, in any case. And a very romantic figure. I think he's every bit as intrigued by her as she is with him, but there's something about him that seems wounded. He doesn't like to talk about his family, and his parents died when he was a baby. God only knows what happened to him as a child, and what scars lie too deep to be seen. And why isn't he already married?" They were normal questions for a parent to ask, but Clarke still thought she was unduly worried.

"He's been busy," Clarke reassured her, as they walked into the living room to join their guests. Kate and Joe were sitting in a corner, deep in conversation, and as her mother looked at them, she knew without a question. They were oblivious to everyone else in the room, and he looked as though he would have died for her, and she for him. It was already too late. All Elizabeth could do now was pray.

4

ON FRIDAY, after Thanksgiving, Joe had picked Kate up at the house and spent the afternoon with her. They had gone for a walk in the Boston Garden, and afterward went to tea at the Ritz. Kate kept him amused the entire time with stories about their trip to Singapore and Hong Kong, and then regaled him with their adventures in Europe. Anyone who had ever flown with him, wouldn't have recognized him. He was more talkative with her than he had ever been in his life, and they spent the entire afternoon laughing.

He took her to dinner that night, and then they went to a movie. They saw *Citizen Kane,* and they both loved it. It was nearly midnight when he took her home, and Kate was yawning when she said goodnight to him.

"I had a wonderful time," she smiled up at him, and he looked down at her with a look of pleasure.

"So did I, Kate." He seemed about to say something more to her, and then didn't. And a moment later, she went inside, and ran into her mother at the top of the stairs. She had just been to the kitchen to check on something.

"Did you have fun?" her mother asked, trying not to look worried. She wanted to ask her what Joe had said, and done, had he kissed her, or done anything he shouldn't. But she was taking her cues from her husband, and didn't press Kate about it.

"I had a really nice time, Mom," Kate said, looking peaceful. She loved being with Joe more than she had ever thought she would enjoy anyone. It was hard to believe this was only the fourth time she'd ever seen him. But their exchange of letters over the past three months had brought them infinitely closer. They felt like old friends, and Kate had no sense of the years between them. He seemed more like a kid at times than an adult.

"Are you seeing him tomorrow?" Kate could have lied to her, but she didn't want to, and she nodded. "He's not taking you flying, is he?"

"Of course not," Kate said. He hadn't mentioned taking her flying all day. He was going back to California on Sunday.

Her mother wished her goodnight then, and Kate walked back to her own room, looking thoughtful. She had a lot to think about, mostly to figure out how she felt about Joe. Or maybe it wasn't important since he hadn't said anything to her to indicate that he had anything other than friendly feelings toward her. There had been no overt suggestion of romance, just the enormous pull they felt toward each other. She felt drawn to him like a magnet, but she was convinced that all he wanted was to be friends.

The next morning when Kate was on her way to the kitchen to get something to eat, she heard the phone ring in the hall. It was early, both her parents were still asleep, and it was a glorious autumn day. It was just after eight o'clock, and she couldn't imagine who was calling at that hour. And much to her surprise, when she answered, it was Joe.

"Did I wake you?" he asked, sounding worried, and a little bit embarrassed. He had been mildly afraid that her mother would pick up the phone, and was relieved when it was Kate instead.

"No, I was up. I was just going to get something to eat," she said, as she stood in the hallway in her dressing gown. They were planning to have lunch that day, and she assumed he was calling to tell her what time he'd come by. But it was a little early to call, and she was glad that she'd been the one to answer the phone. Her mother would have been annoyed.

"It's a beautiful day, isn't it?" he asked, sounding as though he had something else on his mind. "I . . . I have kind of a surprise planned for you. . . . I think it's something you might like a lot . . . at least I hope you will." He sounded like a boy with a new bicycle, and she smiled, listening to him.

"Will you bring the surprise with you when you come to the house?" She had no idea what it was, but he made it sound exciting.

He hesitated before he answered. "I was kind of thinking I'd take you to the surprise. It's a little harder to bring it to you. Does that sound all right to you, Kate?" All he wanted was for her to say yes. It meant the world to him. It was the one gift he wanted to give her more than anything. The best and only gift he had. Her father might have suspected what it was, but Kate had no idea.

"It sounds very intriguing," Kate said, smiling broadly, as she ran a hand through her long dark red hair. "When can I see it?" She was beginning to think it might be a new car, but it didn't make sense for him to buy a car in the East when he was still living in California. But she could hear that kind of male thrill in his voice that men usually reserved for machines and exotic cars.

"What if I pick you up in an hour?" he asked breathlessly. "Could you be ready by then?"

"Sure." She didn't know if her parents would be awake, but she could leave them a note, telling them she'd gone out earlier than planned. Her mother already knew she was having lunch with Joe.

"I'll pick you up at nine," he said hurriedly, ". . . and Kate . . . dress warm." She wondered if they were going walking somewhere, but whatever it was, she assured him that she'd wear a heavy coat.

An hour later, she was waiting outside the house in a duffel coat, a knit cap, and a scarf she wore at school, when Joe came by to pick her up in a cab.

"You look cute," he said with a smile. She was wearing loafers and wool socks, and a kilt and cashmere sweater she'd had for years. And of course, a string of pearls. It was the kind of outfit she wore daily to class. "Will you be warm enough?" he asked with a look of concern, as she nodded and laughed. She suddenly wondered if they were going ice skating. And then she heard him tell the cab driver to drive them to a suburb on the outskirts of town.

"What's out there?" she asked with a look of surprise.

"You'll see." And then, instinctively, she knew. It hadn't even occurred to her that he would take her to see his plane.

She didn't ask anything, and they chatted easily on the way. He told her how much he had enjoyed the past two days, and wanted to do something special for her. And she knew that in his eyes, showing her his plane was the best thing he could do. She already knew from his letters that he was very proud of it, it was one he had designed himself, and Charles Lindbergh had helped him build it. She was only sorry they hadn't brought her father with them. Even her mother couldn't object to their just looking at a plane. And a short while later, they arrived at Hanscom Field, a small private airport just outside Boston. There were several small hangars, and a long narrow airstrip. And a small red Lockheed Vega was landing as they got out of the cab.

Joe paid the driver, and he looked like a kid on Christmas, as he took Kate's hand and walked her quickly to the nearest hangar. He led her in through a side door, and she gasped as she saw the pretty little plane he lovingly patted, and opened the door to show her the cockpit as he beamed.

"Joe, it's gorgeous!" Kate knew nothing about planes, and the only flying she had done was on commercial airplanes with her parents. But for the first time, she felt a thrill just looking at the plane and knowing Joe had designed it. It was a beautiful machine.

He handed her up into the cockpit, and spent half an hour showing her everything about the plane, and explaining to her how it all worked. He had never shared any of it with a neophyte before, and he was amazed by how quickly she caught on, and how enthusiastic she was. She was listening raptly to every word, and she remembered almost everything he said. She only got two of the dials confused, and it was a mistake many young pilots made when they were first learning. He felt as though doors and windows were opening all around him as he talked to her, and he could show her new vistas into a world she had never even dreamed of. Sharing it with her was even more exciting for him than it was for her. He absolutely loved it, and his heart glowed as he saw the intent look in her eyes as she devoured every word and the most minute details.

It was an hour later when he turned to her, and asked if she would like to go up with him for a few minutes, just to see how the plane felt once it was off the ground. He hadn't intended to take her flying, but in light of her acute interest, it was far too tempting, and Kate didn't hesitate.

"Now?" She looked startled and as excited as he did. It was in fact the best gift he could give her. She liked just being with him around the small plane. For all his quiet ways and occasional awkwardness when he was on the ground, when Joe got anywhere near a plane, it was as though he could spread his wings and soar. "I'd love it, Joe . . . can we?" All her mother's warnings and admonitions were instantly forgotten, as Joe went to tell someone what they were doing and came back a minute later with a look of pleasure and a broad smile.

Technically, it was a small plane, but it was still of a respectable size, and thanks to some of the adjustments Lindbergh had helped him make, it was able to go a considerable distance. He started the engine easily, and they rolled slowly out of the vast open mouth of the hangar. And within minutes, they were taxiing down the runway, after Joe made the appropriate checks and told her what he was doing as he did. He was just going to take her up for a few minutes so she could get the feel of it, and as they lifted off the ground, he suddenly thought of something that hadn't occurred to him before.

"You don't get airsick, do you, Kate?" She laughed and shook her head, and he wasn't surprised. He had suspected she wasn't the kind of girl who would get airsick, and he loved that about her as well. It would have spoiled everything if she did.

"Never. Are you going to turn us upside down?" She looked hopeful and he laughed at her. He had never before felt as close to her as he did at that moment, flying together. It was like a dream.

"I hope not. I think we'll save that for next time," he said as they gained altitude.

Joe and Kate chatted comfortably over the sound of the engine for the first few minutes, and then they settled into an easy silence, as she looked around her with awe, and silently watched him. He was everything she had always known he would be, proud, quiet, strong, infinitely capable, in total control of the machine he had built, and master of the skies around him. She had never in her entire life known anyone who seemed as powerful to her, or as magical. It was as though he had been born to do this, and she felt sure that there was no other man alive who could do it better, not even Charles Lindbergh. If she had been drawn to Joe before, he became irresistible from the first moment she saw him fly. It would have been impossible for her not to feel that way. He was everything she had ever dreamed of or admired, and he personified everything her mother wanted her not to see in him. He was power and strength and freedom and joy. It was as though he himself were a proud bird swooping carefully over the countryside, and all she wanted when they finally landed an hour later was to go back up with him again. She had never in her entire life been as happy, or had as much fun, or liked anyone as she did Joe. It was as though they had each been meant to spend that exact moment in time together and it formed an instant bond between them.

"God, Joe, it was so perfect . . . thank you," she said, as he stopped the plane and turned off the engine. Flying was what he did best, and who he had been born to be. And he had shared it with her. It was almost like a profound religious experience for both of them. He looked at her peacefully and said nothing for a long moment. He just sat watching her.

"I'm so glad you liked it, Kate," he said quietly, knowing that if she hadn't, it would have disappointed him. But she did. And now he could feel whatever barriers there had been dissolving between them. He had never felt as close to another human in his life.

"I didn't like it, Joe. I loved it," she said solemnly. Being in the sky with him not only made her feel close to Joe, but to God.

"I hoped you'd like it, Kate," he said softly. "Would you like to learn to fly?"

"I'd love that," she said with bright sparkling eyes that danced as she looked at him. All she wanted to do was go back up with him. "Thank you so much . . ." And then she remembered something. "Whatever you do, don't tell my mother. She'd kill me . . . or you . . . or probably both of us. I promised her I wouldn't." But she hadn't been able to stop herself, and hadn't wanted to. It had been a profoundly moving experience for her, not just the flying, but seeing him in his natural habitat. She knew at that moment that he was the most exciting man she would ever know. There was no one else in the world like him. His skill alone set him apart from all others, and the style with which he did it only made him that much more appealing to her. What she had just seen was precisely what had impressed Charles Lindbergh about Joe when they met when he was barely more than a boy. Flying was in

Joe's soul. He was a rare bird, and everything she had suspected he would be. Neither of them was disappointed by their morning, far from it. After he had turned the engine off, Joe turned and looked at her with pride.

"You're a great copilot, Kate," he praised her. She had known just what to ask, what to say, and when to stay silent and feel the sheer joy and beauty of the sky with him. "One of these days, when we have some time, I'll teach you to fly." He not only made it look effortless with his innate sense for flying, but he also knew how to explain the basics in a way that Kate could understand. But Joe had been particularly impressed by what a natural she was.

"I wish we could spend the day here," she said wistfully, as he handed her out of the plane, and Joe looked pleased.

"So do I. But your mother would have my head if she even thought I'd taken you up for an hour, Kate. It's safer than driving a car, but I'm not sure she would agree." They both knew she would not.

They drove back to town in peaceful silence, and went to the Union Oyster House for lunch. And as soon as they sat down, all Kate could talk about was their brief flight, his impressive ease and skill, and the beauty of his plane. It had been the perfect way for her to get to know him. And once in the restaurant, Joe seemed quiet and somewhat reserved again. He truly was like a bird, one minute soaring effortlessly through the sky, and the next moment waddling awkwardly on land. Once out of his airplane, he was like a different man. But it was the natural pilot and the man of infinite skill whom she had sensed from the beginning, and who drew her irrevocably toward him.

But as they sat at lunch, and she told him stories about Radcliffe, he began to relax again. She had an irresistible way of unwinding him, and he felt even more comfortable with her now that she had seen him in his own world. It was what he had wanted to show her ever since the beginning, and now he sensed that she understood, not only how much flying meant to him, but who he was.

And as she drew him out, he relaxed and let down his defenses again. It was one of the many things he liked about her, even when he couldn't do it himself, she helped him reach out and open up, no matter how shy he felt. It was like cranking down the bridge over the moat to the castle. She facilitated the process, and he loved that in her.

There were so many things he liked about her that sometimes it frightened him. He had no idea what to do about it. She was far too young for him to get involved with, and her family was more than a little daunting. She had sensible, attentive parents, who weren't going to let anything happen to her, and had no intention of letting her have too much freedom. But he didn't want to take anything from her. He just wanted to be with her, and bask in the light she radiated and the warmth she exuded. Sometimes it made him feel like a lizard on a rock, soaking up the sunshine, as he sat next to her. She made him feel happy and warm and comfortable. But even those feelings seemed dangerous to him at times. He didn't want to be vulnerable to her. It would be too easy to get hurt then. He didn't analyze it, he just knew it at his core. He told himself that if she had been older, it might have been different, but she wasn't. She was an eighteen-year-old girl, and he was thirty, no matter how much he had liked flying with her. In spite of all his resistance, and the walls he'd built up over the years, the time they had spent in his airplane that morning had been magical for both of them.

The last day they shared passed all too quickly. They went back to her house for a while, and played cards in the library. He taught her to play liar's dice. She was surprisingly good at it, and actually beat him twice, which delighted her. She clapped her hands and looked like a child as she chortled. And that night he took her out to dinner. They had had a very nice weekend, and when he said goodnight to her, he had no idea when he'd see her again. He was planning to be back in New York by Christmas, but he and Charles Lindbergh had a lot of work to do, on the design for a new engine. Joe knew it would be difficult to garner much of Charles's time. He was so busy making speeches and appearances for the America First movement. And Joe had a lot to do too. For the first few months at least, he doubted if he'd have time to come to Boston. And he hesitated to ask her to come to see him. Asking her to visit him seemed a little too forward, and he didn't think her parents would approve.

She seemed quieter than usual when he said goodbye to her. They were standing on the front steps outside the house, and for the first time in three days, he looked painfully awkward again.

"Take care of yourself, Kate," he said, looking down at his shoes and not at her, and she smiled as she looked at him. She wanted to touch his chin, and force him to look at her, but she didn't. She knew that if she waited long enough, he would meet her gaze again. And in another instant, he did.

"Thank you for taking me flying," she whispered. It was a secret they now shared. "Have a safe trip back to California. How long will it take you?"

"About eighteen hours, depending on the weather. There's a storm over the Midwest, so I may have to fly pretty far south, over Texas. I'll call you when I get there."

"I'd like that," she whispered. Her eyes were full of all the things they hadn't said to each other, and which she wasn't even sure she understood yet, and the new bond they had formed in his plane. She still had no idea what he felt for her, if anything, other than brotherly affection. She had been almost certain that the only thing that had brought him to Boston was friendship. He hadn't indicated anything other than that, and he didn't now. Sometimes he was almost fatherly to her. And yet, there was always an undercurrent of something deeper and more mysterious between them. She was not sure if she was imagining it, or if there was something else there that they were both afraid of. "I'll write to you," she promised, and he knew she would. He loved getting her letters. The intricacy of them, and the skill with which she wrote, amazed him. They were almost like short stories, and more often than not they either touched his heart or made him laugh.

"I'll try to see you over Christmas. But Charles and I are going to be pretty busy," Joe said as she thought that she would have liked to offer to come to see him, but she didn't dare. She knew her parents would have been deeply upset by it. Her mother was already concerned that she had spent so much time with him over Thanksgiving, and even Joe sensed that. He didn't want to push it, and offend them.

"Just take care of yourself, Joe. Fly safely." She said it with a tone of obvious concern, which touched him. She looked so sweet as she said the words.

"You do the same, and don't flunk out of school," he teased, and she laughed. And then, with a funny little pat on her shoulder, he opened the front door for her with her key, and then ran quickly down the stairs and waved to her from the sidewalk. It was as though he had to get away from her before he did something he knew he shouldn't. She smiled as she walked through the front door, and closed it quietly behind her.

It had been an odd three days with him, they had been times of warmth and ease and friendship. And the wonder of flying with him. She told herself, as she walked slowly up the stairs, that she was glad she had met him. One day she would tell her children about him. And there was no doubt in her mind that when she did, they would not be his children. His life was already full, with airplanes and flying and test flights and engines. There was no room for a woman in it, not much anyway, and surely not for a wife and children. He had said as much to her on Cape Cod at the end of the summer, and again over the week-end. People were a sacrifice he was willing to make, for the sake of his passion for flying and planes. He had too little time to give anyone, he had said repeatedly, and she could see that. But at the same time, some deep primal part of her didn't accept that, or believe it. How could he be willing to give up the possibility of a family for his airplanes? But it wasn't for her to argue with him about it, and she knew that. She had to accept what he was saying. And she told herself that whatever she felt for him, or imagined that he felt for her, was only an illusion. It was nothing more than a dream.

On Sunday, before Kate left to go back to school, her mother said nothing about him. She had decided to take her husband's advice and wait to see what happened. Maybe he was right, and Joe would never pursue her any further. Maybe it was just a very unusual friendship between a grown man and a young girl. She hoped so. But no matter how hard she tried to believe what Clarke had said, she was not convinced.

And once back in the house at school, Kate didn't know why, but she was restless. The girls trickled back one by one, and reported on what they had done over the Thanksgiving weekend. Some had gone home with friends, others to their families. She chatted with her friends, but told no one about the visit from Joe. It was too hard to explain, and no one would have believed that she wasn't infatuated with him. She knew she could no longer say it with conviction herself. Sally Tuttle was the one who finally asked her about the man who had called her from California.

"Is he in school out there? Is he an old boyfriend?" She was curious about him, but Kate was noncommittal and avoided her eyes.

"No, he's just a friend. He's working out there."

"He sounded nice on the phone." It was the understatement of a lifetime, and all Kate could do was nod.

"I'll introduce you to him if he comes to Boston," Kate teased her, and then they all went to get ready for classes the next day. One of the girls came back from the weekend with her family in Connecticut, and announced that she had gotten engaged over Thanksgiving. It made everything that Kate felt, and insisted she didn't feel, seem even more awkward. She had a crush on a man who was twelve years older than she, and insisted he never wanted to get married. And he didn't even know she had a crush on him. It was ridiculous really. By the time she went to bed that night she had convinced herself that she was being incredibly stupid, and if she wasn't careful, she'd annoy him and lose his friendship entirely, and he'd never take her up in a plane again. And she didn't want that to happen. She was still hoping that one day he would teach her to fly.

Much to her amazement, Joe called her the next day.

He said he had just landed at the airport. He'd had a tough flight, had to refuel three times, and had flown through two snowstorms. He had even been grounded for a while, due to hail over Waynoka, Oklahoma. Kate thought he sounded exhausted, and the trip had taken him twenty-two hours.

"It was so nice of you to call me," she said, looking surprised and pleased. She hadn't expected to hear from him, and it confused her a little, but she suspected he was just being kind. What he said next confirmed it. He sounded nonchalant and a little cool.

"I didn't want you to worry. How's school?"

"It's okay." She had actually been feeling sad since he left, and she was annoyed at herself for it. There was no reason for her to get attached to him. He had offered no encouragement, and had done nothing to mislead her. But she missed him anyway, even if she knew she shouldn't. In her eyes, it was like having a crush on the governor, or the president, or some lofty person who would forever be just out of reach for her. The only difference was that she and Joe were friends, and she enjoyed his company so much, it was hard not to get too caught up in the pleasure of being with him. And she had seen a side of him few people did, high up in the sky. She had no idea how much it had moved him too.

"I can't wait till Christmas vacation." She made it sound as though her excitement was caused by the holidays and not the fact that he was moving back east again, to work with Charles Lindbergh. But she liked knowing that he would be closer. And she wondered if her parents would let her travel to New York to see him, maybe if one of her friends came with her. But she didn't mention that to Joe. She instinctively knew that if she had, it would have frightened him.

"I'll call you in a few days," he said, sounding drained. He was dying to get some sleep after the arduous twenty-two-hour flight across the country.

"Isn't that terribly expensive? Maybe we should just stick to letters."

"I can call you once in a while," he said cautiously, "unless you'd rather I didn't." He sounded poised for flight, and not nearly as relaxed as he had been with her over the weekend. His awkwardness seemed more pronounced when he called. Calling her was a big step for him.

"No, I'd like it," Kate said quickly. "I just don't want to cost you a lot of money."

"Don't worry about it." It was, after all, cheaper than dinner. He had taken her to some very nice places, which was rare for him. So rare as to be nonexistent. He put every penny he earned into developing new engines and new planes. But he had wanted to do something special for her. She deserved it. And then, his voice sounded husky at the other end. "Kate?" She waited but he didn't say more until she answered. It was as though he wanted to be sure she was there, before he stuck his neck out.

"Yes?" She felt suddenly breathless, not sure what was coming, but sensing something fragile in him.

"Will you still write to me? I love your letters." She smiled then, not sure if she was disappointed or relieved. He had sounded so serious when he said her name that for a moment she'd been worried. He had sounded as though he were about to say something important. It was to him, but not what Kate had hoped for or expected.

"Of course I will," she reassured him. "I have exams next week though."

"So do I," he laughed. He had test flights scheduled all week. Some of them were going to be pretty dangerous, but he wanted to do them himself before he left California, although he didn't say that to her. "I'll be pretty tied up for the next few weeks, but I'll call you when I can." A moment later, he hung up, and Kate went back to her room to study, trying not to think too much about him.

She had been wondering about something all weekend. She hadn't said anything to Joe but her parents were giving her a big party at the Copley Plaza for her coming out just before Christmas. She was going to be presented at the debutante cotillion, and her own party was going to be lovely, but not nearly as lavish as the one where she had met Joe. She hadn't dared broach the subject yet, but she was planning to ask her parents if she could invite him. She wasn't sure if he could come, but she at least wanted to ask him and hoped he would. She knew it would be much more fun for her if he were there, but her mother had been so nervous about Joe, that Kate didn't want to push it. There was still time. The party was more than three weeks away, and Joe was still in California. And she was sure that when he did return, his social calendar wouldn't be full yet.

As it turned out, a week later, to the day, she was talking to her mother on the phone on Sunday at lunchtime, about the ball, and some of the questions she still had, when one of the girls from her house came running down the hall crying. Kate was sure that something terrible had happened to her, some awful news from home, maybe one of her parents had died. She was saying something unintelligible as Kate continued to listen to her mother. Liz had a long list of questions about cakes and hors d'oeuvres, and the exact dimensions of the dance floor. Kate's dress had been ready since October. It had a plain white satin bodice and a tulle skirt, and she looked incredible in it. And over her shoulders there was a haze of white tulle, through which one saw the shimmering bodice. She was going to wear her dark auburn hair pulled back in a neat bun, like a Degas ballerina. As the dressmaker had said, as she looked at Kate admiringly, all she needed were toe shoes. Her mind was full of girlish details as she began to hear people shouting to each other. A group of girls had been just leaving the house for lunch, when the inexplicable shouting began.

"What did you say, Mom?" Kate asked her to repeat the question. There was so much noise coming from the house that Kate couldn't hear a thing.

"I said . . . oh my God . . . what? . . . are you serious? Clarke . . ." She could hear her mother start to cry and didn't know what had happened.

"Did something happen to Dad? Mom, what's wrong?" Her heart began to beat wildly. Then suddenly, as she looked around her, she noticed that a number of girls in the hall were crying too. Then it hit her, this wasn't just about her father, something terrible had happened. "Mom, what's happening? Do you know?"

"Your father was just listening to the radio." He was standing in the kitchen in disbelief, saying something unbelievable to her. An entire nation was as shocked as they were. "Pearl Harbor was bombed by the Japanese half an hour ago. A number of ships were sunk, and a lot of men were killed and wounded. My God, this is awful." As Kate looked down the hall toward the rooms, she could see the entire house was in chaos. Kate heard radios on in every room and she heard the continual sounds of crying. So many girls realized that their fathers and brothers and fiancés and boyfriends were suddenly at risk. There was no way America could stay out of the war any longer. The Japanese had brought it right to their door, and despite all his previous promises, President Roosevelt was going to have to do something radical about it. Kate quickly got off the phone, and hurried back to her room to see what people were saying about the news.

They all sat quietly, tears pouring down their faces as they listened to the news on the radio. One of the girls in her house was from Hawaii, and she knew that there were two Japanese girls in an upstairs room. She couldn't even imagine what they must have been feeling, trapped in a foreign country, so far from home.

It was later that night when she finally called her mother back, and by then, they had all been listening to the radio all day. It was unthinkable, and easy to believe that within a very short time the nation's young men would be sent far, far from home to fight this war. And only God knew how many of them would survive.

All the Jamisons could think of when they heard the news was that they were grateful they didn't have a son. In cities and towns and backwaters everywhere, young men were facing the fact that they had to leave their families to defend their country. It was beyond imagining, and there was considerable concern that the Japanese would attack again. Everyone felt sure that the next attack would be on California, and there was pandemonium spreading there.

Major General Joseph Stilwell had sped into action, and everything possible was being done to protect the cities on the West Coast. Bomb shelters were being built, medical personnel were being organized. There was a general state of controlled panic. Even in Boston, people were frightened. Kate's parents asked her to come home, and she said she would the next day, but she wanted to wait and see what they were telling them at school. She didn't want to just leave.

As it turned out, classes were canceled and the girls were sent home, until after Christmas vacation. Everyone was desperate to get back to where they lived and be with their families. And as Kate was packing her things the morning after the attack, Joe called her. It had taken him hours to get through, the lines were all busy. All the girls had been calling home. The U.S. had declared war on Japan by then. Japan had declared war on the U.S. and Great Britain, who had in turn declared war on Japan.

"Not very good news, huh, Kate?" Joe said, sounding surprisingly calm about it. He didn't want to alarm her more than she already was.

"Pretty awful. What's happening out there?" He was that much closer to Hawaii.

"It's what somebody called discreet panic. No one wants to openly admit that they're terrified, but they are, and maybe with good reason. It's hard to know what the Japs will do now. They're talking about interning the Japanese in the Western states. I can't even imagine what that'll do to California." They had businesses and lives and houses. They couldn't just walk away from them.

"What about you, Joe?" Kate asked, sounding worried. He had already been to England several times to advise the RAF in the past two years, it was easy now to figure out what was going to happen. With America entering the war in Europe as well, he would more than likely be sent there. And if not, he would be involved in the war against Japan. But either way, he would be going somewhere to fly planes. He was exactly the kind of man they wanted, and he wasn't hard to find.

"I'm flying east tomorrow. I can't finish my work here. They want me in Washington as soon as possible. They're going to give me my orders then." He'd had a call from the War Office. And Kate was right, he would be shipping out shortly. "I don't know how long I'll be there. If I can, I'll try to come up to Boston to see you before I leave, if they give me enough time. If not . . ." His voice trailed off, everything was up in the air now. Not just for them, but for the entire country. A nation of men were about to be sent away to war.

"I could meet you in Washington to say goodbye," she volunteered, realizing that she no longer cared what her parents would think. If he was leaving, she wanted to see him. It was all she could think of as she listened to him, and tried to fight back panic. The thought of his being sent to war filled her with fear.

"Don't do anything till I call you. They may send me to New York for a few days. It depends if they want me to train here before I leave, or go straight from Washington to England and train there." He already suspected he would be going there. The only question was when. "I'd rather go to England than Japan." They had spoken to him about it that morning on the phone, and he had said he would go wherever he was sent.

"I wish you didn't have to go anywhere," she said sadly.

All she could think of now were all the young men she knew, the ones she had grown up with and gone to school with, and the girls who were their sisters and girlfriends and wives. It was devastating for everyone, and a number of Kate's friends were already married and starting families. Everyone's lives were about to be disrupted, not just hers or Joe's and people she knew, but the lives of an entire nation. There was no hiding from the fact that many of them were not going to be returning. It was as though a pall hung over everything now. People were talking and whispering and crying, and everyone was frightened of what would happen next. There was even a rumor that all the cities on the Eastern Seaboard were going to be attacked by German U-boats. No one in the entire country felt safe from the minute they heard the news of the attack in Hawaii.

"Just sit tight, Kate. Will you be at school, or at your parents'?" He wanted to know where to find her. It might only be a matter of hours before he had to leave. If so, he wanted to know where she'd be, in case he could see her. There was a possibility that he wouldn't have time, but he was hoping for at least a few minutes with her.

"I'm going to my parents' house this afternoon. We're off until after the Christmas holidays." But it was going to be a grim Christmas this year.

"I'm going to start flying east in a couple of hours, in case I hit a lot of weather. I've got to be in Washington tomorrow. I hate leaving everything out here in midstream." But he had no choice, he had no other option. It was what the entire country was doing. Men everywhere were dropping everything and going to war.

"Is the weather all right for you to leave?" She sounded even more worried. He wanted to promise her everything would be fine, but he couldn't. But just talking to him comforted her. There was something so solid and sensible and unruffled about him. He seemed to have none of the sense of hysteria that everyone else had. He seemed like an island of calm in a stormy sea, which was very much Joe's style.

"The weather is fine out here," he said calmly. "I'm not so sure what it'll look like as we get further east." He was bringing two other men with him. "I've got to go home and pack now, Kate. We're leaving in two hours. I'll call you when I can."

"I'll be at home waiting." There was no point playing games. All her efforts and senses were aimed at seeing him before he was shipped overseas, in whichever direction. It was suddenly past the time to pretend that she didn't care. She did. A great deal.

All the girls bade each other a tearful goodbye, as they left one by one to return to their homes in assorted places, and some had a long way to travel. The girl from Hawaii was going home with a friend from California, but her parents didn't want her to return to Honolulu, in case the Japanese attacked again. Thousands of men had died and been injured at Pearl Harbor, along with a number of civilians.

The girls from Japan had to report to the Japanese consulate in Boston. They were even more frightened than the others, and had no idea what would happen to them. They had no way of contacting their parents, and no idea when or how or even if they would get home.

Kate got home late that afternoon, and when she did, both her parents were waiting for her. They looked frightened and distressed. The radio was on constantly, and they all knew that it was only a matter of hours or days before American troops began to fight.

"Did you hear from Joe?" her father asked her as she set down her suitcase in the front hall. He had sent a driver over to help her with her bags. He hadn't wanted to leave her mother. Elizabeth was looking pale and nervous. Her father was impressed by Kate's composure. She seemed surprisingly calm, and nodded when he asked about Joe.

"He's flying in to Washington tomorrow. He doesn't know yet where they're going to send him." Her father nodded in answer, and her mother glanced at her with concern, but didn't comment about Joe. Kate and Joe seemed to be in alarmingly frequent communication, but admittedly, these were unusual circumstances. Liz couldn't help wondering how often he had called her before.

They ate dinner in the kitchen that night, with the radio on, and none of them said a word. The food sat on their plates getting colder by the minute, and eventually Kate helped her mother clear the table, and scraped the still full plates into the garbage can. It was a long night that night, as Kate lay in her bed, thinking about Joe, and wondering how far east he had come so far, and if she would be able to see him before he was shipped off to war.

It was nearly noon the next day when he called her. He had just landed in Washington, D.C., at Bolling Field Airport.

"I just wanted you to know I got here safely." She was relieved to hear from him, but neither of them could explain why he felt a need to call her. This was definitely more than friendship, but neither of them wanted to talk about it. They didn't have to, or even admit it to each other. It was obvious that he felt linked to her in some silent, secret way that they weren't ready to acknowledge with words. "I'm going to the War Office now. I'll call you later, Kate."

"I'll be here." He was keeping her apprised of his every move. The phone rang again four hours later. He had been briefed all afternoon, and given his orders and commission. He had been made a captain in the Army Air Corps, and would be flying fighter missions with the RAF. He was leaving in two days for London, from New York. He would get his training, in military protocol, and formation flying in England. He had done a fair amount of it in air shows, and it was something he was exceptionally good at. That afternoon President Roosevelt announced to the nation that America had officially entered the war in Europe.

"That's it, kid. I'll be out of here in two days. But I'm going to a very decent place."

He was going to East Anglia and he had been there before to visit the RAF. Within two weeks, they expected him to be flying fighter missions. The thought of it terrified her, particularly when she realized that once the Germans knew he had joined the Allied war effort, they'd be gunning for him. With his reputation as a flying ace, he was just the kind of pilot they wanted to eliminate, and she knew they would do everything they could to shoot him down. He was in far greater danger than the others, and just knowing that turned her stomach. It was un-bearable thinking of him going away for God only knew how long, and being in danger nearly every moment. She couldn't even begin to imagine how she was going to live knowing that, with no news of him. It was obviously going to be impossible for him to call her. But they still had two days, or as much of it as he could spend with her. They had already both assumed that he would spend as much time with her as possible before he flew to Europe. In a matter of hours, everything between them had changed. The pretense of friendship had already begun to slip away, and their relationship had already begun to evolve into something else.

As it turned out, he had to pick up uniforms and more papers, and it was the next day before he could leave Washington. He was flying out the following day at six o'clock in the morning. To be sure he didn't miss the plane, he had to be back in New York by midnight. It was ten in the morning when he took the plane from Washington to Boston, and nearly one o'clock when he landed. His plane to New York was at ten o'clock that night. They had exactly nine hours to spend together. Young couples all over the country were facing the same dilemma. Some got married in the little time they had left, others went to hotels to find what comfort they could with each other. Others just sat in train stations, or coffee shops, or on park benches in freezing weather. All they wanted was to share their last moments of freedom and peacetime, and cling to each other. And as she thought of them, Kate's mother felt even sorrier for the mothers who were saying goodbye to sons. She couldn't imagine anything worse.

Kate was waiting for Joe when he landed at East Boston Airport. He came off the plane looking serious and trim in a brand-new army uniform, which suited him to perfection. He looked even more handsome than he had at their home on Thanksgiving. And he smiled as he strode across the runway and approached her. He looked as though nothing was wrong, and this time when he got to her, he put an arm around her shoulders.

"It's okay, Kate. Relax. Everything will be okay." He could see instantly how terrified she was for him. "I'm one guy who'll know what he's doing over there. Flying is flying." It reminded her instantly of his extraordinary ease and expertise when she had flown with him only two weeks before.

But they both knew that normally, when he flew, no one was trying to shoot him down. Despite what he said to quell her fears, this was going to be very different. "What are we going to do today?" he asked, as though it was an ordinary day, and they didn't have to say goodbye to each other in less than nine hours. Couples all over the country were spending their last hours together, just as they were.

"Do you want to go back to the house?" she asked, looking vague. It was hard not to be distracted, or imagine that you could hear a clock ticking. The minutes were drifting away from them, and almost before it had begun, their last day together would be over, and he would be gone. She could feel a shiver of fear run through her at the thought. She wasn't even aware of it, but she hadn't felt as frightened or bereft since her father died.

"Why don't we go out for lunch? We can go to the house afterward. I want to say goodbye to your parents." She thought it seemed very respectful of him. And even her mother had stopped overtly worrying about his intentions. Whatever she was feeling about him, she was keeping to herself, and Kate was grateful for that. They all felt sorry for him, and millions of other young men just like him.

He took her to Locke-Ober's for lunch, and despite the elegant room and the fine meal, Kate could hardly eat. All she could think of was not where they were now, but where he was going in a matter of hours. The effort to have a civilized meal was essentially wasted on her. They were back at her house at three o'clock. Her mother was sitting in the living room, listening to the radio, as she always did now, and her father was not yet back from the office.

They sat and talked to her mother for a little while, and listened to the news, and at four o'clock, her father came home, and shook hands with Joe while patting his shoulder in a fatherly way. His eyes seemed to say it all, and neither of them found words to express what they were feeling. And after a little while, Clarke took Elizabeth upstairs, to leave the young people alone. They had enough to think about, Clarke felt, without having to worry about entertaining her parents. And both Kate and Joe were grateful to have some time together. It would have been out of the question to take him to her bedroom, to just relax and talk. No matter how well they behaved, the impropriety of it would have offended her mother, so Kate didn't even try to suggest it. Instead, they sat quietly on the couch in the living room, talking to each other, and trying not to think of the minutes ticking by.

"I'll write to you, Kate. Every day, if I can," he promised. There were a myriad things in his eyes, and he looked troubled. But he didn't offer to explain what he was thinking, and she was afraid to ask. She still had no idea how he felt about her, if they had just become very dear friends, or if there was something more to it. She was far more clear about what she was feeling for him. She realized now that she had been in love with him for months, but she didn't dare say it to him. It had happened sometime during their exchange of letters since September, and seeing him over Thanksgiving had confirmed it to her. But she had been fighting it ever since. She had no idea if Joe reciprocated her feelings, and it would have been improper to ask. Even she, with all her brave ways, wouldn't have had the courage to do that. She just had to go on what she knew and what she felt, and appreciate that, for whatever reason, he had wanted to spend these last hours with her. But she also reminded herself that he had no one else to spend them with. Other than his cousins whom he hadn't seen in years, he had no other relatives, and no girlfriend. The only person who seemed to matter to him was Charles Lindbergh. Other than that, he was alone in the world. And he had wanted to be with her.

It occurred to her as they sat close to each other on the couch, talking softly, that he hadn't had to come to Boston. He had only done that because he wanted to see her, and had stayed in close contact with her, ever since they'd heard the news, when Pearl Harbor had been attacked.

Kate told him, as they sat there, that her parents had canceled the coming-out party they'd been planning for her. She hadn't told him about it yet, but had planned to. She hadn't wanted to seem too anxious, but it was irrelevant now. All three Jamisons had agreed that it would have been in terrible taste to give a big party, and there probably wouldn't be many young men there anyway. Her father had promised to give a party for her after the war.

"It really doesn't matter now," she told Joe, as he nodded.

"Was it going to be like the party where we met last year?" he asked with interest, it was a good topic to distract her. She looked so sad that it touched his heart. He realized more than ever that he'd been lucky to meet her when he did. He almost hadn't gone to the ball with Charles Lindbergh the year before. And the fact that he had had obviously been fate, for both of them.

Kate smiled at his question about her canceled party. "Nothing as fancy as that." It was going to be at the Copley, for about two hundred people. There had been seven hundred people at the ball where they had met, with enough caviar and champagne to supply an entire village for a year. "I'm glad my parents canceled," she said quietly. Thinking about Joe in England, risking his life every day, was all she cared about now. She had already volunteered for the Red Cross, for whatever war effort they organized in the next few weeks. And Elizabeth had volunteered with her.

"You'll go back to school though, won't you?" he asked, and she nodded.

They sat quietly and talked for hours, and after a while, her mother brought them two plates of food. She didn't ask the young people to join them in the kitchen. Clarke thought they should be alone, and in spite of herself, Elizabeth agreed with him. She wanted to make things as easy as possible for both of them. They had enough anguish in their lives right then, without adding social burdens to it. And Joe stood and thanked her for the meal she had brought them. But they could barely eat as they sat next to each other, and finally he turned to Kate, and put both their plates on the table, as he took her hand in his. Tears filled her eyes before he could say anything to her.

"Don't cry, Kate," he said gently. It was something he had never been able to deal with, but in this instance, he didn't blame her. There were tears being shed in living rooms everywhere. "It'll be okay. I have nine lives, as long as I'm in an airplane." He had walked away from some incredible crashes in the years that he'd been flying.

"What if you need ten?" she asked, as the tears rolled down her cheeks. She had wanted to be so brave, and suddenly found she couldn't. She couldn't bear the thought of something happening to him. Her mother had been right. Kate was in love with him.

"I'll have twenty lives if that's what I need. You can count on it," he reassured her, but they both knew it was a promise he might not be able to keep, which was why he hadn't done anything foolish with her before he left.

Joe had no intention of leaving her an eighteen-year-old widow. She deserved a lot better than that, and if he couldn't give it to her, someone else would. He wanted to leave her feeling free to pursue anything she wanted in his absence. But all Kate could think of was Joe. It was too late to save herself. She was already far more attached to him than either of them had planned. As they sat on the couch side by side, with his arm around her, she turned to him and told him that she loved him. And as he looked down at her, there was a long, painful silence. There was such vast sorrow in her eyes. And he had no idea of the loss she had suffered as a child. Kate had never spoken of her father's suicide to anyone, and as far as Joe knew, the only father Kate had ever had was Clarke. But suddenly, for Kate, this loss reawakened the sorrows of her past, and made his going off to war that much worse for her.

"I didn't want you to say that, Kate," Joe said unhappily. He had tried so hard to stem the tides not only of her love, but his own. "I didn't want to say that to you. I don't want you to feel bound to me if something happens. You mean a lot to me, you have ever since the day I met you. I've never known anyone like you. But it wouldn't be fair of me to extract a promise from you, or expect something from you, or ask you to wait for me. There's always a chance that I might not come back, and I never want you to feel that you owe me something you don't. You owe me nothing. I want you to feel free to do whatever you want while I'm gone. Whatever we've felt for each other, with or without words, has been more than enough for me since we've known each other, and I'm taking it with me." He pulled her closer to him, and held her so tightly she could feel his heart beating, but he didn't kiss her. For a fraction of an instant, she was disappointed. She wanted him to tell her he loved her. This might be their last chance, for a very long time at least, or worse yet, the only one they'd ever have.

"I do love you," she said clearly and simply. "I want you to know that so you can take it with you. I don't want you to wonder while you're sitting over there in the trenches." But he raised a dignified eyebrow at her suggestion.

"Trenches? That's the infantry. I'll be flying high in the sky, shooting down Germans. And I'll be sleeping in my warm bed at night. It won't be as bad as you think, Kate. It will be for some people, but not for me. Fighter pilots are a pretty elite group," he reassured her. And other than Lindbergh, Joe was about as elite as it got, which was at least a relief for him.

The time sped by unbearably, and before they knew it, it was time to leave for the airport. It was a cold, clear night, and Joe took her to the airport with him in a cab. Her father offered to drive them there, but Joe preferred to go in a taxi. And Kate wanted to be alone with Joe.

There were people milling around the airport everywhere, and boys in uniforms had sprung up overnight. Even to Kate, they all looked like such babies. They were eighteen- and nineteen-year-old boys, and they barely looked old enough to leave their mothers. Some of them had never left home before.

Their last minutes together were excruciatingly painful. Kate was trying to hold back tears unsuccessfully, and even Joe looked tense. It was all so intolerably emotional for both of them. Neither of them had any idea if they would see each other again, or when. They knew the war could go on for years, and all Kate could do was hope it wouldn't. It was finally a mercy when he had to get on the plane. They had nothing left to say to each other, and she was beginning to cling to him in desperation. She didn't want him to go, didn't want anything to happen to him, didn't want to lose the only man she had ever loved.

"I love you," she whispered to him again, and he looked pained. This wasn't what he'd had in mind when he came to spend the day with her. He had somehow felt that they had a silent pact not to say those kinds of things to each other, but she wasn't sticking to it. She just couldn't. She could not let him go without telling him she loved him. In her opinion, he had a right to know. What she didn't understand was how much harder it was for him once she said the words. Until then, whatever his feelings for her, or how powerful his attraction to her, he had been able to delude himself that they were just good friends. But now there was no hiding from the fact that they weren't. They were far more than that, no matter how strenuously he tried to pretend it wasn't so.

Her words were her final gift to him, the only thing she had to give him of any real value. And they brought reality to both of them. For just a fraction of an instant, he sensed his own vulnerability, and glimpsed the possibility that he might never come this way again. Suddenly, as he looked at her, he was grateful for every instant they had shared. He knew that he would never meet another woman like her, with as much fire and joy and excitement, and no matter where he went, or what happened to him, he would always remember her. All they had before they left each other were these last moments to share.

And as they called his flight for the last time, he bent and kissed her, standing in the airport with his arms around her. It was too late to stop the tides. He had been kidding himself, he knew, if he thought he could reverse them or even hold them back. Their feelings for each other were as inevitable as the passing of time. Whatever it was that had happened between them, they both knew without promises or words, that it was very rare, and not something that either of them would have changed, or would ever find again.

"Take care of yourself," he said hoarsely, in a whisper.

"I love you," she said again. She looked him right in the eye as she said it, and he nodded, unable to say the words, despite all that he felt for her. They were words to describe feelings that he had fled for thirty years.

He held her close and kissed her again, and then he knew he had to leave her. He had to get on the flight. With every ounce of strength he had, he walked away from her, and paused for a last instant at the gate. She was still looking at him, and there were tears rolling slowly down her cheeks. He started to turn away then, paused, and looked back at her for a last instant. And then, just before it was too late, he shouted back to her, "I love you, Kate." She heard him, and saw him wave, and as she laughed through her tears, he disappeared through the gate.

5

CHRISTMAS WAS GRIM for everyone that year. Two and a half weeks after Pearl Harbor, the world was still reverberating from the shock. America's sons had begun to go off to war, and they were being shipped to Europe and the Pacific. The names of places no one had ever heard of before were suddenly on everyone's lips, and Kate took small comfort in knowing Joe was in England. From the only letter she had had from him so far, his life sounded fairly civilized.

He was stationed in Swinderby. He told her only as much about his doings as the censors would allow. Most of the letter had expressed his concern for her, and told her about the people he'd met there. He described the countryside, and how kind the English were being to them. But he didn't tell her he loved her. He had said it once, but he would have been uncomfortable writing it to her.

It was obvious to both her parents by then how in love with him she was, and the only consolation to them was the sense they had that he also loved her. But in their private moments, Elizabeth Jamison still expressed her deep concerns to Clarke. They were even more profound now because, if something happened to him, she was afraid that Kate would mourn him forever. He would have been a hard man to forget.

"God forgive me for saying it," Clarke said quietly, "but if something happens to him, she'd get over it, Liz. It's happened to other women before her. I just hope it doesn't."

It wasn't just the war that worried Elizabeth, it was something much deeper that she had sensed in Joe, from the moment she met him, and she could never quite find the words to express to Clarke. She had a sense that Joe was unable to let anyone in, and to love or give fully. He was always standing back somewhere around the edges. And his passion for the planes he designed and flew, and the world that opened to him, was a way for him to escape life. She wasn't at all sure that, even if he survived the war, he would ever make Kate happy.

What she also felt was their unspoken bond, and the deep almost mesmeric fascination they had for each other. They were entirely opposite, each of them was like the dark or light side of the other. But what Kate's mother sensed but could never explain was that in some inexplicable way, they were dangerous for each other. She didn't even know why she was frightened by Kate loving him, but she was.

The date of Kate's canceled deb party came and went, and she wasn't really sorry it had been canceled. She hadn't had her heart set on it, it was more something she felt she had to do for her parents. And that night, as she sat at home reading a book she had to read for school, she was surprised when Andy Scott called. Almost every boy she knew was leaving for boot camp by then, had already left or was getting ready to ship out. But Andy had already explained to her several weeks before that he had had a heart murmur ever since his childhood. It didn't hamper him in any way, but even in wartime, it made him ineligible for the army. He was upset about it, and had tried to get them to take him anyway, but they had categorically refused him. He told Kate he wanted to wear a sign, explaining to people why he wasn't in uniform, and why he was still at home. He felt like a traitor being at home with the women. He was still very upset about it when he called her, and they talked for a while. He wanted to take her out to dinner, but she felt odd going now. It seemed unfair, given the way she felt about Joe, and the fact that he was in England. She told Andy why and said she couldn't. And he tried to negotiate her into a movie anyway. But she wasn't in the mood. They had never been more than pals, but she knew from mutual friends that he was crazy about her. And he'd been trying to start something with her since she'd arrived at Radcliffe in the fall.

"I think you should go out," her mother said firmly, when she asked Kate about the call from Andy. "You can't stay home forever. The war could go on for a long time." And nothing had been settled with Joe. He hadn't asked her to marry him, they weren't engaged, they had made no promises. They just loved each other. And her mother would have been far happier to see Kate out with Andy Scott.

"I don't feel right about it," Kate said, going back to her room with her book. She knew it was going to be a long war if she was going to stay home indefinitely with her parents, but she didn't care.

"She can't just sit here day after day and night after night," Liz complained later to her husband. "There's no commitment between them. They're not promised or engaged." Her mother wanted the real thing for her.

"It's a commitment of the heart, from what I understand," her father said calmly. He was concerned about Joe, and sympathetic to his daughter. He had none of the suspicions his wife did about Joe. He thought he was a great guy.

"I'm not sure Joe will ever make more of a commitment," Liz said, looking worried.

"I think he's being very responsible, he doesn't want to make her a young widow. I think he's doing the right thing."

"I don't think men like him ever make real commitments," she insisted. "He's too passionate about his flying. Everything else in his life will always come after that. He'll never give Kate what she needs. His first love will always be flying," she predicted grimly, and Clarke smiled.

"That's not necessarily true. Look at Lindbergh. He's married, he has children."

"Who knows how happy his wife is?" she said skeptically.

But however they felt about it, Kate continued what she was doing. She stayed home with her parents during the entire vacation, and when she went back to school in January, the other girls looked as unhappy as she did. Five of them had gotten married before their boyfriends shipped out, at least a dozen had gotten engaged, and the others all seemed to be involved with boys who would be going overseas very soon. Their whole life already revolved around photographs and letters, which reminded Kate that she didn't have a single photograph of Joe. But she already had a growing stack of letters from him.

She applied herself to her studies diligently, and saw Andy from time to time. She still refused to go out with him on dates, but they were friends, and he came to visit her often at Radcliffe. They would take long walks across the campus, and go to the cafeteria afterward, and he teased her about the elegance of their dinners together. But as long as all they did was eat on campus, she didn't feel it counted as a date, and she wasn't being unfaithful to Joe. Andy just thought she was being silly, and tried to talk her into going out.

"Why won't you let me take you someplace decent?" he moaned as they sat at a back table eating dry meat loaf and nearly inedible chicken. The cafeteria was famous for how bad the food was.

"I don't think it would be right. And this is fine," she insisted.

"Fine? You call this fine?" He plunged a fork into his mashed potatoes, they were like wallpaper paste, and her chicken was so tough she couldn't eat it. "It takes me two days to get over the stomachache I get every time I eat dinner with you." But all Kate could think about were the rations that Joe was getting in England. It would have seemed shocking to her if she were going to expensive restaurants with Andy, and she just wouldn't do it. If he wanted to spend time with her, he had no choice but to eat in the cafeteria at school.

Other than Kate refusing to go out with him, Andy had an active social life. He was tall, dark, and handsome, and one of the few eligible men left on campus and not going off to war. Girls were practically lining up to go out with him, and he could have had just about anyone, except the one girl he wanted. He wanted Kate.

Andy was consistent about coming to visit her, and over the months, they established a strong bond of friendship. She liked him enormously, but she felt none of the things for him she did for Joe. What she felt for Andy was solid and quiet and comfortable, it had none of the fire and passion and irresistible pull she felt toward Joe. Andy seemed more like a brother. They played tennis together several times a week, and finally around Easter time, she let him take her to a movie, but she felt guilty about it. They went to see *Mrs. Miniver* with Greer Garson, and Kate cried all the way through.

She was getting letters from Joe several times a week, and she could only guess that he was flying Spitfires on missions with the RAF. But as long as the letters kept coming, she knew he was alive and well. She lived in constant terror that she would read in the paper that his plane had been shot down, and her hands shook as she opened the newspaper every morning. She knew that, as well known as he was, and because of his association with Charles Lindbergh, she would read about it before anyone would have a chance to warn her. But so far, in his letters, he seemed to be in good spirits and well. He had complained bitterly about the cold and the bad food all winter in England. And in May, he wrote about how beautiful the spring was, he said there were flowers everywhere, and even the poorest people had lovely gardens. But he hadn't told her he loved her since he left.

At the end of May, the RAF flew a thousand bombers in a night bombing raid over Cologne. Joe never mentioned it, but when Kate read about it, she was certain Joe had been there. In June, Andy graduated from Harvard in three years on an accelerated program, and would be going straight into law school in the fall. Kate finished her freshman year, went to Andy's graduation, and went to work full time for the Red Cross over the summer. She rolled bandages, and folded warm clothes to be sent overseas. They mailed packages, provided medicines, and spent a great deal of time doing small useful things. It wasn't an exciting job, but it seemed like the least she could do for the war effort. Even in her small circle of friends, there had already been tragedies. Two of the girls in her house had lost brothers on ships torpedoed by the Germans, and another one had lost two. One of her roommates had gone home to help her father run the family business. Several fiancés had been killed, and of the five girls who had gotten married over Christmas, one had already lost her husband and gone home. It was hard not to think about it, as one looked constantly into saddened eyes and worried faces. The thought of getting a telegram from the War Department chilled everyone's heart.

Andy was doing volunteer work in a military hospital that summer. He wanted to do something to make up for the fact that he hadn't been able to go to war with the rest of the able-bodied young men. And when he called Kate, he told her horror stories of the wounded men he saw, and the experiences they shared with him. He wouldn't have admitted it to anyone, except maybe Kate, but as he listened to them, there were moments when he was actually glad he hadn't been able to go to war. Most of the men they saw had been in Europe, the ones who were wounded in the Pacific went to hospitals on the West Coast to recuperate. Many of them had lost limbs and eyes and faces, they had stepped on mines or were filled with shrapnel. And Andy said there was an entire ward filled with men who had lost their minds over the trauma they'd been through. Just thinking about it horrified both of them. And they knew that in the coming months, it could only get worse.

After working for the Red Cross for two and a half months, Kate went to Cape Cod, for the last two weeks of the summer, with her parents. It was one of the few places where things seemed the same as they had always been. The community was small, and consisted mostly of older people, so most of the familiar faces she had grown up with were still there. But their grandsons wouldn't be visiting them this year, and most of the boys Kate had grown up with were absent. But many of the girls she knew were there, and on Labor Day, their neighbors gave the same barbecue they always did. Kate went next door with her parents. She hadn't heard from Joe for nearly a week by then. The letters she received had always been written weeks before and sometimes arrived in batches. He could have been dead for weeks and she would still be receiving letters. The thought of it always chilled her when it crossed her mind.

She hadn't seen Joe in nearly nine months, and it was beginning to seem endless. She had talked to Andy a couple of times since she'd gotten to the Cape. He was spending the last week of vacation with his grandparents in Maine, after working at the hospital for three months. She could tell from talking to him that he had grown up a lot over the summer. He was going to be starting Harvard law school when they went back. He had completed his undergraduate work in three years instead of four. Since he couldn't go to war, he was anxious to start working. It seemed like the right decision for him, particularly since his father was the head of New York's most prestigious law firm, and they were waiting for him with open arms.

It was hard not to think of Joe as Kate stood at the barbecue, toasting marshmallows, remembering when she'd seen him there the year before. It had been the beginning of their romance. They had started writing to each other shortly after that, and then she had invited him to Thanksgiving dinner. But she could remember almost every word he'd said that night when they walked along the beach. She was standing lost in thought, when someone standing behind her broke into her reverie. She had been a million miles away, thinking of Joe.

"Why do you always burn them?" the voice said, as she gave a start, and then turned quickly backward to see him. It was Joe, standing right behind her, looking tall and thin and pale, and a little older. He was smiling at her, and in a split second she had tossed the branch with the burning marshmallows into the sand, and he had his arms tightly around her. He was the most beautiful sight she'd ever seen.

"Oh my God . . . oh my God . . ." It couldn't be, but it was. She couldn't even begin to imagine what he was doing there, and as she stepped back from him with a worried look, she saw that he was whole, so at least he wasn't wounded. "What are you doing here?"

"I have two weeks leave. I have to report to the War Office on Tuesday. I guess I must have hit my quota of Germans, so they sent me home to check on you. You look pretty good to me. How are you, baby?" Infinitely better now that she saw him. All she could do was think how lucky she was to see him. And he looked every bit as happy as she did. He couldn't keep his hands off her as they stood pressed closely together. He stroked her hair, and kept her close to him, and every few minutes, he kissed her, and held her tight. Neither of them cared who saw them. Kate was just happy he was alive.

Her father spotted them a few minutes later. At first, he couldn't imagine who the tall blond man was standing with Kate, and then he saw him kiss her, and realized it was Joe, as he hurried toward them across the sand.

He gave Joe an enormous hug, and then stood beaming at him as he patted his shoulder. "It's good to see you, Joe. We've all been worried about you."

"I'm fine. You should be worrying about the Germans. We've been shooting the hell out of them."

"They deserve it," Kate's father said firmly with a smile. He felt toward Joe almost like a son.

"I'm just doing it so I can get home," Joe beamed. He was a happy man, and Kate looked like an ecstatically happy woman. She couldn't believe what had just happened to her. It was a reprieve from the long agonizing months of waiting for him and praying for his safety. Two weeks seemed like a miracle to both of them. All she wanted to do was look at him and hold him. And he hadn't moved an inch from her since he'd first surprised her. He wanted to stand as close to her as he could and breathe her in.

"How's it going over there, son?" Clarke asked him in a serious voice, as Kate tore herself away just long enough to go and find her mother and tell her that Joe was home.

"The Brits are having a tough time," Joe said honestly. "The Germans are just plowing right through them, and bombing all the cities. It's pretty tough when you're living through it. I think we'll get them eventually, but it's not going to be easy." The war news had been discouraging for the past two months. Germany had captured Sevastopol, and then launched a ferocious and relentless attack on Stalingrad. Rommel was pummeling the British in North Africa. And the Australians in New Guinea were engaged in fierce combat against the Japanese.

"I'm glad you're all right, son," Clarke said to Joe. He already felt as though he were part of the family, although no promises had been made yet on either side. And even Elizabeth seemed to have softened as she walked over to see him with Kate. She gave him a kiss and a hug and told him how happy she was that he was all right. And she was, for her daughter's sake.

"You've lost weight, Joe," Elizabeth commented, looking worried. He'd gotten very thin, but he was flying hard, working long hours, and eating very little. The rations they were getting were pretty awful, as Kate knew from his letters. "Are you all right?" Elizabeth asked Joe. She was searching his eyes, as he nodded.

"I am now that I'm here for two weeks. I have to go to Washington tomorrow, for two days, but I'll be back on Thursday. I have another ten days after that. I was hoping to come to Boston." For obvious reasons. And Kate beamed.

"We'd love that," Clarke said quickly with a glance at his wife, and even she couldn't resist the look of sheer joy on her daughter's face.

"Would you like to stay with us?" Elizabeth offered, and Kate looked near tears she was so happy as she thanked her mother. But even Elizabeth knew you couldn't fight the tides forever, at some point, you had to go with them. And if anything ever happened to him, she didn't want Kate to feel that they had done whatever they could to keep her and Joe apart. It seemed better for all concerned to be magnanimous about it, as long as Kate didn't do anything foolish. Her mother was planning to talk to her about it, now that she saw them together. Joe was, after all, a thirty-one-year-old man, with needs and desires that far exceeded what was good for Kate to be doing at this point. But as long as they behaved, Elizabeth was willing to have him stay with them. The burden of how they behaved was going to rest on Kate.

The rest of the night seemed to speed by in a blur, and Joe left her long after midnight, to get to Washington by the next morning. He had to drive to Boston, and then take a train to Washington. There were no planes available to him. And when he left her, he kissed her long and hard, and promised to see her in Boston in three days. She hated the fact that she had to go back to school while he was there, but her parents insisted that she couldn't start late. She would just have to

make the best of the time they had. The only concession they made
was that she could stay at the house with Joe and them, as long as she
went to classes every day.

"I'll take her to school myself, and make sure she stays there," Joe
promised them, and she suddenly felt as though she had two fathers,
not just one. There had always been something very paternal and protective about Joe, which was part of why she felt so comfortable with
him. There were a million reasons why she did, and when he left her to
drive back late that night, he held her for a long moment and told her
how much he had missed her and how much he loved her. Kate looked
at him and savored the words. She hadn't heard them in a long time.

"I love you too, Joe. I've been so worried about you." Far more than
she could ever tell him.

"We'll get through this, baby. I promise. And when it's all over, we'll
have a great time together." It was not the kind of promise that her
mother was hoping for, but she didn't care. Just being with him was
enough.

Joe came back from Washington, sooner than expected, in two days,
and moved into the house with them. He was courteous, considerate,
polite, well behaved, and extremely respectful of Kate, which pleased
her parents. Even her mother was impressed by how he behaved. The
only thing he hadn't done, which would have pleased them more, was
ask for her hand in marriage.

Her father skirted the subject delicately one afternoon when he
came home early from the office, and found Joe in the kitchen sketch-
ing designs for a new airplane. There was no way to get it built now,
but when the war was over, it was going to be his dream plane. He had
already filled several notebooks with intricate details.

Seeing that led to a brief discussion about Charles Lindbergh, who
was helping Henry Ford organize bomber plane production.
Lindbergh had wanted to enlist in the military, but FDR had refused.

And what he was doing with Ford was valuable and important to the war effort. But nonetheless the public and the press remained critical of him, due to the political positions he'd taken before the war. Like the rest of the country, Clarke had been disappointed by his statements on behalf of America First. They had made him appear to be sympathetic to the Germans. And like many others, Clarke had lost some of his earlier respect for him. He had always thought of Lindbergh as a patriot, and it seemed so out of character and naïve of him to have been impressed by the Germans before the war. But he had redeemed himself in Clarke's eyes recently by putting his shoulder to the war effort in whatever ways he could.

The conversation drifted slowly back from Lindbergh to Kate, and Clarke didn't ask him directly, but he made it obvious to Joe that he was curious, if not concerned, about his intentions toward his daughter. Joe didn't hesitate for an instant telling him he loved her. He was honest and up front, and although he looked uncomfortable as he spoke of it, he didn't dally around or beat around the bush. He looked down at his hands for a long moment and then back up at her father. And Clarke liked what he saw there, he always had. Joe had never let him down so far. He was just a little slow moving, slower than Kate's mother would have liked, but Kate didn't seem to mind, and Clarke had to respect that. Whatever their feelings for each other, they seemed to be moving toward what they wanted, and had a keen sense of each other. They were inseparable while he was at home, and obviously deeply in love.

"I'm not going to marry her now," Joe said bluntly, squirming slightly in the narrow kitchen chair, like a giant bird sitting on a perch with his wings folded. "It wouldn't be right. If something happens to me over there, she'll be a widow." Clarke didn't want to say that married or not, she would be devastated either way, they both knew that. She was a very young girl. And at nineteen, he was the first man she had ever been in love with, and hopefully the last, if her mother got what she wanted from him. She had told Clarke the night before that she thought they should get engaged. It would at least clarify his intentions and show some respect for Kate. "We don't need to be married. We love each other. There's no one else over there. I'm not seeing anyone, and I won't," Joe explained to her father. He hadn't spelled that out to Kate, but she instinctively knew it. She trusted him completely, and had laid her heart bare to him. She had no defenses or protective wall around her, she had held back nothing from him, which was precisely what was worrying her mother. She wasn't sure if Joe had done the same, and she suspected he hadn't. He was old enough and cautious enough to keep something for himself. Just how much was, in reality, the question. Kate was much younger, and more naïve, and far more vulnerable and trusting, although she could have also hurt him very badly, but she wouldn't do that. Of that there was no doubt.

"Do you see yourself settling down eventually?" Clarke asked quietly. These were the first deep insights he'd had into what Joe wanted out of life. They'd never had a chance to talk about it before the war.

"I suppose so, whatever that means. As long as I can keep flying around and building airplanes. I know I have to do that. As long as everything else fits into that, I guess I could settle in. I've never thought much about it." It was hardly a proposal, or a firm declaration of intention. It was more of a maybe. He had taken a long time to grow up, and obviously had no deep emotional need to be settled with anyone or anything. As he had told Kate, he had never even really cared if he had children. Just airplanes. "It's pretty hard thinking about the future, when you put your life on the line every day, several times a day. When you're doing that, nothing else really matters." He was flying as many as three missions a day, and every time he took off, he knew he might never come back. It was hard to think beyond that. In fact, he didn't want to. All he could do was concentrate on what he was doing, and the importance of shooting down the enemy. The rest was unimportant to him. Even Kate, at those particular moments. She was a luxury he could allow himself after the important things were accomplished. It was how he thought about his life actually. He had things he had to do, and after he did them, he could allow himself to be with her. But she had to wait until he had taken care of business. And right now, the war was business for him.

"I love Kate, Mr. Jamison," Joe said to Clarke, as he handed him a glass of bourbon, and Joe took it and sipped it. "Do you think she'd be happy with a guy like me? Would anyone? Flying comes first with me. It always will. She has to know that." In his own way, he was a genius, he had brilliant ideas about aeronautical engineering, and he knew every tiny piece of his engines intimately. He could fly in any condition imaginable, and had. He knew all there was to know about aerodynamics. He understood a lot less about women, and he knew that, and Clarke was just beginning to understand. Kate's mother had sensed all that about him from the first.

"I think she'd be happy as long as you provided a stable life for her, and cared about her. I think she'll want the same things all women do eventually, a man she can count on, a good home, children. It's pretty basic." The luxuries they could provide for her, and would through her inheritance, but the emotional sustenance and stability, the security, would have to come from him, if he could provide it for her.

"I don't think that's so complicated," Joe said bravely as he took a long swig of the bourbon.

"Sometimes it's more complicated than you think. Women get upset by the damnedest things. You can't just throw them in the trunk of a car like a suitcase. If you get their feathers ruffled, or don't provide for them, emotionally or otherwise, things don't go very smoothly." It was wise advice, and Clarke wasn't sure Joe was ready to hear it yet.

"I guess you're right. I've never thought about it. I never really had to." He squirmed in his seat again and lowered his eyes. He was look-ing into his drink and not at Clarke as he went on a minute later. "I don't think I can really think about all this right now. For one thing, it's too soon. Kate and I hardly know each other, and for another, all I can think about right now is killing Germans. Afterward, when the war is over, we can figure out what color linoleum we want, and if we need drapes. Right now, we don't even have the house yet. I don't think either of us is ready to make big decisions." It was a reasonable thing to say in the circumstances, and true probably, but Clarke was disap-pointed anyway. He had been hoping that Joe was going to ask him for Kate's hand in marriage. And he hadn't said he wouldn't, but he had admitted that he wasn't ready. Maybe it was better that he was honest about it. Clarke thought that, if Joe had been ready to come forward, Kate would have been thrilled about it. At nineteen, she was more ready to settle down, with Joe at least, than he was at thirty-one.

His life up until that point had been very different. He had been floating around the world, drifting between airstrips, concentrating on flying and the future of aviation. He had lofty dreams, as long as they were about airplanes, but few if any when it came to everyday life. What he needed to do, after the war, in Clarke's opinion, was concen-trate more on what was happening on the ground, instead of looking up at the sky all the time. In some ways, Joe Allbright was a dreamer. The question was, did his dreams include Kate?

"What did he say?" Elizabeth quizzed him that night, after they had said goodnight to Joe and Kate, and had closed the door to their bed-room. She had asked him to speak to Joe if he had the opportunity. And to please her, he had come home early from the office to get some time to talk to Joe, before Kate came home from school.

"In few words? He said that he's not ready. 'They're not ready' was what he said more precisely." Clarke tried not to look too disappointed so he wouldn't upset his wife.

"I think Kate would be ready if he were," Liz said sadly.

"So do I. But you can't force it. He's fighting a war, and risking his life every day. It's a little difficult to convince him that he needs to get engaged." Since Kate loved him so much, they had both agreed that they needed to do what they could to help her. They would have liked to tie things down before he left again. It was a rare gift that he had come home for two weeks, but Clarke could see now that this time anyway, there was not going to be an engagement. Maybe later. "I don't think he's a settled-down kind of guy anyway, but I think he could be, for Kate's sake. I have no doubt whatsoever that he loves her, and he said so. I believe him. He doesn't fool around, he's crazy about her. But he's also crazy about his planes." It was exactly what Elizabeth had been afraid of from the first.

"And what happens if she sits this whole war out waiting for him, and he figures out afterward that he doesn't want to settle down? She wastes years, and he breaks her heart." It was precisely the scenario she didn't want for her daughter, and there was no way to guarantee that wouldn't happen. Even if he married her, he could die, and she'd be a widow, and they both knew it. But maybe in that case, she'd have a baby. At least it would be something. But none of it was something they'd have wished for her. What they hoped for was a husband for Kate, who loved her, wanted to be with her, and had a solid, settled life. Clarke was beginning to think that Joe might always be a little bit eccentric. He was brilliant enough to excuse being a little odd. Clarke wasn't sure it was a bad thing, but it made things a little harder to pin down. His conclusion was that they were all going to have to be patient, which was what he said to Liz, as he repeated the conversation to her. "Do you think he was telling you that he never wants to get married?" Liz was panicked over that, but Clarke was calm.

"No, I don't. And I think he will marry her eventually. I've known other guys like him. They just take a little longer to get into the barn," he smiled at his wife, "not all horses are as docile as others. And this one is a bit of a wild horse. Just be patient. At least Kate doesn't seem upset about it."

"That's what worries me. She'd go to the moon with him. She's absolutely head over heels in love with him, and I think she'd agree to anything he wanted. I don't want her living in a tent by the side of the runway in some airport."

"I don't think it'll ever come to that. We can buy them a house if we have to."

"It's not the house I'm worried about. It's who's living in it, and who isn't."

"He'll get there," Clarke reassured her, and he believed what he was saying.

"I hope I'm still alive to see it," she said ruefully, as he kissed her.

"You're not over the hill yet, my love, by any means." But she was feeling tired these days, and depressed over the fact that she was approaching sixty, and she so desperately wanted to see Kate settled and happy. But this was the wrong time. They were at war.

Kate wasn't unhappy at the moment, except for the fact that Joe was away, fighting the war in England. But her mother didn't feel that her future was by any means secure. Joe was like a wild proud bird, and a totally free spirit. And as far as Liz was concerned, there was no predicting what he was going to do when he came back. She was not as sure as Clarke that he could be counted on to marry their daughter. But at least they had tried, and Joe mentioned the conversation to Kate that night too, and she was upset.

"That's disgusting," she said, looking hurt. She felt as though her parents were trying to force him to marry her and she didn't want that. She only wanted him if he wanted her, and if he wanted to get married. "Why did my father do that? It's like trying to force you to marry me."

"They're just worried about you," he said calmly. He understood, although it had made him uncomfortable too. He had never had to explain himself like that before, what he wanted, where he was going and what he was about. "They don't mean any harm by it, Kate. They want what's best for you, and maybe for me too. Actually, I'm kind of flattered. They didn't tell me to get out of their house, or that I'm not good enough for their daughter, and they could have. They want to know if I'm planning to stick around, and if I really love you. And just so you know, I told your father that I do. We'll just have to figure out the rest when I get back from England. God only knows where I'll be then." But she didn't like the sound of that either. He had always been blown by the wind to the most appealing airstrip. But she didn't want to question him about it. Her father had done enough for one afternoon, and she was really annoyed at him, in spite of Joe's good nature. She was glad that he hadn't been upset by it, and saw no point to the conversation. And she knew that whatever Joe had said that didn't sit right with them, would come back to haunt her, but she couldn't worry about that now.

The time they spent together in September of 1942 was magical. She went to school every day, and afterward he came to meet her. They spent hours talking and walking, sitting under trees and talking about life and all the things that mattered to them. In Joe's case, most of the time it was airplanes. But there were other things too, people, and places, and things he wanted to do. Facing death every day made life even more precious to him. They spent lazy afternoons, holding hands and kissing, and they had already agreed that they wouldn't sleep with each other. As the days went by, it became an ever greater challenge, but they behaved admirably. Just as he didn't want to leave her widowed, if he died, he also didn't want to leave her pregnant when he went back to the war. And if they married one day, he wanted it to be because they chose to, not because they had to. And she agreed with him, although some part of her almost wished that if something happened to him, she would have his baby. But all they could do now was trust the future. There were no promises, no guarantees, no sure things. There were only their hopes and dreams and the time they had spent together. The rest was entirely unknown.

When he left her finally, they were more in love than they had ever been, and knew everything about each other. It was as though they were each the perfect complement to the other, and fit together seamlessly. They were different, but so perfectly matched Kate was convinced they had been born for each other, and Joe didn't disagree. He was still awkward at times, still shy, still quiet now and then, lost in his own thoughts, but she was able to understand that, and she found all his little quirks and mannerisms endearing. And when he left this time, there were tears in his eyes when he kissed her and told her he loved her. He promised to write to her as soon as he got back to England. It was the only promise he made her before he left. And for Kate, it was enough.

6

THE WAR HEATED UP in October that year, and some of the reports were more encouraging than they had been. The Australians and their allies were pushing the Japanese out of New Guinea, and they appeared to be weakening in Guadalcanal. The British were finally wearing down German forces in North Africa as well. And Stalingrad was hanging on against the Germans, though admittedly by a thread.

Joe was flying constant missions, and the one he flew over Gibraltar made history. He and three other Spitfire pilots shot down twelve German Stuka dive-bombers on a reconnaissance mission in advance of the huge Allied invasion campaign known as Operation Torch. The mission had been a huge success.

Joe was decorated, and received the Distinguished Flying Cross from Great Britain, and flew back to Washington to receive the United States Distinguished Flying Cross medal from the President, and this time Kate had ample warning of his return. She took the train from Boston to Washington to meet him, three days before Christmas. They had forty-eight hours before he had to go back to England. But once again, it was a precious gift to them, and one that neither of them had expected. The War Department put him up at a hotel, and Kate took a small room on the same floor. She went to the ceremony at the White

House with him and the President shook her hand, and she and Joe posed for a photograph with him. It all felt like something in a movie to Kate.

Joe took her out to dinner afterward, and she smiled at him after they ordered. He was still wearing his medal. And he was more handsome than he had ever been.

"I still can't believe you're here," she said, beaming at him. He was truly a hero. The ceremony had been a strange mixture of happiness and sadness for Kate, as she realized how easily he could have been killed. Everything about life these days seemed bittersweet. Every day that he lived was a gift, and nearly every day she heard about boys who had died in Europe or the Pacific. The girls she had gone to school with had already lost so many loved ones. So far, she'd been very lucky. She held her breath every day, praying for Joe.

"I can't believe I'm here," Joe said as he took a sip of wine. "And before I know it, I'll be freezing my ass off in England again." But here, because the war wasn't as close, things seemed more festive. There were Christmas trees everywhere, carolers, and children laughing as they waited for Santa Claus. There were still happy faces, in contrast to the pained, hungry, frightened ones in England. Even the children there looked exhausted, everyone was so tired of the bombs and the air raids. Houses disappeared in the blink of an eye, friends were lost, children were killed. In England, it seemed almost impossible to be happy these days. And yet, the people Joe knew there were very brave.

Washington looked like a fairyland to him, and to Kate. After dinner, they walked back to their hotel, and chatted in the living room they provided in the lobby. They sat there for hours because they didn't want to leave each other and go to their rooms. And as the night wore on, the sitting room got increasingly drafty, but she didn't think it proper to sit in either of their bedrooms upstairs. Her parents had wanted to come to Washington with her, not just to chaperone her, but to celebrate Joe at his ceremony. But in the end, they couldn't. Her father had important clients coming in from Chicago, and Elizabeth had to be with him. They trusted her implicitly to go alone, and knew Joe was a responsible person. But in the end, they were both so cold sitting in the lobby, he suggested they sit in his room. He promised to behave, and by then Kate's hands were so cold she could hardly move them, and her teeth were chattering. And outside, it was snowing and bitter cold.

They walked up the narrow staircase to their rooms. It was a tiny hotel, and the room rate was dirt cheap for military personnel, which was why they had booked a room for him there. Kate's room was only slightly more expensive. The rooms themselves were simply decorated and tiny, but for two days neither of them cared. All they wanted was to see each other. Seeing him had been the only Christmas gift she wanted, and she hadn't expected to get it. It was the answer to all her prayers. She had missed him terribly since September. And she felt guilty almost to see him. There were women she knew who hadn't laid eyes on their brothers and fiancés since Pearl Harbor. And she had seen Joe twice in the last four months.

If nothing else, because of the size of the rooms, they were warmer than the lobby. There was a bed and a chair in each room, a dresser and a sink, and there was a shower and a toilet in what must have once been a closet. The only place to hang clothes was on the back of the door, but Kate was grateful to have her own bathroom.

Once they got to his room, Joe sat on the bed and she took the chair. He opened a small bottle of champagne he had bought for them when he got to Washington. It was to celebrate his decoration, which dangled from the breast of his uniform.

Kate still couldn't get over the fact that they'd been to the White

House. Mrs. Roosevelt had been so kind to her, and looked exactly as Kate had expected. For some reason, she had noticed that the First Lady had lovely hands, and she'd been mesmerized by them. Kate knew she'd remember every detail of the afternoon forever. Joe seemed a lot more blasé about it, but he'd been to some pretty interesting places with Charles over the years, and other things impressed him more. Like extraordinary flying feats, or important pilots. But he was pleased with the decoration anyway, although he was sorry for the men he knew who had died in the course of the missions he'd flown. He would have vastly preferred not to get the medal and to have them come home with him. It made it hard for him to celebrate the event, or be genuinely excited about the medal. He had already lost so many friends. They were talking about it as he handed her the champagne.

The chair Kate was perched on was so uncomfortable that he invited her to sit on the bed with him. She knew they were tempting fate, but she also knew that they could trust each other. They weren't going to do anything foolish just because they were sitting on a bed in a hotel room. And without hesitation, she came to sit beside him, and they went on talking. She only had half a glass of champagne, and Joe had two. Neither of them was a big drinker, and after a while she said she should go back to her room.

Before she got up, he kissed her. It was a long, slow kiss filled with all the sadness and longing they had both felt for so long, and the joy they both felt to be together. When he stopped kissing her, she was breathless, and so was he. They both suddenly felt as though they were starving. It was as though all the deprivations of the past year had finally caught up with them, and they couldn't get enough of each other. Kate had never felt as overwhelmed by desire for him, nor had Joe. He wasn't even thinking as he laid her down on the bed when he next kissed her, and gently let himself down on top of her, and much to her own amazement, she didn't stop him. They both needed to catch their breath and stop what they were doing before they went any further, or they weren't going to be able to, and they both knew it. He was whispering hoarsely to her as he told her how much he loved her, and he meant it. More than he ever had before.

"I love you too," she whispered breathlessly, all she wanted to do was kiss him and hold him and feel him on top of her, and without thinking, she started unbuttoning his jacket. She wanted to feel his skin, and to nuzzle him. She couldn't get enough of him, and he knew he couldn't restrain himself much longer.

"What are you doing?" he whispered as she opened his jacket, and he started unbuttoning her blouse. Within seconds, he had her breasts in his hands, and leaned down to kiss them. She moaned as he pulled her blouse away and took off her bra, and by then she had taken off his jacket, and he had pulled off his T-shirt, and he was bare chested. The feel of their flesh on each other was hypnotic. "Baby . . . do you want to stop?" he asked her. He was trying to keep a grip on the situation, but he was losing it quickly. Just looking at her, and feeling her next to him, he could no longer think.

"I know we should stop," she whispered between his kisses, but she didn't want to. She couldn't. He was all that she wanted. They had been so restrained for so long, and now suddenly all she wanted was to be with him. And as she began to abandon herself to him, he pulled away from her and looked down at her, with all the restraint he could muster, because he loved her so much.

"Kate, listen to me . . . we don't have to do this if you don't want to. . . ." It was his last effort to save her, but she didn't want to be saved this time. All she wanted was to love him, and be loved.

"I love you so much. . . . I want you, Joe. . . ." She wanted to make love to him before he left again. After the ceremony that day, she had understood more than ever how ephemeral life was, and how fleeting. He might never come back to her again, and now she wanted to have this with him. He kissed her again in answer to what she had said to him, and he gently peeled the rest of her clothes away, and took his own off, and a moment later they were lying on the bed, their clothes in a heap on the floor beside them. Joe was drawing her exquisite body with gentle fingers, and kissing her everywhere, savoring the moment and the sound and feel of her as she moaned beneath his lips and his fingers. She was kissing him as he entered her, and it only hurt her for an instant, and within seconds she was abandoning herself completely to him. They were both engulfed in passion, and he had never loved anyone as he did her, or given himself so totally. He held nothing back, and it almost frightened him as he felt as though he were going to disappear inside her, his soul blended with hers, his body keening for her. They made love for a long time, and when it was over they were both too spent to move or speak. It was Joe who moved first, as he rolled over carefully on his side, and looked at her more tenderly than he ever had any woman. Kate had opened doors in him he never knew were there.

"I love you, Kate," he whispered into her hair, and traced a lazy finger down her side, and then covered her gently with the blanket. She was half asleep as she smiled up at him. She felt no shame, no regret, no pain. She had never in her entire life been as happy. She was his at last.

She never went back to her room that night, she stayed with him, and he tucked her into bed and then slipped into it next to her. He wanted to make love to her again, but he didn't want to hurt her. But in the morning, it was Kate who reached for him, and within moments, they found each other, and soared to new heights again. New places had opened in their life together, and new feelings had been born. And when Kate got up and looked at him afterward, she realized that a deeper bond had been formed between them. It didn't matter where he had been, or where he was going now, she knew instinctively that for the rest of their lives, she would be his, and he was irrevocably woven into her. She wouldn't have known how to say it to him, but she knew, as she got into the shower with him, that he owned her. Her soul and the deepest part of her were his.

7

LEAVING JOE IN WASHINGTON was even harder this time than
when he had left her in Boston in September. He was part of her now,
and he was even more tender with her. It was as though he sensed that
she was truly his, and all he wanted was to protect her. He warned her
a thousand times to be careful on the way home, to take care of herself,
not to do anything foolish. He wished he could have stayed there with
her, but he had to go back to England to fly his missions.

And when he left her, it was agonizing for both of them. For the first
time in his life, he had held nothing back. He had been vulnerable and
strong at the same time, and just as she had, he had given himself to
her. Not because he had slept with her, but because he had taken responsibility for her. And leaving now was excruciatingly painful for
both of them.

"Write to me every day . . . Kate, I love you," he said, before he left
her. And when he put her on the train at Union Station, she thought
her heart would break as it pulled slowly out of the station. He ran beside it for as long as he could, and then he stood on the platform wav-
ing, as she waved at him and tears rolled down her cheeks. She could
no longer imagine a life without him, and she truly believed that if he
died now, it would kill her. She didn't want to live an hour beyond

121

him. And it reminded her once again of the pain of losing her father, as the train pulled away. Joe awoke feelings of love in her she had never before known. And leaving him brought back feelings of loss she had spent half her lifetime trying to forget.

She sat silently with her eyes closed for most of the trip. It was Christmas Eve, and she knew that he would be on a plane to England before she got home. She wouldn't be back in Boston until late that night, and she knew her parents would be waiting up for her. But she could hardly speak she was so grief stricken when she got off the train and hailed a cab. She could no longer imagine surviving without him. What he had given her, and allowed her to give him, was the glue that would cement them together forever. It had been the final piece of the puzzle. He hadn't asked her to marry him, but he didn't have to. She sensed, just as he did, that the very fiber of their beings had blended and become one.

And when her mother saw her face that night when she came in, as they waited for her in the living room, Kate realized Elizabeth must have thought something terrible had happened. But all that had happened was that Kate missed him so unbearably this time, she couldn't even imagine waiting months or years to see him again, or worse, if something terrible happened. Everything was suddenly different. They had taken down their walls.

"Is something wrong?" her mother asked, looking panicked because Kate looked as though someone had died. Kate shook her head and realized something had, her freedom. She was no longer just a girl in love with a man. She was part of a larger whole, and she felt as though she could not function without him. The past two days had changed everything for her.

"No," Kate said in a small voice, but she was unconvincing.

"Are you sure? Did you have an argument before he left?" That happened to people sometimes, out of pure tension.

"No, he was wonderful," and with that, Kate burst into tears and dove into her mother's arms, while her father watched them, looking worried. "What if he gets killed, Mom? . . . what if he never comes back?" Suddenly all the passion, all the fear, all the longing, all the dreams and needs and excitement and disappointment fused into one giant explosion, like a bomb that had been dropped on her by the fact that he was leaving and going back to England. She could not bear the thought of losing someone she loved again. Just fearing it made her feel like a child.

"We just have to pray that he does come back, sweetheart. That's all we can do. If he's meant to, he'll come back. You have to be brave now." Her mother spoke gently, looking sadly over Kate's shoulder at her husband, with eyes filled with regret.

"I don't want to be brave," Kate sobbed. "I want him to come home . . . I want the war to be over." She sounded like a child, and her parents ached for her. It was terrible, but half the world was facing the same agonies she was. She was not unique in her sorrow. In fact, she was luckier than most. Others had already lost the men they loved, their sons and brothers and husbands. And Kate still had Joe. For now.

She sat down on the couch with them finally, and regained her composure. Her mother handed her a handkerchief, and her father hugged her. They were both sorry for her. And after her mother had tucked her into bed that night, like a little girl, she went back to her bedroom to her husband. She closed the door with a sigh, and sat down at her dressing table.

"This is exactly what I didn't want for her," Elizabeth said sadly. "I didn't want her to love him like this. It's too late now. They're not engaged, they're not married. He's made no promises. They have nothing. They just love each other."

"That's a lot, Liz. Maybe it's all they need. Being married wouldn't keep him alive. It's in God's hands. At least they love each other."

"If something happens to him now, Clarke, she'll never get over it." She didn't say it to Clarke, but watching Kate cry that night had reminded her of how bereft Kate had been when her father died.

"She's in the same boat half the women in this country are in. She'll have to get over it, if something happens. She's young. She'd recover."

"I hope she never has to face that," her mother said fervently.

But the next morning, Kate was in a somber mood for Christmas. Her mother had given her a beautiful sapphire necklace with matching sapphire earrings, and her father was offering to buy her a two-year-old car he had seen, in perfect condition, if her driving improved. But with gas rationing she had little opportunity to practice, and Elizabeth didn't think it was a good idea. Kate had bought each of them lovely presents. But all she could think about was Joe as she sat silently at Christmas dinner, unable to say a word. She knew he was back in England by then, flying bombing missions again.

For the next several weeks, her spirits never lifted. Her mother was seriously worried about her, and even thinking of taking her to a doctor. She looked tired and pale, whenever she came home for an occasional night from college on the weekends. She seemed to have no social life anymore, and Andy called her at home several times, complaining that he hadn't seen her in ages. All she seemed to want to do was sleep and reread Joe's letters. He sounded almost as depressed in England. It had been hard going back again, and the weather had been foul. They had had to cancel several missions, and the men were restless and bored.

It was Valentine's Day when Kate's mother finally began to panic about her. She had seen Kate the previous day when she came home for Sunday dinner. She barely touched her food, looked tired and pale, and she cried every time she talked about Joe. After she left, Elizabeth told Clarke she wanted to take Kate to a doctor.

"She's just lonely," he said, dismissing it. "It's cold and dark, she's working hard at school. She'll be all right, Liz. Just give her time. And maybe he'll get another leave soon." But in February of 1943, he was flying more than ever.

Joe had taken part in the night attack on Wilhelmshaven. He was flying mostly day raids, as the British preferred to do the night flying themselves. But he was nonetheless invited to fly at night with them in the bombing of Nuremberg.

It was another week, toward the end of February, when Kate herself began to panic. She had seen Joe eight weeks before, and she had suspected it at first, and been certain for the past month. She was pregnant. It had happened in Washington when he came home to be decorated at the White House. She had no idea what to do about it, and she didn't want to tell her parents. She had gotten the name of a doctor in Mattapan from one of the girls at school, pretending it was for a friend of hers, but she couldn't make herself call him. She knew it would ruin everything if she had a baby now. She'd have to leave school, and it would scandalize everyone, and even if they wanted to, they couldn't get married. Joe had told her recently that he had no hope of coming home on leave anytime soon, and she hadn't told him why she had asked. She just told him that she missed him. But she would never have wanted to force him to marry her, or even ask him to. But she also knew that if she had an abortion, and something happened to him, she would never forgive herself. Married or not, she would want the baby. Rather than making a decision about it, she was letting time pass, and eventually she knew it would be too late to end it. But she hadn't even begun to think of what she would say to her parents after that, or her embarrassment, when she explained her circumstances to school.

Andy dropped by to see her in the dining room one night, and asked if she had the flu. Everyone at Harvard had been sick, and he thought she looked ill. She had been violently nauseous since early

January, and it was nearly the first of March. She had almost decided to go ahead with the pregnancy by then, she knew she couldn't do otherwise, and in truth she wanted it. It was Joe's baby. She was going to wait to tell her parents until she had no other choice. She also figured that if it showed by Easter, she'd have to drop out of school by then. She would have liked to hold out till June and finish her sophomore year, and she could have come back to school in the fall right after she had the baby. But by June, when vacation would begin, she'd be nearly six months pregnant, and there would be no way she could hide it. Sooner or later, she was going to have to face the music. The only amazing thing, as far as Kate was concerned, was that her mother didn't suspect a thing. But once she did, Kate knew, there would be hell to pay, and she knew her parents wouldn't forgive Joe easily.

She had said nothing to Joe about it, although she wrote to him every day. She had debated, but didn't want to upset him, or make him angry. He needed all his wits about him to fly his missions, and she didn't want to distract him. So she was facing it entirely alone, retching on her bathroom floor every morning, and dragging herself to classes. Even her housemates had noticed that she slept all the time, and the house mother asked her if she needed to see a doctor. Kate insisted she was fine, just studying too hard, but her grades were starting to slip, and all of her professors had noticed that as well. Her life was rapidly turning into a nightmare, and she was terrified of what her parents were going to say, when she told them she was having a baby in September, out of wedlock. She was worried that her father was going to try to force Joe to marry her when he came back, but she was not going to let him do that. She knew what a free spirit Joe was, and he had been very clear about never wanting to have children. He might adjust one day, and fall in love with the baby, but she was not going to let anyone put a gun to his head to marry her. The only thing she was sure of in the midst of all her worries these days was how much she loved him, and the other thing she knew was how much she wanted his child. She made her peace with it in early March, and she was even a little excited about it. It was her secret. She had told no one, and didn't plan to anytime soon.

"So what's happening to you these days?" Andy asked her one afternoon, when he dropped by from Harvard. He was having an excruciatingly busy first year of law school, and was feeling utterly swamped. They were walking slowly through Harvard Yard as he talked to her, and his long lanky good looks and dark hair caught the attention of every girl who walked by. They were beginning to look desperate these days, and Andy was getting a lot of attention from the Radcliffe girls.

"You're spoiled rotten," Kate teased him, and he grinned. He had a beautiful smile, and big dark eyes that were filled with warmth and kindness.

"Hell, somebody has to take care of these girls for our boys in uniform. It's hard work, but someone has to do it." He was actually enjoying being at home these days, and was getting over being embarrassed by being 4-F. He had explained it so many times that he was no longer as sensitive about it. And there were times when he was secretly glad to be home.

"You're disgusting, Andy Scott," Kate reassured him. She enjoyed his company, and they had become good friends in the past two years.

He was going to work at the hospital again that summer. She had been dragging her feet about a summer job, because she knew she'd be showing by then, and as an unmarried mother, no one would want to hire her. She was thinking about staying at their house on Cape Cod until she had the baby. And in a few weeks she was going to advise Radcliffe that she would be taking a leave of absence, starting at Easter. It meant she wouldn't graduate with her class. But with luck, it would only cost her one semester. And she would have a great reward for it, if they would take her back. She would have to tell them why she was leaving. She wasn't the first woman it had happened to, and she had made her peace with it. She wondered what Joe would think of it when he found out. She wasn't going to tell him until he next came home, even if that meant her having the baby without his knowing. And she was such good friends with Andy now, she was almost sorry not to tell him. But she knew she couldn't. And he would probably be shocked when he heard. She worried at times now that he would think less of her once he found out. But it was a price she was prepared to pay.

"So what are you doing this summer, Kate? The Red Cross again?"

"Probably," she said vaguely, but he didn't notice that she was distracted. She looked better than she had in February, and he was trying to convince her to go to a movie with him. She went with him occasionally, more so now that he had given up on her as a potential date, and accepted her as a friend. But she had a paper due the next day, and said that this time she couldn't go with him.

"You're no fun. Well, at least I'm glad you're looking better. You looked like death the last time I saw you." The nausea was actually beginning to abate, she was almost three months pregnant, and nearly at the end of her first trimester. She was getting excited about the baby, and hoped it would be a little boy, who would look exactly like Joe.

"I had the flu," she reiterated, and he had believed her all along. He had no reason to doubt her, or suspect she might be pregnant. It was the farthest thing from his mind.

"I'm glad you're over it. Do your paper so we can go to a movie next week," he said, as he hopped on his bicycle, and waved as he rode off, his dark hair ruffled by the wind, and his brown eyes laughing at her. He was a nice boy, and she had grown very fond of him.

She wondered at times if things would have been different between them if Joe had never existed. It was hard to say. She had deep feelings of affection for Andy but couldn't even imagine feeling for him what she felt for Joe. There was something warm and cuddly and kind about Andy, but he elicited none of the excitement and passion that she felt for Joe. But she knew that one day, Andy would make someone a fine husband. He was responsible and loving and decent, all the things that women looked for in a man. Unlike Joe, who was awkward and vague, and brilliant, and totally obsessed with airplanes, and had no desire to settle down. She had never expected to fall in love with a man like Joe Allbright, let alone have a baby with him, without even being married. Her life had taken several sharp turns recently, in totally unexpected directions. But with his baby growing in her, she had never been more in love with Joe.

She was actually feeling very well that weekend, and not nearly as tired as she had been. She'd finished the work she had to do, and she had three letters from Joe in one day. They tended to arrive in clumps like that sometimes, it had to do with the way the censors sent them, after they cleared them, to make sure that no one gave away sensitive security secrets, or the locations of their missions. Joe's letters to her had never been a problem. He wrote to her about people, and the local countryside, and his feelings for her, all totally safe subjects.

She had been planning to go home that weekend, and at the last minute decided against it. She went to a movie with a group of friends, and saw Andy there with a girl Kate knew from one of her classes. She was a tall blonde from the Midwest, she had a great smile and long legs, and she had recently transferred from Wellesley. She grinned at Andy when the girl turned away to put her cardigan on, and he made a face at her. Kate and the girls she had gone to the movie with all went back to the house on their bicycles afterward. It was the best way to travel around campus and Cambridge. They were almost home, when a boy on a bicycle came whizzing out of nowhere, cut through the group with a holler and a whoop, and hit Kate so hard she went flying off her bike, fell to the pavement, and was knocked momentarily unconscious. By the time the other girls got off their bikes, she was awake again, but a little groggy. And the boy who had hit her was standing next to her looking panicked and disoriented. It was obvious that he was drunk.

"Are you crazy?" one of the girls shouted at him, as two others helped Kate to her feet. She had hurt her arm, and her hip, she had fallen hard on her bottom, but nothing seemed to be broken. But all she could think about as she limped back to her room was her baby. She didn't say anything to anyone, but she went straight to bed as soon as they got back to the house, and one of her friends brought her a couple of ice packs for her arm and her hip.

"Are you okay?" Diana asked in her long, slow southern accent. "These northern boys sure don't have manners!"

Kate smiled at her, and thanked her for the ice packs, but it wasn't her arm or her hip that was bothering her. She had had cramps for the past several minutes, and didn't know what to do about it. She thought about going to the infirmary but it was too far to walk, and she was afraid that might make things even worse. She thought maybe if she just stayed in bed, it would get better. She had obviously shaken up the baby pretty badly. But hopefully, it would settle down.

"If you need anything, just call me," Diana said as she left Kate, and went downstairs to smoke a cigarette with a boy from MIT who had dropped by to visit. And when she came back an hour later to check on Kate, she was sleeping. Everyone was sound asleep by the time Kate woke up again at four o'clock in the morning. She was in agony, and when she rolled over in her bed to try and get more comfortable, she saw that she was bleeding. She tried to keep quiet, in spite of the pain, so she wouldn't wake the other girls sleeping near her. And she was doubled over in pain as she made her way to the bathroom. She didn't see it, but she left a trail of blood behind her as she walked. Her arm and her hip hurt too, from the encounter with the bicycle, but nothing was as painful as her belly. She could hardly stand.

She closed the door to the bathroom as quietly as she could, and turned the light on, and when she looked in the mirror she saw that everything from her waist down was covered in blood. She was hemorrhaging, and knew what was happening. She was losing Joe's baby. But she was afraid that if she called someone, she might get kicked out of school, or they might call her parents. She didn't know what the consequences would be if the administration found out she was pregnant. She assumed she'd be asked to leave.

This wasn't the way she had wanted things to happen. She had no idea what to do, or who to call, or what was about to happen. But she had no time to think about it, the pains that had awakened her were suddenly so severe that she could hardly breathe. She was being hit by wave after wave of powerful contractions. She was on her knees on the floor, gasping for air, with blood everywhere, when Diana, the southern girl, wandered in for a drink of water and found her on the floor.

"Oh my God . . . Kate . . . what happened?" She looked like the victim of an ax murder, and all Diana could think of was that they had to call a doctor, an ambulance, someone, but as she said as much to Kate, she begged her not to.

"Don't . . . please . . . I can't . . . Diana . . ." She couldn't even finish her sentence, but the girl from New Orleans suddenly suspected what had happened to her.

"Are you pregnant? Tell me the truth, Kate." She wanted to help her, but had to know what was happening to her. Her mother was a nurse, and her father a doctor, and she had good experience with first aid. But she had never seen as much blood as the pool rapidly spreading around Kate. She was afraid she'd bleed to death if they didn't call someone to help them. Not getting Kate to the hospital seemed like a big chance to take.

"Yes, I am . . ." Kate choked and admitted she was pregnant, as Diana helped her roll over onto a stack of towels. Kate was crying at each pain now, and biting a towel to stay silent and not make any noise. "Almost three months. . . ."

"Shit. I had an abortion once. My daddy nearly killed me. I was seventeen, and I was afraid to tell him . . . so I went to someone outside town. . . . I was as bad as you are . . . poor baby," she said, putting a damp cloth on Kate's head, and holding her hand now with each contraction. She had locked the door so no one could walk in on them, but what she feared most was that she would cost Kate her life if she didn't get help for her. The bleeding was horrific. But it seemed to slow a little as the pains got worse. Neither of them was sure what was happening, but it was easy to figure out that Kate was going to expel the baby. There was no way it was still alive with all that bleeding.

It was another hour of excruciating pain before Kate's entire body writhed in agony, and within seconds, she lost the baby. She lost more blood, but as soon as it was out, she seemed to be losing less. Diana was mopping up what she could with towels, and she had wrapped the fetus in a towel and put it where Kate couldn't see it. She was too weak to even be hysterical, and when she tried to sit up, she almost fainted. Diana had her lie down again.

It was nearly seven o'clock, and they had been in the bathroom for three hours, before Diana could help Kate back to bed. Everything had been cleaned up, and once she was sure that Kate was safely tucked into bed, she ran downstairs to the garbage room, to dispose of the towel that held the evidence of what had happened to Kate.

The bleeding was less out of control, and she was still in pain, but it was tolerable. Diana explained that it was her uterus contracting to stop the bleeding, which was a good thing. The earlier pains had been to expel the baby. And if she didn't bleed too much more, Diana hoped that she would be all right. She had already told Kate that if it got any worse she was calling an ambulance and sending her to the hospital, no matter how much Kate objected. And Kate had agreed, she was terrified and too weak to argue, and in shock from losing so much blood. She was shaking violently, as Diana put three more blankets on her bed, and the other girls began stirring.

"Are you okay?" one of them asked as she got up. They had class that morning. "You look kind of pale, Kate. Maybe you got a concussion when that guy knocked you off your bike last night." She was yawning as she headed for the bathroom, and Kate said she had a terrible headache, and was still visibly shaking as she lay tucked into her bed.

Diana continued to hover over her, and a girl from another room came in to borrow some towels, and looked worried when she saw Kate's ashen lips, and her face, she was the color of chalk.

"What happened to you last night?" the girl asked, and came over to take Kate's pulse.

"She fell off her bike and hit her head," Diana covered for her, but the other girl knew better. Like Diana, she came from a medical family, in New York, and she knew enough to understand that Kate had more than a headache or a concussion. She was so gray, she looked like she'd lost a lot of blood, and was possibly even in shock.

She leaned her face down close to Kate's ear, and gently touched her shoulder. "Kate . . . tell me the truth . . . are you bleeding? . . ." All Kate could do was nod her head and shake. Her teeth were chattering so hard she couldn't even speak. "I think you're in shock. . . . Did you have an abortion?" she whispered. Kate had always liked her, and was willing to trust her with the information. She knew she was in trouble. She was feeling dizzy and her body had been so traumatized that she was freezing and couldn't stop shaking, in spite of the stack of blankets Diana had put on her. Both girls were standing next to her bed looking worried sick.

"No," Kate whispered to the girl, whose name was Beverly. "I lost it."

"Are you hemorrhaging?" She didn't think so, the bed didn't feel damp around her. She was afraid to look.

"I don't think so."

"I'm going to cut class today and stay with you. You shouldn't be alone here. Do you want to go to the hospital?" Kate shook her head no in answer. It was the last thing she wanted.

"I'll stay too," Diana volunteered, and went to get her a cup of tea. Half an hour later, all the other girls had gone to their classes, and the two caretakers sat on either side of Kate's bed. She was wide awake, and crying intermittently. The entire experience had terrified and depressed her.

"You'll be okay, Kate," Beverly said quietly. "I had an abortion last year. It was awful. Just try to sleep, you'll feel better in a day or two. You'll be surprised how fast you get better." And then she thought of something. "Is there anyone you want me to call?" Obviously, there was another person involved in this, and she didn't know Kate's situation. But Kate shook her head.

"He's in England," she whispered, through teeth that were beginning to clench. She had never felt as awful in her life, the loss of blood had shaken her entire system to the core.

"Does he know?" Diana asked, as she patted Kate's shoulder and Kate looked at her gratefully. She couldn't have gotten through it without her. And this way, no one would know, neither Radcliffe nor her parents. Nor Joe.

"I didn't tell him. I was going to have the baby."

"You can have another one when he comes home." Beverly didn't add "if he lives," which was what all three of them were thinking as Kate started to cry again. It was a long, lonely day for her, and it was another two days before she felt even halfway human.

Diana and Beverly went back to class the next day, and Kate just lay in her bed and cried all day long. It was Wednesday before she got out of bed, and when she did, she looked ghostly and had lost ten pounds. She hadn't eaten since Sunday, but the bleeding had almost stopped. She looked and felt terrible, and there were dark circles under her eyes, but all three girls agreed, she was out of danger. She tried to thank them for what they'd done for her, but every time she did, she started crying again.

"It's going to be like that for a while," Beverly warned. "I cried for a month. It's just hormones." But it wasn't just hormones, it was their baby. She had lost a part of Joe.

No one knew what had happened to her, and they all thought in the house that she was in bed as a result of her bike accident on Sunday night. And she never told anyone anything different. She felt as though she had been on another planet for several days. Everything seemed unreal and different, and the only thing that cheered her up were Joe's letters. But she cried again when she realized that she couldn't even tell him what had happened, and what they'd lost.

She spent the following weekend in bed, studying. She was quiet and pale, and still didn't look well when Andy dropped by on Saturday afternoon. It had been a week since the miscarriage, but she still looked awful. She made her way gingerly downstairs to see him. Beverly and Diana had been bringing her food from the cafeteria all week. And the first time she left her room was to see Andy, as he waited for her in the living room downstairs.

"Jesus, Kate, you look legally dead. What happened to you?" She looked so fragile and pale that he was frightened for her. She was wraithlike.

"I got hit by a bike last Sunday night. I think I had a concussion."

"Did you go to the hospital to get it checked out?"

"No, I'm okay," she said, sitting in a chair next to him, but he was genuinely worried about her.

"I think you should see a doctor. Maybe you're brain dead," he grinned at her.

"Very funny. I feel better."

"I'd hate to have seen you on Monday."

"Yes, you would have," she said, but seeing him brought her back into the world again and she was less depressed when she went back to her room, although she was bone tired. Diana had warned her that she would be anemic for a while, and told her to eat lots of liver.

But by the following week, she seemed more herself, and felt well enough to go back to classes. No one had any idea what had happened to her, and as the weeks went by, she quietly put it behind her. She never told Joe.

8

FOR THE REST OF KATE'S sophomore year, she was busy with school. She got letters from Joe constantly, but there were no leaves on the horizon for him. It was the spring of 1943, and Kate went to see newsreels every chance she got, hoping to catch a glimpse of Joe's face.

The RAF was continuing to bomb Berlin and Hamburg, and other cities. Tunis had been taken by the British, and the Americans had taken Bizerte, in North Africa, back from the Germans. On the eastern front the Germans and Russians had almost come to a dead halt, up to their knees in mud, in the spring thaw.

Kate saw her parents frequently on the weekends, wrote to Joe, and went to dinner or the movies occasionally with Andy. He had a new girlfriend from Wellesley that spring, and was spending time with her. It left him less time for Kate, but she didn't mind. She, Diana, and Beverly had become fast friends after her miscarriage. And that summer she was working for the Red Cross again.

They went to Cape Cod at the end of August, but this time Joe didn't appear to surprise her at the barbecue. He hadn't been home in eight months, since the previous Christmas, when they met in Washington. And she couldn't help thinking, as she took long solitary walks on the beach that, if she hadn't lost the baby, she'd be eight months pregnant by then. Her parents never found out what had happened. And her mother was still talking about the fact that Joe had still made no promises about a future with her. She reminded Kate constantly that she was waiting for a man who had promised her nothing. No marriage. No ring. No future. He just expected her to wait for him, and see what happened when he came home. She was twenty years old, and he was thirty-two, old enough to know what he wanted to do when he returned.

Her mother constantly reminded Kate of it every time she went home, and continued to, as the leaves had begun to turn in late October. Kate was studying for exams, it was her junior year, and the house mother where she lived came to tell her she had a visitor downstairs. Without even questioning it, Kate assumed it was Andy. He was in his second year of law school, and working like a slave.

She ran quickly down the stairs, with a book still in her hand, and a pale blue sweater over her shoulders. She was wearing a gray skirt, and saddle shoes, and the moment her foot left the last step, she saw him. It was Joe, looking tall and incredibly handsome in his uniform. He looked very serious as he waited for her, and her breath caught as their eyes met. He seemed to hold back for an instant, and then without a word she flew into his arms and he held her close. She had the feeling as he held her that he had been through some rough times. He couldn't seem to find the words, but she knew that she not only needed him, but he needed her, as well. The war was taking a toll on everyone, even Joe.

"I'm so happy to see you," she said, still in his arms as she closed her eyes. It had been an agonizing ten months, worrying about him constantly, losing their baby, never knowing how he was.

"So am I," he said, pulling away from her finally, and looking in her eyes. It was easy to see how tired he was. He felt as though he was in the air almost constantly these days, and a heartbreaking number of their planes had been shot down. The Germans were getting desperate and hitting hard. He looked at her somberly then, and she realized that he felt awkward with her again. It took him time sometimes to open up with her, and readjust. His letters were so easy and candid with her that she forgot sometimes how shy he was. "I've only got twenty-four hours, Kate. I have to be in Washington tomorrow afternoon, and I'm going back tomorrow night." He was in the States for meetings involving a top secret mission, and he had been flown in with great difficulty. But he could share none of that with her, and she didn't ask. Something about the way he looked told her that there was very little he could say. And it was even stranger to realize that if she hadn't lost the baby in March, he would have returned to find he had a one-month-old child. But he knew nothing of all that. "Can you leave school for a while?" It was almost dinnertime, and she had no plans. She would have canceled them for him anyway.

"Sure. Do you want to go to my house?" It would be nice to have some privacy, and if they sat in the visiting room at school, they had to adhere to all the college's codes and visiting rules. After ten months, they both wanted more freedom than that.

"Can we be alone somewhere?" He just wanted to relax, and be with her. Even after all this time, he didn't want to talk. He just wanted to look at her, and feel her next to him. He was too tired to find the right words. Kate could sense viscerally how disheartened he was.

"Do you want to go to a hotel?" she asked in a voice no one could hear. There were other people standing around in the hall. He looked at her with relief, and nodded. He just wanted to lie next to her for a while. And Kate's mind raced, as she made plans. "Why don't you call the Palmer House from the phone booth outside. Or the Statler. I'll be back in a few minutes." She went to the desk to sign out to go home for the night, and she called her mother from the phone in the hall upstairs. She told her she was spending the night at a friend's, so they could study peacefully for exams, and she didn't want her mother to worry if she called. Her mother thought that was sweet of her, and said she appreciated the call. Kate knew it would never even occur to her mother that the story was a lie.

Five minutes later, Kate was back in the lobby again, and Joe was waiting for her outside. She had brought a few things in a small bag, and she had packed a diaphragm. Beverly had given her the name of a doctor, and Kate had gone to him and said she was engaged. After what had happened the last time, Kate wanted to be prepared when Joe came home.

"They had a room at the Statler," he said nervously.

They both felt a little awkward going straight to a hotel, but they had so little time, and they wanted to be alone. He had borrowed a car, and they talked as they drove to the hotel. She couldn't take her eyes off him. He was as handsome as ever, although he was very thin. And he looked considerably older than he had a year before, or maybe just more mature. There were so many things she wanted to say to him, things she felt awkward putting in her letters to him, and so many things he wanted to ask her.

As they drove to the hotel, they both started to unwind. It was as though they had seen each other just yesterday, and in another sense, she felt as though she hadn't seen him in years. But the odd thing was that after sleeping with him the last time, and then losing their baby, she felt almost married to him. She didn't need a piece of paper, or a ceremony or a wedding ring. No matter what the legalities, she was his.

Joe took a small bag out of the trunk of the car when they got to the hotel, and then parked the car in the garage. He met Kate in the lobby and signed in. They were registered as Major and Mrs. Allbright, and they were treated with considerable respect. The desk clerk had recognized his name. And a bellhop offered to carry his bag upstairs.

"No, we'll be fine." Joe smiled at him, as the desk clerk handed him the key.

Joe and Kate took the elevator upstairs without saying a word, and she was relieved to see when he opened the door that it was a pretty room. She had expected something depressing and small, not that it mattered to them, but there was something a little tawdry about checking into a hotel with a man. She had never done that before, and it seemed very bold to her. But she was not going to miss the opportunity of spending the night with him, particularly if it was the only night he had on leave. Like everyone else in their circumstances, they were living each day as though it were going to be their last, as well it might be.

There was a moment of awkwardness again between them once they got to the room, but as Joe sprawled out on the couch with a nervous look and patted the seat next to him, she smiled as she sat down.

"I can't believe you're here," she said with a look in her eyes that told him how much he had been missed.

"Neither can I," he said. Two days before he had been providing fighter escort cover for bombers over Berlin, and they had lost four planes. And now suddenly, he was sitting in a hotel room in Boston with her, and she was prettier than ever. She looked so young and so fresh and so far from the life he had been leading for nearly two years. They had given him two hours' notice of the trip, and he was lucky they'd given him leave, no matter how brief. On the way over, he had been afraid that he wouldn't be able to see her at all. The night at the Statler was an unexpected gift. And to Joe, at least, it seemed somewhat surreal. They were like homing pigeons that always came back to each other, no matter where they had been. They always found each other, whether in Cape Cod, or Washington, or here, and they would pick up the familiar threads again. Remarkably, no matter how long they'd been away from each other, the same fire and magic was always there.

He kissed her then, without saying another word. It was as though he needed her to comfort him, to soothe the wounds in his soul. He just needed to drink from the peaceful fountain she offered him. It was as though she understood exactly what he needed from her. And in turn, when she was with him, no matter how limited the words, she always knew how much she was loved. It was a perfect exchange.

A few minutes later, he walked over to the bed with her. He felt a little guilty as they undressed. He had planned to take her to dinner, and spend some time talking to her before they made love, but neither of them wanted to be around people or in a restaurant. They just wanted to be alone with each other and what they felt. They didn't even need words.

He kissed her with gentleness and passion as they lay on the bed, and as he undressed her, he realized how hungry for her he had been. Much to his own surprise, there had been no one else. In the ten months that they'd been apart, he hadn't wanted anyone but her. And Kate only wanted him.

She was embarrassed when she left him to go to the bathroom for a few minutes, and he didn't ask her about it until long after they had made love, and lay in each other's arms, sated and quiet, and drifting in their isolated, safe, little world. And feeling shy about it, she told him about the diaphragm, and he seemed relieved.

"I worried about that for months after last time," he said honestly. "I kept wondering what we'd do if you got pregnant. I couldn't even have come back to marry you," he said, and she was touched by his words. It was nice to know he thought that way, and had been concerned for her. She had had no idea how he'd react, and she felt safe enough now to tell him what had happened to her.

"I got pregnant last time, Joe," she said in a soft voice, as he held her close. Her head was on his shoulder, and her hair was brushing his cheek. And he turned his head to look at her.

"Are you serious? What did you do about it?" He looked as though a lightning bolt had just hit them both. It had long since slipped his mind, she'd never said anything to him, and it had never dawned on him that they might have a child by then. "Or . . . do we . . . did you . . ." She smiled at the look on his face. It wasn't so much fear as astonishment. And he wanted to know why she had never told him. She grew immeasurably in his eyes when he realized that, whatever had happened, she had handled it on her own.

"I lost it in March. I didn't know what to do, but I knew that if something happened to you, I'd never forgive myself if I'd done anything about it. I had to have it, if that was meant to be. I was almost three months pregnant when I lost it," she said, and there were tears in her eyes as she told him. He tightened his grip wordlessly around her.

"Do your parents know?" He could easily imagine that they were furious with him, and justifiably so. He felt guilty as hell knowing what she'd been through.

"No, they don't," she reassured him, snuggling closer to him. Whatever comfort he hadn't been able to give, he was offering her now. "I was going to leave school in April, and tell them then. There was nothing else I could do. I got hit by a kid riding a bicycle, and I guess that started it. He hit me pretty hard, and it knocked me out. I lost the baby that night."

"Were you at the hospital?" He looked horrified. This had never happened to him before, although it had happened to many of his friends. But he'd never gotten a girl in trouble before, and he'd always been careful, except with her.

"I was at school, but two of the girls in my house took care of me," she said discreetly, and spared him the details. She knew he would have been even more upset if he had seen the state she'd been in. It had taken months to feel like herself again. She had lost so much blood, it took a long time to get fully back on her feet. But she was fine by then. Joe was amazed too by the thought that if the pregnancy had come to full term, they would have had a one-month-old child. It was mind-boggling to him.

"You know, it's funny. I thought about it for a long time. I kept thinking you were going to tell me that had happened. I don't know why, but when I got back to England, it was all I could think about, I was so sure. But you never said anything, and I didn't want to ask. I didn't know if anyone reads your mail at school. And then I guess I forgot about it. But for a couple of months, I just had this weird feeling. Why didn't you tell me, Kate?" He looked sad that she hadn't, but he understood. And he admired her for it, more than she knew. She had handled it all herself, and recovered from it, seemingly with no bitterness toward him. He was grateful for that, and touched by how brave she had been. He could sense by the way she spoke of it, that it had been hard for her, in a number of ways.

"I thought you had enough to worry about, without adding that." He nodded, and pulled her even closer to him.

"It was my baby too." It would have been, and she was sorry all over again. There was nothing she wanted more than to be with him, and have his child, but it hadn't been meant to be, so far at least. And given what was happening in their lives, it seemed to be for the best, even to her, and surely to him. "I'm glad you're being careful now." He had brought prophylactics with him too this time. He didn't want to be irresponsible with her, and take a risk. And the last thing he felt they needed was a child to complicate their lives.

They talked about the war for a while then, and she asked him how long he thought it would go on. He sighed as he answered her. "It's hard to say. I wish I could say it'll be over soon. I don't know, Kate. If we pummel the hell out of the Krauts, maybe a year." That was part of why he was going to Washington, to see if they could speed up the pummeling with some extraordinary new planes. It had been discouraging so far, the Germans just kept coming at them relentlessly in waves. No matter how many Germans the Allies killed, or how many cities and factories and munitions dumps they destroyed, they always seemed to have more. They were a seemingly indestructible machine.

And the war in the Pacific hadn't been going well. They were fighting a people from a culture and on a terrain that was completely unfamiliar to them. Kamikaze planes were bombing aircraft carriers, ships were being sunk, planes were being shot down. And by the fall of 1943, Allied spirits were low.

It seemed to Kate these days that an incredible number of people she knew had died. It was devastating. A number of boys she had met at Harvard and MIT in the past two years were already gone. She was just grateful that nothing had happened to Joe.

They talked a lot that night, which was unusual for him, but they had so little time, so much pulling at them. They didn't have time to unwind, to warm up, to coast along. They just had to be there, and be all they could, in the little time they had. And for the rest of the evening, they both tried not to think about the war.

They made love again late that night, and never went out. They ordered dinner in the room, and the room service waiter asked if it was their honeymoon, and they both laughed. They never spoke of the future that night, or of any plans. All she wanted for him was to stay alive. She couldn't think of what she wanted for herself, she just wanted to be with him, when and where she could, for however long. More than that was like asking for a miracle at this point, a childish dream. She knew her mother wouldn't have approved of it, but she didn't understand. An engagement ring on her finger wouldn't have

145

changed anything, and it wouldn't have kept him alive. And Joe asked nothing of her, except what Kate wanted to give of her own free will, and to the best of her abilities, she gave it all.

They both slept fitfully that night, holding each other and then drifting apart, and waking with a start when they realized that it wasn't a dream, and they were really together.

"Hi," she said sleepily, as she smiled and opened an eye early the next morning. She had felt his warmth next to her all night, and she could feel his strong powerful legs next to her as she stretched, and he leaned over and kissed her. The night he had spent with her had been a far cry from what he was used to now.

"Did you sleep all right?" he asked, and put an arm around her as she snuggled closer to him. They were lying on their backs, whispering. She loved waking up next to him.

"I kept feeling you next to me, and thinking I was dreaming." Neither of them was accustomed to sleeping with anyone next to them, and it had kept them from sleeping deeply, no matter how happy they were together.

"So did I," he smiled, and thought about their lovemaking the night before. He wanted to savor every moment he spent with her and take the memory of it with him.

"What time do you have to leave?" she asked, with a sad edge to her voice. It was impossible to forget that these were only borrowed hours.

"I have to be on a plane to Washington at one o'clock. I should drop you off at school around eleven-thirty." She had cut all her classes that morning, and she wouldn't have cared about the consequences, nothing would have made her leave him earlier than she had to. "Do you want breakfast?" She wasn't hungry, except for him, and within minutes, as they kissed and his hands began to wander, they found each other again.

At nine o'clock they got up and ordered breakfast. When room service came, they had showered separately, and were wearing the hotel's terrycloth robes. They had orange juice and toast, and ham and eggs, and shared a pot of coffee. It was beyond lavish to Joe, who had been living on military rations for so long he had almost forgotten what real food was. To Kate, it was far more ordinary, but what wasn't was the sheer joy of looking at him across the table. His almost stern, sharply chiseled face looked beautiful to her as he sat drinking his coffee and reading the paper for a minute. And then his eyes moved toward hers, and he smiled.

"Just like real life, isn't it? Who'd know there's a war on." Except the newspaper was full of it, and none of it sounded good. He put the paper down and smiled across the table at Kate. They had shared a wonderful evening, and whenever he was with her, it was like finding the missing piece of him. It was as though there was a void in him he was never aware of, until he saw her. The rest of the time, other things seemed to fill it. He wasn't a person who needed a lot of people. But this one woman in particular touched him deeply. As few had in fact, or any. He had never known anyone quite like her. It struck him again as he sat across the table, looking at her. Her eyes were so deep and so powerful, there was something so direct and open and unafraid about her. She was like a young doe sniffing the air, and liking what she sensed. She always looked excited about life, and as though she were about to burst into laughter, and this morning was no different. As she put her coffee cup down, she was suddenly grinning at him.

"What are you smiling about?" he asked, with a look of amusement. Her good humor was contagious. By nature, he was far less jovial than she was. It wasn't that he was unhappy, he was just serious and quiet, and she liked that about him.

"I was just thinking of my mother's face if she could see us."

"Don't even think about it. It makes me feel guilty. And your father would kill me, and I can't say that I blame him." Particularly after what she had told him about getting pregnant and losing the baby. He knew that the Jamisons would have been horrified, as well they should be. "I'm not sure I can ever face them again," Joe said, looking worried.

"Well, you may have to, so you'd better get over it." As she had. Particularly now that she'd seen Joe. She was almost sorry she'd used the birth control device, she really wished she could have his baby. She wanted that much more than she wanted to be married. Because Joe never talked about their getting married, in order to make her peace with it, she was beginning to tell herself that marriage was something old people did, everyone made such a big deal of it, and her friends that got married all seemed like silly children, or so she said. She claimed to Joe at least that all they cared about were the wedding presents and the bridesmaids, and afterward they complained that the boys they'd married spent too much time with their friends, or drank too much, or were mean to them. They all seemed like kids pretending to be adults. But having his baby was a bond like no other. It was real and deep and important, and had nothing to do with other people. Even knowing the problems it would cause for her, she had loved knowing she was having his baby, when she'd been pregnant. She knew then that she would have a part of him with her forever, and probably the best part. She had been hoping she'd have a little boy, and she was going to teach him all about airplanes just like Joe. Kate was always terrified now of losing Joe to the war. And a baby would be a piece of him that would remain forever hers.

Joe could see, as he looked at her, that Kate was having tender thoughts about him, and he reached a hand across the table and took hers, and then lifted it to his lips and kissed it. "Don't look so sad, Kate. I'll be back. This story isn't over. It never will be." He didn't know how prophetic that would prove to be. But she felt exactly as he did.

"Just take care of yourself, Joe. That's all that matters." It was up to the fates now. He was over there risking his life every day, and who survived and who didn't was in God's hands. In comparison to that, everything else seemed unimportant to them.

After breakfast, they dressed, and they almost didn't leave the room on time. He was kissing and holding her, and they could hardly keep their hands off each other. But he had to drop her off at school and get to the airport on time. He couldn't be late for his meeting in Washington, or worse, miss the plane. What had brought him back from England was serious business, and important to the outcome of the war in Europe. He loved Kate, but he had no choice but to keep it all in perspective. He had important things to do that didn't include her.

As he drove her back to school, they were both quiet as Kate glanced at him. She wanted to remember what he looked like at this exact moment, to keep her warm in the days to come. She felt as though everything they were doing was in slow motion. And they reached the Radcliffe campus all too quickly. They got out of the car, and she stood looking up at him with tears in her eyes. She couldn't bear seeing him leave again, but she knew she had to be brave about it. The night they had just spent together had been an unexpected gift.

"Stay safe," she whispered as he pulled her close to him. "Stay alive" was what she really wanted to say. "I love you, Joe." It was all she could say to him, as she felt a sob strangling in her throat. She didn't want to make this any harder than it was for either of them.

"I love you too . . . and next time something important happens to you, I want you to tell me." There was always the chance that she could get pregnant again, even with birth control, it had happened to plenty of others. But he still appreciated the fact that she hadn't wanted to burden him, and he loved her all the more for it. "Take good care of yourself. And say hello to your parents, if you tell them you saw me." But she didn't plan to. She didn't want them to suspect that she had gone to a hotel with him. She just prayed that no one had seen them entering or leaving the hotel.

They clung to each other for a long moment, praying that the gods would be good to them, and then she watched him drive away as tears streamed down her cheeks. It was a familiar scene these days, like so many others. There were wounded soldiers in every city and town, who had come home from the war injured and maimed. There were little flags in windows to honor loved ones who were fighting some-where. There were soldiers and young girls saying tearful goodbyes to each other, and screams of joy when they returned. There were small children standing at the graves of their fathers. Kate and Joe were no different than the others, and luckier than some. It was a serious time for everyone, and a time of tragedy for far too many. All Kate knew for certain was that she was lucky to have Joe.

She stayed in her room for the rest of the day, and cut the rest of her classes that afternoon. She didn't go to dinner that night, in case he called her. And he did, at eight o'clock, after his meeting. He was just about to leave for the airport, but couldn't tell her how his meeting had gone, what time his flight was leaving, or where he was flying to, it was all classified information. She just wished him a safe trip back, and told him how much she loved him, and he did the same. And then she went back to her room, and lay on her bed, thinking about him. It was hard to believe they had known each other for nearly three years now, and so much had happened since they'd met in a ballroom in New York, in his borrowed tails and her evening gown. She had been seventeen then, and a child in so many ways. At twenty, she felt very much a woman. And better yet, she was his.

She went home to her parents that weekend, to study for exams, and get away from the girls in the house. She didn't want to see anyone, she had been pensive and quiet since Joe left. Her mother noticed it as she sat silently all through dinner. She asked Kate if she was all right, and if she'd heard from Joe. Kate insisted she was fine, but neither of her parents believed her. She seemed to be getting older and more mature every day. College had seasoned her certainly, but her relationship with Joe had catapulted her into adulthood in an instant. And worrying about him constantly made her look and feel older still. Everyone was growing up overnight these days.

Her parents talked about it that night in their room, but they both agreed that Kate was far from unique in her worries about Joe. Most of the young girls and women in the country were worried about someone, brothers, boyfriends, husbands, fathers, friends. Almost every man they knew had gone to war.

"It's a shame she didn't fall in love with Andy," her mother said unhappily. "He'd be perfect for her, and he's not even in the army." But maybe he was too obvious a choice for her, or possibly just too dull. For all his kindness and good breeding, Andy simply could not compare to Joe. Everything about Joe was dazzling and exciting. He was the personification of a hero in every way.

For the next four weeks, Kate kept busy at school. She did well at her exams, despite the fact that she was distracted. She got letters from Joe regularly, and she was both relieved and disappointed to discover three weeks after he left that she wasn't pregnant. She knew it was better that way. Along with the agony of worrying about him, she didn't need the problems that would have created for her.

When she went home for the Thanksgiving weekend, she looked better than the last time they saw her. And she seemed a little more peaceful. She talked about Joe at dinner with their friends, and was surprisingly knowledgeable about what was happening in Europe. And understandably, she had strong opinions about the Germans, and didn't mince words.

In the end, much to everyone's relief, it proved to be a very pleasant Thanksgiving. And she went to bed that night grateful that she had seen Joe only a month before. She had no idea when he'd come home again, but she knew that the closeness they had shared would hold her for as long as it had to. It was hard to believe he'd already been away for two years.

She slept badly that night, in a sleep filled with odd dreams and strange feelings that woke her through the night. She told her mother about it in the morning, and she teased Kate that she'd probably eaten too much chestnut stuffing.

"I used to love chestnuts when I was a child," Elizabeth said, making breakfast for her husband, "and my grandmother always said they'd give me indigestion. They still do, but I love them anyway." Kate felt better that morning. She went shopping with a friend that afternoon, and they had tea at the Statler, which made her think of Joe and the night they'd spent there. And by the time she came home, she was in good spirits. But even when she was, she was more serious these days. She seemed more sensible, and not as mischievous as she had been before she went to college. It was as though knowing Joe, or maybe just fearing for him in the circumstances he was in, had turned her further inward. She kept to herself more than she ever had.

She went back to school on Sunday night, and had nightmares again, and as she woke from a bad dream, she could still remember seeing planes falling all around her. The dream had been so loud it seemed real. It made her feel so panicky that she got out of bed and went to get dressed long before any of the others had risen, and she went to the dining room for breakfast very early, and sat there quietly alone.

She didn't know why, but she had bad dreams all week, and couldn't sleep at night. She was exhausted when her father reached her on Thursday afternoon, and Kate was startled to hear Clarke's voice. He had never once called her at Radcliffe. He asked if she'd like to come home for dinner that night, and she told him she had work to do, but the more she tried to get out of it, the more insistent he became, and she finally relented and agreed. It seemed odd to her, and she was a little concerned. She wondered if one of them was sick, and they wanted to tell her. She hoped not.

As soon as Kate walked into the house, she knew something had happened. Her parents were waiting for her in the living room, and her mother had her back to her so Kate wouldn't see her crying. She was devastated for her.

It was her father who told her the news. He felt more capable of it than Kate's mother did. As soon as Kate sat down, he looked straight at her and told her he'd gotten a telegram that morning, and he had called Washington himself to find out everything he could.

"I don't have good news," he said, as Kate's eyes grew wide. This wasn't about them, she suddenly realized, it was about her, and she could feel her heart pound. She didn't want to hear what he was saying, but she knew she had to. She didn't make a sound as she watched his face. "Joe listed you as his next of kin, Kate, along with some cousins he hasn't seen in years." Kate's mother had accepted the dreaded telegram, and called Clarke at the office, as she opened it. And Clarke had immediately called someone he knew in the War Department for further details, none of which were good. He didn't waste more time then. Kate was holding her breath. "He was shot down over Germany last Friday morning." It had been a week, and on Thursday night she had begun having those hideous dreams about planes free-falling through the sky. It had been Friday morning in Europe. "They saw his plane go down, and they have a rough idea of where he landed. He parachuted out at the last minute, and he may have been killed on the way down, or he may have been captured. But they've had no word of him through their underground sources since. There's been no sign of him on the lists of officers who've been captured. He's flying under a different name, but neither the one he's using, nor his real name has

153

shown up. There's some concern that he may be being held secretly, or that the Germans have killed him. I believe he may have been aware of classified information, which would make him of considerable interest to the Germans, if they're aware of who he really is. Joe is quite a prize because of his own history, he's a real plum for them, because he's a national hero." She was staring at her father dumbly, trying to absorb what he had told her, and for a moment, there was no reaction whatsoever from her. "Kate . . . Allied Intelligence doesn't think he made it," he summed up for her. "And even if he did, the Germans won't let him live long. He's probably dead by now, or either the Americans or the British would have heard something about him." She stared at her father with wide eyes, and was too stunned to speak for a minute, as her mother moved closer to her and put an arm around her shoulders.

"Mom . . . is he dead?" she asked in the voice of a lost child, trying to understand what someone speaking a foreign language had just told her. She couldn't absorb it. Her heart refused to know. It was like a terrifying echo of the day her mother had told her that her father died. And in some ways, this was worse. She had loved Joe too much.

"They think so, dear," her mother said softly, aching for her only daughter. Kate was sheet white and looked shell-shocked. She started to get up, and then sat down, as her father looked at her with eyes filled with sympathy and regret.

"I'm sorry, Kate," he said sadly. She could see that there were tears in his eyes, not only for Joe, but for her.

"Don't be," Kate said sharply as she stood up. She wasn't going to let this happen to her. She couldn't. Or to him. She didn't believe it, and never would, until they were sure. "He's not dead yet. If he were, someone would know it," she insisted as her parents exchanged an unhappy glance. It was not the reaction they had expected, or one she had planned. She refused to accept it. "We just have to know that Joe is going to be okay, Mom . . . Dad . . . that's what he'd expect of us."

"Kate, the man landed in Germany, surrounded by Germans who were out looking for him. He's a famous flying ace. They're not going to let him out alive, even if he was alive when he landed. You have to face that." Her father's voice was firm. He didn't want her deluding herself.

"I don't have to face anything," she shouted at him, as she ran out of the living room, up the stairs, and slammed her bedroom door.

Her parents looked stunned as they watched her go, and had no idea what to say to her. They had expected her to be devastated, and instead she was enraged at them and the rest of the world. But once in her room, with the door firmly closed, Kate threw herself on her bed and began to sob. She lay there and cried for hours, thinking of him and how wonderful he was. She couldn't bear the thought of what had happened to him, it wasn't possible, it wasn't fair, all she could think of now were her terrible dreams for the past week, and how he must have felt when he was shot down. And he had promised her he had a hundred lives.

It was late that night when her mother finally dared to slip into the room, and when Kate turned to look at her, her mother saw that she had red, swollen eyes. She went to sit next to her on the bed, and Kate sobbed in her arms.

"I don't want him to be dead, Mommy . . . ," she said, crying like a child, as tears of pain for her only child slid down her mother's cheeks.

"Neither do I," Elizabeth said. For all her qualms about him, he was a decent man, and didn't deserve to die at thirty-three. And Kate didn't deserve a broken heart. None of it was fair. Nothing had been fair in the past two years. "We just have to pray that he'll be all right." She didn't want to continue to reason with Kate that he was probably already dead. That would come in time. It was hard enough to accept that he'd been shot down. And if they didn't find him eventually, even Kate would have to accept that he was gone. She didn't have to face it now, it was obviously far too painful for her. Her mother stayed with her until late into the night, and stroked her hair lovingly until she fell asleep, making the little snuffling sobs that come after a child has cried for too long. It nearly broke her mother's heart.

"I wish she didn't love that man so," Elizabeth said to Clarke when she finally came to bed. He was so worried about Kate that he had waited up for his wife. "There's something between those two that frightens me." She had seen it the year before in Joe's eyes, and she could see it now in Kate's. It defied reason and time and words, it was like a tie between their souls that even they did not understand. And what frightened Kate's mother now was if the tie proved to be unseverable by death as well. It would be a terrible fate for Kate.

Kate was silent and grim at the breakfast table the next day, and any attempt to speak to her went ignored. She said nothing to either of them, drank only a cup of tea, and then drifted back upstairs like a ghost. She stayed home from school, and for the rest of the weekend, never left her room. Fortunately, she only had one more week of school, before the Christmas break.

But on Sunday night, she dressed and went back to Radcliffe, and never even said goodbye to them. She was like a disembodied soul. She spoke to no one in the house, and when Beverly came to say hello to her and ask if she'd been sick over the weekend, Kate never told her that Joe's plane had been shot down. She couldn't bring herself to say the words, and she cried herself to sleep every night.

Everyone in the house at Radcliffe knew something had happened to her, and it was several days later that someone saw a small article in the newspaper that he had been shot down. Military Intelligence had decided to keep it as low key as they could, so as not to demoralize people at home. They said he was missing in action, and the newspaper was noticeably vague. But it told them all they needed to know. All the girls in her house knew that Joe Allbright had visited Kate.

"I'm sorry . . . ," some of them whispered as they passed her in the hall. And all she could do was nod and look away. She looked terrible, lost weight, and she looked tired and ill when she went home for the Christmas break. And all her mother's efforts to comfort her were in vain. All Kate wanted was to be left alone, as she waited for news of Joe.

She asked her father to call his contact in Washington again before the holidays, but there was no further news. There had been no sign of Joe, and no word through underground sources. The Germans had not reported capturing him, and in fact had denied it when they were asked. No one identified by the name on his papers had surfaced anywhere. And if they knew they had captured Joe Allbright, they would have said so and counted it as a real victory against the Allies. And no one had seen him escape, or alive since he'd gone down. There was no sign of him anywhere.

There was no Christmas for any of them that year. Kate hardly did any Christmas shopping, didn't want any gifts from them, took forever to open the ones she got, and spent most of her time in her room. All she could do was think of him, where he was, what had happened to him, if he was still alive, if she would ever see him again. She thought constantly of the times they had, and she regretted even more bitterly now having lost the baby they had conceived the year before. She was inconsolable and unreachable, she hardly ever slept anymore, and she was rail thin.

She scoured the newspapers for some word of him, but her father had already assured her that they would be called before anything more appeared in the press. And he suspected that there would never be. He had probably been dead for weeks by then, and was lying somewhere in Germany in a shallow grave. To Kate, the thought of it nearly drove her insane. It was as though part of her very being had been cut away, or some deep internal piece of her that she didn't even know was there had been gouged out. She either lay on her bed, staring at the wall, or paced her room at night, feeling like she was about to explode out of her own skin, and nothing helped. She even got drunk one night, and her parents said nothing to her about it the next day. They were desperate, and had never seen anyone as grief-stricken. She was keening for him, and nothing was going to help her now except time.

When she went back to school, she failed an exam for the first time. Her advisor called her in, and asked if something had happened over the holidays. Kate looked terrible, and in a strangled voice she explained that a close friend of hers had been shot down on a mission over Germany. At least it explained her grades. The woman expressed her sympathy, and hoped that Kate would feel better soon. She was very kind and very sweet, she had lost her own son in Salerno the previous year. But nothing anyone said to her offered any solace to Kate. And when she wasn't feeling devastated, she was consumed with rage, at the Germans, at the fates, at the man who had shot him down, at him for letting it happen to him, at herself for loving him so much. She wanted to be free of it, but she knew nothing would ever free her of him. It was too late.

And when Andy saw her after she got back from Christmas break, at first he felt sorry for her, and then he scolded her. He told her she was feeling sorry for herself, that she always knew it could happen to him. And in Joe's case it could have happened anytime, anywhere, while he did death-defying stunts in planes, aerobatics, or raced. Thousands of other women were in the same boat she was in. She and Joe weren't married, they didn't have kids, she wasn't even engaged. But what Andy said to her only made her furious with him.

"Is that supposed to make me feel better? You sound like my mother. Do you think a ring on my finger would make any difference to me? It wouldn't mean a goddamn thing to me, Andy Scott, and it wouldn't change what happened to him. Why is everyone so obsessed

with social rituals? Who gives a damn? He's probably in some goddamn awful prison camp being tortured for what he knows. Do you
think a ring on my finger would make a difference to them? Of course
not. And it wouldn't to Joe. It wouldn't have made him love me more,
or me love him more. I don't care about the ring," she started to sob, "I
just want him to come home." She folded into Andy's arms like a broken doll.

"He's not going to, Kate," Andy said as he held her, while she
sobbed. "You know that. The chances that he'll come home are a million to one." If that.

"It could happen. Maybe he'll escape." She refused to let hope die.

"Maybe he's dead," Andy said, trying to force her to face the truth.
More likely than not, he was. Kate knew it too, but she didn't want to
hear it from anyone. She couldn't face it yet. "Kate, I can only imagine
how hard it is, but you have to get over this. You can't let it tear you
apart." The worst thing was she had no choice. She was doing the best
she could, but she was drowning in her fears for him, her own sense of
panic and loss. She had no idea how she was going to exist if he was
gone. And yet, even at her worst, she had an inexplicable sense that he
was still alive. It was as though there were a part of her that hadn't let
go of him yet, and she wondered if she ever would. She felt bound to
him for life.

She and Andy went to dinner at the cafeteria, and he forced her to
eat. And that weekend he insisted that she come to watch him at a
swimming meet against MIT. She actually had a good time, in spite of
herself, and forgot her miseries for a short while. And everyone was excited when Harvard won.

She waited for him afterward, and they went out to eat, and then he
took her back to the house. She looked better than she had a few days
before, and he felt sorry for her when she told him that she'd had a
dream about Joe. She was convinced he was still alive, and Andy was

sure her mind was playing tricks on her. She wasn't willing to accept the possibility that he had died when he was shot down.

Eventually, it became a sore subject with her, whenever the topic came up with family or friends. People would tell her how sorry they were to have heard about Joe, and then she would insist that he was probably in a German prisoner of war camp somewhere. In time, people stopped mentioning it to her at all.

By the time summer rolled around, Joe had been gone for seven months. His last letters to her had come a month after he had been shot down, and she still read them at night, and lay in bed for hours, thinking of him. Everyone said she had to let go of him, that he was gone, but her heart refused to open and release him like a bird from a cage. She kept him deep within her, in a secret place in her heart. She knew it was a place where no one would ever go again, and she knew they were right when people said she had to get over the tragedy, but she had no idea how. He was like a color she had become, a vision she had seen, a dream she had had, and there was no way to separate herself from him now.

Her parents urged her to go on a trip that summer, and after much arguing, Kate finally agreed to go. She went to visit her godmother in Chicago, and from there on to California to see a girl she knew who was going to Stanford. It was an interesting trip, and she had a good time, but she always felt now as though she were only making the motions, and not living her life anymore. It was a relief finally when she came home on the train. She had three days to herself to stare out the window and think about him, all that he had been, and hopefully still was. But even she was beginning to think now that he was no longer alive. By the time she returned to Boston at the end of August, he'd been gone for nine months. And no one had heard anything about him, or seen him in any of the prisoner of war camps. Both Washington and the RAF had finally agreed that he was dead.

Kate didn't go to Cape Cod that summer. It had too many memories for her, even though she had only seen him there twice. She came
home from California just in time to start her senior year at Radcliffe.
She was majoring in history and art, and had no idea what she was going to do with it. Teaching didn't appeal to her, and there was no other
career path that held any particular lure for her, nor did anything else.

She saw Andy a few weeks after they got back, he was starting his
third year of law school, and had almost no time to see her anymore.
He loved it, and was working too hard. Several of her friends hadn't
come back to school that fall, two of them had gotten married over the
summer, and another girl had moved to the West Coast. Another had
gone to work to support her mother, her father and both her brothers
had been killed in the Pacific the previous year. It seemed to be a world
supported and staffed by women, bus drivers, mailmen, all the jobs
that had previously been done by men were being performed by
women. Everyone had gotten used to it, and Kate teased her parents
and told them she was going to be a bus driver when she grew up.
Unfortunately, there was nothing else she wanted to do more.

She was twenty-one years old, and soon to become a graduate of
Radcliffe. She was intelligent, beautiful, interesting, fun to be with,
and well-informed. By all rights, her mother insisted, if there hadn't
been a war on, she would have been married and had kids by then, if
not with Joe, then with someone else. But she hadn't even been on a
date since he died. Several of the boys from Harvard had asked her out,
a couple of the excessively brainy ones from MIT, and even a nice boy
from Boston College, but she turned all of them down. She had no interest in anyone, and she still expected to get a call from Washington,
telling her that Joe was still alive, or even from the visiting room downstairs that there was someone waiting for her. She expected to see him
as she got on buses, walked around corners and crossed streets. It was
impossible to adjust to the idea that he had vanished into thin air, that

he no longer existed anywhere on the planet, and no matter how much she loved him, would never come back to her. The whole concept of death was incomprehensible to her.

The holidays meant very little to her that year, although they were less painful than they had been the year before. She had calmed down a lot, and was warm and kind to her parents, but when her mother urged her to go out, Kate would either change the subject or leave the room. Her parents were beginning to give up hope, and her mother had confided to Kate's father that she was afraid Kate would be an old maid.

"I hardly think so," he laughed at Elizabeth. "She's twenty-one years old and there's a war on, for God's sake. Wait till the boys come home."

"And when will that be?" Elizabeth asked with a mournful look.

"Soon, I hope." But there was no sign of it yet.

Paris had been liberated finally in August. Russia had prevailed against the Germans, and Russian troops had moved into Poland. But the Germans had increased their bombing raids over England since September. And their offensive in the Ardennes Forest was going badly for the Allies. And the Battle of the Bulge over Christmas had cost a vast number of lives and disheartened everyone on the home front.

It was the last day of the Christmas vacation when Andy Scott dropped by the house with a group of friends, and convinced Kate to go skating with them. They were driving to a nearby lake, and her mother was relieved when she saw her leave with them. She was still hoping that Kate would pay more attention to Andy one day, but Kate always insisted that she had no romantic interest in him, he was just a friend. But they had gotten noticeably closer year by year, and Elizabeth hadn't entirely given up hope. She thought he would have been the perfect husband for Kate, and Kate's father didn't disagree, but he thought that was best left up to Kate.

They spent a wonderful afternoon skating on the lake, falling down, skating backward, pushing each other over. The boys organized a mock hockey game, and Kate skated in graceful circles in the middle of the lake. She had loved figure skating as a child, and was fairly good. And afterward, they all went out for hot toddies, and then went for a long walk in the crisp night air. Kate fell back from the group after a while, and Andy joined her. He was happy to see her looking better and finally having some fun. She said Christmas vacation had been okay, although she admitted that she hadn't done much, and he noticed that for once, she hadn't mentioned Joe. He hoped it was a turning point for her.

"What are you doing next summer?" he asked her calmly, as he tucked her mittened hand into the crook of his arm. He had shining dark hair, and deep brown eyes, and he was wearing earmuffs and a warm scarf from their outing to the lake.

"I don't know, I haven't thought about it," she said vaguely, as the vapor from their breath swirled ahead of them in the cold night air. "What about you?"

"I had kind of a fun idea," he said as they followed the others, "we're both going to graduate in June," she from Radcliffe and he from law school. "My father says I don't have to start work till September at the law firm. I was thinking it might be fun to go on a honeymoon." She was nodding as she listened, and then frowned as she looked at him.

"With who?" Her breath caught for a minute. There was a funny look in his eyes as they stopped walking, and he looked down at her.

"I was thinking maybe you," he said softly, as Kate let out a long sigh. She had thought they had put all that behind them. She had treated him like a brother for years. But Andy had always had a crush on her. And like her parents, and his own, he thought it would be a good match for both of them.

"Are you kidding?" she asked hopefully, but he shook his head, and she leaned her own against him.

"I can't do that, Andy, you know that. I love you like a brother."

And then she smiled up at him sadly. "It would be incest to marry you."

"I know you've been in love with Joe," he said honestly, "but he's gone now. And I've always loved you. I think I could make you happy, Kate." But not the way Joe had. Joe had been passion and excitement and danger. Andy was hot chocolate and ice skates. They were both important to her, but in different ways, and she felt certain that she would never feel for him what she had for Joe. They had stopped walking by then, and the others were far ahead, with no idea of what was happening behind them.

"I don't think it would be fair to you," she said honestly, snuggling close to him as they started to walk again. He had been wanting to ask her all day, and hadn't had the opportunity he wanted at the lake. He'd gotten too busy playing hockey with their friends. And she had gone off to skate by herself. She was very solitary these days. "I still can't believe that he's gone and never coming back," although she had begun to try the idea on for size recently, and it didn't feel good, and probably never would.

"You weren't even engaged to him, Kate. Lots of people have romances with other people before they get married. Some people even break engagements when they meet someone else," he grew more serious then, as he looked at her. "There are going to be a lot of women in your position after the war. There are widows even younger than you, and some of them have kids. They can't just lock themselves away for the rest of their lives. They're going to have to live again, and so are you. You can't hide forever, Kate."

"Yes, I can." She was beginning to think that what she'd had with Joe had been so unusual and so special that it would sustain her for the rest of her life, and there would be no one else.

"It's not good for you. You need a husband and kids and a good life, and someone who loves you to take care of you." What he was saying would have been music to her mother's ears, but not to Kate's. She wasn't ready to think about anyone else. She was still in love with Joe.

"You deserve better than someone who's in love with a ghost." It was the first time she had admitted to anyone that Joe might be dead, and Andy thought it was a first step.

"Maybe there's room in our life for a ghost." Andy felt certain that Kate would eventually let go of Joe one day.

"I don't know," she answered, sounding vague. But so far, she hadn't actually said no.

"We don't have to get married next summer, Kate. I just said that to see what you'd say. We can take as long as you want. Maybe we could just date for a while."

"Like real people?" she asked, as she looked at him, but she couldn't imagine being in love with him. To her, even at twenty-three, he still seemed like a kid. Joe was exactly ten years older than he. And they were very different men. Kate had been drawn to Joe from the moment she met him, he was like an explosion of light in her heart. Andy had always seemed like a cuddly person and a good friend. It was what her mother said husbands were supposed to be.

"So what do you think?" he asked hopefully, and she laughed. It was like having a boy ask you if you wanted to see his tree house, or go on a first date. She couldn't take him seriously.

"I think you're crazy to even want me," she said honestly.

"And?" he asked expectantly, "what about you?"

"I don't know. I can't imagine what it would be like going out with you. Let me think about it." She had been trying to fix him up with her housemates for the past three and a half years, but Andy had always been more interested in her. "It sounds like a crazy idea to me," she said most unromantically, but he wasn't discouraged. Things had gone better than he expected, and he looked pleased. He had been trying to get up the courage to ask her for months, but he'd been afraid it was too soon. But now it had been over a year since Joe had disappeared.

"Maybe not as crazy as you think," Andy said softly. "Why don't we just see how things go for the next few months?" he suggested, and she nodded. She had always liked him, and maybe her mother was right.

But that night, after he took her back to her parents' house, it depressed her thinking about it. Even letting Andy talk to her about it seemed like a betrayal of Joe, and thinking of Andy only made her miss Joe more. They were not only different, they existed in different worlds. Everything about Joe was exciting, fascinating, mesmerizing. She had always been enthralled by his flying tales, and flying with Joe had been one of the high points of her life. But beyond what Joe said to her, and what they did together, there had always been a powerful, almost irresistible unspoken attraction between them. It was a kind of chemistry that neither of them could have explained. And she had none of that with Andy Scott. Instead of a bright light burning somewhere deep within her, all Andy represented in her mind was a comfortable warm place. It would have been a huge adjustment to make. And when she saw him at school again a few days later, she started to say as much to him.

"Sshhhh!" he said firmly, putting a finger to her lips. "I know what you're going to say. Forget it. I don't want to hear it. You're just scared." But the trouble was she wasn't in love with him. She had said nothing to her parents about what Andy had said to her. She didn't want to raise her mother's hopes, or have her go crazy about it. Kate wasn't sold on the idea yet herself. Far from it, she was having cold feet about even dating him. She felt silly going out with him. "Just give it a chance," he continued. "How about dinner on Friday night? And we could go to a movie on Saturday." Suddenly, she felt as though she were being asked to go steady by a high school kid. He was bright and kind, and friendly and solid, but having stayed home while everyone else went to war, he also seemed less mature in Kate's opinion, certainly than Joe.

In spite of herself, she got dressed for dinner on Friday evening. She wore a black dress her mother had given her for Christmas, high heels, a little fur jacket, and a string of pearls. And she looked very pretty with her shining auburn hair when he came to pick her up, wearing a dark suit. He looked like every senior's dream. But not Kate's.

They had a lovely time at an Italian restaurant in the North End, and he took her dancing afterward, but somehow, no matter how hard she tried, she just felt like it was a joke. She would much rather have been eating at the cafeteria with him, as they always did. But she didn't say it to him.

Andy was very circumspect when he took her home at the end of the evening, and he didn't kiss her. He didn't want to scare her off, and he was very sensible about the fact that it was too soon. And the following night, he took her to see *Casablanca* again, which was more relaxed, and they went out for hamburgers afterward. Kate was surprised at how much fun she had. It was actually enjoyable going out on a date, and it was easy being with him. But for her at least, it wasn't exciting or romantic being with him. He was just a friend, and she couldn't imagine, or not yet at least, feeling more than that for him. But at least she was making the effort to give it a chance.

It was Valentine's Day before he finally tried to kiss her. Joe had been gone for fifteen months, but Joe was all she could think of when she felt Andy's lips on hers. He was handsome and sexy and young, and he was an attractive young man in many ways. But she felt as though there were something terribly wrong with her. It was as if everything inside her, in her heart, in her head, in her soul, were numb. When Joe's light went out in her, everything in her had gone dark. Her heart had left with him.

Andy appeared not to notice, and for the next few months, they went on a date once a week, and he kissed her when he brought her home. He never tried to go further than that, which was a relief to her. She knew that Andy would never expect her to risk her reputation, and she suspected that he had no idea that she had ever made love to Joe. He told her he loved her constantly, and she loved him too, in her own way. Her parents were ecstatic that she was going out with him, but she kept insisting that it wasn't serious yet. And when her father looked into her eyes, it almost broke his heart. He could read all too easily what was and wasn't there. All he saw was immeasurable pain. It was like looking into a bottomless pool of grief. The fact that she chatted and smiled and had begun to laugh again didn't fool him.

And when her mother was rhapsodizing about Andy one day, when she and Clarke were alone having dinner at the house, he tried to discourage her. He thought that what she was doing was dangerous for Kate.

"Don't push them, Liz. Let them find their own way."

"They seem to be doing fine. I'm sure they're going to get engaged." But what did that mean? he wondered to himself. That she had been profoundly in love with one man, and had to be married to someone, anyone, to replace him, whether she loved him or not? To him, it seemed an abysmal fate. He and Liz had been married for thirteen years, and he was still in love with her every day. He didn't want anything less for Kate.

"I don't think she should marry him," Clarke said sensibly.

"Why not?" Elizabeth looked incensed. She didn't want him to spoil anything.

"She's not in love with him, Liz," he said quietly. "Look at her. She's still in love with Joe."

"He was never right for her, and he's gone, for Heaven's sake."

"That doesn't change how she felt about him. She may not get over it for years." What he was beginning to fear most was that she never would. And marrying Andy might only make things worse, particularly if she did it to please them. It might break her spirit entirely, or fill her with despair. In that case, she was better off alone, no matter how nice a boy Andy was. "Just leave them alone, and let them figure it out," he urged, and Liz shook her head as she looked at him.

"She needs to get married and have kids, Clarke. What do you expect her to do when she graduates in June?" She made marriage and children sound like occupational therapy, which was upsetting to him.

"I'd rather she get a job than marry the wrong man." He was very firm.

"There is nothing 'wrong' with Andy Scott." She was beginning to wonder where her husband got his crazy ideas. Maybe he had been a little dazzled by Joe Allbright too. But however dazzling he had been, Joe Allbright was gone. And Kate had to go on with her life.

In spite of her parents' arguments and concern over her, Kate continued to go out with Andy every weekend, and do her best to feel more than just friendship for him, but it was an uphill fight. And by spring, everyone's attention was riveted on England and France and Germany. The tides were beginning to turn.

U.S. troops were winning the Battle of the Ruhr in March, and had taken Iwo Jima in the Pacific. Nuremberg had fallen to the Allies in April, just as the Russians reached the suburbs of Berlin. Mussolini and his cabinet members were executed at the end of April, and the German armies in Italy surrendered the following day, just two weeks after President Roosevelt's death. Harry Truman had been made President by then. Germany surrendered on May 7, and President Truman declared May 8 V-E Day.

Kate and Andy followed the news avidly, and argued about what they read. The war meant more to her than it did to a lot of girls her age, because it had cost her so much. And others were constantly holding their breath, praying that their men would come home. By then, nearly two years after he'd been shot down, even Kate had lost hope that Joe would turn up at the end of the war. He had been gone for seventeen months, and everyone had come to assume he was dead, even Kate. His files were closed, although his flying records still stood, and would for a long time.

Kate was in class on V-E Day when she heard the news. The door was open, and a teacher came in with tears streaming down her face. She had lost her husband in France three years before. All the girls stood up and cheered and embraced each other. It was over . . . finished . . . done . . . the boys could come home at last. All they needed now was victory in Japan, but everyone was sure it would come soon.

Kate went to see her parents that afternoon, and her father was jubilant. She and her father talked about it for a while, and then he noticed the profoundly sad look in her eyes. It was easy to see what had crossed her mind, and there were tears in her eyes when she looked up at him. He instantly understood, and touched her hand.

"I'm sorry he didn't make it, Kate."

She nodded at him. "So am I," she said, with tears rolling down her cheeks as she wiped them away. She went back to the house where she lived a little while after that, and lay on her bed, thinking about Joe again. He was always there, somewhere, close to her. He was never far. And when one of the girls came to tell her Andy was on the phone, she told her to tell him she was out. She just couldn't talk to him. Her mind and heart were too full of Joe.

9

GRADUATION WAS ANTICLIMACTIC after the victory in Europe, and Kate looked wonderful in her cap and gown. Her parents were proud of her, and Andy was there. He had talked to her about getting engaged that week, and she had asked him to wait awhile. He was going to travel around the Northwest that summer, and go to work for his father in New York in the fall.

She went to his law school graduation after hers, which was understandably quite small. But it was very dignified, and she was happy for him. She had gotten him to agree to wait until the summer to discuss marriage with her again. And to Kate, it felt like a reprieve.

But once he left on his trip in June, she found that she missed him more than she would have thought, and she was relieved to find that she actually had feelings for him. She was never sure exactly what she felt for him, and she knew that it was because of Joe. The power of her emotions still felt dim, as though all the power had been turned off in her. But it was slowly coming back. And she was grateful for Andy's kindness to her, and his patience. She knew she had given him a hard time, and by the end of June, she was actually anxious for him to come back. He called her as often as he could, and sent her postcards from everywhere. He was heading for the Grand Tetons and eventually Lake

Louise. He had friends in Washington State, then he was going to San Francisco on the way back. And from what he was telling her, he was having a great time, but he missed her a lot. And she was surprised to see how much she missed him. Kate found herself actually thinking about getting engaged to him in the fall, and maybe getting married the following June. But she knew that, if nothing else, she needed another year. And she was working full time for the Red Cross again.

There were hordes of young men coming in from Europe every day, and hospital ships bringing the wounded in. She had just been assigned to working on the docks, helping the medical personnel wade through the men who came off the ship, and sending them off to hospitals where they would spend the next several months, or even years. Kate had never seen people so happy to be home, no matter how damaged they were. They knelt down and kissed the ground, they kissed her, and anyone near at hand if their mothers and sweethearts were not there. But although it was exhausting work, in a way it was a happy job. Many had injuries that were horrifying, yet all of them still looked so young, until you saw their eyes. They had all seen too much. But they were thrilled to be home. Just watching them limp off the ship or embrace their loved ones constantly brought Kate to tears.

Kate spent hours with them, holding hands, smoothing brows, taking notes for men who had lost their sight. She got them into ambulances and on military trucks. She came home filthy and tired every day, but at least she felt she was doing something useful with her time.

She came home very late one night, after a long day working in a packed hospital ward. Because she was so late, she knew her parents would be concerned. But the moment she walked in and saw her father's face, she knew something was terribly wrong. Her mother was sitting on the couch next to him, dabbing at her eyes with a handkerchief. Kate didn't know who, but she suspected instantly that someone had died. She felt a chill run down her spine.

"What's wrong, Dad?" she asked quietly as she walked further into the room.

"Nothing, Kate. Come and sit down." She did as she was told, and smoothed her uniform. There were stains all over it, and her cap was askew. It had been an incredibly long day, and she was hot and tired.

"Are you okay, Mom?" she asked gently, and her mother nodded, but didn't say a word. "What happened?" She looked from one to the other, and there was an interminable pause. She had no living grandparents, no uncles or aunts, so she knew it had to be one of their friends, or maybe one of their friends' sons. Some of the wounded hadn't survived the trip home.

"I got a call from Washington today," her father said, and it meant nothing to Kate now. All her bad news had come and gone. It gave her great compassion in the work she did. She knew what it was like to lose the person you loved most. She was watching her father's eyes for a clue to what had upset them so much, as her father hesitated and went on. "They found Joe, Kate. He's alive." She was so stunned that his words hit her like a rock, and she couldn't make a sound.

"What?" It was all she could say. Her face had gone dead white. "I don't understand." She felt as though she were going into shock. It reminded her of the night she had lost their child. "What do you mean, Dad?" Even after hoping for so long, it no longer seemed possible to her. Kate had finally come to believe Joe was dead. And now, hearing the words she had given up hope of ever hearing, her mind reeled, and she was completely confused.

"He was shot down just west of Berlin," her father said, as tears rolled down his cheeks. "He had a problem with his parachute and badly damaged both his legs. He was hidden by a farmer, and then eventually tried to make his way to the border, but he was caught and taken to Colditz Castle Prison near Leipzig. He had no way of contacting anyone before that, and from what the War Office told us before, we know he was carrying identification with a false name. They were afraid to let him fly over Germany with papers showing his correct name, because it would have been even more dangerous for him," her father said, wiping away his tears, as Kate stared at him. It was almost beyond her comprehension, as she tried to concentrate on what was being said. She felt as though she herself were being brought back from the dead, not just Joe. "He was kept in solitary confinement, and for some reason the Germans did not report him on their list of prisoners, even under the alias he had used. No one knows why, they may have suspected the name he was using was in fact not correct, and they tried to torture any information he had out of him. He was in Colditz for seven months, and then finally escaped. He had been in Germany for nearly a year by then. And this time, he made it all the way into Sweden and was trying to board a freighter when he was caught again. He was shot that time, and very badly injured. They think he was either delirious or unconscious for several months, and then put in Colditz again. He had been using false Swedish papers, which is why he didn't turn up on the list of American prisoners again. I'm not sure they even knew who he was. They found him in solitary confinement in Colditz weeks ago, but he wasn't able to tell them who he was until yesterday. He's in a military hospital in Berlin now. And Kate . . . ," her father's voice drifted off for a minute as he tried to control his voice, "he seems to be in pretty bad shape. They said he was barely alive when they took him out. But somehow, God bless him, he's managed to hold on till now. They think he'll make it, barring any complications. He has managed to stay alive and unidentified for all this time. His legs are still badly damaged, and had been broken again. He still had bullet wounds in his legs and arms. He's been in hell for all this time. And if they can get him well enough to travel, they're going to put him on a hospital ship in two weeks and bring him home. He should be here sometime in July."

Kate still hadn't said a word and, like her father, all she could do was cry. Her mother was looking at her in despair. She knew, without being told, that Kate's life was about to alter radically. Andy Scott and everything he had to offer her had just vanished in a puff of smoke. And no matter how much Kate loved Joe, her mother was sure that because of it, he would destroy her life. But it was obvious to both of them how much he meant to her, it had been impossible to overlook for the past two years. All her father wanted for her was her happiness, whatever it took, and whatever that meant to her. He had always had a deep respect for Joe.

"Can I talk to him?" she asked finally, her voice barely more than a croak, but her father doubted that she could call. He had written down the name of the hospital for her, but communications with Germany were worse than sketchy these days.

She tried calling late that night, but the operator said it was impossible to get through. She sat in her room instead, looking out at the moonlit night and thinking of him. All she could remember now was how sure she had been for so long that he was still alive. It was only in the past few months that she had actually begun to believe he was dead.

She felt as though she were moving underwater for the next few weeks. She went to work on the docks every day, and in the Red Cross facility between ships. She went to visit men in hospitals, wrote letters for them, helped them eat and sit up and drink. She listened to a thousand painful tales. And when Andy called, she sounded vague when she talked to him. She didn't want to tell him on the phone that Joe was alive, and she didn't know what to say. She had tried so hard to talk herself into loving him, and she might have one day, but in the face of Joe coming home, she could barely talk to Andy anymore. But it didn't seem fair to ruin his trip by telling him while he was away.

She went to work at five in the morning the day Joe's ship was due in. She knew they were expected at six o'clock when they came in with the high tide. They had been just offshore the night before, and had radioed in. She wore a clean uniform and her cap, and her hands were shaking when she pinned it on. She couldn't even imagine seeing him. It was all beginning to seem like a very strange dream.

She took the streetcar to the docks, reported in to her supervisor, and checked their supplies. There were seven hundred wounded men on the ship, and it was one of the first from Germany. The others had been coming in from England and France. There were ambulances and military transport vehicles lined up all along the docks, and they would be sending the men to military hospitals over a range of several hundred miles. She had no idea where they were going to be sending Joe. But wherever it was, she was going to be there with him as much as she could. She had never been able to get to him by phone in Germany in the past few weeks, and she'd been told that even a letter wouldn't make it in time. They had had no contact at all since October, nearly two years before.

The ship steamed slowly in, and the decks were lined with men, on crutches, wearing bandages, and you could hear them shouting and screaming and whistling and see them wave long before the ship reached the dock. It was a scene she had seen often by then, and it always brought tears to her eyes. But this time, she stood watching them, straining her eyes, scouring the decks for him, but she doubted if he was in any condition to be standing up. From the sound of it he would be one of the men on stretchers lying flat on the deck. And she had already spoken to her supervisor about going on board.

"Anyone you know?" Usually, the volunteers waited for the men to be unloaded on the dock, but now and then they went on board to lend a hand. But the retired nurse in charge of the volunteers could see how anxious Kate was. With her dark red hair framing her face, she had never seen anyone as pale and still standing up.

"I . . . my . . . my fiancé is on board," she said finally. It was too complicated to explain what he meant to her and where he had been for two years. It was easier to just tell her a diplomatic lie.

"How long has it been since you've seen him?" she asked Kate, as they watched the ship come in. She had already given Kate permission to go aboard.

"Twenty-one months." And then she looked at the young woman with her enormous dark blue eyes. "We thought he was dead until three weeks ago." The woman could only imagine what that must have been like for her. She had lived through her own private hell, she was a widow and had lost three sons.

"Where did they find him?" she asked, more to distract Kate. The poor girl looked like she was about to break in half.

"In Germany. In prison," she said simply. The nurse could only guess at the kind of damage that had been done. "He was shot down on a bombing raid," Kate still had no idea what kind of injuries he'd had. She was just grateful he was alive.

It took them over an hour to berth the ship, and then one by one the men came down the gangways to land. People were cheering and crying and there were countless tearful scenes being played out on the dock. But this time, Kate wasn't crying for them, she was crying for Joe, as tears streamed down her cheeks as she watched. It was another two hours before she could get on the ship. They were ready to unload the stretcher cases by then, and she went up with a group of orderlies who were going up to take them off. She had to fight to control herself, and not shove her way past them, and she had no idea where to find him on the huge ship. She saw quickly that the orderlies on the ship and the crew were bringing out men on litters and laying them on the upper deck. And she carefully threaded her way amongst wounded and dying men. There was the stench of sick and sweating bodies heavy in the air, and she had to struggle not to gag.

Some of them reached out to her, tried to grab her hands, and touch her legs. And she had to stop every few feet to talk to them. No matter what she felt, she couldn't just walk by. She had been walking a cautious path among them, careful not to step on anyone, and she stopped for what must have been the hundredth time when a man with no legs reached up and took her hand. He had lost half his face, and she could see from the way he turned his head, that his remaining eye was blind. He just wanted to talk to her and tell her how glad he was to be home, and she could tell from his accent that he was from the Deep South. She was still bending down talking to him, when a hand behind her gently touched her arm. She finished talking to the southern man, and then turned to see what she could do for the man who had touched her arm, and he was lying there, looking up at her with a broad smile. His face was thin and pale, and there were small scars from beatings he had sustained from the Germans, but in spite of that she knew who he was. She fell to her knees next to him, and he sat up and took her in his arms. There were tears rolling down his cheeks, as they mingled with hers. It was Joe.

"Oh my God . . ." It was all she could say.

"Hello, Kate," he said quietly in a shaking but nonetheless familiar voice. "I told you I had a hundred lives." She was crying so hard she couldn't talk to him, and he gently wiped the tears from her face with a roughened hand. He had lost an incredible amount of weight, and she could see as she sat back and looked at him that both his legs were in casts, they had reset them in Germany, but the doctors weren't sure yet if he would walk again. His captors had broken them during interrogations and shot him in both legs when he tried to escape. He had hung on to the merest thread of life, and he had come back to her. Kate couldn't even imagine the condition he'd been in, it was hard to believe that it could have been worse than what she saw now, but she knew that it had.

"I never thought I'd see you again," he said softly, as the orderlies carried his stretcher off the ship, and Kate walked beside him, holding his hand, as he used the other one to wipe his eyes.

"Neither did I," she said, as her supervisor spotted them, she had been crying silently as she watched them reach the dock. It was a scene they had all seen now a thousand times, but this one touched her particularly because she liked Kate so much. Someone deserved to win in all this, she told herself. There had been enough tragedy in the past four years.

"I see you got your guy. Welcome home, son," the woman said, and patted his arm. He had a death grip on Kate's hand. "Do you want to ride in the ambulance with him, Kate?" They were sending him to a VA hospital just outside of Boston, and it would be an easy commute for her to visit him. The tides of fortune had finally turned. And Kate knew that, whatever else happened to them, she would be grateful forever for the gift of Joe's life.

She got in the ambulance, and sat on the floor next to him. She had brought a bar of chocolate for him in her purse and she handed it to him as the ambulance pulled out. There were three other men riding with them, and she divided up another bar of chocolate among the three of them, and one of them started to cry.

They had all been in Germany, two of them had been in prisoner of war camps, and the fourth man had been caught trying to escape into Switzerland. He had been tortured for four months and then left to die. They had all gotten nightmarish treatment while in German hands, but in each case, civilians had saved their lives, except for Joe, who had been hidden by a farmer at first, but then had simply hung on to life while in prison, until he was found.

"Are you okay?" Joe was looking her over like a mother hen. He had never seen a sight as beautiful as her hair and her skin and her eyes, and the other three men riding with them couldn't take their eyes off her. They just lay on their litters and stared at her, while Joe held her hand.

"I'm fine. I always thought you were alive," she said in a whisper as she sat close to him. "I just knew you weren't dead, in spite of what everyone said."

"You're not married or anything, I hope," he laughed and she shook her head. But if he had taken much longer, it might have been a close call. "Did you finish school?" He wanted to know everything. He had thought of her a million times, and fell asleep thinking of her at night, and wondering if he'd ever see her again. For her sake, and his own, he had refused to die.

"I graduated in June," she filled him in, but after all this time, there was too much to say. There were eighteen months to fill in, and it would take time. "I'm working for the Red Cross as a volunteer."

"No kidding," he laughed through painfully cracked lips that she had already kissed several times, and he knew with utter certainty that there was nothing in life as sweet. "I thought you were just a friendly nurse." He couldn't believe it when he saw her standing next to him on the ship. He hadn't even been able to contact her before they sailed. And it was fortunate that they had shipped him to Boston and not New York. At least here she could visit him every day.

She stayed with him while they settled him in the hospital, but after that she had to ride back to the dock with the ambulance and finish work.

"I'll come back tonight," she promised him. And by the time she got back to her parents' house after work, and borrowed their car, it was after six o'clock. It was nearly seven when she got to him, all clean and neatly tucked into clean sheets by then, he was sound asleep. She sat next to him, without disturbing him, and she was surprised when, two hours later, he stirred. He turned, grimacing painfully, and then sensed her watching him, and opened his eyes.

"Am I dreaming? Or am I in Heaven?" he said with a sleepy smile.

"That can't be you sitting there, Kate. . . . I never did anything in my life to deserve this."

"Yes, you did." She gently kissed his cheeks and then his lips. "I'm the lucky one. My mother was afraid I'd be an old maid."

"I figured you'd have married that kid Andy by now, the one you always said was just a friend. Guys like that always wind up with the girl when the hero dies."

"Guess not," she said cryptically, "the hero didn't die."

"No," Joe said, rolling on his back with a sigh. His legs were encased in heavy plaster casts. "I never thought I'd get out of that prison again. I was sure they were going to kill me every day. I guess they were having too much fun to let me die." They had tortured him mercilessly. She couldn't even imagine eighteen months in the hell he had known, or how he had survived, but thank God he had.

She stayed with him until after ten o'clock, and then finally went home, more because she could see how tired he was than because she wanted to leave. And they were going to give him medication for the pain in his legs. He was dozing off again when she left, and she stood for a minute, looking at the strong, distinct face that she had dreamed of a million times.

And when she got home, her father was waiting up for her.

"How is he, Kate?" he asked, looking concerned. He'd still been at the office when she came to pick up the car.

"He's alive," she beamed, "and in surprisingly good shape. His legs are in casts, and his face is a mess." He'd had hair to his waist when they fished him out, but they had cut it at the hospital in Germany. Joe said he had looked a lot worse then. "It's really a miracle he's with us, Dad." He smiled at the look on his daughter's face. It had been years since he'd seen her smile like that. It warmed his heart to see her happy again.

"He'll be flying again in no time, if I know him." Clarke smiled.

"I'm afraid you may be right." They still had to see about his legs, and maybe operate again, and there was a chance he would have a limp. But there were far worse fates. He had come back from the dead, and whatever was left of him would be enough for her.

Her father looked serious for a moment then. "Andy called when you were out. What are you going to say to him, Kate?"

"Nothing till he gets back." She had been thinking about it on the way home, and felt badly for him. It was just blind luck, and she hoped he would understand. "I'll tell him the truth," she said honestly. "As soon as I tell him Joe is back, he'll know. I'm not sure I could ever have married him, Dad. He knew I was still in love with Joe."

"So did your mother and I. We hoped you'd get over it, for your sake, if he was gone. We didn't want you to pine for him for the rest of your life. Will you two be getting married now?" he asked. It seemed pretty obvious to him that they would, after all they'd been through. It was clear to him at least that they were bound together for life.

"We didn't talk about it. He's still pretty sick, Dad. I don't think it's a big issue at the moment."

When Clarke Jamison went to visit Joe the next day, he could see why not. He was shocked at how terrible he looked, it was worse than he'd imagined. Kate had seen so many wounded men by then that it hadn't startled her as much as it might have otherwise. She had actually expected him to look worse than he did.

Joe was thrilled to see him, and they talked for a long time. Clarke didn't ask him about his experience in Germany, he thought it was best not to talk about it, but eventually Joe told him what it had been like, and about getting shot down. It was an incredible story, but Joe was in amazingly good spirits in spite of it. And his eyes lit up when he saw Kate. She had come to visit him while her father was still there. He left them to each other a few minutes after that, and Kate inquired about his legs. The doctors had examined him, and thought that things looked hopeful. They'd done a good job in Germany of setting his legs.

For the next month, Kate visited him every evening after work, she sat with him every weekend, and rolled him into the garden in his wheelchair. He called her the angel of mercy. And when no one was looking, they kissed and held hands. By the time he'd been home for two weeks, he was threatening to leave the hospital and take her to a hotel, and she laughed at him.

"You wouldn't get very far with those on," she pointed at his casts. But she was as anxious to get her hands on him as he was on her. They had to content themselves with clandestine kisses for the time being. He wasn't well enough to go anywhere, but with each day he was better able to move his legs, in spite of the casts. And when they took them off four weeks after he arrived, much to everyone's amazement, he started walking. He could only take a few steps at first, and he was on crutches, but the prognosis was very good.

Both her parents had come to see him by then, and her mother had brought him books and flowers. She was very pleasant to him, but the day after their visit, she cornered Kate in the kitchen, with an earnest look in her eyes.

"Have you and Joe talked about getting married yet?" she asked pointedly, as Kate sighed in irritation.

"Mom, have you seen the condition he's in? Why don't we get him on his feet first?"

"You cried over him for two years, Kate. And you've known him for nearly five. Is there some reason you two aren't making plans, or is there something I don't know here? Is he married?"

"Of course he's not. He's not going anywhere. I just don't think it's important. He's alive, that's all I wanted, Mom."

"That's abnormal. And what about Andy?" Kate sat down with a serious look in answer to her question.

"He's coming home this week, I'll tell him then."

"Tell him what? There doesn't seem to be anything to tell him. Maybe you'd better give it some thought before you decide you can't see him anymore. Kate, mark my words, as soon as Joe is on his feet, he's not going to be heading down the aisle with you, he's going to be running for the nearest airstrip. All he did was talk about planes yesterday. He's a lot more excited about flying than about being with you. Maybe you'd better face that, before it's too late."

"It's what he loves, Mom." But her mother was right. He was already talking constantly about flying. He was dying to get in an airplane, almost as much as he wanted to go to bed with her, but she couldn't say that to her mother.

"How much does he love you, Kate? I think that's a far more relevant question."

"Can't he love both? Does he have to make a choice?"

"I don't know, Kate. Can he love both? I'm not sure he can. One may be exclusive of the other."

"That's crazy. I don't expect him to give up flying. It's his life. It always has been."

"He's nearly thirty-five years old, and he's just spent two years damn near dead. If he's going to settle down and get married, and have a family, I'd say this would be a good time." Kate didn't disagree with her, but she didn't want to pressure him. They hadn't talked about it yet. Kate just assumed it would happen eventually. She wasn't worried about it. She might as well have been married to him anyway, they were totally devoted to each other. He had no interest whatsoever in other women, just in airplanes.

Andy came to the house to see Kate the day he got home. He had just gotten off the train from Chicago, after spending the last weeks of his vacation in San Francisco. He was a little disappointed that she hadn't met him at the train, but he also knew how hard she was working. It was a hot day, and she looked thoroughly wilted when she got home. They had unloaded two ships that day. Andy looked thrilled to see her, far more than she did him. He knew instantly that something had happened while he was gone.

"Are you okay?" he asked when her parents left them alone. Her mother went upstairs to her dressing room, and she cried when she thought of what Kate was going to say. She knew it was going to crush him, but Liz knew that Kate had to be honest with him. And she was of no use to any man now, except Joe. She adored him.

"I'm fine, just tired," she said, brushing her hair back. He had tried to kiss her when her parents left the room, and she seemed uncomfortable and awkward with him. She knew she couldn't wait any longer. "No, I guess, I'm not fine . . . or I am . . . but we're not."

"What does all that mean?" He looked worried, and he already sensed some of what was coming. But she knew that the news that Joe was alive, and home again, was going to stun him, almost as much as it had her.

She turned to face him bravely then, she hated hurting him. But she had no choice. Fate had dealt them a tough hand, and Joe an extremely good one. It obviously wasn't meant to be for her to be with Andy. They both had to accept that. But it would be easier for her to accept than for him. All her dreams had just come true, and Andy's were about to end. And as he looked at her, he knew, even before he heard the words.

"What exactly happened while I was gone, Kate?" His voice sounded strangled as he asked.

"Joe came home," she said simply. That said it all for him. It was over between them. He had no illusions about what she felt for him.

"He's alive? How did he manage that? Was he in a prisoner of war camp?" It seemed impossible that the War Office had thought he was dead for nearly two years, and now he was back.

"He was in prison, under a false name, and he escaped and was caught again. They never knew who he was. It's a miracle that he's alive, although he's pretty badly wounded." All Andy could see in her eyes was what she felt for Joe. There was nothing for him.

"And where does that leave us, Kate? Or do I even need to ask?" The love in her eyes when she spoke of Joe told the entire story. "I guess I don't need to ask, do I? He's a lucky guy. You never stopped loving him for a second the entire time he was gone. I always knew that. I figured you'd get over it in time. It never occurred to me that you might be right and he could be alive. I thought you just didn't want to face his being dead. I hope he knows how much you love him."

"I think he loves me just as much," she said softly. She hated the look in Andy's eyes. He was being gentlemanly, but he looked devastated by what he'd just heard.

"Are you getting married?" Andy wanted to know, and wished she had told him before he'd gotten home, although he understood why she hadn't. It would have been an even bigger shock hearing it on the phone. But he had spent the whole summer thinking about her, and planning their engagement and subsequent marriage. He'd been planning to pick out a ring for her as soon as he got back to Boston.

"Not for the moment. Eventually, I guess. I'm not worried about it."

"I wish you luck, Kate," Andy said nobly, "both of you. Offer Joe my congratulations." He only hesitated for a moment then, and she reached out a hand to him, but he didn't take it. He walked quietly out of the house, got in his car, and drove away.

10

JOE LEFT THE HOSPITAL two months after he'd arrived, on canes, with stiff legs, but they were coming along. The doctors thought he might be walking normally by Christmas. No one could believe the recovery he'd made, least of all Kate. It still seemed like a miracle to her that he was with them.

Two days after he left the hospital, he got his discharge papers. They had already spent an afternoon at the Copley Plaza Hotel by then. She couldn't get away for an entire night, now that she was living with her parents. And he had accepted their kind invitation to stay with them. But he was well aware that he couldn't live with them forever, and he wanted privacy with Kate.

Joe had already called Charles Lindbergh long before he left the hospital, and he was planning to go to New York to see him. His mentor had some interesting ideas he wanted to discuss with Joe, and there were some people he wanted him to meet. Joe was going to stay in New York for several days, and then come back to Boston.

Kate drove him to the train on her way to work the week after he'd gotten out of the hospital. It was the end of September by then, and the war was over. Victory in Japan had finally come in August. The nightmare had ended at last.

"Have fun in New York," she kissed him before he left the car. She had found a way of sneaking into his room at night without waking her parents. It was too hard for him to get to her. And they both felt like mischievous children as they whispered in his bed every night.

"I'll be back in a few days. I'll call you. Don't pick up any soldiers while I'm gone, please."

"Then don't stay gone too long," she warned, and he wagged a finger at her. She still couldn't believe how lucky she was, how lucky they both were. He had been wonderful to her. Even her mother had finally relented. Despite the fact that he loved flying, he was a good man, and a responsible person, and it was obvious to everyone how much he loved her. Her parents were expecting them to get engaged any day.

She hadn't heard from Andy again since she'd told him Joe was back. She knew he was in New York by then, working for his father. And all she could hope was that he was feeling better, and he'd forgive her someday. She missed his presence in her life. It felt like losing her best friend. But she still wasn't convinced that his warm friendship would have been enough to make her love him as a husband. Things had obviously worked out the way they should.

She waved as Joe hobbled off toward the train. He was getting around surprisingly well, and was very independent. She drove off to work, thinking about him, and for the rest of the day, her mind was occupied with the men she was helping there.

She had hoped he would call her that night, but he didn't. He called her instead early the next morning.

"How's it going?" she asked him.

"Very interesting," he said cryptically, "I'll tell you about it when I get back." He was rushing off to a meeting, and she had to go to work. "I'll call you tonight. I promise." And this time, he called her. He'd been in meetings all day with the men that Charles Lindbergh had introduced him to. And much to Kate's delight, Joe made it back to

Boston by the weekend. And she was more than a little bowled over by what he had to say.

The men Charles had introduced him to wanted to start a company with him, to design and build the most advanced airplanes. They had been buying land since the beginning of the war, had remodeled an old factory, and they even had their own airstrip. They were setting up the entire operation in New Jersey, and they not only wanted Joe to run it, but to design and test the planes. He was going to wear a lot of hats at first, but eventually when things settled down, he would run the whole operation. They wanted to put up the money. He would be the brains.

"It's the perfect setup, Kate," he said with an ecstatic grin that warmed the chiseled face. Nothing made him happier than airplanes. But she had to admit it sounded perfect for him. "I get fifty percent ownership, and if we ever become a listed company, I get half the stock. It's a sweet deal, for me at least."

"And a lot of work," she added. But the entire project sounded as though it had been tailor-made for him.

Joe explained it to her father that night, and Clarke was extremely impressed by everything Joe said. He knew of the investors by name, and said they were very sound. It was a once-in-a-lifetime opportunity for Joe.

"When do you start?" he asked with interest.

"I have to be in New Jersey a week from Monday. It's not a bad place. It's less than an hour from New York. I probably won't leave the factory much at first, and we have to make some changes to the airstrip." His mind was already spinning with everything he was going to do. His own expertise was going to serve him well, and Clarke agreed with Kate enthusiastically, it was perfect for him.

And as Clarke congratulated him, Kate's mother spoke unexpectedly, and startled them all.

"Does this mean you two will be getting married soon?" she asked, and as Joe looked at Kate, there was silence in the room.

"I don't know, Mom," Kate tried to fob her off, but her mother had long since gotten tired of waiting for Joe to come up with the idea himself. As far as she was concerned, it was time to ask him directly about his intentions toward their daughter. Kate was blushing when she answered her mother. And Joe looked equally embarrassed, and didn't know what to say.

"Why don't you let Joe answer the question. It sounds like you've landed yourself a wonderful opportunity with this job, not just for work temporarily, but for a real future. What are your plans now for Kate?" She had waited for him for two years, and loved him for another two before that. It had been five years since they met, long enough, as far as Liz was concerned, to not only figure out his intentions, but declare them to her.

"I don't know, Mrs. Jamison. Kate and I haven't discussed it," Joe said, avoiding her gaze, and Kate's. What her mother was saying was making him feel trapped, in spite of all he felt for Kate. Her mother was treating him like a wayward, irresponsible child, and not a man worthy of respect.

"I suggest you give it some thought. It damn near killed her when you got shot down. I think she deserves a little recognition for her loyalty and courage. She waited a long time for you, Joe." Listening to Elizabeth Jamison was like being told he was a naughty boy. And all he could feel was anger and guilt. Hearing her made him want to run away.

"I know," Joe said calmly. "I didn't realize marriage was that important to her." She had never said anything to him about it, and they were having a great time sneaking into each other's bedrooms at night. But the burden of guilt her mother was forcing on him weighed heavily on him, although nothing showed.

"If marriage isn't important to her," Liz said, as her husband watched her with amazement. She had stolen the show for the moment, but he didn't disagree with her. It was just a more direct approach than he would have used, if he had chosen to broach the subject with Joe. "If it isn't important to her, Joe, it should be. And maybe it's time we reminded you both of that. Maybe this would be a fine time to announce your engagement." He hadn't even asked her to marry him, and he didn't look overly happy to be pressured by her mother, but he could also appreciate their point of view. There was no question in his mind that he loved her, and maybe they needed to know that. But he didn't feel ready to do as they wished. His freedom was something he had to be willing to give, not something they could take from him. And he had a firm grip on it still.

"If you don't mind, Mrs. Jamison, I'd rather wait to get engaged until I get my feet wet in this new job, and get the project well in hand. It's going to take a little time, but then I'll really have something to offer your daughter. I thought by then, we could live in New York, and I could commute to New Jersey." He had already been planning ahead. But he hadn't even started the job yet. And he wasn't ready for marriage. Kate knew that. And she could also see the look of panic in his eyes. What her mother was saying was making him want to run. Joe was not a man you could push or force into a cage.

"That sounds reasonable," Clarke stepped in then. It was beginning to sound like the Spanish Inquisition, and he gave his wife a sign that he felt the conversation should end. She had made her point, and everyone got it. And what Joe said made sense. There was no real hurry, and he needed to establish himself. He had undertaken an enormous job.

The evening broke up shortly afterward, and later that night, Kate was irate when she joined him in his room.

"I can't believe the way my mother behaved at dinner. I apologize.

My father should have stopped her. I thought she was incredibly rude to you." Kate was furious with her, which in turn allowed Joe to be magnanimous toward Kate.

"It's all right, sweetheart. They care about you, and they want to be sure I'll make you happy, and that I'm a serious guy. I'd have done the same thing if you were my daughter. I just didn't realize how much a concern it was to them, right now at least. Have you been worried about it?" He put his arms around her and kissed her as he asked her. He didn't look as nervous as he had when Kate's mother had been grilling him.

"No, I haven't been worried about it. And you're much too generous. I thought she was disgusting. I'm really sorry." Kate looked deeply chagrined, which was a relief to him.

"Don't be. My intentions are honorable, Miss Jamison, I promise. Although, if you don't mind, I'd like to take advantage of you in the meantime." As he slipped her nightgown off, she giggled. The last thing on her mind at that particular moment was marriage. She was divinely happy just being with him. All she wanted was his love, not a leash.

The scene in her parents' bedroom was a little less romantic. Her father had been scolding her mother for taking the bull by the horns.

"I don't see why you're upset," she told Clarke. "Someone had to ask him, and you wouldn't." It was an accusatory tone he had learned not to react to over the years.

"The poor boy just returned from the dead moments ago. Give him a chance to get on his feet again, Liz. It's not fair to push him so soon." But she disagreed with him. She was a woman on a mission, and she would not be swayed.

"He's not a boy, Clarke. He's a thirty-four-year-old man, he's been back for two months, and he's seen her every day. He's had ample opportunity to propose to her, and he hasn't." That spoke volumes to her, if not to Clarke.

"He wants to get set with his job first. That's entirely reasonable and respectable, and I approve."

"I wish I were as sure as you are that he's going to do the right thing. I think once he gets into a plane again, he's going to forget all about marrying her. He's obsessed with airplanes and not nearly as interested in marriage. I don't want her hanging around forever waiting for him."

"I'll lay you a wager tonight that they're married in a year, maybe before that," Clarke said confidently, as his wife glared at him, as though he were to blame. But he was used to it.

"That at least is a bet I will enjoy losing," she said, as he smiled at her. She was like a lioness defending her cub, and he admired her for it, but he wasn't nearly as sure that Kate and Joe had enjoyed it. Joe had looked particularly awkward while he was under attack, and more uncomfortable than Clarke had ever seen. It had made Clarke feel sorry for Joe.

"Why don't you trust him, Liz?" Clarke asked her as he got into bed with her. He knew she didn't, she made no secret of it, although she admitted that she liked him, but not necessarily for Kate. Liz would have been much happier if Kate had married Andy. In her eyes, he would have been a much better husband than Joe.

"I think men like Joe don't marry." She explained to Clarke. "And if they do, they botch it. They don't really know what marriage is. It's something they do in their spare time when they're not playing with their toys or their friends. They're not bad guys, but the women in their lives are less important to them. I like Joe a lot, he's a decent man and I know he loves her, but I'm not sure he'll ever pay attention to her. He's going to spend the rest of his life playing with his airplanes, and now he's going to get paid to do it. And if it's a success, he'll never marry her."

"I think he will," Kate's father said firmly. "And at least he'll be able to support her. In fact, he might wind up making quite a lot of money, from what he said. I don't think you're right, Liz. I think he can manage both a wife and a career. He's a bright guy. In fact, sometimes I think he's brilliant. He's a genius with airplanes, and God knows he can fly them. He just has to come down to earth once in a while to keep her happy. They love each other, that ought to be enough."

"Sometimes it isn't," she said sadly. "I hope it will be, for them. They've come through an awful lot, they deserve some happiness now. I just want to see Kate settled with a man who loves her, a nice home, and some kids."

"She'll get there. He's crazy about her." Clarke was sure.

"I hope so," she said with a sigh as she slid down into her bed, and cuddled up next to her husband. She wanted Kate to be as happy as she was, and that was a lot to ask. Men like Clarke Jamison were rare.

But in his room, Kate was lying in Joe's arms, happy and sated, and pressed up close to him, as they drifted off to sleep together.

"I love you," she whispered, and he smiled sleepily in answer.

"I love you too, sweetheart. . . . I even love your mother." She giggled, and a moment later they were fast asleep, as were Liz and Clarke. One pair lovers, the other married. It was hard to say who was happier that night.

11

WHEN JOE LEFT for New Jersey, he promised to have Kate come down to spend the weekend with him after he settled in. He thought it would take him a couple of weeks, but it was a month before he found an apartment. There was a hotel nearby where she could stay, where he had been living for the past month. But the truth was he had no time to spend with her. He was working night and day, and staying in the office until well after midnight. And he was working weekends too. Sometimes he even slept in his office on the couch.

Joe was hiring people, setting up the factory, and redesigning the airstrip. He never seemed to come up for air, but the aeronautics industry was beginning to get interested in what he was doing in a major way. The whole plant they were setting up was going to be highly innovative, and there had already been several articles about it in business sections and trade papers. He barely managed to call Kate at night, and it had been six weeks since he left Boston when he finally let her come to see him for a weekend. He looked exhausted when she arrived. And when he explained to her all that he'd been doing, Kate was enormously impressed. It was a fantastic operation, and Joe loved the fact that when he explained it to her, she understood it all.

They had a wonderful weekend together. They spent most of it at the plant, and even got some flying time in a brand-new plane he had designed. When she got back to Boston, she described it all to her father. He was dying to see it too. People in the business world were beginning to realize that Joe was making history with his ideas.

Two weeks later, Joe came up to spend Thanksgiving with them. But he was having problems with the factory, and on Friday morning he had to go back. He had responsibilities he'd never had before, and an entire industry was resting on his shoulders. Sometimes it felt like the whole world. Joe was handling it well, but it left him no spare time to play, or even call Kate much of the time. And by Christmas, in spite of her enthusiasm about his work, she was complaining to him. She had seen him twice in three months, and she was lonely in Boston without him. And every time she said it to him, he felt consumed by guilt, but there was nothing he could do.

Kate was beginning to think her mother was right, and they should get married. At least they'd be together then, instead of miles apart. She said as much to Joe when he came to spend Christmas with them, and he looked surprised.

"Now? I'm home about five hours a night, Kate. That wouldn't be much fun. And I can't move to New York yet." Marriage still didn't make sense to him.

"So we'll live in New Jersey. At least we'd be together," Kate said reasonably. She was tired of living with her parents. And she didn't want to get her own apartment in Boston, if they were going to get married. She felt as though she were living in suspended animation, waiting for him to set up his business, and have time for a life. But it was no easy task for him. He had taken on a mammoth project, and he was only just then beginning to realize how much time and effort it was going to take to do it right. In three months, he had barely scratched the surface. He was working a hundred and twenty hours a week, or more.

"I think it's silly for us to get married now," he explained to her on

Christmas Eve, after he snuck into her bedroom. To Kate, it was beginning to seem like a crazy way to live, and a frustrating way to see each other. She felt like a child, still living with her parents. By then, most of her friends were married. Those who hadn't gotten married before or during the war, were all getting married now, and having babies. She was suddenly anxious to get started or at least live with him. "Just give me time to set this up, and then we'll find an apartment in New York and get married. I promise." A year before he'd been in prison in Germany, being tortured by the Germans. And suddenly he was running a major empire. It was an enormous adjustment for him. And he didn't want to get married until he had time for her. He thought it wouldn't be fair to her otherwise. But neither was this.

He spent a wonderful Christmas with her family, and managed to spend three days in Boston. Kate and Joe went flying again, and they even spent an entire day in bed in a hotel, and by the time he left, Kate was feeling better. He was right. It made more sense to wait until he had a good grip on the business. Kate understood that. Things were winding down at the Red Cross, so she decided to look for a job. And she found something she liked right after New Year's. She had spent New Year's Eve in New Jersey with Joe, and it made her realize again how lucky they were. The year before she'd been crying for him, thinking he was gone forever. She would have given anything then for what she had now, even if she seldom saw him. At least they had a whole life ahead of them, and a rosy future once they got married.

January was difficult for both of them. She was adjusting to a new job in an art gallery, and he had a terrible battle with the unions. For him, the entire month was a nightmare, and February was worse. He didn't make it up for Valentine's Day, in fact he forgot it completely. They had failed to get their final permit for the airstrip. It was crucial for them, and he had to spend three days romancing politicians and lobbying petty officials to get it. He only remembered that it had been

Valentine's Day when she called him two days later, crying. They hadn't seen each other in six weeks by then, and he promised to make it up to her, and suggested she come down again for the weekend.

They had a great time while she was there. She helped him organize his office, and he even managed to take her out to dinner. He stayed at the hotel with her, and she went back to Boston on Sunday night smiling and happy. She enjoyed it so much, she wanted to come down every weekend, which sounded good to him. He was lonely and he missed her, but he also knew he had to work eighteen hours a day, even on weekends, just as he did on weekdays. He felt terrible about Kate, but for the moment, there was nothing he could do. He felt as though he were on a constant merry-go-round, trapped between feeling guilty about Kate and running a business that devoured his every waking hour. And the worse he felt about Kate, the less time he seemed to have. It didn't even make sense to him. Finally, in desperation, three weeks later, he let her come down for a week, so they could be together. And he was surprised by how smoothly things went when she helped out in the office. He only caught glimpses of her all day, but she seemed blissfully happy. And at least they could sleep together at night, and have breakfast together at the coffee shop in the morning. The rest of the day's meals he ate at his desk or on the run. The only time he actually sat down to dinner at a restaurant was when she came to visit him in New Jersey, and then he felt guilty for the time it cost him. He felt like a man being pulled in ten thousand directions at once. And he was.

Things didn't even begin to fall into place until May. And by then, she quit her job, and came down to work for him for the summer. It worked perfectly, and although she kept a room at the hotel for the sake of respectability, she stayed at his apartment with him. She had never been happier in her life, and he had to admit it suited him too. She was no longer complaining about not seeing him. It seemed like the perfect arrangement, to them, if not to her parents. They weren't pleased about her visiting Joe in New Jersey, but she was twenty-three years old, and she told them she stayed at the hotel. She had the room at the hotel in case they called.

Joe had been home for a year by then, and neither of them ever talked about an engagement. They were far too busy thinking about his work. It was only when he took a week's holiday and went up to the Cape with them, that her father took him aside, and had a serious talk with him. It had been nearly a year since Liz's last outburst. And she was furious by then with both Joe and Kate. She had begun to suspect what their living arrangements were, and she disapproved vehemently, if she was right. What if Kate got pregnant? Would he even marry her then? She fumed every time she looked at Joe. And more than ever, Kate's mother made Joe feel like a wicked child. Whenever he saw her, it made him want to run. She was like a constant guilt machine, spewing at him, even when she didn't say a word. She didn't need to anymore. And Kate felt torn between her parents and Joe.

By then, Clarke wasn't happy either, it had gone on for too long, and he said as much to Joe as they took a walk on the beach in Cape Cod. Joe had flown up from New Jersey in a beautifully designed plane that his company was making. They were pulling in huge money. Joe's life was in a far distant place than it had been in a year before, when he was taken off the hospital ship in Boston. He was becoming a very rich man. But he was too busy to breathe. And Clarke was worried about both of them. He was fond of Joe.

Joe took Clarke up in his new plane, and they agreed not to tell Liz, who was even more furious now that she knew that Kate often flew with Joe. Despite his history as a flying ace, and his years as a war hero, she was still convinced he was going to crash and kill them both. She had been beside herself when she discovered that Joe was giving Kate flying lessons. Kate had slipped and told her inadvertently. But Joe was confident about how capable Kate was. He had taught her well, although she hadn't had time to qualify for her license yet. She was too busy working for him.

Clarke was vastly impressed by Joe's fabulous new plane, and afterward on the way back to the house they stopped at a roadhouse for some beers. It was a hot summer day, and Joe was happy with his plane. But Clarke had a lot on his mind, his daughter's happiness, his wife's sanity, and he wanted to offer Joe some fatherly advice. It was why he had gone flying with Joe, although he had enjoyed the plane.

"You're working too hard, son," he began. "You're going to miss out on life, and at the speed you're moving, you could make some important mistakes that will cost you in the long run." Joe recognized instantly that he was talking about Kate, but he also knew that all was well with them. It was her mother who was in a constant frenzy about the status quo.

"Things will settle down in a while, Clarke, the business is young," he said confidently.

"So are you, but you won't be for long. You should enjoy it now."

"I am. I love what I'm doing." He did, and it showed. But he also loved Kate, and Clarke knew that too. Enough so that he felt justified violating a promise he had made to Liz years before, to not talk about her late husband's suicide, or even that Clarke wasn't Kate's father, to people who hadn't been around then. When Clarke had adopted Kate, Liz had told him she didn't want John Barrett's suicide hanging over Kate like a dark cloud for the rest of her life. But Clarke knew better than Liz that in a silent way it had anyway. And he thought that Joe should know. It was an important piece of who Kate was, and couldn't be ignored. It wasn't fair to her, or even Joe. And Clarke thought it might open Joe's eyes, and his heart, if he knew.

"There's something about Kate I think you should know," Clarke said quietly after they had finished their second round of beers and switched to gin. He knew that Liz wouldn't be pleased if they both came home drunk, but at the moment he didn't care. He had made up his mind about telling Joe, and needed to steel himself for the task.

"That sounds mysterious," Joe said with a grin. He liked Clarke, and for his entire life, he had been more comfortable with men. Kate was the only woman he had ever felt open and easy with, and even she frightened him sometimes. Particularly when she got wound up about something, which fortunately, was rare. But when she did, any sense of intensity or criticism drove him away. He'd never explained it to her. He thought telling her when she frightened him might make him even more vulnerable. After his early years with his cousins constantly telling him how worthless he was, any hint of that in the years since made him want to run. It was the button Kate's mother pushed in him, with unpleasant results every time.

"It is mysterious," Clarke confirmed to him about Kate. "Not so much mysterious as dark. And I don't want either Liz or Kate to know that we talked about this. I mean that, Joe," he said fervently on their second gin. Clarke was beginning to feel tight, and Joe was grinning a lot. He always got expansive when he drank. It took some of the pressure off him.

"So what's the dark mystery?" Joe asked with a boyish smile. He was growing ever more fond of Clarke, and always had been. He thought he was a good man. They respected each other and had from the first.

"I'm not her father, Joe," Clarke said quietly, suddenly sober again. He had never in thirteen years said those words. And as he looked at Joe, the younger man's smile faded as their eyes met.

"What does that mean? It doesn't make sense." He looked worried now. He could sense something ugly lurking near.

"Liz was married before. For a long time. Nearly thirty years. We've only been married for fourteen. Feels like forever though at times," he said with a grin and Joe laughed. But he also knew how much Clarke loved Liz. He had to, to put up with her. "Her husband was a friend of mine, he was a good man, gentle, kind, from a great family. His brother and I went to school together, which was how I met John. He lost everything in the crash of '29, not only his own and his family's, but all of the money of the people whose investments he handled, and some of Liz's fortune as well. Fortunately, her own family had kept a tight rein on most of hers, and they were luckier than John. Most of her money was intact after the crash. But John lost it all." It was a story Clarke didn't want to tell, and Joe was suddenly afraid to hear. "It damn near killed him at the time. He was the most honorable man I knew, and it destroyed him on the spot. It took him two years, locked in a bedroom upstairs, sitting in the dark. He tried to drink himself to death, but it didn't work. So he shot himself in '31. Kate was eight when he died."

"Was she there? Did she see him do it?" Joe looked horrified at the image Clarke had conjured for him, but the older man shook his head.

"No, thank God. Liz found him. I think Kate was in school. It was all over by the time she got home. But she knew how he died. I had known Liz and John and Kate for years and years, all of Kate's life, and most of John's. I did what I could for them afterward, with no other motive, I might add, except to lend a hand. Liz was in shock. I had lost my own wife several years before. Eventually things developed between Liz and myself, but I think I fell in love with Kate even before I fell in love with Liz. She was a terrified, heartbroken little girl after her father died. I never thought she'd be the same again. She was eight then. I married Liz a year later, and adopted Kate a year after that, when she was ten. It took me another two years to bring her back from the cave she'd been hiding in since John killed himself. I don't think she really trusted me, or anyone else, for years, particularly men. And Liz adored the child, but I'm not sure she really knew how to reach out to her, she was too shocked by his death herself. There was a terrible moment when Liz got sick right after we got married. It was nothing more than a bad case of influenza. But you could see Kate panic. She was terrified to lose her mother. I'm not sure Liz really understood it. It's taken Kate her entire life to become the woman she is now. Strong, confident, happy, funny, capable. The woman you love was a terrified, broken little girl for a long time. I think for years she was afraid that I would abandon her in some way too, like her father. Poor bastard, he couldn't help himself. He didn't have the stamina to survive what happened to him, no matter how much money Liz had. It destroyed all his self-respect, his manhood, his pride. But when he killed himself, he destroyed Kate, or damn near."

"Why are you telling me this?" Joe asked suspiciously, still looking shocked by what he'd heard.

"Because it's an important part of Kate. She loved her father and he adored her. And then she came to love me. And now you. You went off to the war and she thought you were dead for nearly two years. It would have been a tragedy for any girl, but it was more than that for Kate. It opened all her old wounds again, I could see it in her eyes every day. It was a kind of loss that could have destroyed her this time, if she weren't as strong as she is. And then, miraculously, you came back from the dead. Life was kind to her this time. But there's a broken piece in her that you need to see, if you're going to love her. Every time you leave her, or reject her, or make her feel abandoned in some way, you remind her of everything she's ever lost. She's like a wounded doe, you need to be gentle with her, and give her a good home. If you're kind to her, she'll be good to you forever, Joe. But you need to know about that broken piece. She's like a bird with a broken wing, no matter how well you think she can fly. You have to be gentle with that wing. . . . She's the most beautiful little bird I've ever seen, and she'll fly farther than anyone for you. Just don't frighten her, and you won't, if you know what she's been through." Joe sat in silence for a long time, pondering Clarke's words. It was a heavy dose of reality to be sharing on a summer day over a couple of gins. But he was right, it was an important piece of Kate, and it explained a lot to him. There was a sense of panic about her when he was away from her. She never expressed it openly, but when he left her to go somewhere, he could always see it in her eyes. And that look of terror had frightened him at times. It was like the shadow of the leash he had fled from all his life.

"What are you saying to me, Clarke?" Joe asked, but more important, he was wondering why.

"I think you should marry her, Joe. Not for the reasons Liz wants for her. She wants pomp and circumstance and respectability, a big party and a white dress. I want to know she's got a good home. She deserves it, Joe, more than most. Her father took something from her that none of us will ever be able to give back. But you can, not entirely, but enough to make a difference for the rest of her life. I want her to feel safe and to have the comfort of knowing you're going to stick around."

Listening to him made Joe want to scream "what about me?" Marrying her was exactly what he feared most. A leash. A cage. A trap. No matter how much he loved her, and he did, the marriage itself was an enormous threat to him. More than Clarke could ever suspect.

"I'm not sure I can," Joe said honestly, with the assistance of the gin.

"Why not?"

"It feels like a trap. Or a noose around my neck. My parents deserted me in a different way. They died and left me to people who hated me. They were rotten to me, and whenever I think of marriage, or families, or getting tied down, it just makes me want to run."

"She'll be good to you, Joe. I know her well. She's a good girl, and she loves you more than life."

"That scares me too," he said honestly, "I don't want to be loved that much." Clarke watched his eyes and saw fear peering out at him. A deeper fear than he'd ever seen there before. "I'm not sure that I can give her the love she needs and wants. I don't want to disappoint her, Clarke, or let her down. I couldn't stand the guilt if I failed somehow. I love her too much to do that to her."

"We all fail at some time. We learn from it. She's good for you. You'll teach each other, even if it hurts sometimes. Love heals a lot of wounds. Liz has healed a lot of mine." It was a side of her Joe had never thought of before, but he was willing to believe Clarke. She had obviously been through a lot. "You'll be a lonely man one day if you don't let someone love you, Joe. It's a high price to pay for letting yourself run."

"Maybe so," Joe said noncommittally, staring down at his glass.

"You need each other, Joe. She needs your strength, and knowing that you won't run out on her, that you love her enough to marry her. And you need her strength too, and her warmth. It's cold out there alone. I was there for a long time after my wife died. It's a sad life. A girl like Kate won't let you be sad, if you let her in, even just a little bit. She'll make you mad as hell sometimes, but she won't break your heart. She may scare the hell out of you, but she won't break you, you're a lot stronger than you think. You're not a kid anymore, no one can do to you what your cousins did. You're a man now, Joe, they're gone. They're just ghosts. Don't let them run your life."

"Why not? It's worked so far, hasn't it? I'd say I have a pretty good life." Joe smiled cynically.

"That's my point. You'll have a better life if you share it with her. You'll be a sad man if you lose her one day. And you might. Women are funny that way. They leave when we least expect them to. You can lose anyone if you try hard enough. She won't leave you though, unless you force her to. She loves you too much. Grab her while you can. For both your sakes. I want this for both of you. Trust me, son. It will be good for you both. And if you give her a chance to grow up, you'll have a good woman on your hands. I think now she's probably afraid that sooner or later you'll run out on her."

"I might," Joe said, looking Clarke squarely in the eye.

"I hope you don't. But even if you do, I hope you'll be man enough to come back and give it another chance. It's rare to see what you two have. You won't get away from each other now, no matter what you do, or how far you run. What you've got runs too deep and it's too strong. I see it in your eyes, and hers. You'll both lose if you run. The kind of love you two have is for life, Joe. Whether you're together or not." It was a life sentence of sorts to Joe, and yet behind his own fears, even Joe sensed that Clarke was right and what he said was true.

"I'll think about it," Joe said quietly, and Clarke nodded. There was nothing more he could say. He had spoken from the heart, out of love for both Kate and Joe.

"She still has some growing up to do. Give her a chance, Joe. And don't tell her what I told you today about her father. I think she's ashamed of it. She'll tell you herself one day."

"I'm glad to know." Although in truth it complicated things for him. Knowing how she felt about her father's suicide, and what she perceived as his abandoning her, put an even greater burden on Joe. It didn't seem fair somehow. He had his own problems from the past. And yet one thing Clarke had said he knew was true. Joe had never loved anyone as much in his life, nor had Kate. And he could easily believe that what they shared would not come again. But the irony was that he had a need to run away, to flee, to be free, and she had a need to hang on for dear life. It was like a tug-of-war to see who would win. And yet, he sensed that if they could each relax their grip, it could work between them. But knowing what he did of her now, he wondered if she ever would. And could he? If nothing else, learning the dance with each other would take time. And Clarke knew that too. But they both had lots of it. They were young. The only question Clarke had was if they were both wise enough to stick with it long enough to make it work for both of them. He could only pray that they would be. They had too much to lose if they were not.

Joe drove them back to the house, although he'd had a lot to drink. And Clarke confessed that he was properly drunk. Liz noticed it as soon as they walked in, but she didn't say anything. And Clarke walked over and gave her a hug. And for once, Joe was relieved to see that she didn't scold either of them, she just laughed and brought two cups of steaming coffee out for both of them, as Clarke accepted one regretfully and said that he hated to spoil a good drunk, and then winked at Joe. A deeper friendship had formed between them that afternoon, and Joe knew that whatever happened between him and Kate, he would always have a soft spot for Clarke.

Joe and Kate took a walk down the beach after dinner that night. They were going back to New Jersey the next day. And Joe surprised her when he put an arm around her and kissed her with a tender look in his eyes. What Clarke had told him that afternoon had changed things in a subtle way. Joe was still afraid of being strangled by a commitment to her, and yet at the same time he wanted to protect her not only from the world, but from herself. He could still sense the lonely child in her, whose father had committed suicide. No matter how bright the outer trappings were, he could see in her now the bird with the broken wing she had been as a child. And in some ways, it made him love her more. She had grown strong, and she flew well, as far as the world was concerned, but within, she was still a frightened little girl. Just as he had once been a lonely little boy. They had found each other by fate, or destiny, drawn to each other for some deep reason that was perhaps meant to be from the first. He could still remember how she had dazzled him the first time they met. Maybe it had been meant to be after all.

"You sure got my father drunk today," she laughed as they walked down the beach hand in hand.

"We had a good time."

"That's nice." Listening to her, he wondered if she'd turn into her mother one day. And if she did, what it would be like for him. And yet, in spite of his own fears, it was hard to ignore the wisdom of Clarke's words. A lot of what he had said had touched Joe's heart.

"I think we ought to get married one of these days," Joe said casually, and Kate stopped in her tracks and stared at him in surprise.

"Are you still drunk?" She wasn't sure if he was serious or not.

"Probably. But why not, Kate? It might work out fine." He didn't sound totally convinced, but for the first time in thirty-five years, he was willing to give it a try.

"What made you decide that? Did my father put the heat on you today?"

"No. He told me I'd lose you one of these days, if I don't get smart. And maybe he's right."

"You're not going to lose me, Joe," she said softly as they sat down on the sand, and he pulled her close to him. "I love you too much. You don't have to marry me." She almost felt sorry for him. She had come to understand how much his freedom meant to him.

"Maybe I want to marry you. How would that be?"

"Wonderful," she said, smiling at him, and he had never loved her more. "Very, very wonderful. Are you sure?" She was stunned. It had finally come.

"Sure enough," he said honestly. Clarke had made a lot of sense. He saw something in them that Joe saw too, when he was brave enough to look. A love that was both powerful and infinitely rare. "I don't think we should rush into it or anything," he said cautiously. "Maybe in six months or a year or so. I need time to get used to the idea. Why don't we keep it to ourselves for now."

"That's fine," she said quietly. They sat together without saying anything for a while, and then they walked back to the house hand in hand.

12

THEY WENT BACK TO New Jersey to work side by side, and things changed subtly between them as soon as they decided to get married. Kate seemed to feel more confident and more secure, and Joe liked the idea for a while. They talked about plans they were going to make, the house they were going to buy, where to go on their honeymoon. But after several conversations, Joe started to look irritated when she talked about it. It was a nice idea, but too much of a good thing made him nervous.

He didn't have time to think about getting married. They were talking about building a second factory, and his business was exploding into new levels, and to new heights almost every day. By the fall, marriage was the last thing on his mind.

Things there were busier than ever for both of them. So much so that they didn't go to Boston for Thanksgiving, but managed to spend a week with her parents between Christmas and New Year's. By then her mother was so upset about their not being engaged that no one dared to mention marriage anymore. It had become far too sensitive a subject. But Kate was also beginning to realize that as long as she lived with him, there was no particular rush for them to get married. Joe had so much on his plate that she didn't want to press him about their plans. He was just too busy. And too frightened by the commitment he'd made. She could sense it: As soon as he'd proposed to her, he started to back away.

Kate didn't say anything about it until spring, it was 1947 by then, and she was beginning to wonder if he really did want to get married. She mentioned it once or twice, and he was always too preoccupied to discuss it with her. She had just turned twenty-four, and Joe was thirty-six, and the most important man in aviation. The business he had helped start a year and a half before had turned into a gold mine. He took her father up in one of his newest planes when he came to visit them. She was still keeping up the myth that she was staying at the hotel, and her father was discreet enough not to press them about it, but he was worried about her. And Joe seemed to be spending all his time either in meetings or in the air. He had given her a real job by then, she was handling PR for him, and earning a sizable salary. But it wasn't money she needed, the Jamisons had more than enough for her. As far as they were concerned, she needed a husband. Clarke was certain by then that his conversation with Joe the summer before had fallen on deaf ears, and Liz was pressing Kate to come back to Boston to live with them. By summer, Joe had not said a word about their getting married in months.

It was a full two years after he'd come home and a year after he'd proposed to her that Kate sat him down finally and asked him a blunt question. Whatever he was thinking, she wanted to know.

"Are we ever getting married, Joe? Or have you decided to skip it entirely?" Even he had to admit that he'd been avoiding the issue. He had liked the idea when he talked to Clarke, and he saw some merit to it, particularly for Kate, given her history, but it just seemed so unnecessary to him, from his point of view at least. And the truth was, he finally admitted to her again, he didn't want to have children. He had thought about it repeatedly, and knew it wasn't for him. It just wasn't what he wanted out of life. All he wanted were his business and his planes, and Kate to come home to at night. He didn't want kids or need marriage. He didn't want to be that tied down. What he was doing was too exciting. The prospect of screaming babies in the house and diapers to change horrified him. He had hated his own childhood, and had no desire to share, much less deal with, someone else's. "Are you telling me that if we get married, you don't want kids?" It was the first time he had actually spelled it out for her. She knew he wasn't enthusiastic about them, but it had never occurred to her that he had made a firm decision. And he had never before shared that with her quite as directly. He thought it was better not to. And she had been so incredibly helpful in his business that he had no desire to lose her to some screaming brat. Marriage seemed ominous enough to him without adding children to it.

"I think that is what I'm saying," he said honestly. He had never lied to her, he just didn't discuss it. "In fact, I know it. I don't want kids." That decision had made him question the point of getting married, in spite of everything Clarke had told him a year before.

"Wow," she said, sitting back in a chair in his apartment. She had no home of her own, just his sparsely furnished place, her hotel room, and her parents' home in Boston. She felt as though she had been slapped after what he'd just said. "I've always wanted to have children." It was a huge sacrifice for her to make for him, but she also knew how much she loved him, and she didn't want to lose him. Not after losing him for nearly two years during the war. She knew what that felt like. She wondered if he'd change his mind about having kids once they got married. It was a risk she could take, but he wasn't suggesting they get married either. All discussions of that had ended months before. "What do you think, Joe?" she asked him after he had told her about not having children.

"About what?" He looked at her awkwardly. He felt cornered by the questions she had asked.

"About marriage. Have you ruled that out too?" She was upset that he hadn't told her he'd decided he didn't want children. It seemed unfair not to have at least said so, but admittedly, he was busy and had other things on his mind. He thought of his growing empire all the time, and nothing else these days.

"I don't know," he said vaguely. "Do we need to? If we're not going to have kids, why get married?" His walls had gone up and there was a look of panic in her eyes.

"Are you serious?" She was staring at him as though he were a stranger, and she was beginning to think he had become one. She wasn't quite sure when. But everything had changed again. She couldn't help wondering if his decision not to tell anyone the year before that they had decided to get married was so that he would have the freedom to change his mind. And apparently, he had.

"Do we have to talk about this now? I have an early meeting tomorrow." He looked annoyed, and wanted the conversation to end. Just talking about it made him feel trapped, and worse yet, guilty for not wanting to marry her. And guilt was the one thing Joe couldn't stand. It struck terror in his heart, and it was a pain more acute than any he had ever known. It brought back each and every nightmare from his past, especially the echoed voices of the cousins who had relentlessly told him how "bad" he was as a child.

"This is our life we're talking about, our future," Kate insisted, "I think that may just be important." There was an edge to her voice that was like fingernails on a blackboard to him. Her tone reminded him of her mother instantly.

"Do we have to settle it tonight?" He was irritated, but she was more so. She could feel him withdrawing, which made her want to clutch at him, and only drove him away more. They were trapped in a deathly dance. She was feeling abandoned by him, and sensing that in her, and the panic it caused, made him want to run.

Joe wanted to escape, and hide somewhere to lick his wounds, but Kate wasn't wise enough to leave him alone. Panic was a powerful force she could not control.

"Maybe we don't have to settle it at all," she said unhappily, and hearing her tone made him feel guiltier and even more desperate to flee. Joe felt guilt like a physical blow she was dealing him. "Maybe you just did settle it," she said. "You're telling me you don't want kids, and you don't see any reason to get married. That's kind of a big switch in decisions, isn't it?" His decisions affected her entire future, and she suddenly felt even more panicky. She had been patiently waiting for the right time for him, for two years. And she had suddenly come to understand that there was no right time, as far as he was concerned, and never would be. Marriage was no longer an option for him. Or for her, as a result.

"I have a business to run, Kate. I don't know how much energy I'd have left for a wife and kids. Probably none." He was frantically seeking refuge from her, and in his own way, his panic was as great as hers, but for Joe, it translated to something very distant and cool, which frightened her as much as her advances did him.

"What are you saying to me?" she said, as her eyes filled with tears. He was destroying everything she'd hoped for, and all her dreams with him. She had only come to New Jersey to work for him to facilitate their life together, and speed things up so they could settle down. But it was the business he was in love with now. And the airplanes. Always the planes. There were no other women in his life. His planes were his mistresses, his children, and his wives.

"I guess I'm saying that this is it," he answered her finally, since she was pressing him. "This is as good as it gets, for me at least. I don't need the rest. I don't need marriage, Kate. I can't do it. I don't want it.

I need to be free. We have each other. What difference does it make if we have a piece of paper? What does that mean?" It meant nothing to him, but it meant a lot to her.

"It means you love me and trust me, and care about me, and want to stay with me forever, Joe," that was the key issue for her. And *forever* was a word that frightened him. "It means you stand up and say you believe in me, and I believe in you. It means we're proud of each other. Somehow I think we owe each other that by now." He hated hearing that. It sounded painful to him. He felt like she was trying to nail him to the floor. Or the cross. He felt engulfed suddenly and overwhelmed by what she needed from him, and he was determined to protect himself at all costs. Even if it meant losing her.

"We don't owe each other anything, except to be here if we want to be, on a day-by-day basis. And if we don't want to anymore, we do something else. There are no guarantees." Joe was shouting at her by then, which offended and frightened her. It was his way of trying to keep her at a safe distance. He was running away. What Kate saw, and felt, was that Joe was abandoning her, just as her father had, which only made her pursue him more.

"When did this happen?" she asked, her voice rising beyond what she intended, but he had pushed her too far. She felt as though she was spiraling down into an abyss. She felt desperate, frightened, and out of control. "When did you decide not to get married?" she asked plaintively. "When did everything change? And why didn't I understand that this was what you were thinking? Why didn't you tell me, Joe?" She was beginning to sob, and it was hard to breathe. "Why are you doing this to me?" He cringed, listening to her, and felt her words pierce him like knives.

"Why can't you just let it be?" he begged.

"Because I love you," she said miserably. But he was no longer sure he loved her. Or if he ever could, enough to make up for her father killing himself when she was a child. By then, Joe felt as desperate as she. As desperate as she was to avoid his abandoning her. It was Kate who was actually causing him to flee.

"Can we go to bed now, Kate? I'm tired." He looked like he was drowning. They both were. They were like two terrified children clawing at each other, and neither of them was able to be adult enough to stop. They were both too scared, she of abandonment, and he of being devoured.

"I'm tired too," she said in a tone of despair. She felt lonelier than she ever had in her life. She went to take a shower, and she stayed in it for a long time. She felt shell-shocked and unloved as she stood there and cried. When she got into bed, he was already asleep. She got into bed next to him and looked at him for a long time, wondering who he was. She stroked his hair cautiously, as though he might attack her again, and he murmured in his sleep, and turned away. She knew that in spite of what he said, he loved her, and she loved him, maybe even enough to give up all her dreams. But she couldn't see how anymore. He was afraid of loving her. He felt safer running away. And all she wanted was to be close to him.

She had made a decision in the shower that night. She knew she had to leave before they destroyed each other. He was never going to marry her. It was time to go. Her mother had been right about him all along.

She told Joe the next morning, over breakfast. She said it quietly and reasonably, and succinctly. "I'm leaving, Joe." Their eyes met across the table and he looked confused. He was still reverberating from the pain they had caused each other the night before.

"Why, Kate?" He looked shocked, but he didn't tell her not to go.

"After what you said last night, I can't stay here anymore. I love you. With all my heart. With all my life. I waited two years for you, unable to believe you were dead. I didn't think I could love anybody else after you, and I still don't. Not the way I love you. I never will. But I want a husband and children and a real life. You don't want the same things I do." There were tears in her eyes as she spoke, but she was trying to stay calm, despite the sinking feeling of panic in her stomach, or the knife in her heart. She wanted him to take back everything he'd said the night before, but he didn't say a word.

Joe finished his breakfast silently, and then he looked at her. It was one of those hideous moments in a life that you remember forever, visually and word by word. "I love you, Kate. But I have to be honest with you. I don't think I ever want to get married. I don't want to. I don't want to be married to anyone, except maybe my planes. I don't want to be tied down. I don't want to be 'owned.' There's room for you here, if you want to share my work with me. But that's all I can give you. It's all I have to give. Me and my planes. I probably love them as much as I love you. Maybe more some days. I can't love you more than that, I'm too afraid. Kate, it's who I am, and all I have to give. I don't want kids. Ever. I don't have room for them in my life. I don't need them. And I don't want them." Joe realized with regret that right then, he didn't want her either. She was too big a threat to him. He wanted his business and his planes, and her after that. But Kate was a twenty-four-year-old girl, and she wanted babies and a husband and a life, not just the opportunity to work for him. What he had just said to her struck her like a blow, and confirmed all of her worst fears.

"I don't want a business, Joe. I want children. I want you. I love you, but I'm going home. I guess I should have asked these questions a long time ago." She felt like an utter fool. And she felt the same way she had the day her father died. Overwhelmed by immeasurable loss.

"I don't think I knew how I felt when we started the business. Now I do. Do whatever you have to do, Kate."

"I'm leaving you," she said simply, as their eyes met.

"Is it worth leaving the business?" He couldn't imagine her doing that. He thought she'd be crazy if she did. Didn't she understand what he was doing here? It was something that had never been done before, and he wanted to share it with her. It was the best he could give. But right then, she didn't care.

"It's not my business, Joe, it's yours." He hadn't thought about that. That clarified things for him, or at least so he thought.

"Do you want stock?"

She smiled at him. "No. I want a husband. My mother was right, I guess. Eventually, it matters. To me anyway."

"I understand," he said, and believed he did. He wanted to. But they both had a lot to learn. Joe picked up his briefcase and looked at her. "I'm sorry, Kate." After all they'd been to each other for seven years, in one form and another, he had to let her go. He wasn't willing to be forced into marrying her. He had too many other things to think about. In public life on the exterior, he knew that he had become an important man, but deep inside, no matter how important he was, he was still a frightened, lonely little boy.

"I'm sorry too, Joe," Kate whispered.

It was like a death scene. Their relationship was dying. He was killing it. He had made disastrous choices about their life without even consulting her. But he felt he had no other choice.

He didn't kiss her goodbye. He didn't say anything. And neither did Kate. He just walked out the door with his briefcase, without looking back, as Kate watched him go.

13

KATE'S PARENTS KNEW she had come home for good, but they didn't know why. She never explained it to them, never said anything about Joe or what had happened in New Jersey. She felt too bruised and broken to discuss it with them. And she was crushed when he never called her. She kept hoping that he would wake up and miss her unbearably, and call to tell her that he wanted to marry her and have children with her after all.

But he meant what he had said. He sent her a small box of clothes a few weeks later, things she had forgotten in his apartment, and there was no note with it. Her parents could see how much pain she was in, but they didn't press her, although her mother suspected what had happened. Kate spent three months in the Boston winter, going for long walks and crying. And it was a painful Christmas for her. She thought of calling Joe a thousand times, and she desperately wanted to, but she wasn't willing to live with him as his mistress. In the long run, it would have made her feel like an outcast. She went skiing for a few days after Christmas, and came back to spend New Year's Eve with her parents. She didn't reach out to Joe, and he never called her. She felt as though part of her had died when she left him, and she couldn't imagine a life without him. But now she had to. She had taken a brave stand, and now she had to live with it, and make the best of it. She had no other choice.

She made an effort to see a few old friends, but she no longer seemed to have anything in common with them. Her life had been too entwined with Joe's for too many years. Not knowing what else to do, and determined to have a life of her own again, she decided to move to New York in January and take a job at the Metropolitan Museum, as an assistant to the curator in the Egyptian wing. At least it called into play her art history studies from Radcliffe, although these days she knew a lot more about airplanes. Her heart wasn't in it at first, but she was surprised to find, once she got there, that she loved her job, far more than she had expected. And by February, she had found an apartment. All she had to do now was get through the rest of her life. The prospect seemed grim and endless and depressing and incredibly empty without him. Night and day, she missed everything about him. Even when she was working, Joe was all she thought of. She read about him constantly in the papers. Seven years ago he had been in the news for setting flight records, and now the whole world was talking about him building fantastic airplanes. And when he wasn't working on them, he was flying them.

She saw in the paper in June that he had won a prize at the Paris Air Show. She was happy for him. And miserable, and lonely for herself. She was twenty-five years old, more beautiful than she knew, and her life was more boring than her mother's.

She never went on dates, and when people asked her out, she told them she was busy. It was just like when his plane was shot down, she was mourning him, and missing him intensely. She didn't even go to Cape Cod that summer because she knew it would remind her of him. Everything reminded her of him. Talking, living, moving, breathing. Even going to restaurants and eating. Cooking. It was absurd and she knew it, but he had become part of her essence. All she had to do now, she was convinced, was wait a lifetime to forget him. It could be done, she told herself, she just wasn't sure she could do it. She woke up every morning feeling as though someone had died, and then she remembered who. She had.

She had been in New York nearly a year when she was in the grocery store one day buying dog food. She had just gotten a puppy to keep her company, and even she laughed at herself and admitted that it was pathetic. She was checking out the different brands, when she looked up and was startled to see Andy. She hadn't seen him in more than three years, and he looked very grown-up and handsome in a dark suit and a Burberry. He had just come home from work and was obviously buying groceries. She assumed by then that he was married, although she didn't know that for sure.

"How are you, Kate?" he asked, smiling broadly. He had long since recovered from the blow she had dealt him, although even thinking about her had pained him for a long time, and he had thrown away all his pictures of her. But he was fine now.

"I'm fine, how've you been?" She didn't tell him that she'd missed him. Good friends were hard to come by, and it had been a long time since she'd had someone to talk to like him.

"I've been busy. What are you doing here?" He seemed happy to see her.

"I live here. I work at the Metropolitan. It's fun."

"That's nice. I read about Joe everywhere these days. That's an incredible empire he started. Do you have kids yet?" She laughed at the question. It made an obvious assumption, which was not only incorrect, but now obsolete.

"No. I have a puppy." She pointed at the dog food, and then decided to correct the assumption for old times' sake. "I'm not married." He looked stunned when she said it.

"You and Joe didn't get married?"

"No. He's married to his airplanes. It was a good decision for him."

"What about you?" he asked honestly. He had always been straight-forward with her, it was one of the things she liked about him. "How was it for you, his decision, I mean?"

"Not so great. I left. I'm getting used to it. It's been about a year now." It had been fourteen months, two weeks and three days, but she thought she'd spare him the details. "What about you? Married? Kids?"

"Girlfriends. Many of them. Safer. No heartbreak." He hadn't changed at all, and she laughed at his response.

"Good for you. I'll see if I can find you some more. There are lots of cute girls working at the museum."

"You among them. You look great, Kate." She had cut her hair shorter, mostly out of boredom. Her big excitement these days were manicures and haircuts, and the dog.

"Thank you." It had been so long since she'd talked to a man her own age for more than five minutes that she wasn't sure what to say to him.

"How about a movie sometime?"

"I'd like that," she said, as they wheeled slowly toward the check-out. He had bought cornflakes and some soda, she noticed. And he was carrying a bottle of scotch he'd just bought at the liquor store. A bachelor's diet. "Shouldn't you at least have toast or milk with that?" she suggested and he grinned. She hadn't changed either. "Or do you just put the scotch on your cornflakes? I'll have to try that."

"I drink it neat as a chaser."

"What do you do with the soda?"

"I use it to clean my carpets."

They were enjoying the banter that reminded them both of the old days at school, and he insisted on paying for her dog food. He had always been generous with her, and chivalrous and kind.

"Are you still working for your father?" she asked as they walked out of the store.

"Yes, it's worked out pretty well. He gives me all the divorce cases, he hates them."

"That's cheerful. Well, at least I was spared that."

"Maybe you were spared more than that, Kate. Men like that are never easy. Too brilliant, too creative, too difficult. You were so in love with him, I don't think you saw it." She had, and she had loved it. Much as she had loved Andy as a friend, he had never seemed exciting enough to her. Joe was like a shining star, just out of reach, and always what she wanted, perhaps all the more because of that.

"Are you suggesting I look for a dumb one?" She was amused by the implication, but he was serious when he answered.

"Maybe just someone a little more human. He was hard to measure up to, and a tough act to follow. You deserve better." She was grateful for Andy's kindness in reassuring her. He was such a wonderful, kind man, she was surprised he hadn't married. "I'll call you," he said as they started to head in opposite directions. "How do I find you?"

"I'm listed, or call the museum."

He called her two days later, and took her to a movie. And then ice-skating at Rockefeller Center. And out to dinner. They had been together almost constantly by the time she went home for Christmas three weeks later. She didn't tell her parents she'd seen him, she didn't want her mother to get excited. But she answered the phone when he called her in Boston on Christmas morning. And she was happy to hear him. It was almost like the old days, except she liked him better now. He was comfortable and easy and kind to her. He had none of Joe's brilliance, but he cared about her. Just as she had never gotten over Joe, he had never gotten over Kate completely.

"I miss you," he said when she answered. "When are you coming back?"

225

"In a couple of days," she said vaguely. She was disappointed that she hadn't heard from Joe for Christmas. He could have done that much. It was as though he had forgotten her completely, as though she'd never existed. She had thought of calling him, but decided it was better if she didn't. It would just depress her, and remind her of everything they'd had, and then lost.

"When did you start seeing Andy again?" her mother asked with interest when she hung up the phone.

"I ran into him a few weeks ago, in the grocery store."

"Is he married?"

"Yes. And he has eight children," she teased her mother.

"I always thought he'd be good for you," her mother said.

"I know, Mom. We're just friends. It's better that way. No damage on either side." She had hurt him badly three years before. And she was still wounded. And suspected she would be for a long time. Maybe forever. It was impossible to forget Joe. They had had too much together. And he represented a third of her lifetime.

She went back to New York after two days, and was happy to see her puppy. She had left her with a neighbor. And Andy called her almost as soon as she walked in the door of her apartment.

"What do you have? Radar?"

"I'm having you followed." He asked her to a movie that night, and she went. And they spent New Year's Eve together, drinking champagne at El Morocco. It seemed very glamorous to Kate, and very grown-up, as she said to Andy.

"I am grown-up," he said with amusement. He had gotten very sophisticated, and she couldn't help but compare him to Joe. Joe who was unusual and beautiful and sometimes awkward. But she had loved that about him. Andy was smoother, in ways that Joe didn't care about at all.

"I skipped the grown-up part," Kate confided after her third glass of champagne. "I went straight to old age. Sometimes I feel older than my mother."

"You'll get better. Time. It heals everything," he said wisely.

"How long did it take you to get over me?" she asked, feeling slightly tipsy. But he didn't seem to notice.

"About ten minutes." It had taken him two years, but he didn't tell her that. And he still wasn't over her, which was why he was spending New Year's Eve with her. There were half a dozen women he'd been seeing who were furious about it. "Should it have taken longer?"

"Probably not," she said sadly. "I didn't deserve it. I was rotten to you." She was getting slightly morose from the champagne she'd been drinking. And in spite of herself, she kept wondering where Joe was, what he was doing, and with whom that night.

"You couldn't help it, Kate," Andy said, and meant it. "He was a great love, you were crazy about him, and he came back from the dead. It's hard to beat that. Better then than if we'd have been married."

"That would have been awful," she said, horrified.

"Yes, it would have. So I guess we were lucky. And you needed to get him out of your system once and for all."

"What if I never do?" she said miserably, and he laughed at her.

"You will. But not if you become an alcoholic. You're drunk, Kate."

"I am *not*," she said, looking outraged, and a little vague.

"You are, but you're cute that way. Maybe we should dance before you pass out or get any drunker."

It had been a nice evening, and she had a terrific headache the next day, but he brought her croissants and aspirin and orange juice at her apartment. Kate wore dark glasses while she made breakfast for them.

"Why didn't you bring your scotch and cornflakes? That would have been better," she said mournfully, with her headache.

"You're turning into a lush," he said as he played with her puppy and smiled.

"Heartbreak does that." She burned the croissants, spilled the orange juice, and broke the yolks when she made fried eggs for him, but he ate all of it and thanked her afterward. "I'm a terrible cook," she confessed.

"Is that why he left you?" It was the first time he had asked her.

"I left him," she corrected, hiding behind the dark glasses. "He didn't want to marry me, or have kids. I told you, he's married to his planes."

"He's a very rich man now," Andy said admiringly. There were a lot of things one had to admire about Joe, his skill, his genius, his talent, but not his judgment about women. Andy thought he was a fool for not marrying Kate, but he was glad he had been.

"Why aren't you married?" Kate asked, sprawling out on the couch, and taking off the dark glasses finally.

"I don't know. Too scared, too young, too busy. No one terrific. Since you. I ate worms for a while, and then I started having too much fun. I've got time. So do you. Don't rush it. I see too many divorces at the law firm."

"Not according to my mother, about having time, I mean. She's panicked."

"I would be too, in her shoes. You're not easy to get rid of. Just don't cook for them. Let them find out later. I'd forgotten what a lousy cook you are. I'd have made breakfast myself if I'd remembered."

"Stop complaining. You ate everything."

"Next time, scotch and cornflakes."

They went for a walk that afternoon, in Central Park. It was a crisp winter day, and there was a thin blanket of snow on the ground, and Kate felt better when they got back to her apartment. They had taken the dog with them. It all seemed so comfortable and normal. He was easy to be with. Just like the old days. And that night they went to a movie. They were spending a lot of time together. And she was suddenly less lonely. It wasn't high romance, it was more like high friendship.

For the next six weeks, they saw a lot of each other. Dinners, movies, parties, friends. He came to have lunch with her at the museum. On Saturdays they went grocery shopping together, and he did errands with her. It was nice having someone to do things with. Kate realized in all her time with Joe he never had time for any of that. He was too busy building the business, although she had loved building it with him. But it was fun being with Andy. He had more time for her, and he enjoyed spending it with her.

On Valentine's Day he appeared at her apartment with a bouquet of two dozen red roses in his arms, and a huge heart-shaped box of candy.

"My God, what did I do to deserve all this?" she asked, grinning broadly. She had been missing Joe all day, and reminded herself that she had to forget him once and for all. Even after all this time, it still seemed like an insuperable challenge to her. It seemed incredible to Kate that someone she had loved so much for so long was perfectly able to live without her. It seemed so wrong, after all they'd been through, that they hadn't been able to work it out and end up together. They had each gotten tangled up in their own fears. It was depressing to realize that fairy tales didn't have happy endings, they had sad ones. It wasn't the way life was supposed to be.

"What are you looking so gloomy about?" He could see it in her eyes. She couldn't hide it from him.

"Feeling sorry for myself again."

"How boring. Have a chocolate. Eat the flowers, whichever you prefer. Get dressed. I'm taking you to dinner."

"What about all your other girlfriends?" She felt guilty monopolizing him. She was still in love with Joe anyway, it wasn't fair to Andy. But she also enjoyed him, more than she admitted. She hadn't been as sad lately. He was good for her.

"My other girlfriends are joining us for dinner. You'll love them, all fourteen of them."

"Where are you taking me?"

"You'll see. It's a surprise. Wear something fancy. And try not to get drunk this time."

"That was New Year's Eve, you turkey. Besides, I'm entitled."

"No, you're not. Your time's running out. Besides, he loves his airplanes better than he loves you. Remember that."

"I try to." But lately, she didn't even mind that. She had been thinking about Joe a lot lately, and wondering if she had made the right decision. Maybe it didn't matter if he married her, or they had children. Maybe it was worth the sacrifice, just to be with him. But she didn't say it to Andy and she wasn't sure of that herself.

He waited while she got dressed, and there was a hansom cab waiting downstairs when they left her apartment. She was bowled over by it. It seemed incredibly romantic. And the horse clip-clopped along as they rode to the restaurant while passersby and cab drivers smiled at them. And she was cozy and warm under a heavy blanket, in the closed carriage.

The carriage turned on Fifty-second Street, and dropped them off at the '21' Club, while Kate smiled at him.

"You spoil me."

"You deserve it," he said, as they walked into the restaurant. She was surprised to see heads turn as they entered. They made a very handsome couple. And a few minutes later, they were shown to a quiet corner table upstairs.

It was a wonderful evening and a delicious meal, and they were talking quietly when dessert came. He had ordered a tiny heart-shaped cake for her, and when she cut into it with her fork, there was something hard in it. She pushed the cake away with her fork, and saw that it was a jeweler's box.

"What's that?" she asked, looking puzzled.

"Better open it and see. Maybe there's something good in it. It looks pretty good to me," but she could suddenly feel her heart race. And when she looked up at him, he was smiling, and spoke softly. "It's okay, Kate, don't be afraid . . . it'll be all right, you'll see."

"What if it isn't?" She knew what he was doing and she was frightened. Joe had hurt her very badly, and she had hurt Andy. She didn't want to do that again, or make a mistake they'd both regret.

"It will be. We'll make it all right. It's up to us to do that, it doesn't just happen." It was everything she had wanted, just not with the person she wanted. But maybe it worked that way, you only got half your wish in life, not the whole one. She no longer believed in happy endings anymore. And Andy's version was happier than most.

She very carefully opened the box, and licked the cake off her fingers, and as she opened it, she saw a diamond ring sparkling at her. It was an engagement ring from Tiffany, and Andy slipped it on her finger. "Will you marry me, Kate? I'm not going to let you run away this time. I think this is the right thing for both of us . . . and by the way, I love you."

"By the way?" she said. "What kind of proposal is that?"

"A real one. Let's do it. I know we'll be happy."

"My mother always said you were the right one."

"My mother said you were a bitch when you dumped me," he laughed and then kissed her. Kissing him was better than she'd remembered. And as she pondered it, she realized that she loved him. Not as she had Joe. She would never have that again. This was different. It was comfortable and easy and fun. They would make good traveling companions for a lifetime. Maybe you couldn't have it all in life. A great love. And passion. And dreams. Maybe in the end, one was better off with a small love and no dreams. Or at least that was what she told herself when she kissed him.

"Your mother was right, about me, I mean. I was horrible to you, and I'm so sorry," she said after he kissed her.

"You should be. I'm going to make you spend the rest of your life paying for it. You owe me, big time."

"I promise. I'll put scotch in your cornflakes forever. Every morning."

"I'll need it, if you're cooking breakfast. Does that mean you'll marry me?" He looked hopeful and happy.

"I have to," she said sensibly, "I like the ring. I guess that's the only way you'll let me keep it." She was wearing it, and it looked beautiful on her. And as he smiled at her, he kissed her.

"I love you, Kate. I hate to say it, but I'm glad it didn't work out with Joe," he said honestly, and she felt her heart ache. She wasn't glad, but she had to learn to live with it, and maybe Andy would help her. She hoped so.

"I love you too," she whispered. And then she looked at him with a grin. "When are we getting married?"

"June," he said decisively, and Kate laughed and threw her arms around him. She was happy, and she knew she'd made the right decision. Or he had.

"Wait till I tell my mother!!" she said, and they laughed.

"Wait till I tell mine!" Andy said as he rolled his eyes.

14

KATE CALLED TO tell her parents the day after Andy had proposed to her, and predictably, they were thrilled. Her mother was ecstatic and asked about plans for the wedding, and she was even happier
when Kate told her they were getting married in June. This was the real
thing. At last.

For the next four months, Kate and her mother were up to their ears
in details for the wedding. Kate only wanted three bridesmaids,
Beverly and Diana from Radcliffe, and an old friend from school. She
selected lovely pale blue organza dresses, her mother came to New York
to help her pick her wedding gown. It was elegant and simple, and
Kate looked incredible in it. Her mother cried at the first fitting, and
so did her father when he walked her down the aisle.

There had been four months of parties given mostly by friends of
Andy's parents in New York, and another round of events in Boston in
May. There were showers and luncheons and dinner parties. Kate had
never had so much excitement in her life. And they had decided to go
to Paris and Venice on their honeymoon. It was all incredibly romantic, and she kept reminding herself of how lucky she was.

Some secret part of her hoped to hear from Joe after her engagement
was announced, as though he would sense what she was about to do,

and return to stop her and reclaim her. But she was more sensible than that, and didn't really expect him to call. She realized that it was probably just as well. It would have cut her to the quick to hear his voice again. She tried not to let herself think of him often, but he crept into her mind late at night, and in the morning as she lay in bed, thinking of him. It had been their favorite time of day. He was always there, on the fringes of her life, and her heart ached instantly when she thought of him. She continued to wonder if she had done the right thing, if she should have sacrificed marriage and children to be with him. She still loved him as she always had, that was the hard part, but she kept telling herself she was doing the right thing. And all he cared about were his planes. She never told Andy, or anyone, how often she still thought of Joe.

The wedding was perfect, and Kate looked exquisite. The long satin wedding gown made her look like Rita Hayworth, and behind her was a long elegant lace train. She wore a full veil, and when Andy looked into her eyes as she reached the altar, he saw something tender and sad that touched him to the core.

"It'll be all right, Kate . . . I love you . . . ," he whispered, as two little tears spilled from her eyes. She couldn't have told anyone, and she knew she was wrong to do it, but all morning, she had been longing for Joe. She felt as though she were leaving him all over again. But she knew she'd have a good life with Andy, he was a kind man, and they loved each other. Not with passion, but with tenderness and understanding. Whatever she still felt for Joe Allbright, Kate knew she had made the right choice with Andy and would work hard to make it a marriage that worked for both of them.

The reception was at the Plaza, and they spent the night in a fabulous suite looking out over Central Park. It was lovely and romantic, and they were both exhausted after the wedding. They didn't even make love until the next morning. Andy didn't want to rush her, they had the rest of their lives. They had never made love to each other before the wedding, and he hadn't wanted to ask her if she was a virgin. He had never wanted to know the details of her long involvement with Joe and still did not. And she didn't offer any. It wasn't the sort of thing she felt she should talk about with her husband, and he wasn't sure if it was painful for her or not, but they enjoyed making love. She seemed innocent and shy and somewhat cautious, which he assumed was lack of experience on her part. In truth, it was more that it seemed odd to Kate to be in bed with him. They had always been friends. But with a little time and effort, she found that she was surprisingly comfortable with him. He was gentle and playful and tender, and desperately in love with her. And by the time they left for the airport that morning, they seemed less like young lovers than old friends. But it meant a lot to Kate to be at ease with him. What they shared had none of the pain or the passion or the fire of what she and Joe had shared. It was easy and friendly and funny, she trusted Andy completely, and her heart was far less at risk with him than it had been with Joe.

Her mother had suspected that Kate wasn't madly in love with Andy when she'd agreed to marry him, and it didn't worry her at all. She had said something to Kate about it during one of the fittings and told her that passion of the kind she'd had for Joe was a dangerous thing. If you let it, it owned and controlled you. She would be better off, her mother assured her, married to her best friend, and Andy was.

Their honeymoon was everything it should have been. They had romantic dinners at Maxim's and little bistros on the Left Bank, explored the Louvre, did lots of shopping, and went for long walks along the Seine. It was the perfect time, the perfect season, the weather was warm and sunny, and Kate realized she had never been happier in her life. And Andy was proving to be a gentle and skilled lover. By the time they got to Venice, she felt as though they had been married for years. He suspected by then that she hadn't been a virgin, but he never asked her about it. He preferred not knowing, and he didn't like asking her about things that reminded her of Joe. He sensed more than knew that it was still a sore subject, and suspected that it would be for a very long time. But she was his now, and no longer Joe's.

Venice was even more romantic than Paris, if that was possible. They ate delicious food, drifted around looking at the sights in a gondola Andy had hired, and they kissed for good luck as they passed under the Bridge of Sighs.

They went back to Paris for one night, and then flew back to New York. They had been gone for three weeks and it was the perfect honeymoon. They came home happy and relaxed and bonded to each other. And they were looking forward to a long and happy life.

Andy went back to work the day after they got back from Paris, and Kate got up to cook him breakfast. He showered and shaved and dressed, and when he walked into the kitchen, she had a bowl of cornflakes on the table and a bottle of scotch.

"Darling, you remembered!" he said, throwing his arms around her in movie star fashion, and then crunched a mouthful of cornflakes and downed a shot of scotch. He was a good sport and a nice person and had a warm and funny sense of humor. And best of all, he was crazy about her. "My father's going to think you've turned me into an alcoholic, if I go to work smelling of scotch. We've got meetings all day."

He left for work and she stayed home to tidy up the apartment. She had given up her job at the museum the month before the wedding. Andy didn't want her to work, and at the time she had too much to do. But now she had nothing whatsoever to occupy her until he came home from the office in the late afternoon. And when he did, she was so bored that she dragged him into bed, and then suggested they go out to dinner, even when Andy was tired. She didn't know what to do with herself all day. She talked to him about going back to work, she had no idea what to do to keep occupied. Married life left her with too much time on her hands.

"Go shopping, go to museums, have fun, have lunch with friends," he told her, but her friends were all either working or in the suburbs with their kids. She felt like the odd man out.

They had talked about getting a bigger apartment, but they both liked Andy's and for the time being it was fine. It had two bedrooms, so even if they had a baby, there would be enough room for all of them.

Three weeks after they got back from Europe, Kate smiled at him shyly over dinner, and told Andy she had news for him. He imagined she had done something fun that day, or talked to her mother or one of her friends. He was startled when instead she told him she was sure she was pregnant. They had only been married for six weeks, and she thought it might have happened the day after their wedding, the first time they made love.

"Did you go to a doctor?" He looked both thrilled and worried, cleared the table for her, insisted that she take it easy, and asked her if she felt sick or wanted to lie down, and Kate laughed.

"No, I didn't go to the doctor yet, but I'm sure." She had felt this way before, five years before with Joe's baby, but she couldn't tell Andy that, and wouldn't have. "And it's not a terminal illness, for Heaven's sake, I'm fine."

He made love to her ever so gently that night, afraid to do anything that might hurt her or the baby, insisted that she go to the doctor as soon as she could arrange it, and was disappointed when she wouldn't let him tell their parents yet.

"Why not, Kate?" He wanted to shout it from the roof, which she thought was sweet. He was even more excited than she was, and she was pleased. She wanted a baby, it was one reason she had left Joe after all, and this would be a further bond between her and Andy. This was what she had wanted, a real married life. And yet at the same time, with all the happiness she felt, and love she felt for Andy, there was always an empty space in her that she could never quite fill, despite all her efforts. She knew what it was, but not how to cure it. It was Joe. All she could hope was that the baby would fill the immeasurable void Joe had left in her.

"What if I lose it?" she said sensibly in answer to her husband's question. "It would be awful if everyone already knew."

"Why would you lose it?" He looked puzzled. "Do you feel like something's wrong?" The possibility hadn't even occurred to him.

"Of course not," she said, looking happy. "I just want to be sure that everything's all right. They say there's always a risk of miscarriage in the first three months." Particularly if you got hit by a boy on a bike. Andy had never heard about the first three months being sensitive before.

Kate went to the doctor a few days later, and he told her that everything was fine. She told him, in confidence, about the miscarriage she'd had five years before, and he was disturbed that she hadn't had medical attention, but he felt it was an isolated incident, not due to any weakness on her part, but because she'd been hit by the bike. He told her to be sensible, rest, eat well, and not to do anything foolish like ride horses or skip rope, which made her laugh. And he sent her home with vitamins and some written instructions to share with her husband, and told her to come back to see him in a month. The baby was due in early March.

And as she walked home to their apartment, she strolled along the edge of Central Park, thinking how lucky she was. She was happy, loved, married, had a great husband, and she was having a baby. All her dreams had come true, and she knew finally that she had done the right thing when she married Andy. They were going to have a great life.

They told her parents about the baby finally when they went to stay with them for a week at the end of August, in Cape Cod. Her mother was beside herself with excitement, and her father was pleased for them.

"I told you he'd be perfect for her," Elizabeth beamed at her husband after Kate and Andy went back to New York.

"Why? Because he got her pregnant?" Clarke teased her. He had been fond of Joe, but he agreed with her, Andy was the right husband for Kate, and he was happy for them.

"No, because he's a good man. And having a baby will do her a world of good. It'll ground her and settle her down, and make her feel closer to him."

"And give her lots of work!" Clarke laughed. But she had nothing else to do. She was ready for a family. She was twenty-six years old, which was certainly old enough, and older than most of her friends when they'd had their first babies. Most of the girls she'd gone to school with already had two or three. There had been a wave of young people who'd gotten married right after the war, and were having babies every year to make up for lost time. Compared to them, and those who had gotten married before the war, Kate was off to a late start.

Kate felt well during her entire pregnancy. And by Christmas, Andy said she looked like a balloon. She was nearly seven months pregnant, and she herself thought she was huge. She hadn't gained weight anywhere, it seemed, except around the baby, the rest of her looked elegant and thin. She went for long walks every day, slept a lot, ate well, and was the picture of good health. There was only one small scare on New Year's Eve. They went dancing with friends at El Morocco, they had an active social life these days, mostly with friends of Andy's, or people he met through work, and when they got home at two o'clock in the morning, she started having contractions. She felt guilty because she'd danced a lot and had several glasses of champagne. Andy called the doctor and he told them to come to the hospital right away, and when he checked her, the doctor told her he wanted her to stay for the rest of the night, just to make sure she didn't go into labor. Kate looked terrified, and Andy said he'd spend the night with her, and one of the nurses set up a cot for him next to her bed.

"How do you feel, Kate?" he asked as they lay there, she on the comfortable hospital bed, and he on the narrow cot beside her.

"Scared," she said honestly. "What if I have the baby early?"

"You won't, I think you just overdid it a little. I think it was that last mambo that did you in." She guffawed, and he grinned.

"That was fun," they always had a good time together, and he was so good to her.

"Apparently, the baby didn't think so. Or maybe he did."

"What if something happens and we lose the baby?" She rolled over on her side to look at him, and he reached up and took her hand and held it in his.

"What if you stop worrying for a few minutes? How about that?" And then he asked her something she hadn't been prepared for. He had been wondering about it for a while. "Why do you worry so much about losing the baby?" He met her eyes squarely with his. His were the color of melted chocolate, his dark hair was tousled, and he looked very handsome as he lay on the cot, looking up at her.

"I think everyone worries about that," she said, and looked away from him.

"Kate?"

There was a long pause. "Yes?"

"Have you ever been pregnant before?" It was a question she didn't want to answer, but she also didn't want to lie to him.

The pause this time was even longer. "Yes," she looked down at him sadly, she didn't want to hurt him, and was afraid that she had.

"I thought so." He didn't seem too devastated by the information. "What happened?"

"I got hit by a bike at Radcliffe, and lost it," she said simply, looking sad.

"I remember that, the bike incident, I mean," he said pensively, "you had a concussion. How pregnant were you?"

"About two and a half months. I had decided to have it. I never told Joe while I was pregnant, or my parents ever. I told Joe about it much later, when he was home on leave."

"Your parents would have loved that," he said, looking at her. But it didn't matter, except that he was sorry for the pain she'd been through. But she was his now, and as she lay on the hospital bed talking to him, he smiled at the sight of her enormous stomach. "Everything's going to be fine this time, Kate. You'll see. We're going to have a beautiful baby." He leaned over and kissed her as he said it, and she was reminded once again of how lucky she was to have him. She wouldn't even let herself think of Joe. Perhaps now, it would finally be over, maybe she could be free of him at last.

They left the hospital the next morning, hand in hand, and she spent the rest of the week resting. And after that she was fine, and had no more contractions, until early one Sunday morning, when she woke him. She had been lying in bed for two hours, while he slept, timing contractions. And finally, she nudged him.

"Hmm . . . yeah? . . . time for scotch and cornflakes?"

"Better than that," she smiled at him, feeling remarkably calm, "time for baby."

"Now?" He sat up with a start, looking panicked, and she laughed at him. "Should I get dressed?"

"I think you'll look silly going to the hospital like that. Cute though." He had been lying in bed naked.

"Okay, okay. I'll hurry. Did you call the doctor?"

"Not yet." She smiled at him as he hurried around the room, picking up clothes and dropping them. She looked like the Mona Lisa. And he looked nervous and disorganized, but very sweet.

Half an hour later, she was showered and dressed, her hair was neatly combed, and he looked slightly disheveled but very attentive. He had an arm around her and was carrying her suitcase. And when they checked into the hospital, the nurse said she was making good progress. And as soon as she said it, they dismissed Andy. He was sent to the waiting room to smoke with the other fathers.

"How long will it be?" he asked the nurse nervously as he left Kate.

"Not for a while, Mr. Scott," she said, closed the door firmly behind him, and returned to her patient. Kate was getting uncomfortable, and she wanted Andy, but it was against hospital policy for him to be there. And for the first time then, she was frightened.

Three hours later, she was still making progress, but it was slow going, and Andy's nerves were frayed while he waited. They had gotten to the hospital at nine, and by noon he had heard nothing. And whenever he inquired, they brushed him off, it seemed to be taking forever for the baby to come.

It was four o'clock when they took her to the delivery room, which was right on schedule from their point of view, but by then Kate was miserable and crying. All she wanted was Andy. He hadn't eaten all day by then, and had seen other fathers come and go, and some who had waited longer than he had. It seemed like an endless process, and all he wished was that he could be with her. The baby seemed to be taking an eternity to get there, and he was hoping things would be easy for her. In fact, they weren't, she was having a big baby, and it was going slowly. It seemed interminable to both of them.

At seven o'clock that night, the doctors contemplated performing a cesarean section, but ultimately decided to let Kate continue to go normally for a while longer, and finally two hours later, Reed Clarke Scott appeared, named for both their fathers. He weighed just under ten pounds, and had a shock of dark hair like his father's, but Andy thought he looked like Kate. He had never seen anything more beautiful than Kate, lying in bed afterward with her hair combed, in a pink bed jacket, holding their sleeping baby.

"He's so perfect," Andy whispered. The twelve hours in the waiting room, worrying about them, had nearly driven him crazy. But she looked remarkably calm and happy as she held Andy's hand, she was tired but she looked fulfilled and peaceful. Her dreams had finally come true. Her mother had been right. She had done the right thing, and now she was sure.

Kate and the baby stayed in the hospital for five days, and then Andy took them home with a nurse they'd hired for four weeks. He had bought flowers for her and put them all over the house, and he held the baby while she settled into bed in their bedroom. The doctor wanted her to have three weeks bed rest, which was standard for new mothers. And they had put a bassinet next to their bed, where the baby slept, and whenever he woke, she nursed him, as Andy watched in fascination.

"You look so beautiful, Kate." He was thinking that they had both been worth waiting for. Good things were, in his opinion. And the baby absolutely delighted him. He was pink and round and perfect.

Kate was twenty-seven when Reed was born. She was a lot older than most of her friends when she had her first baby, but she was ready for him. She was calm and mature, and she was wonderful with him, and loved nursing. She felt as though she had waited an entire lifetime for this time in her life, and she thoroughly enjoyed it, and her husband. They had never been as happy in their lives.

15

REED WAS TWO AND A HALF months old in May when Andy came home from work one night, looking excited. He had been named to be part of a commission going to Germany to hear testimony in the ongoing war trials. They had been going for quite some time, and lawyers of varying specialties were being recruited for several months each. Andy had been getting various kinds of legal experience at his father's law firm, and being invited to participate in the war crimes trials was an enormous honor for him.

"Can I come with you?" Kate was excited, it sounded challenging and interesting and she wanted to be there to watch him work.

"I don't think so, sweetheart. We're going to be billeted in military barracks. The accommodations are bare bones, but the work is going to be wonderful." He was thrilled to be going, although he hated to leave her and Reed.

"How long will you be there?" It occurred to her that it didn't sound like a two-day trip, maybe not even a two-week one.

"That's the hard part," he said apologetically. He had considered it carefully before he accepted. They had wanted to know on the spot if he would do it, but he was sure that Kate would want him to be part of something so exceptional. It was an opportunity he had wanted, but never expected. "I have to be there for three or four months," he said, looking unhappy, and Kate was startled.

"Wow! That's a long time, Andy." And he was going to miss so much time with the baby.

"I asked if we can get away for a few days for a break, maybe in the middle, but they said it would be impossible. I'm going to be stuck there and none of the men are taking their wives. There are no accommodations for them." For three or four months, it would be like being in the army, in the legal corps, but since he'd never done military service, or been in the war, he felt that this was an opportunity to serve his country. "I'm sorry, baby. We'll do something nice afterward, like take a vacation." He wanted to take her to California because he had loved it there.

"Okay, well, I guess I'll just have to keep busy."

"I think the young prince will take care of that for you." He seemed to keep Kate on her toes tending to his needs and nursing. At least she had him, otherwise she would have been really lonely in Andy's absence. "Do you want to go to Boston and stay with your parents?"

Kate shook her head in answer. "My mother would love it, having Reed there. But she'd drive me crazy. We'll stay here and keep the home fires burning. Just don't forget to take scotch for your cornflakes."

"Thank you for being a good sport about it, Kate," he said, as he kissed her.

"Do I have a choice? Can I be bratty?" She smiled. She knew she'd miss him but she was pleased for him. It was an honor to be asked.

"You could be bratty, but I'm glad you aren't. I really want to do this. It's important work." She had been a very good sport, and he loved her all the more for that.

"I know it is." She respected him a lot for it, and wouldn't have done anything to stop him. "When do you go?" He still hadn't told her.

"In four weeks," he said, grimacing, and she threw a pillow at him.

"You turkey. You'll be gone all summer." And then some. He was leaving on the first of July and they had told the attorneys who had agreed to go not to expect to be back in the States until late October. They were coming from all over the country and flying to Germany on a military plane.

As Kate helped Andy organize his papers and pack in the ensuing weeks, she began to realize how lonely it was going to be for her, being in the apartment alone, with the baby. In a year of being married to Andy, she had gotten used to his company, and now she couldn't imagine being without him. Four months was going to seem endless, to both of them.

Two days later, on their first anniversary, he gave her a beautiful diamond bracelet from Cartier. She was bowled over. She had bought him a watch at Tiffany, but it wasn't nearly as impressive as the bracelet he'd given her.

"Andy, you spoil me!" She looked thrilled and he was pleased. He was good to her, and enjoyed doing it, he was happy with her, far more than even he had expected. She was a good wife, a wonderful mother, and a terrific companion. He loved being with her, and making love to her, and laughing with her. They truly were best friends.

"That's for being a good sport above and beyond the call of duty."

"Maybe you should go away more often," she said, smiling at him. They had a wonderful evening at the Stork Club.

And when he left on the first of July, they were both sad. She brought the baby when she took him to the airport and saw him off. There were five attorneys leaving from New York, on a military flight. The others were all coming from other cities. Andy kissed her and held her for a long moment before he left. He said he'd try to call her, but didn't think he'd have the chance too often.

"I'll write to you," he promised, but she suspected more than he did that he wouldn't have time. It was going to be a long, lonely four months without him. As hesitant as she had been about marrying him, now she couldn't imagine a day without him in it. He kissed the baby, and her again, and then ran to catch the plane before he missed it. He was the youngest of the group leaving from New York, and the other wives all smiled at her, as she carried the baby out of the terminal. Reed was three and a half months old, and he would be doing all kinds of things by the time Andy saw him again. She had promised to take lots of pictures.

Kate spent the Fourth of July in New York, and it was sweltering. She and the baby hardly ever went out, since they had air conditioning, and the rest of the month was scarcely better. She would take the baby to the park early in the morning, and try to be home by eleven, and then they'd stay in all afternoon, and go out at the end of the day to get some air as the streets started to cool. But in spite of the baby, and the effort she made to keep herself busy, she was surprisingly lonely without Andy. She missed him a lot.

She was pushing Reed in his pram late one afternoon, after they'd been to the zoo, and she wandered past the Plaza Hotel and down Fifth Avenue to look in the store windows. She had just crossed Fifth Avenue when someone dashed across the street and bumped into her. It startled her, and she looked up from checking the baby, they were still standing in the middle of the street, and she found herself looking into the eyes of Joe Allbright. She just stood there for a minute staring at him, she had thought of him so often and never expected to see him again, except in the newspapers.

"Hi, Kate." It was as though they had seen each other that morning. Nothing had changed. He looked exactly the same. Except there was none of the hardness she had seen on that last day, none of the cruel words, or the disappointment. There was just that incredible face and those blue eyes boring into her, looking as though he'd been waiting for her, but she knew that was an illusion. He could have called her and never had. There were times when, even shy as he was, Joe could be incredibly charming. And he looked that way now. As though he'd been waiting for her for three years.

Horns were honking at them as the light changed, and he took her by the arm, as she pushed the pram, and escorted her to the corner. He helped her up onto the curb, and then smiled as he looked at the baby.

"Who's that?" he asked, with a look of amusement, as the baby crowed at him, as though he was happy to see Joe.

"That's my son Reed," she said proudly. "He's three months old."

"He's a handsome guy," he said thoughtfully, and then smiled gently at her, "he looks just like you, Kate. I didn't know you were married, or are you?" The question would have been insulting from anyone else, but that was the way Joe was. To him, having a baby did not automatically mean one had to be married. He was a little advanced in his thinking, or maybe just backward. Sometimes it was hard to decide which.

"I've been married for a year, almost exactly."

"You didn't waste any time having the baby," he said, but that didn't surprise him. He knew that was what she wanted. She had made that clear when she left him. He hadn't seen her in nearly three years, but she looked no different. If anything, she looked better, as did he. He was thirty-nine years old, but no one would have guessed his age. He had an eternally boyish look about him, particularly with his sandy blond hair falling toward his eyes. He pushed it back, as he always had, in a gesture that Kate had always found endearing. She had thought of it a thousand times at night, when she cried for him. And now he was standing in front of her, and it was a strange, sad, empty feeling. She would have liked to be able to say she didn't care, and was unaffected by him, but she had the same odd clutch in the pit of her stomach, like a rock that was turning slowly. She had always thought that was what love meant. But she had never felt the rock in her gut with Andy. With him, she always felt peaceful. And now, with Joe standing inches from her, she felt intolerably nervous. He was just a piece of her past, she told herself. But a very big piece. There was the same electricity between them as he looked into her eyes. She wondered if those feelings ever went away.

"Who's the lucky guy?" he asked casually. He seemed to have no inclination to leave her.

"Andy Scott, my old friend from Harvard."

"Your mother always said you should marry him. She must be happy." There was a faint edge to his voice. He knew her mother had hated him.

"She is," Kate said, feeling dazed. It was as though he exuded some strange scent that mesmerized her. She could already feel it, and told herself she had to leave. But she felt paralyzed, and lulled by his voice, and went nowhere. "She loves the baby."

"He's a cute guy. The business is doing great, by the way." She smiled at the understatement. It was one of the most important corporations in the country, and Andy had told her several times that Joe had made millions. The last thing she'd read about him was that he was starting an airline called AllWorld.

"I read about you a lot, Joe. Are you still flying as much?"

"As much as I can. I don't have enough time. I still test my own designs, but that's a different kind of flying. We're developing commercial airlines now, capable of transoceanic passages. Charles and I flew to Paris together a few weeks ago. But most of the time I'm stuck in the boardroom or my office. I have a place in town now," he said. They were like old friends catching up on old times, standing on the corner shooting the breeze, except they weren't. The breeze they were shooting was a strong one, and there were dangerous currents in the waters they were wading into. Kate tried to tell herself that wasn't true, but instinctively she knew it was. "We have an office building here now, one in Chicago, one in L.A. I go to the West Coast a lot, but I'm actually in New York more than anywhere else," he volunteered. He had been leaving his office when he ran into her on Fifty-seventh.

"You're an important man, Joe." She remembered when he hadn't had anything, and she'd loved him then. In some ways he was different now. He had the aura of a man in power, and yet when he looked at her, he was still the same, awkward, shy, hesitating to look at her one minute, and then gazing directly into her eyes the next, as though he were looking straight into her soul and knew what she was thinking. There was no way she could avoid the power of his eyes.

"Do you need a lift somewhere, Kate? It's too hot for you to be out with the baby."

"We were just getting some air. I live a few blocks up. I don't mind walking."

"Come on," he said, taking her arm, without waiting for her reaction. There was a car waiting across the street for him, and as though swept downstream on a rushing river, he pushed the pram across the street with the baby, as she followed, and before she knew it, she was sitting in the back of his car, holding the baby, the driver had put the pram in the trunk, and Joe had climbed in beside her. "Where do you live?" She gave him the address, and he told the driver, as she sat back against the seat next to him with her baby. "I only live a few blocks from you. In the penthouse because it gives me the feeling I'm flying. So what about you, what are you doing this summer?"

"I don't know . . . we . . . I . . ." She was beginning to feel overwhelmed by him, he was so strong and so powerful that he just swept one along, like a riptide. She felt as though she were about to go over Niagara Falls in a barrel. He had always had that effect on her. She had never been able to resist him, or the electricity she felt when she was near him. There was an intensity to it, and to him, that left her breathless. And much to her dismay, even after three years, it seemed no different. It was just the way she reacted to him, and the way he handled people, particularly now that he was so successful. He was used to getting everything he wanted. "I don't know what our plans are," she said vaguely, trying to keep her wits about her, and not feel the effect of him. Being with him was like a drug, and sitting with him in the car she felt the tug of her old addiction. She knew she had to resist. She was married now.

"I was going to Europe next week," he chatted as they drove uptown, "but I just canceled. I've got too much work here with the airline. We're having the same old union problems we had in the beginning in New Jersey." He drew her instantly into his circle of familiarity, talking about things she knew about and had been part of. It was a clever way of reminding her she had been his before she was Andy's. And as he sat next to her, Joe looked over at her with the smile that had cut right through her from the first moment they met. He didn't know what he was doing, it was instinctive, just like the pull he felt toward Kate as he sat beside her. They were like two animals sniffing the air and circling each other. "You and Andy should come flying with me sometime. Would he like that?" Probably. With anyone but Joe. He was a little sensitive on the subject, with good reason. He more than anyone knew how much Joe had meant to her. And she had been honest with him about how hard it had been to leave him. He also knew that if she hadn't, she would never have married him. He had never been able to compete with the glamour of Joe Allbright, or the magic Kate felt for him.

She didn't know what to say, so she told the truth. In a matter of minutes, he had already thrown her. And as soon as she said the words, she was sorry. It wasn't smart to give Joe too much information. He was liable to use it.

"He's away, in Germany. He's one of the counsel in the war crimes trials."

"That's impressive. He must be a good lawyer," he acknowledged, but his eyes never left Kate's, and were asking other questions, to which she had no answers, and if she did, she wouldn't give them to Joe.

"He is," she said proudly. And with that, the car stopped at her building, and she got out as quickly as she could. The driver took the pram out of the trunk an instant later, and she put Reed in it, as Joe watched her. He was always watching. He saw everything, he always had, even what she didn't want him to see. And she knew him just as well. They were each like the inside of the other, two halves forming a whole, and held together by a magnetic force so powerful that they could barely resist it. And never had before. But she intended to this time. He was out of her life and he was going to stay that way. For her sake, as well as Andy's. She stuck out a hand formally to him and thanked him for the ride. She was suddenly a little more distant and chilly. It wasn't fair really, she was angry at him for what she felt, and had felt for him. It wasn't his fault that she was so irrevocably drawn to him. It just was. But she assured herself that now it meant nothing to her.

"You know where to find me," he said somewhat arrogantly. Half the world did. "Call me sometime. We'll go flying."

"Thanks, Joe," she said, feeling like a young girl again. She was wearing a skirt and blouse and sandals, and he could see that even after the baby, her figure was still perfect. He remembered it distinctly. Three years hadn't dimmed the memories, or the feelings. "Thanks again for the ride," she said, as he stood watching her roll the pram into the building. She didn't turn back to look at him, or wave. And she hoped that their paths wouldn't cross again. She felt breathless when she and Reed got back to the apartment. The whole experience of seeing him had made her feel uneasy. She wanted to say something to someone, to hang on to something solid, to explain that she hadn't felt anything for him, that she was over him, and glad she had married Andy, and had Reed. It was as though she had to excuse herself, or defend what had happened. She wanted to convince someone that he meant nothing to her. But she knew that if she had, she would have been lying. It was just the same as it had always been, for ten years.

16

KATE WOKE UP the morning after she ran into Joe, feeling heavy. She had had bad dreams all night, and woke when the baby cried, with an uncomfortable feeling, as though she had betrayed Andy. And then over a cup of coffee, after she put Reed down for a nap, she told herself that she had done nothing wrong. She hadn't been inappropriate, hadn't shown any interest in him, hadn't encouraged him in any way, hadn't said she'd call him. But without knowing why, she felt guilty about seeing him at all, as though she had been responsible for running into him, or had planned it, which of course, she hadn't. It was an unpleasant sensation and stayed with her all day. And that night, after she'd written Andy a letter and enclosed photographs of Reed, the phone rang. It was probably her mother, she decided, as she answered. But the voice at the other end nearly ripped her heart out. It was that same velvet roll of thunder that had always had the same effect on her, and she had longed for, for years.

"Hi, Kate." He sounded tired and relaxed. It was late. And he was still in his office.

"Hi, Joe." She didn't offer anything more than that. She waited. She had no idea why he would call her.

"I thought maybe you were bored with Andy away." It was a clever

255

choice of words. He said "bored," not "lonely." She was both in fact, but she had no intention of admitting it to him. "Would you like to have lunch, for old times' sake?" He sounded gentle and youthful, and almost humble. And safe, which was deceptive. Even if he meant it, he was not, and never would be for her.

"I don't think so." It wasn't a good idea, and she knew it.

"I've always wanted you to see the building here in town. It's incredible. One of the most beautiful in the country. You were in on the beginning, I thought you'd want to see where it all went after . . . after you . . ."

"I'd like to, but I don't think we should."

"Why not?" He sounded disappointed, and it touched her. Danger! Danger! It was like a sign flashing. But she chose to ignore it anyway.

"I don't know, Joe," she said, sighing. She was tired. And he was so familiar. It was so comfortable talking to him, it made her want to turn back the clock. It suddenly made her think of the two years of agony when everyone thought he'd been killed, and seeing him on the ship for the first time when he came back from Germany. There were so many threads left from those days, dangling off her heart, but it wasn't enough to hang on to. "There's been a lot of water under the bridge since I left New Jersey."

"That's my point. I want you to see what the dam looks like. It's a beauty."

"You're hopeless," she laughed at him. But she was feeling more comfortable with him.

"Am I? Why can't we be friends, Kate?" Because I still love you, she wanted to answer. Or did she? Maybe it was just the memory of love that looked like the real thing. Maybe all it had ever been was an illusion. What she had with Andy was real love. She was sure of it. Joe was something else, an illusion, a dream, a hope that refused to die, a childish fairy tale that she always wanted a happy ending for and couldn't have. Joe was a disaster waiting to happen, and she knew it. They both did. "Have lunch with me . . . please . . . I'll behave. I promise."

"I'm sure we both would," she said firmly, "but why put ourselves through it?"

"Because we enjoy each other's company, we always did. What are you worried about anyway? You're married, you have a baby, a life. All I have are airplanes." He tried to sound pathetic and she laughed at him.

"Don't give me that, Joe Allbright! That's all you ever wanted. More than you wanted me, in fact. That's why I left you."

"We could have had both," he said sadly, and this time he sounded as though he meant it. She hated him for saying it now. It was much, much too late.

"I tried telling you that, you wouldn't listen," she said sadly.

"I was incredibly stupid and scared of getting tied down. I'm smarter now, and braver. I'm older. And I know what I lost when you left me. I was too proud to admit to you or myself then what you meant to me. My life has been meaningless without you, Kate." Joe sounded just as he had when she loved him most and it was everything she had always wanted to hear from him. It was a cruel trick of fate to hear it now. Too late.

"I'm married, Joe," she said softly.

"I know. I'm not asking you to change that. I understand that you've made a life for yourself. I just want lunch. A sandwich, an hour. You can spare me that. I just want to show you what I've done." He sounded so proud of it, and as though he had no one to share it with, which was his own fault. She had to believe there had been other women since she left, but knowing him maybe not, or maybe no one important. He was consumed by his planes and his business. And he had long since been recognized as the world's most important airplane designer. He was a genius. "Will you do it, Kate? Hell, you can't have much else to do with Andy gone. Get a sitter and come to lunch with me, or bring the baby." But she wouldn't have done that. She had already used several baby-sitters when she and Andy went out for the evening, and she had some good ones to call. She wouldn't have taken Reed to an office building, in case he disturbed the people working there.

"All right, all right," she said with a sigh. It was like arguing with a kid. He was so damnably persuasive. "I'll do it."

"You're wonderful, Kate. Thank you." What difference did it make? she asked herself. Why on earth did he care if she saw his office? She had to keep reminding herself that she was married to Andy. "How about tomorrow?" he suggested.

She thought about it for a long moment, and then nodded. "Okay." She wanted to get it behind her and prove that she could do it, without falling for him again, or wanting him, or being drawn to him. It had to be possible. It was like a reformed alcoholic proving to himself that he could walk past a bar without drinking. And she knew she could do it, no matter how appealing he was.

"Do you want me to pick you up?" he offered, and she declined. She said she'd meet him at the restaurant. He suggested Giovanni's, and she said she'd meet him at twelve-thirty.

She arrived at the restaurant the next day, precisely on time, in a white linen suit, with her hair pulled back and a big straw hat she had bought at Bonwit Teller. She looked very chic, and Joe was waiting for her. He kissed her on the cheek, and several people looked at them. He was a very distinctive figure, and easily recognized after all the press he got, and she was a beautiful woman in a great hat. But no one knew who she was.

"You always made me look good," he said as they sat down in a corner booth that gave them a little privacy.

"You do fine on your own," she smiled at him. It was fun to go out to lunch, and she was surprised to realize that she hadn't done it since before the baby was born. With Andy gone, she had nothing to do except take care of Reed, and it was nice to be out in the world again like a grown-up. She loved Reed, but she had no one to talk to. Her childhood friends were all in Boston, and she had lost track of most of them during her years with Joe. Her passion for him and the time she'd spent helping him set up his business had isolated her from everyone she'd ever known. And in the time since, she'd gotten wrapped up in Andy's life and their baby. She hadn't had the time or desire to make new friends.

She and Joe talked about a thousand things at lunch, about his company, his designs, his problems, his latest airplane. And then they spent an hour talking about his airline. He was involved in a multitude of exciting projects. It was a far cry from her own life. She was leading a quiet, happy little life with her husband and her baby.

"Are you going to get a job now, Kate?" he asked her. He had been a perfect gentleman all through lunch, and she was surprised to find how comfortable she was with him.

"I don't think so. I want to be home with the baby." But she had thought of it. Andy really didn't want her to, and for the moment she had agreed not to. She had enjoyed her job at the Metropolitan, but she had no burning desire for a career.

"He's a cute kid, but it must be pretty boring," Joe said honestly, and she laughed.

"It is, sometimes. But it's fun too."

"I'm glad you're happy, Kate," he said as he searched her face, and she nodded. She didn't want to talk about that with him. It opened too many doors to the past, and she didn't think they should talk about Andy, it seemed disrespectful to her. She knew he wouldn't have liked her having lunch with Joe, but she had felt it was something she had to do to prove something to herself. And it had been harmless. All they had done really was talk about aviation. It was still his favorite subject, and she knew a fair amount about it, or used to. He had always valued her advice, and he had loved it when she worked in the business with him in the beginning. It was why she understood so much of what he was doing. But the business had grown exponentially since then. And she knew nothing about his airline, except what she read in the papers.

They got in his car when they left the restaurant, and she was enormously impressed when she saw his office building. It was an entire skyscraper filled with the people he employed, both for his design company and his airline.

"My God, Joe, who would have thought it would have grown into all this?" In five years, he had built an empire.

"It's kind of amazing when you think I started out as a kid hanging around an airstrip. That's what this country's about, Kate. I'm very grateful." He sounded humble, which touched her a lot.

"You should be grateful." She whistled when she saw his office, on the top floor, overlooking all of New York. It really was like flying. It was wood-paneled, and there were handsome English antiques around the room, and paintings that she recognized. He had some very important art, and extraordinary taste. He was a remarkable man, and well on his way to becoming one of the richest men in the world. But, she reminded herself, she could have shared all of this with him on his terms—no marriage, no children. But no matter what he had accomplished, or acquired, it still wasn't a life she would have wanted, no matter how much she loved him. Even more so perhaps because she did. She preferred what she had with Andy, and their baby. For Kate, it had never been about money. It had been about love and commitment and kids, which was what she had now. But not with Joe. She had made her peace with the idea that she couldn't have everything she wanted a long time since.

She walked into the conference room with him, and he introduced her to several people, including his secretary, who had been with him right from the beginning and was thrilled to see Kate again. Her name was Hazel and she was a very sweet woman.

"I'm so happy to see you! Joe says you just had a baby. You sure don't look it!" Kate thanked her, and they went back to sit in Joe's office for a few minutes. But she had to get back to Reed soon. She had told the sitter she would be back at three-thirty and it was nearly that now. And she needed to nurse him soon.

"Thank you for having lunch with me," he said as she began to make noises about leaving.

"I think I wanted to prove to myself, as much as to you, that we can be friends." It had been a formidable challenge. But she had met it well.

"And, did I pass the test? Can we?" He looked innocent and hopeful, and she smiled.

"You didn't need to pass the test, Joe," she said honestly, "I did."

"I think we passed with flying colors." He seemed pleased.

"I hope so," she said, looking prettier than ever beneath the big straw hat. Her eyes looked to him like they were dancing. Everything about her had always fascinated him. She was so full of life, and so young and so pretty. She had been everything he wanted in a woman. But she wanted more from him than he could give her, or any woman. She had wanted too much.

She stood up then and kissed his cheek, and he closed his eyes as he smelled her perfume. For an instant, it was painfully familiar, just as the feel of his skin was to her and the way he held her. There were a lot of things, maybe too many things, that they both remembered. The memories were under their skin and in their hearts and their bones.

"Let's have lunch again," he said as he took her downstairs to put her in the car. He was sending her back uptown with his driver.

"I'd like that," she said softly.

He closed the door of the limousine for her, and she waved as they drove away. He stood watching his car for a long moment, and then went back upstairs and sat down at his desk, and frantically began drawing airplanes.

It was a week later, on a hot night, when she sat in the air conditioning, watching television. The baby was asleep when the phone rang. It was Joe, and she was surprised to hear him. She had been relieved by how well their lunch went, and she was proud of herself about it. It had been bittersweet, and kind of fun, but not agonizing. And afterward, she had been happy to get home to her baby and a letter from Andy. Joe was entirely a thing of the past now.

"What are you up to?" he asked, sounding relaxed. He was at home, doing nothing, and he'd been thinking about her.

"I'm watching TV," she said, still surprised to hear him.

"Do you want to go out for a hamburger? I'm bored," he confessed and she laughed.

"I'd love to, but I don't have a sitter."

"Bring the baby."

She laughed at the suggestion. "I can't, Joe. He's sleeping. And if I wake him up, he'll cry for hours. Believe me, you wouldn't enjoy it."

"You're right. I wouldn't. Have you eaten?"

"More or less. I ate some ice cream this afternoon. I'm not really hungry. It's too hot."

"What if I bring a hamburger over to you?" he suggested as an option.

"Here?"

"Well, yes. Where else would I take it?"

It was an odd suggestion. It seemed strange to have him come to the apartment she shared with her husband, but on the other hand, they were both alone with nothing to do, and they were friends now. She could do this. She had proven it the week before.

"Are you sure you want to do that?" she asked him.

"Why not? We both have to eat." It sounded reasonable, and finally she agreed. He knew the address, and he said he'd be there in thirty minutes.

He was there in fifteen, with two big oozing cheeseburgers in a white paper bag, just the way they both liked them. She hadn't had one like that in years, and as they dripped and dropped ketchup all over the place, and licked their fingers, they laughed at each other as they sat at the kitchen table.

"You're a mess," he said, as he watched her. And she giggled, and sounded seventeen again.

"I know. I love it." She handed him a stack of paper napkins, and eventually they both cleaned up the mess. And she offered him ice cream from her freezer. It was just like the old days, when he was staying at her parents' house in Boston, and afterward in New Jersey. She had missed that, although she had fun with Andy. Joe was like a giant bird who swooped down, and then settled in for a while, and after that took flight again and disappeared. But she had enjoyed seeing him again. She had forgotten what good company he was, and how much they liked each other. He loved her stories, and she made him laugh at silly things. She was good for him. She always had been. He had been good for her too, once upon a time, but she had worked hard to forget that. It had taken years.

After they ate, they watched TV. She was wearing sandals, and he kicked off his shoes, and she teased him when she saw there were holes in his socks.

"You're too successful to wear socks like that," she scolded him.

"I don't have anyone to buy me new ones," he said, trying to make her feel sorry for him, but she didn't.

"You like it that way, remember? Have Hazel do it." But his secretary had other things to do, so he never got them. He just wore the socks with holes.

"I don't like it that way. I just don't want to get married so I can have decent socks. That's a high price to pay for socks without holes in them," he said, as they sat on the couch and the TV chattered in the background.

"Is it, why?"

"I don't know. You know me. I'm afraid to be tied down. I'm afraid I'm going to miss something, or someone will take too much from me. Not money. But me. A part of me I don't want to give them." He had always been afraid of that. It was the real reason he hadn't married her. But he wasn't afraid of her now. For some reason even he couldn't fathom, he finally trusted her. It had taken a long, long time.

"No one can take what you won't give them," Kate said calmly.

"They can try. I guess I'm scared I'll lose me in the process." He nearly had with her. She had taken a big piece of him with her, but he suspected she didn't know that. And he wished now that he could reclaim it, and her.

"You're too big to lose, Joe," she said honestly. "I don't think you have any idea how big you are. You're enormous." He was the biggest man she had ever known. He had an enormous spirit and a brilliant mind.

"I always think I'm invisible, or want to be," Joe confessed, sounding like a boy.

"I don't think anyone sees themselves as they really are. In your case, you have a lot to be proud of," she said generously. It was odd sitting there with him. If anyone had told her a month before that would happen, she wouldn't have believed them, but she was enjoying his company, and they were friends again. There was great comfort in it. For both of them.

"There's a lot I'm not proud of, Kate," he confessed, looking boyish again, and it touched her heart. There was a side of him she had always loved, and knew she always would, and another side of him she had very nearly hated, the side that had hurt her so badly when she left. "I'm not proud of the way I treated you," he continued, and she was surprised to hear it. "I was rotten to you before you left. I was working you too hard, using you, I wasn't thinking about you, just about myself. But you scared the hell out of me. You loved me so damn much, and it made me feel so inadequate and so guilty. So trapped, I guess. I just wanted to run away and hide. You were right to leave, Kate. It damn near killed me when you did, but I don't blame you. That's why I never called, as much as I wanted to. You were right to go. There was nothing in it for you. I couldn't give you what you needed. I didn't understand how lucky I was. It took me a long time to calm down and figure that out." And by then she'd been long gone.

"It's nice of you to say that," she said generously, "but it never would have worked anyway. I realize that now."

"Why not?" He frowned, nothing woke Joe up more than a challenge.

"Because this is what I wanted," she said with a wave around the apartment and in the direction of the baby. "A husband, a baby, a regular life. You need a lot more than that in your life, you need power and success and excitement and airplanes, and you're willing to sacrifice everything for it, even people. I'm not. This is what I wanted."

"We could have had this, and more, if you'd waited."

"Not from what you said then."

"It was the wrong time for me, Kate. I was starting a business. That was all I could think of." It was true, but she knew that his aversion to marriage and kids and responsibility ran deeper than he was admitting. She had seen it. She knew him better than he knew himself. He had been too terrified to let her in.

"And now?" she asked skeptically. "Are you dying for a wife and a bunch of kids?" She smiled at him. "I don't think so. I think you were right, you'd hate it." She was convinced of it now.

"It depends on who the wife is. But no, I'm not looking. I found the right woman a long time ago, and I was foolish enough to lose her." It was a nice thing to say, but it made Kate uncomfortable. There was no point talking about that now, and she didn't want to. But he didn't want to let it drop yet. "I mean that, Kate. I was an incredible fool, and I want you to know that."

"Oh, I knew it," she laughed at him, "I just didn't think you did." And then she grew more serious. "I appreciate knowing how you feel about it, Joe. Things happen the way they're meant to."

"That's bullshit," he said bluntly. "They happen a certain way because we screw things up, or we're scared, or we're stupid, or just plain blind sometimes. It takes a lot of brains and courage to do things right, Kate, and not everyone has that. Sometimes it takes time to figure it out, and then it's too late. But you have to fix it if you can. You can't just sit back and leave things screwed up, and say that was how they were meant to be. Only fools do that." And they both knew he was no fool.

"You can't change some things," she said quietly. She understood what he was saying, but she wasn't sure she liked it. There was no point rehashing the past.

"You didn't give me enough time," he said, looking deep into her eyes that were the same color as his own. They were like mirrors of each other. They were so alike in some ways, and so diametrically different in others. And it was all so perfect when it worked.

"I waited two years, after I left you, to get married," she said sternly. "You had all the opportunity in the world to change your mind and come get me. And you didn't."

"I was mad. I was scared. I was busy. I hadn't figured it out yet. But I have now," he said pointedly, and she felt her heart do a somersault when she saw the look in his eyes. He wanted what they had had before, but now it belonged to someone else. That was hard for Joe. He always wanted what he couldn't have. "Look, Kate, I get it. I have a great life, I've built a solid business, but none of it means as much to me without you."

"Joe, don't let's talk about this. There's no point."

"Yes, there is, Kate," he said, looking at her. "I love you." And before she could say another word, he kissed her, and then put his arms around her as they sat on the couch. She felt as though she were drifting into another world with him, floating through space, as her heart soared, and a moment later she fell to earth as she pulled away.

"Joe, you have to go."

"I won't until you talk to me about it. Do you still love me?" He had to know.

"I love my husband," she said, looking away from him so he couldn't see her eyes.

"That's not what I asked you," he persisted, and finally she looked into his eyes. "I asked you if you still love me."

"I have always loved you," she said honestly. "But it's not right. And it's impossible now. I'm married to someone else." She looked agonized as she talked to him. She hadn't wanted this to happen. She had convinced herself they could be friends.

"How can you love me and be married to Andy?" Joe said, looking profoundly upset.

"Because I didn't think you loved me, you didn't want to get married . . ." She had gone over it a hundred times. A thousand. A million. And it was too late.

"So you married the first guy who came along?"

"That's a rotten thing to say. I waited two years."

"Well, it took me longer to figure it out." He sounded like a child, but no matter what the words were, it didn't matter. What mattered was what she had felt when he kissed her, what she saw in his eyes when he looked at her, and felt in her heart. She was still in love with him and knew she always would be. Kate felt like she had been condemned to a life sentence, there was nothing she could do about it now.

"I can't do this to Andy," she said simply. "He's my husband. We have a child." She stood up with an unhappy expression. "It doesn't matter anymore what happened, what we did or said or why. We did it, we said it. I left, and you wanted me to go. If you didn't, you'd have stopped me, you'd have asked me to come back. That was all I wanted for two long years, for you to want me back. You were too busy playing with your airplanes to give a damn. And too scared to risk being swallowed up. And the truth is, I still love you. I always will. But it's too late for us, Joe. I'm married to someone else. I have to respect that, even if you don't." She looked at him miserably then, and stood up. "You have to go. I can't do this to myself, or to him. He doesn't deserve this, and neither do I."

"You're punishing me because I wouldn't marry you," he said, as he stood up to his full height, and looked down at her with regret.

"I'm punishing myself because I married a man who deserves a real wife, not someone who has always been in love with someone else. That's not right, Joe. We have to forget each other. I don't know how the hell to do it, and by God, I've tried. But I swear, if it kills me, I'll do it. I can't be married to him and in love with you for the rest of my life."

"Then leave him."

"I love him, and I won't do that. We just had a baby."

"I want you back, Kate." He said it like a man who was used to having his way, and wouldn't settle for anything less.

"Why? Because I'm married to someone else? Why now? I'm not a toy, or an airplane, or a company you own or want to buy. I waited two goddamn years while everyone said you were dead in Germany some-where. I was always there, waiting for you. I was just a kid, and I couldn't even look at anyone else. And I pined for you for a year three years ago after you told me you'd never get married. Why now?" She was crying, as he shook his head.

"I don't know. I just know that you're part of me. I don't want to live the rest of my life without you, Kate. We've come too far. We've known each other for ten years, we've been in love for nine."

"So what?" she said unkindly. "You should have thought of that be-fore. It's too late."

"That's ridiculous. You don't love him. Is that what you want for the rest of your life?"

"Yes!" she said firmly, as the baby began to cry. "You have to go, Joe," she said, still crying. "I have to feed the baby."

"Aren't you supposed to be calm when you feed a baby?"

"Yes, but it's a little late for that." He took a step closer to her then, and wiped her eyes. "Don't, please . . ." she cried harder, and he pulled her into his arms as she sobbed. All she wanted was to be with him, and she couldn't. It was a cruel twist of fate that he wanted her back. She couldn't abandon Andy and take their child, no matter how much she loved Joe. And she loved Andy too, but in a different way.

"I'm sorry . . . I shouldn't have come here tonight." He felt guilty for the state she was in.

"It's not your fault," she admitted, drying her eyes, "I wanted to see you too. It was so wonderful seeing you the other day, and being with you. . . . Oh Joe . . . what are we going to do?" she said as she clung to him. They were lost, and so obviously still in love.

"I don't know, we'll figure it out." He held her and then kissed her. All she wanted was to be with him. She left him then to get the baby, and brought him out to lie between them on the couch. He was a beautiful baby, and Joe looked at him silently and then at her. "It'll be all right, Kate. Maybe we can see each other once in a while."

"And then what? We'll always wish we were together. That's not a life."

"It's all we've got, for now. Maybe it's enough." But she knew it wouldn't be for long. They would always want more than just stolen moments and knowing that they loved each other and couldn't be together. It sounded like a lifetime of torture to her. He looked at her then, she looked so tormented, and so unhappy, and he knew she had to feed the baby. "Do you want me to go, or wait till you've fed him?" She knew he should go, but she didn't want him to. She didn't know when or if she'd see him again.

"If you want, you can wait." She went in the other room, while he watched TV, and when she came back, Joe had fallen asleep on the couch. He had had a long day, and it had been an emotional evening for both of them. She looked more peaceful after feeding the baby, and Reed was sound asleep in his bassinet.

Kate sat watching Joe for a while, she touched his hair, and gently stroked his face. It was all so familiar. He had belonged to her for so many years, and she to him. They had so much history together, it was a powerful bond. She just sat there holding him for a long time, until after a while he opened his eyes.

"I love you, Kate," he whispered, and she smiled.

"No, you don't. I won't let you," she said in a whisper back to him, and he kissed her. They lay on the couch kissing for a long time. It was an impossible situation, with an impossible man. "You've got to go," she whispered. He nodded, but made no move to leave the couch, and kissed her again and again, and after a while, she no longer cared if he left or not. She didn't want him to go. She didn't want to have left him, she didn't want to hurt Andy, or their son . . . she didn't want any of it to happen, but the force of what tied them to each other was stronger than they were. He picked her up in his arms and laid her on her bed. She knew she should tell him to go, but she couldn't. Instead, she let him peel away her clothes as he had so many times, and then he took off his own. They made love with all the longing that had haunted them for three years, and afterward, they fell into a deep, peaceful sleep in each other's arms.

17

Whenn kate woke up the next morning, she smiled feeling Andy beside her, and turned to face him, and when she did, she saw Joe. It hadn't been a dream or a nightmare. It had been the culmination of all the years she had loved him, and the three years they'd been apart. But she had no idea what to do now. They had to forget each other, she told herself, as she watched him slowly stir. The baby was still sound asleep.

Joe woke a few minutes later, and when he saw her, he smiled.

"Am I dreaming? Or did I die and go to Heaven last night?" It all seemed so simple to him. He wasn't married to anyone, and wasn't in danger of destroying anyone's life, except hers and his own. That was enough.

"You look disgustingly happy," she accused him, but as she did, she snuggled close to him. The time they spent in bed, in the morning, cuddled close to each other, and talking, had always been her favorite part of their day. "You must have no conscience at all."

"None," he confirmed. He smiled as he kissed the top of her head. He hadn't been this happy in years, for that moment at least, all was well with the world. "Is the baby okay? Is he supposed to still be sleeping?" It was new to him.

"He's fine. He sleeps late," she said, touched that he was concerned.

He began kissing her then, and they took advantage of the fact that Reed was still asleep to make love again. It was all like a dream. It was almost as though he had never left, except that they had both grown up in the past three years, and she was married and had a child. But what she shared in bed with Joe, and everywhere else, she had never had with any other man. All the feelings they had for each other ran deeper than either of them was able to understand. It was like some kind of primal pull. They had to be together. They were so different, so separate, each so unique, and yet in some part of them, they were as one. It needed no explanations and few words. Most of the time, it needed none at all. The words were only the external excuse for what they felt. The apologies they made. The promises they could no longer keep. The words didn't matter at all. It was the rest that bound them to each other's souls.

The baby woke up finally with a healthy cry. Kate nursed him while Joe took a shower, and afterward she made breakfast for them. He wanted to linger over breakfast with her, and he laughed when the baby grinned at him from his little seat. And then he said regretfully that he had a meeting that morning, and had to go. He would have loved to spend the day with them.

"Can you have lunch?" he asked Kate as he stood up and put his jacket on.

"What are we doing, Joe?" she asked him with deep, worried eyes. They still had time to stop. It could be one time, one moment that she could atone for, for the rest of her life. It was early enough to stop before they destroyed everything, and everyone in their wake. She had far more to lose than he. It was up to her to stop, she knew, but she couldn't bear losing him again. Deep in her soul she knew it was already too late.

"I think we're doing the best we can, Kate. That's all we can do.

We'll figure it out as we go." He had a way of not wanting to see the
pitfalls that lay ahead, except when building planes.

"That's dangerous," she said as she smoothed the lapels of his coat.
She loved the way he looked, his height, his chiseled face, the cleft
chin, the very male square of his shoulders, the eyes that followed her
everywhere, the long legs. She was drunk on him. He was her dream,
and had always been, since she was seventeen. It was too great a force
to fight. And it was no different for him. He had been mesmerized by
her since the first time he saw her, drawn to her like moth to flame.

"Life is dangerous, Kate," he said calmly, as he smiled at her and
then kissed her. He couldn't get enough of her, or she him. "Maybe it's
not worthwhile unless it is. Good things come at a high price. I've
never been afraid to pay for what I want, or believe." But they were
paying this time with other lives than just their own. "Do you want to
meet me for lunch?" She hesitated, and then nodded. She wanted to be
with him for as long as she could. She realized now that she had no
choice.

"I'll get a sitter. Where do you want to meet?"

He suggested Le Pavillon, which had always been one of her favorite
places, and they agreed to meet at noon. After he left, she nursed the
baby again, and sat quietly on the couch. There were pictures of her
and Andy all around the room, and a portrait taken at their wedding
the year before. Being with Joe again made Andy seem like a distant
dream. She knew she loved him, she reminded herself, he was her husband. But he always seemed like a boy in comparison to the man Joe
already was. There was something about Joe that intoxicated her every
time she saw him. He was right, it was dangerous, but at that exact
moment in time Kate knew it was too late to turn back, and the risks
seemed worth the happiness they shared.

She put the baby back in his bassinet, and called the sitter. And at
noon, she met Joe at Le Pavillon, and walked in wearing a pale green

silk dress, with a watery emerald pin her mother had given her years before. She looked beautiful and delicate, and the dress looked incredible with her dark auburn hair. Joe sat staring at her, as she walked across the room, just as he had ten years before. There was a certain danger in their being so visible and public, but they had discussed it and decided that their having lunch openly would seem less suspicious, if someone saw them, than if they appeared to be hiding somewhere.

"Aren't you Joe Allbright?" she whispered as she sat down next to him. And he grinned. He loved the way she looked and played and smelled, loved the way she sauntered across a room, totally unaware of how spectacular she was. Together, they made an extraordinary pair. They were not an obvious match, but they looked incredible together, and always had. It was part of the magic they exuded and shared.

"Do you want to go flying this weekend?" he asked her over lunch. She had always loved his planes, and she hadn't flown herself in three years. He told her he had a cute little model that had just been delivered the day before. "You'll love it, Kate," he grinned, looking more than ever like a handsome boy.

"Sure." She had nothing else to do. She was free for the next three and a half months, and she realized now that whatever happened after that, this time belonged to them. There was no point fighting it. She had abandoned herself to the fates. The tether that bound them could not be cut. Or at least not yet.

They stayed at lunch for a long time, and were very circumspect, and then he went back to the office and she went home. She was going to take Reed to the park, and she found a letter from Andy when she got home. It was so funny and loving, and he missed her so much, that it cut through her like a knife. She sat there holding it for a long time, crying. She had never felt as guilty in her life, and she knew that what she was doing was wrong, but she couldn't stop. No matter how much she cared about Andy, she needed to be with Joe.

She was quiet that night when Joe came back. He had had a busy day at the office, and he was tired. She fixed him a scotch and water and handed it to him, and then poured herself a glass of wine. The baby was already asleep.

"I had a letter from Andy today. I feel awful, Joe. If he ever finds out, this will break his heart. He'd probably divorce me," she said, looking depressed.

"Good. Then I'll marry you." He'd been thinking about it all day, and had almost made up his mind. But he had wanted to ponder it some more before saying anything to her.

"You're just saying that because I'm married to someone else. If I were free," she smiled at him, "you'd run like hell."

"Try me."

"I can't."

"Let's not talk about it, and enjoy the time we have," he said calmly. Which was exactly what they did.

For the next month, they had lunch several times a week, dinner together every night, at home and out, went flying on the weekends, went to movies, talked, made love, laughed, and cocooned themselves in their own little world. Joe even played with the baby when he came home every night, and got wildly excited when he discovered Reed's first tooth. It was as though they were a perfect family, and Andy didn't exist. The only reminder of him was Andy's mother, who came to see the baby once a week, on Tuesday afternoons, but Kate was careful that there was never any sign of Joe's presence anywhere in the house. And when they went out, Kate and Joe were discreet enough for anyone to believe they were just friends and not romantically involved. But they felt more like husband and wife. They were an inseparable pair.

She wrote to Andy almost every day, but the letters were stilted and felt strange. She only hoped he didn't notice. Mostly, she talked about Reed, and said very little about herself. It seemed best that way. And what he had told her about the trials was fascinating. But he also told her how much he missed her and loved her and couldn't wait to come home to Reed and her. Each letter was like a slice to her heart. She had no idea what they would do, and she and Joe had agreed not to try to figure it out until the fall.

In August, she had promised her parents that she would spend a week with them in Cape Cod, but she hated the thought of leaving Joe. They had so little time. They were already halfway through the four months Andy would be gone. But she knew that if she didn't go to the Cape with the baby, her parents would know something was amiss, and might even come to New York and discover Joe living with her. He had moved in at the end of July. So she decided it was best to go. Joe said he'd keep busy while she was gone, and they agreed that she would call him. Her mother would have recognized his voice on the phone if he called. It was strange being so deceitful, and not something she was proud of, to say the least, but they had no choice. If this was what they wanted, what they felt they had to have, they had to play by what rules they could.

She'd already been at the Cape for five days, the night of their neighbor's annual barbecue. She left the baby with a sitter and went next door with her parents. She was in good spirits, and knew that in two more days she would see Joe. She could hardly wait.

She was having drinks on the terrace just above the dunes, when she turned around and saw him walk in. And mercifully, she looked appropriately surprised. In fact, she looked stunned. Joe had surprised her and come up to visit his friends, and had come to the barbecue with them. Their hosts were pleased to see him, and remembered him from several years before. Joe Allbright was not a man one forgot, and they hadn't. He was making his way slowly across the terrace, shaking hands and greeting people, when Kate's mother spotted him.

"What's he doing here?" she asked Kate.

"I have no idea," Kate said, turning away, so her mother couldn't see her face. But she thought Joe had been foolish to come. It was tempting fate. And Kate wasn't sure either of them could pull it off.

"Did you know he was coming?" The inquisition started, as her father walked across the terrace to shake Joe's hand. He was pleased to see him, in spite of the rift between him and Kate. That was all behind them now, she was married to another man. The past was the past, or so he thought.

"Why would I know he was coming, Mother? He has friends here. He's been here before."

"It just seems strange. He hasn't been here for three years. Maybe he wanted to see you."

"I doubt it." Kate had her back to him, but she could almost feel him approaching, and sense her mother watching them. She could only hope that they didn't betray themselves, but she didn't trust either of them, particularly herself. Her mother knew her too well.

Joe finally reached where she was standing, politely said hello to her mother, who shook his hand reluctantly and gave him an icy stare.

"Hello, Joe," she said in frigid tones, and he gave her a warm smile.

"Hello, Mrs. Jamison. It's nice to see you." She didn't answer, and then he turned to Kate. Their eyes met, and Kate kept an iron rein on herself as she said hello to him. "It's good to see you, Kate. I hear you had a baby. Congratulations."

"Thank you," she said coolly, and moved away to talk to someone else. She knew her mother would be relieved, and hopefully put off the scent. She whispered as much to Joe when she stood next to him later on the beach. They were roasting hot dogs and hers were already burned. All she was interested in was talking to him. "It was crazy for you to come up here. If they figure it out, they'll have a fit."

"I missed you. I wanted to see you," he said, sounding earnest and young.

279

"I'll be home in two days," she whispered back, wanting to kiss him or put her arms around him, or feel his around her. But she didn't dare even look at him.

"Your hot dog is turning to ash," he whispered again and she laughed, and their eyes met for an instant. And when she turned away, she saw her mother watching them.

"She hates me," Joe commented, as he handed Kate a plate. It wasn't totally inconceivable that they would talk to each other, but it was obvious that her mother didn't approve. She looked like she wanted him dead, or at the very least as far away from Kate as he could get.

In the end, her parents left early because her mother had a headache, and she and Joe went for a walk on the beach, as they had years before. They had history between them, a lot of it. Ten years was a long time, and counted for a lot. For them, if no one else. As long as they had never married, her mother discounted whatever they had ever felt. As far as she was concerned, they were wasted years, and she had often said as much to Kate. Kate didn't see it that way. They had been the best years of her life.

It was nice to just get away, and walk on the sand in the moonlight. They lay side by side far down the beach, and kissed, and held hands on the way back. They let go long before they reached the house, and once back, they were very circumspect. Kate left the party before he did, and her parents were already in bed, and Reed was sound asleep and didn't even want to be nursed. And Kate lay in bed, thinking about Joe. They had such a good time together, and such a good life. Everything they had each wanted had happened, her baby, his success, but there seemed to be no way to put it together, and if they tried to, someone would get hurt. It was like a Chinese puzzle, or a maze, but in this case, she knew, there was no way out.

She got up early with the baby, and her mother was in the kitchen, when Kate came downstairs trying not to make any noise, which was difficult with Reed. He was cooing and crowing and laughing and squealing, and she quietly closed the kitchen door and then saw that her mother was sitting quietly at the kitchen table, reading the local newspaper, and drinking a cup of tea.

She didn't raise her eyes as she spoke to Kate, but kept them on the paper, as Kate put the baby in his chair.

"You knew he was coming last night, didn't you?" her mother said in an accusing tone, and then finally looked up at her.

"No, I didn't," Kate said truthfully. "I honestly had no idea."

"There's something between you, Kate. I can feel it. I've never seen two people more drawn to each other. You can sense it even when you're standing across the room." It was why Kate never seemed to be able to let him go, nor he her. "It's almost like some kind of animal fascination with each other. You can't leave each other alone."

"I hardly talked to him last night," Kate said as she handed a tiny piece of banana to the baby, and he put it in his mouth.

"You don't need to talk to him, Kate. He feels you, just like you feel him. He's a dangerous man. Don't let him near you. He'll destroy your life." But it was already far too late. "It was rude of him to come here. He did it because he knew you'd be here. I'm surprised he had the gall . . . although nothing surprises me anymore," she said angrily. She still thought Joe was a threat, particularly with Andy gone. And she was right.

"Nor me," her father said cheerfully as he walked into the kitchen and kissed the baby, and glanced at his wife. He could see that she and Kate had had words, although he had no idea about what, and didn't care to guess. He preferred to stay out of their fights. "It was nice to see Joe last night. I've been reading about his airline, it's going to be a colossal success, and already is. He says they're going to open offices in Europe. Who'd have thought all of this would happen five years ago?" he said, looking impressed, as his wife put her cup of tea in the sink.

"I think it was rude of him to come," her mother reiterated for her husband's sake, and he looked surprised.

"Why?"

"He knew he'd see Kate. She's a married woman, Clarke. He shouldn't be chasing her all the way to Cape Cod, or anywhere else." Nor living with her, which he was, Kate thought. Her mother would have had her committed if she knew that. And maybe she should. "He knows that. He just did it to press himself on her."

"Don't be silly, Liz. That's water under the bridge. That was years ago. Kate's married, and he probably has someone else. Is he married, Kate?"

"I don't think so, Dad. I don't really know."

"I saw him talking to you on the beach," her mother accused.

"There's no harm in that," Clarke intervened. "He's a good man."

"If he were, he'd have married your daughter, instead of making her wait for him for two years during the war and using her for two years after he got home," his wife snapped. "Thank God Kate came to her senses and married someone else. It's a shame Andy wasn't here last night."

"Yes, it is," Kate said softly, but her mother saw something in her eyes she didn't like. There was something guarded and hidden, as though she had a deep secret, and everything in her told her it was Joe.

"You're a fool if you have anything to do with him, Kate. He'll just use you again, and you'll break Andy's heart. Joe's never going to marry anyone. Mark my words." She had always said that, and so far she'd been right. But Kate also knew he wanted to marry her now, or so he said, although it was easier to say it now when she was married to someone else. After a while, she took the baby and went outside to sit in the sun on the porch. And as she looked up, she saw a plane doing loops overhead. It was easy to guess who it was. He was such a kid, but it made her smile.

Her father came out to see it, and grinned up at the sky. "Pretty little plane," he commented, still looking up.

"It's his newest design," Kate said before she could stop herself, and her father lowered his gaze to look at her.

"How would you know, Kate?" There was none of the accusation of her mother, only concern.

"He told me last night."

He sat down next to her after that, and patted her hand.

"I'm sorry it didn't work out, Kate. Some things just don't." He knew how much she had loved him, and how much pain it had caused her when they broke up. "Your mother's right though. It would be very wrong if you started things up with him again now." He was suddenly worried about her. She looked so sad.

"I won't, Dad." She hated lying to him, but she had no choice. And she knew what she and Joe were doing was wrong. But it seemed impossible to her to let him go. There wasn't a man in the world who made her feel as he did, in bed or out. It was as though he completed her, just as she did him. They each had the missing pieces the other needed to be whole. She had no idea what they would do when Andy got home, but at least it was another two months away. She and Joe had time to figure out what they were going to do then.

He was still flying around overhead, doing loops and rolls, and he did a terrifying stall, which made her put her hand over her mouth. She was sure he was going to crash. And her father watched her eyes. It was worse than he thought, and he was beginning to wonder if Liz was right, and something was going on after all. But he didn't want to ask Kate. She was an adult, and he didn't feel it was his place to pry.

She went back to New York the next day, and Joe called her the minute she got home. She scolded him for the stall that had terrified her, and he laughed. He knew he had been in no danger at all. He never was.

"It's more dangerous crossing the street in New York, Kate. You know that." He was amused that she'd been concerned. "Did your parents give you a rough time?" He figured they would after seeing him at the barbecue, and he was right.

"Only my mom. She thinks something's going on."

"Very observant," he said admiringly. "Did you say anything to them?"

"Of course not. They'd be horrified. And I guess, when I think about it, so am I." She had thought about it all the way home, and he didn't like the sound of her voice. She was consumed with guilt, Andy was so innocent in all this. He had no idea what was happening at home. Somehow, Joe felt he had seniority, and a right, because he had known her for so long. But it was Andy who had married her a year before, and given her a child. And it was Joe who owned her heart, and always had.

"Is it still all right if I come back tonight, Kate?" he asked her so humbly that it touched her heart. No matter how guilty she felt, there was no way she could bring herself to say no.

He came over half an hour later, and as always, they fell into bed. Their longing for each other was like a tidal wave, it swept everything in its wake, and left them gasping for air. Not being together for a week had seemed far too long.

September flew by as soon as Labor Day was past. Joe had to go to California for a few days, and then he flew to Nevada for a test flight. He invited Kate to come along, but she didn't think she should. There was no way to explain it if Andy called. He had only called once or twice in the two months he'd been gone, it was almost impossible for him to call, but he wrote to her faithfully every day.

By the end of September, Kate and Joe had been living together for two months. It had begun to seem comfortable and normal, as though they were married. He was so relaxed that one night, when her mother called, he almost answered the phone. Kate grabbed it from his hand before he could say anything, and they both looked startled when they realized what he'd almost done.

She flew with him every weekend, went to the factory with him, he asked her opinions and she gave him advice. And the people in his office had begun to treat her as his wife. But remarkably, they hadn't run into anyone she knew in restaurants or movie theaters, or even walking down the street. Part of their good fortune had been that many of the people she knew went away for the summer. But even after Labor Day there had been no chance encounters with people who might suspect she and Joe were having an affair. They had found an easy rhythm that worked for them. And then, in mid-October, Kate looked devastated when Andy called to tell her he was coming home. He told Kate how grateful he was, how well she had done, how uncomplaining she had been. Her letters had been wonderful, and he was dying to see her and Reed again. The photographs she'd sent were adorable, and Andy said the baby looked even more like Kate than before, except for the color of his hair. He told Kate that the trials he had participated in, in Germany, had gone extremely well. But he was anxious to wrap up his work in the next two weeks and come home.

Kate and Joe sat in the kitchen for hours, discussing it, the night he called.

"What are we going to do?" she asked miserably. Now that she had to face reality, she had never been so tormented in her life. Someone was going to get hurt, possibly all of them, even her son. There was no way out. There were choices to be made, and she and Joe had to come to some kind of agreement or decision in a matter of days.

"I want to marry you, Kate," he said quietly. "I want you to get divorced. You can go to Reno and stay for six weeks. We could be married by the end of the year." It was all she had ever wanted from him. But in order to do that now, she had to destroy Andy's life. It seemed a blow too cruel for anyone to take, and so unfair to him. He had done nothing to deserve this fate, and it wasn't his fault that she had fallen prey to Joe's charms again.

"I don't even know what to say to him," she said, looking at Joe, and feeling sick over it. His parents were going to be distraught, and hers. But for Andy it would be the worst of all. And he had no suspicion whatsoever what was about to befall him.

"Tell him the truth," Joe said practically. It was easy for him to be the winner in the piece. All he had to do was stand back and let Kate deliver the fatal blow. "What other choice do we have, Kate? Walk away from each other again? Is that what you want to do?" It was the only other choice they had, or else to continue a clandestine affair, and Kate knew the pressure and deceit of that would drive her insane, and Joe agreed. He wanted to live with her, be married to her, he even wanted to be with Reed, and if they were married, he would. "I feel sorry for him," Joe said decently, "but he has a right to know."

"Are you serious about getting married, Joe?" She still remembered her mother's words, and Kate knew him well. Joe loved his freedom and his planes. But he also loved her. And he was nearly forty years old. She believed he was finally ready to settle down and make a serious commitment to her this time, or so he said. She just wanted to be sure before she asked Andy for a divorce. Other than being devastated over losing her, she knew he would be heartbroken not to be living with his son.

"I'm serious," Joe said emphatically. "It's time, Kate." For her, it would have been time three or four years before. Or even five. He had taken his time getting there. And her parents would have been happier if they'd gotten married before or during the war. But whatever path they had taken to get there, he had arrived, and now he wanted her to do what she had to, to make it work for them. It was in her hands. He couldn't do more than assure her that he was serious, and wanted to marry her.

"I'll tell him when he gets home," she said. She wasn't looking forward to it, but they both agreed, it had to be done.

She found a sitter, and they spent a weekend at a cozy inn in Connecticut in an out-of-the-way place. Joe had stayed there once before, and no one had bothered or intruded on him. It seemed the perfect hideaway for them. Often, people recognized him wherever they went, and with ordinary strangers, he introduced her as his wife. She didn't respond at first when the woman at the inn called her by Joe's name. She realized it was going to be strange to give up Andy's name. She had been calling herself Kate Scott for more than a year. It had been hard enough to adjust to giving up Jamison after twenty-six years. And now she would have another name. She felt as though she were on a merry-go-round. It was where she wanted to be, and had wanted to be for years, but now that it was happening, it all felt strange.

Joe moved his things out the night before Andy came home, but he spent the night with her anyway. The baby was teething and cried all night, Kate's nerves were raw, and by morning even Joe looked strained. All she wanted now was to get it over with. She was going to tell Andy that night, and she had already convinced herself that it was going to be a gruesome scene of heartbreak and regret.

She felt as though she and Joe had lived in isolation for four months. She had been avoiding whoever she knew in order to keep their secret, and she had seen none of her few friends. But so far, no one seemed to have figured out what was happening. And in the next few weeks, everyone would know. After she told Andy, she was going to tell her parents, and she knew that wasn't going to be a pretty scene. She had already played out all of it in her head, and with Joe. It was their destiny to be together, she knew. It had always been that way. She was just sorry that she was going to cause Andy so much pain. She never should have married him, she realized. It hadn't been fair to him. But she had never expected Joe to come back into her life again. And if he hadn't, maybe she and Andy could have made it work. They would never know. And at least, this way, she had Reed. Although Joe was certain he wanted Kate and Reed, he was still unsure about having their own kids. They had talked about it several times, and he wasn't convinced that having children would improve the quality of their life. But he was enough now for Kate.

Joe left for the office at nine the next day, and she was picking Andy up at the airport at noon. She had told Joe she'd call him when she could, but she didn't know if it would be possible that night. Out of respect for her husband, she had to see how it went. But she promised Joe she would call him no later than the next day.

They made love that morning before he left, and he kissed her one last time, and blew Reed a kiss.

"Try not to worry about it, sweetheart. I know you'll do the best you can. Better now, after a year, than five years from now. You're doing him a favor ending it this soon. He'll get married again and have a good life." It irked her that Joe was so practical about it. It was easy being the winner. She was sure it was not going to seem quite so simple to Andy when he heard the news.

Kate took a cab to Idlewild at eleven o'clock. She had brought Reed with her, and she was wearing a plain black dress, and black hat. She realized that she looked a little funereal when she left the house, but it seemed appropriate. For them at least, this was not going to be a happy day.

She checked the list of arriving flights when she arrived at the airport, and saw that his flight was on time. And then, holding the baby close to her, she went to wait for him at the gate.

Andy was one of the first passengers off the plane. He looked tired from the flight, and four months of hard work, but he smiled broadly the moment he saw his wife and son, and kissed her so hard he knocked off her hat.

"I've missed you so much, Kate!" He took the baby out of her arms and couldn't believe how much he'd grown. Reed was nearly eight months old by then. He had eight teeth and could almost stand up by himself. And as Andy held him, he reached for his mother and started to scream.

"He doesn't even know who I am anymore," Andy looked crushed, and as they walked out of the airport, he put an arm around her. He felt as though he'd been gone for years. He not only felt as though the baby didn't know who he was, he could tell that Kate was ill at ease with him, and when he looked at her as they drove home in a cab, she looked strange. She said she was happy to see him, but she looked like someone had died. She asked him about Germany, and the trials, but when he tried to hold her hand in the cab, she pulled it away to look for something in her purse. She didn't want to mislead him more than she already had.

Kate made lunch for all of them when they got home, and put Reed down for a nap afterward. All she wanted was to get it over with. She couldn't wait. She didn't want to play out a farce with him. He deserved more respect from her than that.

"Kate, are you all right?" he asked after she put the baby to bed. She looked suddenly older and more serious in the somber black dress. He didn't know what had happened while he was gone, but he knew something had. The atmosphere around them seemed incredibly tense, and Kate kept avoiding his touch, his arms, his eyes.

"Can we sit down and talk?" she said, as they walked into the living room and she sat down on the couch. Andy sat down across from her, and all she could think of as she looked at him was Joe.

This was the worst thing she had ever done in her life, to anyone, she knew. When she had left Joe three years before, it had been an entirely different situation than walking out on a man who she knew loved her, and taking his child with her. But there was no escape now. They had to face the truth, both of them. She had been foolish to marry him and think that their love would grow, but she had meant well. She was very attached to him, and they had had lots of happy times. But all of it had meant nothing the moment she saw Joe.

"What's wrong, Kate?" Andy asked quietly. He looked upset, but he was very much in control. He looked as though he'd matured in the past four months. He had seen and heard of atrocities that had made his blood run cold. There was no way not to grow up with all the responsibility that had rested on him. And now he had come home to something even worse. He could see it in her eyes.

"Andy, I've made a terrible mistake," she began, sitting well away from him. She didn't try to sit near him, or take his hand. And she wanted to get it over with as fast as she could, for both their sakes.

"I don't think we need to talk about this," he suddenly cut into what she'd just said, and she looked surprised.

"Yes, we do," she went on. "We have to talk about it. Something happened while you were gone." She was planning to tell him that she had met Joe again, and that, as a result, everything had changed. But Andy was holding up a hand to stop her, as though he could turn back her words, and she saw something in his eyes she'd never seen there before. It was a kind of strength and dignity she had never known he was capable of, and he took the control of the situation away from her.

"Whatever happened, Kate, I don't need to know what it was. In fact, I don't want to know. You're not going to tell me. It's not important. We're what's important, and our son. Whatever you were going to say to me, don't. I won't listen to it. We are going to shut the door behind us now, and go on." She was so stunned that for a moment, she couldn't say a word.

"But Andy, we can't . . ." She could feel tears filling her eyes. He had to listen to her. She was going to divorce him, and marry Joe. She didn't want to be married to Andy anymore. And Joe wanted to marry her. She wasn't going to lose him now, after all these years. But Andy had something to say about it, and she couldn't divorce him, unless he agreed. He had obviously figured it out, or enough to know that their marriage was on the line, and he was not going to lie down and let her roll over him. He had already made a decision about it, no matter how she felt. And as far as Andy was concerned, the subject was closed.

"Yes, Kate, we can," he said in a tone that frightened her. "And we will. Whatever you wanted to say to me, you're going to keep to yourself. We're married. We have a son. We'll have more children soon, I hope. And we're going to have a good life. And that's all you're going to say to me. Is that clear? I probably shouldn't have stayed away as long as I did. But I think we did something important in Germany, and I'm glad that I was part of it. And now you're going to be my wife, Kate, and we'll go on from here." Kate was stunned by the power of his words and the steel in his eyes. It was very unlike him.

"But Andy, please," the tears were rolling down her cheeks. "I can't do this . . . I can't . . ." she sobbed. She was in love with Joe, and not with him. She had never felt so trapped in her life as she just had, listening to him. He was not going to let her out, she knew, no matter what she said. Her only choice then would be to run away with Joe, and live with him. She couldn't even take Reed with her if she wasn't divorced and didn't have custody. Andy might as well have put her in jail and locked her in. And they both knew he just had. She had not yet consulted a lawyer, she had wanted to tell Andy first, but she knew that she could not divorce him without grounds to do so. And she had none against him. Her hands were tied, unless he agreed. "You have to listen to me," she pleaded with him. "You don't want me like this." She was sobbing, and his eyes were hard.

"We're married, Kate. That's the end of it. You'll feel better about it in a while, and you'll thank me for this one day. You were about to make a terrible mistake, and I'm not going to let that happen to us. I can't. Now, I'm going to shower and take a nap. Would you like to go out to dinner with me tonight?" When she looked up at him, her eyes were bleak. She didn't want to go anywhere with him. She didn't want to be married to him. She was his prisoner now. Not his wife.

She never answered him about dinner, and he didn't wait to hear her response. He left the room and closed the bedroom door. He was shaking when he walked into the bathroom and locked the door, but Kate didn't know that. For the first time in the years she'd known him, she hated him. All she wanted was to be with Joe, but she couldn't leave her son. Andy knew he had her by the throat. She would never abandon Reed. And if Andy would not agree to divorce her, she was trapped.

When she heard him turn on the shower, she called Joe. He was in a meeting, but she asked Hazel to get him out, and a moment later, he was on the phone.

"What's up? Was it very bad?" He sounded worried. He'd been thinking about her all day, wondering how it had gone when she told Andy she was leaving him.

"Worse than that. He won't even listen to me. He won't give me a divorce. And if he doesn't, I can't take Reed."

"He's just bluffing you, Kate. He's scared. Just hold firm."

"You don't understand. I've never seen him like this. He says the matter is closed. It's done. He wouldn't even let me talk about it." She hadn't even had the chance to tell him about Joe, which had seemed fair and she thought would convince him. But he wouldn't let her speak, and Kate felt as though he had surrounded himself with a wall of stone.

"Then take the baby and walk out," Joe said, sounding stern. She felt trapped between the two men, like their pawn. "He can't force you to stay there."

"He can force me to come back with Reed, if he takes me to court." She sounded scared, and she was. The way Andy had looked at her, she knew she had good reason to be. Andy did not intend to lose her or his son.

"He won't. The two of you can stay with me." It would be an even bigger scandal than it was, if she did. She knew she had to get Andy to agree with her, to let her out. It was the only way she could go.

"I'll talk to him tonight," she said. He went back to his meeting, and she hung up as Andy got out of the shower. She called a sitter and agreed to go to dinner with him that night, but the atmosphere between them was extremely unpleasant when she did. He was icy with her and his tone was hard. He wanted her to know that he meant everything he'd said. She was hoping to convince him over dinner, but she got nowhere.

"Andy, please, listen to me. . . . I can't do this. You don't want to be married to me like this." She was pleading with him. And in order to win him over, it suddenly seemed like the wrong time to tell him it was Joe.

"Kate, when I left, everything was fine. It was great. It's going to be great again. Trust me on this. You're hysterical, you don't know what you're doing, and I'm not going to let you destroy our life." He was ice cold and firm, and she felt as though he had a grip on her throat. She could barely speak.

"Things have changed. You've been gone for four months." She felt desperate as she tried to explain it to him. And she had an eerie sense that he knew what had happened and with whom. But he didn't seem to care. No matter what Kate did or said, Andy would not let her go. He didn't want to know who or why. He wanted to hear none of it, and they spoke not a word to each other as they went home in a cab.

Kate felt almost as though she had lost her strength to move or walk or speak to him.

She got a sitter and went to Joe's office the next day. She was panic-stricken, and Joe was visibly upset. But she needed support and direction from him. It was as though Andy had grown into someone she didn't even know while he was in Germany. He was immovable and invincible. And she sat talking to Joe in tears.

"He can't just keep you there, Kate. You're not a child, for Heaven's sake. Pack your bags and get out."

"And leave my son?"

"You can go back for him afterward. Take Andy to court, for chrissake."

"And say what? That I cheated on him? I have no grounds for divorce. And he'll say that I abandoned my son. I'll never get Reed back again. They'll say I'm an unfit mother for having an affair with you and leaving my son. Joe, I can't leave." Not unless Andy agreed.

"Are you telling me you're going to stay married to him?"

"What else can I do?" Her eyes looked like two dark blue pools of pain. "I have no choice. For right now anyway. Maybe he'll give in eventually, but right now he's refusing to be reasonable. He won't even let me talk about it."

"Kate, this is insane." She knew it was. But Andy had been very clever about it, and he was fighting like a tiger to keep her, whether she wanted to be there or not. She had to admire him for that. But however much she admired Andy, it was Joe she loved. He came around his desk and put his arms around her while she sobbed uncontrollably.

"I never should have left you three years ago," she cried. Now she was trapped, and she realized that Andy would never let her out. She had lost her chance to be with Joe. And she wouldn't give up her son, even for him.

"I didn't give you much choice. I was a damn fool to let you walk out on me three years ago, and tell you you'd never be as important as my planes." He still remembered the speech he'd made. Three years later, he knew how wrong he'd been, but for the moment at least, it appeared to be too late. "Do you want me to talk to him, Kate? That might put the fear of God into him. What about buying him off?" It was a crass idea, but Joe was willing to do whatever would work, but Kate shook her head.

"He doesn't need your money, Joe. He has his own. This isn't about money. It's about love."

"Owning someone isn't love, Kate. That's all he's got. He owns you right now because of your son. It's the only hold on you he's got." But it was a powerful one. He had checked it out with an attorney that day. If she left the boy, she ran the risk of losing him. And if she took him, Andy could force her to bring Reed back, unless she kidnapped him and disappeared. But that was impossible for either of them. She could hardly go into hiding as Joe's wife.

"I'm trapped, Joe. I can't get out," she said miserably. She had felt so sorry for Andy for the past four months, and now he was squeezing the life out of them. He had their future in his hands and he was turning it to dust.

"Just wait awhile. You can't live like this forever. You're too young, and so is he. He'll give up eventually. He's got to want something more than this in his life." He was fighting for his family, his wife, his son, and he wasn't willing to give any of it up, nor lose Kate.

Joe kissed her before she left, and she went home. And when Andy came home that night, she tried to talk to him again, to no avail. He lost his temper this time, and threw a porcelain candy dish at the wall. It had been a wedding gift from one of her friends and it smashed to smithereens, while Kate cried. She had expected Andy to be hurt but reasonable. She had never expected him to do any of this. There was no way out.

"Why are you doing this to me?" she sobbed, as he sat down across from her with a look of despair.

"I'm doing it to protect our family, since you won't," he said, looking distraught. "Years from now, you'll be grateful I did." But in the meantime, it was a nightmarish time.

And what Kate did not know, or even suspect, was that Andy had instantly surmised it was Joe. It was written all over her face. He remembered too well their college days when she had been deeply in love with him, and waiting for letters from him. It was the same look Andy had seen in her eyes when Kate told him Joe was not dead, and ended their relationship. He knew that look well. There was only one man in the world who could make Kate look and feel that way. And he knew he was seeing it again and precisely who had walked back into her life again. He didn't need to hear the words.

He was so certain of it that he didn't even bother to call Joe. He just showed up in his office the day after Kate had been there to tell Joe all her tales of despair. Andy strode right into Joe's office building, and asked his secretary to announce him. She looked more than a little stunned when she asked if Andy had an appointment, and he said no, but assured her that Joe would see him, and then he sat down to wait.

He was right. Less than two minutes later, the secretary led him into a staggeringly impressive office full of the art and treasures and memorabilia Joe had collected since the advent of his success. Joe did not rise to greet him, but sat watching him like an animal being stalked, from behind his desk. They had only met once years before. But they each knew who the other was, and why Andy was there.

"Hello, Joe," Andy said calmly. His cool demeanor was a better hand of poker than he had ever played in his life. Joe was taller, older, smarter, more successful, and Kate had been in love with him for most of her adult life. He would have been an awesome opponent for any man. But Andy knew he had the winning hand, and for once Joe did not. Andy had their son. And Kate.

"This is an interesting move, Andy," Joe said with a lazy smile. Neither of them showed what they felt. Both were angry, both felt ill used and put upon. Each would have liked to kill the other, and instead Joe waved Andy to a chair. "Can I offer you a drink?" Andy hesitated for a fraction of a second and then asked for scotch. He rarely if ever drank before dinnertime, but he knew that in this case it might help to steel his nerves. Joe poured it over the rocks himself and handed it to Andy before he sat down again. "Do I need to ask what brings you here?"

"I assume not. We both know. Not a very elegant move on your part, I might add," Andy said bravely, and tried to pretend he didn't feel like a boy in Joe's office. In other circumstances, he would have liked to look around. The view was extraordinary and took in all of New York, with both rivers, and Central Park. "She's married now, Joe. We have a child. She's not going anywhere this time."

"You won't win her this way, Andy. You can't force a woman to love you by holding her hostage. Why don't you just chain her to the wall? It's not as subtle but it works just as well." Joe was not afraid of him, he didn't even hate him. He was an important man, and knew he had nothing to fear. He could have bought and sold Andy a thousand times, and to Joe that meant a lot. It was something he couldn't even have contemplated once upon a time. But those times had come and gone. Joe was on top of the world, and Kate was his, whether Andy held the key to her jail cell or not. He had never owned her heart as Joe did, or even at all, in Joe's eyes. She felt sorry for him, she pitied him, she had never loved him as she did Joe. She and Andy had never shared what they did, and never would. And as Joe looked at him, he pitied him. "Why are we here, Andy? Let's get to the point. What is it you want?" He still could not believe that Andy would refuse to let her go in the end, and felt certain that, with enough pressure from Joe and Kate, he would cave in. But he had no idea, nor had Kate till now, what a ruthless and determined fighter Andy could be. This time, he did not intend to lose, whatever it took.

"I want you to understand who she is, and what it is you're chasing after with such passion. I don't think you know what you're lusting after, Joe." Joe was amused at the choice of words, and smiled from behind his desk, as Andy took a swig of the scotch.

"You think I don't know her after ten years? I don't want to shock you, but I'm sure Kate told you we lived together for two years."

"As a matter of fact, she did, although it's somewhat indelicate of you to put it that way. I believe she was living at a hotel at the time."

"If that's what she said," Joe said noncommittally, but Kate had told Andy the truth. He just didn't like hearing it from Joe.

"And what were your conclusions after 'living' with her? I gather that you weren't anxious to marry her then. Why now?"

"Because I was a fool, as all three of us know. I was building my business, I had a lot on my mind. I didn't feel ready to take on a wife. That was three years ago. I didn't have time for her then. I do now."

"Was that the only reason you didn't marry her? Or were there things about her that worried you, Joe? Was she too needy, too demanding, did you feel trapped? Did you want to run?" Kate had told him all of it when she and Andy met again, but Joe couldn't know that as he listened to him. He felt a vaguely familiar sense of what it had been like then, and they weren't pleasant memories for him. He had felt everything that Andy had described. It wasn't that Kate he wanted, it was the one she had become now. The one who appeared to understand what had gone wrong. "She's the same woman, Joe. She looks panicked every time I leave the house. She calls me everywhere I go. If I go out to lunch, she has my secretary track me down. When she was pregnant, she nearly drove me insane. I had to go home to see her in the middle of the day. Is that what you want? Is that the kind of time you have available, Joe? You must be a very successful man indeed to have that kind of time on your hands. You'll have to be with her night and day. How will you take her with you when you travel? She won't leave Reed. And she wants to get pregnant again. She wants more babies. And she'll get them with whatever ruse she has to use to see to it that that happens. I know Kate. She did it to me with Reed. I didn't mind. You will." They were lies, all of them, but Kate had long since given him a map of all of Joe's terrors, and Andy was systematically playing each one of them. And he was winning. He could see it in Joe's eyes, although he felt some obligation to defend Kate. But he was scared. Andy could sense his terror heavy in the air.

"She's not in love with you," Joe said firmly. "She'll be different when she's with me." But he didn't sound quite as sure.

"Really?" Andy asked, as he finished his scotch. "How different was she in New Jersey?" He knew all about the fights that had brought them down, her panic over feeling abandoned, his terror of being engulfed. Kate had explained it all, in retrospect, to him. And Andy was using it all now. For a good cause, he thought.

"That was three years ago. She was a kid then," but he no longer sounded quite as convinced. He wouldn't have admitted it to anyone, but he was beginning to wonder if Andy was right. He could feel a feather of terror tracing its way down his spine. Just listening to Andy describe her painted a picture of everything he didn't want, no matter how much in love with her he was.

"She's still a kid," Andy said smugly, longing for another scotch, but he wouldn't have dared. The one had been just right to give him courage. But he didn't want to get sloppy now. He could see the worry in Joe's eyes. His demons had been reborn. "She'll always be a kid, Joe. You know what happened to her as a child. So do I."

For once, Joe looked surprised. He was the better fighter of the pair, but this time Andy had him on the ropes. He was the small speedy devil who was going to bring down the champion, and he could already taste the prize. He didn't care what he had to do to keep her, but he wasn't going to lose her to Joe this time. No matter what. And he knew that if he played it right, Joe would never even tell her he'd been there. It was the perfect crime, and the only way to keep from losing her. He had to make Joe want to run.

"Did she tell you about her father?" Joe asked. There was a trace of hurt in his voice. Kate had never admitted it to him in ten years. All he knew he had heard from Clarke, that day in Cape Cod. But once again, Andy didn't hesitate to lie to him. She hadn't told Andy either, and he had learned it from Clarke too, shortly before they were married.

"She told me when we were in college. I've always known. We were good friends." Joe nodded, and said nothing. "Do you know what that must have been like for her? How terrified she is of losing the people she loves? She couldn't survive without us. She couldn't live through a day on her own. She is the most dependent woman I've ever met, and you know it too. Do you realize that she wrote to me twice a day while I was in Europe?" Even that was a lie. She had written him hastily scribbled notes that only mentioned their son. Andy had suspected that something was wrong then, but there was nothing he could do about it from Europe. He had had to wait till he got home. "Do you have any idea how desperately insecure she is? How frightened? How unbalanced? I don't suppose she told you she tried to commit suicide after she left you in New Jersey." As he said the words, Andy knew he had hit his mark. Kate had told him when they first met again how consumed by guilt Joe had been, how painful that had been for him. "Intolerable" was the word she used. And at what Andy had just said, Joe looked like he had just dropped to his knees.

"She *what*?" He was stunned.

"I didn't think she'd tell you. It was on Christmas, I think. We hadn't met again yet. She was in the hospital for a long time." Andy was shameless. But he was a desperate man. And he was convinced that if he could get Kate away from Joe this time, she would be his for the rest of his life. But he didn't know his wife. The only way to have wrested Joe from her would have been to kill her or him. Anything less wouldn't have worked. She loved Joe that much.

"I can't believe that." Joe looked appalled, and Andy looked sad. "A mental hospital?" This time Andy nodded, seemingly unable to speak he was so chagrined. But the poisoned dart he had aimed at Joe had done its job. The venom was coursing through Joe's veins. The very thought of her committing suicide because of him was more than he could bear. It terrified him and would have made him not only the bad little boy he had been accused of being as a child, but a truly evil man as an adult. And a hidden fragile part of him could not allow him to risk that, just as Andy had hoped.

"What are you going to do about her wanting more children? She told me only yesterday she wants two more." Andy continued to hone in with blow after lethal blow.

"Yesterday?" Joe looked shocked. "I think you must have misunderstood. I've been very clear about that."

"So has Kate. She's a lot like her mother, in a far subtler way." Andy also knew from Kate how much Joe had hated Liz. "And we haven't spoken about the most important issue to me, my son. Are you really prepared to bring him up, to play baseball with him, to sit up with him at night when he has an earache or a nightmare or he throws up? Somehow, I don't see you doing that." Andy was letting it all sink in. And Joe looked visibly sick. He and Kate had discussed none of those things. Or at least he thought they had. She had said she would be content with only one child, and would have a nurse for him so she could travel with Joe from time to time. But Andy was painting a far more vivid picture than she ever had. Particularly of Kate. The knowledge that she had attempted suicide when she felt abandoned by him three years before nearly drove him insane. It was guilt of the purest kind, and highly toxic to him. "So where are we now, Joe? I don't want to lose my wife, or my son's mother. I don't want her feeling abandoned when you travel and perhaps trying something foolish again. She's very fragile, far more so than she looks. It's in her family. Her father committed suicide after all. She could easily follow in his footsteps one day." It was an evil trick to play on Kate, and such a cruel one. She had no idea what Andy was doing to her, in Joe's eyes, or to Joe. Andy was playing all Joe's worst fears like keys on a piano, and Joe was so anxious he could hardly speak. All he wanted to do was run, and all he could remember was Clarke describing her as a bird with a broken wing. Joe had no way of knowing that Kate had never even contemplated suicide, and no matter how unhappy she'd been over him, it had been the farthest thing from her mind. But Andy's ploy had accomplished just what he had wanted it to. No matter how much he loved her, Joe realized again now that marrying her was not a responsibility he could undertake. He had known that before. And Andy had convinced him with a few brief brushstrokes that he'd been right. He was gone.

"So where are we now?" Andy asked innocently, in the guise of talking man to man. But what he had done was not worthy of any man. It was something Joe would never, ever have done, to her, or anyone else. But his own fears were so rampant, he couldn't see Andy's ploy for what it was. The act of a desperate man. He took it as truth. And he wanted to cry as he sat at his desk.

"I think you're right. I think no matter how hard I try, the way I live my life, and have to with my work, will cause her irreparable damage.

Imagine if she killed herself while I was on a trip." He couldn't even bear thinking about it, the very idea made him feel sick, and overwhelmed.

"I think she could," Andy said thoughtfully, as though weighing the possibility, as he met Joe's eyes. And all he could see in Joe's eyes was fear.

"I can't do that to her. At least you can keep an eye on her. Weren't you afraid to leave her when you went to Europe for four months?" Joe asked, looking puzzled for a moment, but Andy was quick to explain.

"My parents promised to keep an eye on her, and hers of course. And she sees her psychiatrist twice a week."

"Psychiatrist?" Joe looked shocked again. "She sees a psychiatrist?"

Andy nodded. "I gather she didn't tell you that either. It's one of those dark secrets she keeps."

"She seems to have a lot of them." But he could see why. In his eyes, it wasn't something to be proud of, nor was her father's suicide. Her secrecy about that had set the stage for everything else Andy chose to say. Kate had never seen a psychiatrist in her life, as he knew full well, nor attempted suicide, nor chased after him when he went to work. Nor had he ever come home to her in the middle of the day. It was all lies. But it had worked. "I don't know what to say to her," Joe said with a look of despair. He loved her, and she him, but he believed now that attempting to share his life with her would more than likely destroy her, or even kill her. It was a danger he was not willing to risk. And a guilt he could never have borne.

All Joe wanted now was to get Andy out of his office, and to be alone. He had never felt as unhappy in his life, not even when she left New Jersey. This was far, far worse. He had been so sure he was going to marry Kate, and that in time Andy would step aside. But he could see now that it was better for Kate if she stayed with him. It was safer for her, and best for their child. There really was no choice. And to signal that the battle was over, he stood up and looked dour as he shook Andy's hand.

"Thank you for coming here," Joe said somberly, "I think you did the right thing for Kate." He loved her too much to put her in jeopardy, and the fear of her committing suicide was too great a risk to take, not to mention the terrors Andy had awakened in him as well.

"So did you," Andy said, as Joe showed him to the door of his office, and Andy left. And as the door closed, Joe went to sit at his desk again, and stare at the view. All he could think of was Kate as tears rolled slowly down his cheeks. He had lost her again.

Kate never knew what had happened between Joe and Andy that day. She never even knew that they had met. Andy came home quietly that afternoon and said nothing to her. But there was an air of victory about him that made her feel sick. Her jailer, who had once been her husband, was pleased with himself. And she hated him all the more. Any hint of love had vanished between them, and for her at least was forever gone.

Two days later, Joe asked her to lunch. They met at a small dark restaurant where they had gone to lunch before, and neither of them touched their food. He told her simply that he had thought about it, and knew that he could not drag her out of her marriage, at the risk of her losing her son. It was something he could not do. And listening to him, she could see the guilt in his eyes. He was in great pain. Far greater than she knew. All he'd been able to think of since seeing Andy was her attempted suicide three years before, and all because of him supposedly. It was more than he could stand. And so he was leaving her. It was an agonizing lunch for both of them, and afterward Kate cried all the way home in the cab. Joe had told her that they had to let each other go, had to forget each other. The pain had to end for both of them. He was afraid to say too much to her, for fear of driving her to suicide again.

And as she lay on her bed and cried after she got home, she knew she'd never see Joe again. She wished she were dead, but not enough so to take the matter into her own hands. The thought never even crossed her mind.

And Joe did what he knew best. He ran. He flew to California that night. And when Andy saw her when he came home from the office that afternoon, he knew that the deed was done. He had won, whatever the price.

18

THE ATMOSPHERE BETWEEN Andy and Kate was tense for months. They barely spoke to each other, she was obviously depressed, and she lost a shocking amount of weight. They hadn't made love with each other since he got home. She stayed as far away from Andy as she could. She talked to Joe from time to time. But just as he knew it would, the time and space between them began to force them apart, no matter how deeply they still felt for each other. Andy had executed his plan brilliantly. The fatal damage had been done. But Kate knew that no matter how long he kept her prisoner, he would never change what was in her heart. He lost her forever the moment he had forced her to stay with him, and blackmailed her with her son. She had stopped feeling anything, even sympathy for him. For Kate, it was over from that moment on. She hated him, and would have hated him more if she'd known what he'd said to Joe.

Things improved slightly after Reed's first birthday in March. Andy had been home from Germany for eight months by then, and it had been a very rough time.

Her parents had commented on it, but this time neither of them dared ask what was going on. Whatever it was that had happened to them, it had taken a tremendous toll.

They went to Cape Cod that summer, as they always did, and this time Kate and Andy slept in separate rooms. Andy could force Kate to stay married to him, but he couldn't force her to make love. Their life had become a nightmare, their marriage an empty shell. And Kate looked like a ghost as she walked around the house.

Kate stayed home from the barbecue that year, and when her parents came back, her father commented that Joe Allbright hadn't been there that year. As he said the words, Andy looked at Kate, and the look of hatred between them was so strong that Clarke was stunned. Her parents were in despair over what they'd seen after Kate and Andy went home.

Reed was walking by then, and when they got home, she called Joe, as she did from time to time, just to see how he was. Hazel said he was in California, doing test flights again, and Kate asked her to send him her love when he called. All she heard from him by then were cryptic postcards once in a while. They hadn't talked in a long time.

It was nearly Thanksgiving when Andy looked at her one night. The nightmare that their marriage had become had gone on for a year. "Is there any chance we could at least become friends again? I miss talking to you, Kate." They had lost everything between them when he had refused to let her out. He had won an empty victory, all that was left of Kate now was a shell. "Why don't we at least try to be friends?" But even as he said the words, he saw in her eyes that there was no hope. She was gone. He had been her enemy for too long.

"I don't know," she said to him honestly. In the past year, she had felt nothing for him. The only man she still cared about was Joe, and he was out of her life and back to his own, and his other love. His airplanes had become his passion again, and had always been. It was only for a brief time that he had finally understood he could have both. And now that she was gone, they were all he wanted, and all he had. There had been no other woman in his life.

They went to Andy's parents for the holidays that year, and after that, out of sheer loneliness, she at least began talking to him again. But that was all. She hadn't slept with him, or made love to him in eighteen months. She had moved into the second bedroom with Reed. They spent New Year's Eve with friends, and actually danced with each other, and Kate drank an inordinate amount of champagne. He actually heard her laugh that night, and she was so drunk she flirted with him on the way home. It was the most fun he'd had with her in a year and a half, and it almost reminded him of old times. He helped her out of her coat when they got home, and the strap of her dress slipped off her shoulder, and revealed parts of her he hadn't seen in far too long. He'd had a fair amount to drink himself, and suddenly found himself kissing her, and fondling her, and was amazed to feel her respond.

"Kate? . . ." He didn't want to take advantage of her when she was drunk, but the temptation was far too great, for both of them. They were married after all, and living a celibate life. She was twenty-eight years old, and he had turned thirty that month, and they had just spent one of the loneliest years of both their lives.

She followed him into the bedroom they no longer shared. She was still living in the bedroom next to his, and Reed was still sleeping in a crib next to her. He was twenty-one months old, and sound asleep when the sitter left that night.

"Would you like to sleep with me tonight, Kate?" Andy offered tentatively, and without a word, she took off her dress and slipped into his bed. He had no illusions that she was in love with him. They were two drowning people lost in a stormy sea, clutching at anything they could to survive. Each other, if all else failed.

Afterward, she hardly remembered making love to him that night. All she knew was that she'd woken up in his bed, and then scurried back to her own. When he woke up on New Year's Day, she was gone.

They both had fearsome hangovers and said very little that day. She was profoundly upset by what had happened the night before. She had vowed to herself fourteen months before that she would never sleep with him again. And she hadn't, until then. But she was so lonely, the champagne had unleashed a torrent of desire that had gone unquenched for too long.

They made no mention of it and went back to their separate solitude, and it was only at the end of January that she told him the news. She had been devastated when she found out. It was yet another bond to him, but she had long since given up hope of getting out. Andy had made it perfectly clear to her. He owned her for the rest of her life. And now, she was expecting another child.

He hoped it would bring them closer to each other, but it drove them even further apart. She was constantly sick, day and night. She took to her bed and stayed there most of the time. She was in bed all through the spring, and only got up briefly in the afternoons to take Reed to the park. Her illness was yet another way of shutting Andy out.

They dined in silence at night, and the only sounds in the apartment once Andy got home, were Reed's chatterings. Andy and Kate rarely spoke to each other anymore. And in June, Kate saw in the newspaper that Joe had gotten engaged. She called to congratulate him, and found he was in Paris. He never called her anymore. At twenty-nine, she felt as though her life was over. She was married to a man she felt nothing for, was having a child she didn't want, and had lost the only man she'd ever loved. The baby was due in September, and Kate didn't seem to care. The only joys in her life were her son, and her memories of Joe.

It was Andy who finally came to her, just before their second child was born. She was lying on her bed, reading late at night, Reed was in bed next to her, sound asleep. He had turned two in March, and was a beautiful, loving child. She looked up when she saw Andy come into the room. Looking at him now was like seeing a stranger. It was hard to imagine they'd ever been close or thought they were in love, or were even friends.

"How do you feel?" he asked, sitting next to her on the bed. It was the closest they'd been to each other in eight months. It was hard to believe it had been that way between them for almost two years. The only decent time they'd ever shared was their first year of marriage, before he left for Germany and Joe came back.

"I feel large," she smiled. Talking to him was like talking to a distant friend, someone you had met years before and hadn't seen in a long time.

"I thought you'd like to know. I'm moving out after the baby comes." He had made the decision weeks before, and rented an apartment that afternoon. He couldn't live that way anymore. Anything they'd ever shared or dreamed had long since died. And he knew now that he could no longer keep her like a bird in a cage. Her spirit had long since flown. The victory he had won over Joe was meaningless, he knew now. Kate had never been Andy's to lose. She was always Joe's.

"Why are you moving out?" she asked quietly, putting her book down.

"Why stay? You were right. It was a mistake. I'm sorry I got you pregnant on New Year's Eve. This complicates things for you."

"Destiny, I guess. That word again." It was the thing that made people come and go, or stay, or wish they could, and not make the right decision when they should. Chance. "The baby will be good for Reed," she said quietly. "Where are you going?" It was like asking a fellow traveler on a train, not a man she had once loved. She was no longer sure she ever had. Probably not. They had been better as friends. She had just been so heartbroken after she left Joe. But they had both paid a high price for what they'd done.

"I should have listened to you two years ago," he said. She nodded and said nothing. The two years he'd taken to agree to a divorce had cost her Joe. She wondered if he was married yet. The papers hadn't said, only that he'd gotten engaged several months before. And she had to respect that now. It was too late for them. And certainly for her, she felt. Andy had wasted her life, and destroyed her dreams. They belonged now to the woman who was going to marry Joe. And Kate had none.

"You were probably right to try," she said to Andy, trying to be fair. But she had been too much in love with Joe to even consider it. The marriage to Andy had ended the moment she saw Joe again.

"Go back to him, Kate," he said softly, looking like the friend he had once been as she watched his eyes. "I've never understood what you two had, or why, but whatever it is, it's powerful for both of you, you deserve to have it, if you want it that much." She had all but died when he left. There was nothing left. She felt dead inside. "Tell him you're free now. He has a right to know." Andy had spent two years feeling guilty over the lies he'd told Joe, particularly once he saw that Kate had closed all doors to him. But he had no idea how to undo the damage he had done to her, in Joe's eyes. And he didn't have the courage to tell Kate. But as much as she and Joe loved each other, or had, Andy suspected Joe would forgive her anything.

"He's engaged to someone else," she said with somber eyes.

"So what?" Andy smiled. "We were married when he came back. If he loves you, he'll want you now, no matter what."

"Is that how it works?" She smiled back at Andy for the first time in a long time. For two years, he had been her jailer and nothing more. Maybe now, in freeing her, they could at least be friends again. It was what he had hoped when he had decided to let her go. Even he wanted more. "It's too late for us." Andy knew she was talking about Joe. "Our timing is pretty grim. He's engaged."

"I remember when everyone thought he was dead, and you still believed he was alive. You've been dead for two years, Kate. You need a life again. All you've ever wanted was to be with him."

"I know," she said softly. "Crazy, isn't it? I always did. The first time I met him, I was hooked. It was the damnedest thing. Like some giant fishhook in my gut. We never seem to be able to cut the line."

"Then don't. Swim back to him. Do whatever you have to do, but follow your dream." He had, but the dream he had followed had belonged to someone else, and he knew it always would. She had always been Joe's and never his.

"Thank you," she said, and he bent down to kiss her cheek.

"Get some sleep," he said, and left her room.

She lay in bed thinking about Andy after he left her room that night. It was strange how little she felt, not sadness, not relief. She felt nothing at all, and hadn't for two years. She had been numb. She thought of what he'd said to her about Joe, and wondered if it was even possible anymore. Follow your dream . . . swim . . . fly . . . go to him . . . She smiled as she turned over and went to sleep. It was hard to believe that the dream would ever be hers. It had always been just out of reach. And it was again. He was engaged, or maybe even married by then. She felt she had no right to turn his life upside down again. Whatever he had now, he had a right to it. And it was odd to realize that in the end she had lost them both, Andy and Joe. Whatever Andy said now, out of guilt, she knew it was too late to call Joe. Her gift to him this time was to let him go.

Andy took her to the hospital when the baby came. It was a little girl this time. They named her Stephanie. And two weeks later, Andy moved out. It was surprisingly unemotional. Everything between them had been dead for so long that neither of them felt anything but relief.

Kate left for Reno with both children and a nurse when Stephanie was four weeks old. She stayed for six weeks, and came back on the train, divorced, on December 15th. She had been legally married to

Andy for three and a half years, and in reality only for one. She heard from a friend that Andy was going out with someone else by then, and supposedly madly in love. She hoped he was. They had both been lonely for long enough. She wished for him that he would marry again and have more kids. He deserved a lot better than she'd given him, although they both loved Stephanie and Reed. He was going to see them every Wednesday afternoon, and alternate weekends. It had all been so neatly and quietly done, as though it had never happened at all. Now that it was over, it seemed like a dream. Her parents mourned the marriage far more than either she or Andy did. They had never fully accepted or understood why it died.

A week after they got back from Reno, she took Reed to buy a Christmas tree, and she felt like herself for the first time in years. They sang Christmas carols as they walked along, and when they got to the lot on the corner, Reed picked an enormous Christmas tree. She was telling the men where to deliver it, as Reed jumped up and down clapping his hands, when she saw someone get out of a car with his head down in the cold. It had just started to snow. He was wearing a hat and a dark coat, and she knew it was him even before he turned around, and as soon as he did, he saw her. It was Joe. He stopped and then smiled at her. They hadn't talked on the phone in months, or seen each other in two years.

As he walked toward her, she smiled in spite of herself. Destiny. There he was. Just seeing him reminded her of the magic they had always shared. Their paths crossed and then disappeared again, separately, and then suddenly there he would be. At the barbecue, on the ship, at the ball when she was seventeen. It had been twelve years since then. And just seeing him brought back the dream.

"Hello, Kate." He had come to buy a Christmas tree. She didn't even know where he was anymore. California, New York. Somewhere else. She hadn't called or written to him. They had put each other through enough two years before. It was done, she had told herself. If nothing else, she owed him peace. But some power or force had intervened, and brought him back to cross her path yet again.

"Hello, Joe." She smiled at him. It was so good to see him in spite of everything. He looked the same. And her heart ached at the sight of him.

"How's your life these days?" There was a lot he wanted to know, but it seemed awkward to ask with a lot of people milling around, and Reed standing next to her. He was old enough to understand what they said.

Kate laughed, remembering Andy's words before he left. Tell him. Call him. Find him. He had found her. She decided to jump in. "I'm divorced."

"When did that happen?" He looked startled, but pleased.

"We got back from Reno last week. I took the kids with me."

"Kids?" he seemed surprised.

"Stephanie. She's three months old. I got drunk last New Year's Eve." It was a lot of information to share over a Christmas tree, after two years, and Joe looked amused. "What about you?"

"I got drunk last New Year's Eve too, but I don't have anything to show for it. I got engaged in June. Things are a little rocky these days. She hates my planes."

"That won't work," Kate said sensibly. She was basking in the pleasure of just looking at him. They both knew, just standing there, that nothing had changed. It was still there for both of them. Just the way it had been since the first day. What they had shared had been infinitely rare, and still was.

"Will we work, Kate?" he asked, as he moved closer to her. They had already put each other through a lot of pain. Maybe it was too late for them, there was always that possibility. Or the chance that they'd get lucky this time if they tried, if they dared. Maybe one day they'd have to be brave enough to take the chance, and do it right. And as he looked at her, all the terrifying things Andy had said about her two years before no longer mattered to him.

"I don't know. What do you think?" She was game. But she didn't want to say it to him.

There had been so much water under the bridge, oceans of it. Wars, and the empire he'd built, her marriage, their affair two years before, and now her divorce. They had come together and apart so many times, in so many ways, and yet the bond was still there, the magic, the flame. They could both feel it as they stood looking at each other in the snow.

"Go home, Mommy," Reed said, tugging at her arm, he was getting impatient waiting around, and he didn't know who the man was.

"In a minute, sweetheart." Kate gently touched the child's cheek with her hand.

"What do you say?" Joe asked, looking at her intently with his blue eyes, as his hat got slowly covered with the falling snow.

"Now? You want to know *now*?" She stared at Joe in disbelief.

"We've waited twelve years, Kate," he said calmly. It seemed long enough to him.

"Yes, we have. If I had to give you an answer right now, I'd say we give it a try." After she said it, Kate held her breath, not sure what he would think or say, or if her willingness would frighten him and make him run away. But he wasn't going anywhere this time. He looked down at her and stood firm.

"I'd say you're right. We're probably crazy. God knows if this would ever work. Our timing has been rotten so far, but maybe this is our time." It had never been before. They were always wanting something different from each other than the other could provide at that moment. It was as though the fates had conspired to keep them apart.

And now suddenly there they were. And with any luck at all, maybe this was finally the right time, for both of them.

"What about your fiancée?" Kate looked concerned. Andy had ended it for them two years before, maybe now she would. Or someone else.

"Give me an hour. I'll tell her the design has been canceled, she failed the test flight." He smiled at Kate.

"What about kids?" She was curious about that in case she wanted more. It was a crazy conversation, but so typical of them. They were like lightning flashing through the sky, lighting up each other's worlds.

"You have two kids, I think. Do we have to settle all this right now? I didn't even know I was going to run into you. Is there a chance I'll ever see you again, so we can discuss the rest?" He was laughing at her. And she could see in his eyes that he was happy and no longer afraid. Or at least not then.

"That could be arranged." She was grinning at him. Life had a way of taking the strangest turns. When you least expected it, you walked right into your dreams, and found yourself where you no longer expected to be. It had been the story of their lives till then.

"Same address?" She nodded. "I'll call you tonight. Just don't get married, or go back to Andy, or run away. Sit tight for a couple of hours and try not to get into trouble, will you please?" he said, looking firmly at her.

"I'll try." All she could do was smile.

"Good." He came over and put his arms around her, as Reed stared up at them, still wondering who he was. "Welcome back, Kate." Her life had been a wasteland since they'd left each other, and his had mostly been filled with work and planes and recently a woman who got airsick in an elevator and hated flying with him, unlike Kate. Their lives had taken some very crazy turns, and some extremely unusual ones. There was the time he spent in Germany for nearly two years, and her marriage to Andy, and the last two lonely years before he finally let her go. It was hard to believe that their time had finally come. Neither of them was entirely sure it had, but it looked like it. And suddenly there didn't seem to be a moment to waste. He wasn't going to wait another twelve years to work it out. He wasn't going to let her get away this time, or run away himself. "I'll call you in two hours, and I'll come by tonight. There's something I have to do first." Kate had already figured out what that was. He had an engagement to break. And for once, Kate didn't care what it took for him to come back. She just wanted him. They had climbed Everest to find each other again, and she wasn't going to share the prize with anyone. Joe was hers. She had earned the right to be with him fair and square.

He called her two hours later, and came by at eight o'clock that night after the children were asleep. They were so hungry for each other that they didn't waste any words. They closed her bedroom door and nearly devoured each other. They were like starving people, and they had been for far too long. It had taken them forever to get here, but they were safe at last. Or they hoped they were. It was impossible to know. But at least they had to try. There were no guarantees, there were only dreams, and as they fell asleep in each other's arms that night, they each knew they were where they wanted to be, and always had.

Joe played with Reed the next morning, while she fed the baby, and then they decorated the tree. He spent Christmas with them, and two days later, he and Kate went to City Hall. They went alone, hand in hand, with no friends and no witnesses, and no false hopes. And they called her parents when they got home. The suddenness of it came as a shock to them, but it was not a total surprise. Her mother reminded her father that she had finally lost a bet to him, over Joe marrying Kate. She had been convinced he never would.

"I never thought I'd see this day," Liz said in amazement as they hung up the phone. And neither did Kate and Joe. It had taken so long, on an endlessly curvy road.

"Happy?" Joe asked her, as she cuddled up next to him in bed that night.

"Totally," she said, with a broad smile. She was Mrs. Joe Allbright at last.

He lay looking at her for a long time that night after she fell asleep. Everything about her had always fascinated him, and now she was finally his. He didn't see how it could go wrong. It seemed like the perfect combination to him. He had always been her passion, and she was his dream. Her happy ending had come. And theirs.

19

THE FIRST DAYS OF Joe and Kate's marriage were blissful and exactly what they'd each expected them to be. They were happy and busy. She had hired a nurse to help take care of the kids, so she could have plenty of free time with him. She visited him at the office, gave him advice on some of his projects. She flew with him on weekends, and when he came home at night, he played with the kids. She went to California with him in January, and was enormously impressed by his entire operation there. She even went to Nevada with him, and watched him do his test flights, and afterward, he took her up for a spin. She loved all the wild and crazy things he did. And best of all, he was hers.

"It's a good thing I didn't marry Mary," he said with a grin after a particularly dicey flight over the desert. He had dazzled Kate with a series of loops and stalls. She had always loved doing that with him. She said it was better than a roller coaster, and nothing he did, no matter how scary, ever made her airsick. She loved flying with him, no matter what he did, although she didn't fly herself anymore. It had been too long.

"She probably cooks better than I do," Kate said cheerfully as she got out of the cockpit with him, and he had mentioned his ex-fiancée.

"That's for sure. She'd have thrown up all over me after that flight."

She had flatly refused to go up in a plane with him, and didn't even like hearing about what he did. He had known even then that getting engaged to her had been foolish, but he'd been bored and lonely when Kate stayed with Andy, and he wanted to prove to himself that he could have a life with someone else. But the only woman he'd ever really loved was Kate.

In his opinion, Kate had saved him from a fate worse than death, if he'd ever gone through with it, which he'd begun to doubt anyway. Kate was perfect for him, in every way. She loved flying, loved him, loved his planes. And she put something in his life that, without her, was never there. She was full of mischief and childlike spirit and fun. She trusted him and loved him. She was serious when he wanted her to be, and smarter than any woman he'd ever known, and most men. She loved him more than life itself, and he loved her. They had it all. And they made a couple so striking and so handsome that wherever they went, people stopped to stare. Everyone knew who he was, and his quiet, powerful style was the perfect counterpoint to her wit, charm, and poise.

She and her children moved into his apartment a month after they got married, and she brought her dog. There was enough room for all of them, and even the nurse for the kids. And little by little, she added pretty things to his apartment and feminine touches, which made it more livable for all of them. They were even talking about buying a house.

They talked about a lot of things. Nothing was sacred now to either of them. He had even brought up her "attempted suicide" one day. It had haunted him ever since Andy had told him about it two years before. And Joe told her how sorry he was. Kate had looked blank as she listened to him.

"What are you talking about?" She looked mystified by what he had just said.

"It's all right, Kate. I know," Joe said quietly. But he didn't tell her how. He had never told her that Andy had come to see him that day. He didn't think she needed to know.

"You know what?" Kate asked, still sounding confused, and Joe thought she was being coy.

"That you tried to kill yourself, after we broke up years ago." He had nearly forgiven himself for it, but not quite. He was still trying to make it up to her. He had felt guilty about it for the past two years.

"Are you nuts? I was out of my mind over you, but I wasn't totally insane. What on earth made you think I tried to kill myself?" The way she looked at him suddenly made him pause.

"Are you telling me you never tried to commit suicide, Kate?" She wasn't sure if he was angry or relieved, and neither was he.

"That's exactly what I'm telling you. That's the most disgusting thing I ever heard. How could you even think I would do something like that? I love you, Joe. But I've never been out of my mind. That's a terrible thing to do," as she knew only too well. But there was a thunderous look on Joe's face as he looked pointedly at her.

"Did you ever see a psychiatrist?"

"No," she looked startled. "Do you think I should?"

"That sonofabitch!" he said, exploding out of the chair where he'd been sitting, and suddenly pacing around the room in what looked to Kate like a rage.

"What are you talking about?" He was making no sense to her, but it all made perfect sense to him now.

"I'm talking about that rotten little bastard you were married to. I don't even know how to tell you what he did, or what a fool I was." He felt even guiltier now for believing him. But he understood perfectly what Andy had done, and why. He had played right into every one of Joe's old fears. And Joe felt sick thinking about how he had taken the bait and the line. It had cost them both another two years of wasted time.

"Are you saying that Andy told you I tried to kill myself?" She stared at Joe in disbelief. "And you believed him?" She looked amazed as well as hurt.

"I think we were all a little crazy then. It was right after you told him you wanted a divorce, and he was refusing to let you go. You came to the office to tell me he wouldn't agree to the divorce, and the next day, he showed up. And I hate to admit it to you, but he played me like a harp. He told me how desperate and insecure you were, and how unstable, that you'd tried to kill yourself when we broke up before, and he got me so panicked that I was afraid I'd drive you to it again if I ever did anything wrong or hurt you again. He told me you were seeing a psychiatrist several times a week, and I started to think that if you felt abandoned at any point, you might do it again. I wasn't willing to take the risk." And he had also been terrified of everything Andy had described to him, including her terrors of being left, and wanting more kids.

"Why didn't you ask me?" Kate stared at him in utter astonishment at everything he'd just said.

"I didn't want to upset you more than you were, and push you over the edge. But I see what he did now, that bastard. He played me perfectly. He knew how guilty I'd feel thinking you had tried to kill yourself over me once before, and how panicked I'd be that you might do it again." She could see it all now too, and it made her hate Andy more than she ever had before. He had used everything she'd ever said to him to manipulate Joe. It had been an incredibly cruel thing to do, although she knew Andy had been fighting for his life then, and trying to preserve their family. But it was Andy who had driven Joe away. It was something she knew she'd never forgive him for. He had nearly cost her her happiness with Joe. It was a miracle that they had found each other again. "He made it sound so real, all of it. I was too upset myself at that point to question it, or be suspicious of him. What he was describing was something I knew I couldn't take on. I felt guilty for months after that, just thinking about it."

"How could he do a thing like that?" And then as she thought about it, she realized that there was more that he must have said, which might have given added credibility to the lies he told. It was the one thing she had never told Joe, and she wondered now if he knew. She sat very still as she looked up at him, and all she could see was the love in his eyes. "Did he tell you about my father too?" She hated talking about it, and never had before. But there was nothing she couldn't say to Joe. She knew she was safe with him.

"Clarke told me about that before I asked you to marry me in Cape Cod. He thought I should know," Joe said gently as he took her hand in his own, and pulled her close to him. "I'm sorry, Kate. That must have been awful for you."

"It was," she said, with tears in her eyes. "I remember that day so perfectly. . . . I remember everything about it. . . . The funny thing is I don't remember much about him. I should, but I just don't. I was eight when he died, but he pulled away from everyone two years before that." She looked sad as she spoke of it. It had been the greatest trauma in her life, other than losing Joe. "It must have been so awful for my mother too, but she never talks about him. Sometimes I wish she would. There's so little I know about him, except that Clarke says he was a nice man."

"I'm sure he was." He could see in her eyes how painful it still was for her. It was the root and core of all her fears, fears of loss and grief and abandonment. Unwittingly, her father had caused her so much pain. But she was happy and at peace with Joe. She had found a safe harbor at last.

"I'm glad you know," she said quietly. It was the only secret she had ever kept from him.

And that night, when they went to bed, they talked about Andy's betrayal of them both again. It was horrifying to Kate, worse yet to think that Joe had believed what he'd said, and in using Joe's guilts and frailties so brilliantly, Andy had succeeded in driving him away. They both agreed that it had been despicable of him, but an ingenious plan. Kate hadn't thought him capable of anything so devious, and it told her a great deal about him. She wanted to take some time to think about it, but she knew she would confront him about it one day. In the end, even after having used every ruse he could, he had lost her anyway. In spite of that, in the end, she had found her way back to Joe, and she was grateful for the kindness of the fates every day.

During the spring, Joe started spending more time in California. He needed a bigger base for his airline out there. By summer, he was spending half the month in L.A., and he wanted her with him. She took both children and the sitter, and they lived at the Beverly Hills Hotel. She enjoyed it a lot at first, she went shopping, played with the kids, and hung out at the pool watching movie stars come and go. Joe was constantly at the office, and came back to the hotel after midnight most nights and left again at six the next day. He was trying to spread his operation into the Pacific, and he wanted to establish new routes where they had never been before. It was an enormous undertaking, establishing numerous bases overseas, and planning all the logistics for an airline emerging as one of the most important in the world.

By September he was spending a lot of time in Hong Kong and Japan. They both agreed it was too far for her to go, and she hated leaving the kids for weeks on end. And it didn't make sense for her to sit in a hotel and wait for him in L.A. So she spent her time waiting for him in New York. He called her every night, no matter where he was, and filled her in on what he was doing. And from what she could see, he was doing a million things at once. Running New York, reaching out in the Orient, designing planes, running an airline, and doing test flights himself whenever he could. Understandably, he was crazed, and even when he called Kate, he sounded tense. In spite of competent people in all the various arms of his organization, he acted like he was a one-man band. And he complained constantly that he didn't have enough time to fly his planes. Or see his wife.

When he came back in early October, he hadn't been home in four weeks, and Kate pointed out that she never saw him anymore.

"What am I supposed to do, Kate? I can't be in fourteen places at once." He had been in Tokyo for two weeks, making deals and setting up routes, Hong Kong for a week, battling with the British, and L.A. for five days. And one of his best test pilots had crashed just before he left, for no apparent reason, in a plane Joe had previously cleared himself. He had gone to Reno for the night, to inspect the wreckage and see his widow, and by the time he got back to New York, he was half dead.

"Why can't you try to run things from here?" Kate said sensibly. But it was more complicated than that.

"How can I do that?" he asked in exasperation, his temper was short these days. He was always tired, always running, always on a plane to somewhere. And Kate was bored at home, and felt more anxious when he was away. His lengthy absences were beginning to wear on her. She knew Joe loved her, but she was lonely when he was gone. "How the hell do you expect me to sit in an office here, when I have employees halfway around the world? Why don't you do something to keep busy? Do Red Cross work again or something. Play with the kids." He was too tired to deal with it, and most of the time brushed her off. And when he was traveling, he was irritable and his temper was short. But from Kate's perspective, she was thirty years old, had a husband she was crazy about, and spent most of her time alone.

She went to dinner parties without him, spent weekends with the children, went to sleep alone at night, and had to explain to people who wanted to see them that her husband wouldn't be there. All of New York wanted to invite them, the Allbrights were much in demand, he had become the most important man in aviation in eight short years, and he was only forty-two years old. He had achieved what he had totally on his own, and he was not only admired for his skill as a pilot, but for his genius in business. Everything Joe touched turned to gold. But the money he was making didn't keep Kate warm at night. She missed Joe, more than she had in a long time. And for her, his absences stirred up old ghosts. But Joe was too busy to see the signs. All he observed was that she complained about his absences the moment he got home, which made him withdraw, and in turn made Kate even worse. She needed him, and he was hard to find.

"Why don't you come with me? You'd love it," he suggested to her. She hadn't been to Tokyo in years, since she'd gone with her parents as a young girl. And Joe had taken her to Hong Kong. "You can go shopping or go to museums or temples or something," he said, trying to come up with a compromise that would work for both of them. But they both knew that even if she went, she wouldn't see much of him. He worked constantly while he was away, just as he did at home.

"I can't leave the kids for weeks at a time, Joe. They're one and three years old."

"Bring them," he said curtly.

"To Tokyo?" she asked in horror.

"They have kids in Japan, Kate. I swear. I saw one once. Trust me." But she thought it was too far for them to go. And what if they got sick while they were there? She couldn't talk to the doctor, and what point was there in all of them sitting in a hotel room waiting to see Joe? It made more sense for them to wait for him at home.

He was in Europe for Thanksgiving, and she went to her parents' with the kids. He called from London and spoke to Clarke and Liz. Her father wanted to know all about what he was doing. And her mother made a comment about it to Kate that night, which unnerved her more than she wanted to admit.

"Is he *ever* home, Kate?" Even now, her mother didn't approve of him. She had always suspected that he broke up Kate's marriage to Andy, and she blamed him for it, more than Kate. She thought it had been a terrible thing to do. And even though he had married her, he was never around.

"He's not home much, Mom. But he's building something amazing. In a year or two, it'll settle down." Kate was, in fact, sure it would.

"How do you know? In the old days, it was his planes. Now it's his business, and his planes. When does he get to you?" In hours and days between trips, Kate thought silently, when he was too tired to even talk to her, or too exhausted to sleep, so he'd go to the office at four A.M. By Thanksgiving, they hadn't made love in two months, he was just too tired to even think about it in the few days he was at home. He wanted to, he wanted all of it, to be with her, to have sensual nights and lazy mornings, but there was no time anymore. He had a thousand forces pulling at him. "You'd better take a good look at what you've got, Kate. You've got a guy who's never going to be there for you, no matter what. He can't. And what do you think he's really doing on those trips, Kate? He's got to have a woman sometime, he's a man." The very idea of it cut through Kate like a knife, and she always told herself it wasn't true. She had thought about it herself, but rejected the idea. Joe wasn't that kind of man, he never had been. He was driven by his passion for flying and obsessed by his work. He was building a fortune and an empire, which was as addictive for Joe as a drug. She was almost certain that in the year they'd been married, he had never cheated on her. And she would never have done it to him.

But the rest of what her mother said hit its mark. He was never around. Whatever the reasons, however good, he wasn't there. And when he got home, there were papers and problems, and threats from the unions. He was on the phone to California and Europe and Tokyo and the White House, or Charles Lindbergh. It was always someone or something that ate his time and seemed more important than Kate. She had to stand in line with everyone else, and most of the time, she got last place. That was just the way it worked. And if she wanted a life with him, which she did without question, it was what she'd get. He couldn't slice off more pieces of himself than he already had, and he expected her to understand. And most of the time she did. She loved him, and admired his success. She was happy for him. It was exciting, and he was amazing. But sometimes it hurt anyway. She was lonelier for him than he understood. And although she tried to reason with herself, at times she felt abandoned when he was gone.

She tried to explain it to him calmly one afternoon when he was home. It was the week after Thanksgiving, and he was watching football on TV. He had come home early that morning, and hadn't slept at all the night before. And he was just staring at the television set, drinking a beer and relaxing. It was a rare treat for him.

"Christ, Kate, don't start on that again. I just got home. I know I've been gone for three weeks, and I missed Thanksgiving with your parents, but the Brits were about to cancel my routes." He looked beat. And he was in desperate need of some time to relax, without pressure from her.

"Can't someone else negotiate with them once in a while?" He was becoming an egomaniac, he had to do it all himself. But he had built the business, and the truth was he did it better than anyone else. When he went in and handled things, they turned out right. That was just the way it was. He didn't want to risk having someone else destroy what he'd built.

"Kate, this is who I am. If you want someone to sit at your feet all the time, get another dog." He slammed his beer down on the table, and it spilled all over the floor. Kate made no move to clean it up, as he

glared at her. She was on the verge of tears. She wanted him to understand what she was saying to him, but he didn't want to hear.

"Joe, can't you understand? I want to be with you. I love you. I get
it. I know what you have to do. But this is hard for me." Harder than
he understood. But the more she tried to reach out to him, the more
he pulled away. She was making him feel guilty again. His nemesis.
The one thing he couldn't stand, from her, or anyone else.

"Why? Why can't you just accept the fact that I'm doing something
important with my life? I'm not just doing it for me, I'm doing it for
you. I love what I'm building. The world needs it." He was right, but
she needed him too. "I don't want to come home to you bugging me
all the time. It's not fair. At least enjoy it when I'm here."

In his own way, he was begging her not to reproach him. It hurt too
much. But she couldn't understand that, any more than he could understand how abandoned she felt. The vicious cycle of their early years
had begun again.

There was no arguing with him, no way to balance what he was ac-
complishing in business, and the pressures on him, with what she
wanted from him. One of them had to back down, and Kate knew it
had to be her. It was just a fact of their life, but it was killing her, particularly when she thought he was withdrawing from her. That only
panicked her more.

In December, he was there even less. He had gone back to Hong
Kong to meet with bankers there, and they were giving him a tough
time. And she knew he still had to stop in California on the way home.
There were problems at the plant, and the engine for one of his latest
designs had failed. There had been yet another death, and he took the
blame. He was sure that this time, it was an error of design. But he had
sworn to her that, no matter what happened, he would be home on
Christmas Eve. And she was counting on him. He had promised that,
come hell or high water, he would be home that day. He had even told

her that he would skip the trip to California, if he had to, and go back after the holidays. The last thing she'd heard was that he'd be home on Christmas Eve.

The phone rang in the morning while she was decorating the tree with Reed. He was squealing with excitement, and she was humming to herself when the phone rang. She had talked to Hazel, Joe's secretary, after breakfast, and she hadn't had confirmation, but she was sure Joe was on the flight back. He had told her it was what he planned to do, when she spoke to him the day before. And he had said as much to Kate.

She answered the phone, and it was Joe. She could hear immediately that it was long distance. The operator put through the call, and she could hardly hear him. He was shouting into the phone.

"What? Where are you?" She shouted back.

"I'm still in Japan." She could hardly hear his voice, but her heart sank at the words.

"Why?"

"I missed my flight." There was static and interference on the line, but she could hear him a little more clearly as she tried not to cry. "Meetings . . . had to go to more meetings . . . very difficult situation here. . . ." There were tears in her eyes and she knew she had to say something, but there was a long pause. "I'm sorry, baby . . . be home in a few days. . . . Kate? . . . Kate? . . . Are you there? Can you hear me?"

"I can hear you," she said, as she wiped her eyes. "I miss you. . . . When are you coming back?"

"Maybe two days." Which probably meant three or four or five. It was always longer than he said, through no fault of his. He was trying to do too much.

"I'll see you when you get back," she said, trying not to sound upset. She knew how much he hated that. And at this distance, there was no point arguing about it. It wouldn't change anything. She didn't want to badger him, or drive him even further away. She wanted so much to be a good wife to Joe, whatever that entailed.

"Merry Christmas . . . kiss the kids. . . ." His voice was fading out.

"I love you!" she shouted back into the phone, hoping he could hear her. "Merry Christmas! . . . I love you, Joe!" But he was gone. They had lost the line. And as Reed watched her standing next to the Christmas tree, she sat in her chair and cried.

"Don't be sad, Mommy." He came and got on her lap and she held him. She wasn't angry, she was bitterly disappointed. She knew it probably wasn't his fault, but it was painful anyway. He wouldn't be there for Christmas, and then she forced herself to remember what it had been like when he'd been shot down. She thought he was dead. Now at least she knew he was coming back. She set Reed back on his feet, and went to blow her nose. There was nothing she could do about it. They'd just have to make the best of it, and celebrate Christmas with him when he came home. She was determined not to let him know how upset she was.

Christmas was quiet without Joe. She and the children opened their presents. Her parents had sent her hers, and there were a few from friends. She suspected correctly that Joe probably hadn't had time to shop. But it didn't matter anyway. All she wanted was him.

Andy came to pick Reed up on Christmas Day and take him to his place for a few hours, and he looked serious when he appeared at the door. She had just heard he was getting married, and she was happy for him. She hoped that this time he made the right choice. She hadn't been for him. And even if things weren't easy with Joe, she thought it was better being married to someone you really loved, problems and all.

"Hello, Kate," Andy said, standing in the doorway awkwardly. They had been civil to each other since the divorce, but never close. And

Kate had finally confronted him about his lies to Joe about her, and he had apologized and admitted that it had been a rotten thing to do. He was deeply embarrassed about it, and had been for a long time.

Kate knew he still visited her parents, whenever he was in Boston, but she didn't mind. He was her children's father after all, and her parents had always liked him. And they felt sorry for him after the divorce. Her mother was the one who'd told her Andy was getting married. He had been seeing the girl for a year, which seemed reasonable to Kate.

"Merry Christmas," Kate said, and invited him to come in, but he hesitated, and she added politely, "It's okay. Joe's not here. He's away."

"On Christmas?" He looked shocked, as he stepped into the front hall of the apartment that had been Joe's before he married Kate. "I'm sorry, Kate. That must be hard for you."

"It's not great, but he couldn't help it. He got stuck in Japan." She tried to make it sound more tolerable than it was.

"He's a busy man," he said, as Reed appeared and gave a whoop, and Stephanie toddled behind him, but she was going to stay home with her mom.

"I hear you're getting married," she said when Reed went to get his coat. She didn't know if Andy had told him yet, the child hadn't said anything.

"Not till June. I'm taking my time." They both smiled, he didn't want to say "So I don't make another mistake," but Kate knew that was on his mind, and should have been.

"I hope you'll be happy. You deserve it," she said as Reed reappeared with coat and cap and mittens on, and took his father's hand.

"So do you. Merry Christmas, Kate," he said as they left. He was bringing Reed back at eight o'clock. And she and Stephanie went to play in her room.

It had been a lonely holiday for Kate. She tried to call Joe at his hotel, but she couldn't get through. And he probably had the same problem, or was stuck in meetings, because he didn't call her. And all she could do was tell herself that it didn't matter. They'd have Christmas together next year. Sometimes things worked out that way, and she knew she had to be grown up about it. But she almost cried when her parents called, and then assured them she was fine.

She didn't hear from Joe for another two days. He called to tell her he was leaving Tokyo the next day, and stopping in L.A. on the way home.

"I thought you said you'd go later," she said, trying not to whine. But he was always changing plans, and disappointing her. And her tone of voice conveyed to him how she felt about it, even when her words did not.

"I can't. I have to go now. The unions are acting up. Besides, it's not right, Kate. There's a widow out there who lost her husband because of one of my planes. I think I at least owe it to her to stop and make a condolence call. That's the least I can do." Kate didn't disagree with him, he always had good reasons, but she had to fight herself not to scream "What about me?" She always seemed to be the last priority on his list, and yet she understood how much he had to do. But he had just missed Christmas with her, and she wanted him to come home.

"When are you coming home?" she asked in a tired voice.

"I'll be home for New Year's Eve." Maybe. If nothing else happened to stall him in L.A. She was no longer counting on him. They were scheduled to go out for dinner and dancing that night with friends, and she'd been looking forward to it. But if he didn't come home in time, she'd stay home with the kids. She didn't want to be a fifth wheel on New Year's Eve.

As it turned out, he flew back on December 31, and it started to snow in New York before he left L.A. The weather was almost totally socked in by the time he got to New York, and their arrival was delayed. He walked into the apartment at nine o'clock that night, looking beyond exhausted. He had flown the company plane himself. He didn't trust anyone else to bring him in in one piece in conditions like that. Kate was waiting for him, she had already taken off her dress, and was in bed with a book. She didn't even hear him come in, and suddenly he was standing in the room, looking at her sheepishly. But the look in his eyes instantly melted her heart. Joe was irresistible to her, and always had been.

"Do I still live here, Kate?" He knew the last few weeks had been rough on her.

"Could be," she said, grinning at him, as he came to sit down next to her. "You look pretty good."

"I'm so sorry, baby. I screwed up all your holidays. I really wanted to get home. I'm sorry I'm such a jerk. Do you want to go out?" She had a better idea, as she got up and closed the door to their bedroom. He had taken off his jacket and was loosening his tie, as she walked over to him, and started unbuttoning his shirt. "Should I get dressed?" He was willing to do anything she wanted, to make up to her for the time he'd missed.

"Nope," she said, unzipping his pants for him, and he grinned.

"This looks serious," he said, as he kissed her.

"It is . . . it's the price you have to pay for standing me up for Christmas." She was teasing him and laughing as she kissed him, and despite how tired he was, she managed to instantly arouse him.

"If you'd told me about this, I'd have come home a lot sooner," he whispered as he slipped into bed with her.

"It's here anytime you want it, Joe," she said as she kissed him in all the places he loved best, and he moaned softly.

"Next time, remind me . . . ," he said, as they abandoned themselves to each other. It was the perfect New Year's Eve.

20

By THE TIME KATE and Joe had been married a year, at the beginning of 1954, they had settled into a routine of his being away much of the time, and she was at home with the children. She started doing some charity work to keep occupied while he was gone. And Joe found another project for her that spring. He wanted to buy a house in California. He was spending so much time there these days, it made sense to him, and he thought that decorating it would keep Kate busy and amused.

They found a beautiful old mansion in Bel Air, hired a decorator, and as soon as Kate got busy on it, Joe started spending more time in Europe. He was establishing new routes to Italy and Spain, and when he wasn't in Rome or Madrid, he was in Paris or London. He still had to go to L.A. every month at least, but he was no longer spending as much time in Asia. And it was beginning to seem to Kate that wherever she was, he was on the opposite side of the world somewhere. No matter what they did, she was hardly ever with him.

She met him in London once or twice, joined him in Madrid and Rome, and they spent a fabulous week in Paris. But whenever she went, she felt guilty about leaving the children. His life was a constant rat race, traveling on planes, and hers was an eternal relay race between

Joe and her children. She was always feeling guilty about not being with one, when she was with the other. But at least she was enjoying decorating the house in California. It had become a joke with them, whenever she went out to work on it, he flew to Europe. And when he was in L.A., she was in New York with the kids.

The house was finally ready for them in September, and Joe loved it. It was comfortable and warm, and elegant, a home away from home for him whenever he was in California. And he told everyone what a great job Kate had done on it. He even encouraged her to do some decorating for friends in her spare time, but she didn't want to be tied to any projects. She wanted to be free to join him on his trips whenever she was able. He was gone so much that she wanted to do whatever she could to keep their marriage intact.

He was home for most of October that year, which was rare for him. But for once he had no fires to put out anywhere, things were calm, and he had a number of important meetings in New York and New Jersey. Kate loved having him at home every night, although she hated to admit to herself that she could see Joe was getting restless. He was flying a lot on weekends, and one Sunday, they even flew up to Boston to visit her parents. And on the way back he let her take the controls for a while, which was fun for her.

They were on their way home and he was back at the controls again when she broached a subject to him that she had wanted to discuss with him for a long time. Usually, he wasn't home long enough to warrant bringing up sensitive topics, but he was in such a good mood, and so happy with the plane he was flying, that Kate decided to brave it. She wanted another baby. His.

"Now?" He looked horrified.

"Well, don't crash the plane for Heaven's sake, while we talk about it."

"You already have two kids, Kate. And you're tied down as it is." Stephanie had just turned two, and Reed was four. Andy had remarried in June, and they were already expecting a baby. Reed was none too pleased about it.

"We've been married for a year and a half, Joe. It would be nice to have one of ours, wouldn't it?" The look on his face didn't suggest that he thought so. He had never been enthusiastic about kids, with the exception of Reed and Stevie. Reed thought Joe walked on water. And Joe was crazy about him.

"We don't need more kids, Kate. We have enough going on in our lives as it is."

"You've never had one," she said pleadingly. She had wanted his baby for more than ten years. It had been eleven and a half since she lost the one at Radcliffe.

"I don't need one," he said bluntly. "I've got Reed and Stevie."

"That's not the same thing," she said sadly. He didn't sound as though he was open to the subject at all.

"It is to me, Kate. I wouldn't love them more if they were my own kids." He had always been wonderful to them, which was what always made her think he'd be a terrific father. And she wanted another baby. To her, it seemed the normal outcome of how much she loved him. "Besides, I'm too old to have kids now, Kate. I'm forty-three years old. By the time they go to college, I'll be in my sixties."

"My father was older than you are when I was born. And Clarke is older than that. He's still pretty lively."

"He was never as busy as I am. My kids won't even know me." It was one of his rare admissions that he was seldom around. But this time it served his purpose. "Why don't you find something else to keep you busy?" It was more than just a matter of keeping busy, she really wanted to have their baby. But he looked annoyed that she'd even brought up the subject, and even more so when he saw that she was disappointed. "There's always something with you," he complained as they started to approach the airport. "Either you're bitching about my being gone, or now you want a baby. Can't you just be happy with the way things are? Why do you always need more, Kate? What's wrong with you?" He was busy landing the plane and she didn't want to argue with him, but she didn't like the way he said it. It was up to her to fit in and adjust to his needs, and seldom the reverse. What she wanted didn't seem to matter. He had gotten spoiled over the years, and some of it was her fault. He was home so rarely, and for so little time, that everything revolved around him when he was there. Between public adulation over his flying record, his heroism during the war, and his enormous success in business, all he ever heard was how remarkable he was, and Kate's was just one more voice added to the others.

But on the drive home from the airport, she was quiet. He knew why, and he refused to discuss it with her any further. He had told her for years that he didn't want children. There were enough children in the world, the baby boom had repopulated the world, and he didn't feel he needed to add to it. And when Reed threw his arms around Joe's neck when they got home, he looked over his head at Kate, as though to prove his point. They had two kids, they didn't need more. As far as he was concerned, it was the end of the conversation. For him, at least.

The subject didn't come up again, and he made a point of being home for the holidays that year. Kate had never let him forget the fact that he had missed Thanksgiving and Christmas with her the year before, so he arranged his entire schedule to accommodate her, and he thoroughly enjoyed it. They went to Christmas parties and a coming-out ball, took the kids ice-skating, and made snowmen in Central Park with the children. And he bought Kate an incredible diamond necklace with matching earrings for Christmas. They had been married for two years, and had never been happier in their lives. Their dreams had all come true. And when they danced on New Year's Eve, and kissed at midnight, Kate knew she had never been as happy in her life.

He was watching football on television the next day, while she took the decorations off the tree. Both kids were having naps, and despite a mild hangover from the night before, Joe was in good spirits. The holidays had been perfect. He was leaving in two days for a four-week trip to Europe, and in February, he was going back to Asia, but Kate had made her peace with it, and was going to meet him on his way back in California.

She brought him a sandwich while he watched the game, and she was laughing at something he said, when he suddenly saw an odd expression in her eyes, and she turned deathly pale. Just looking at her, he was frightened. He had never seen her look like that.

"Are you okay?" She was turning green as he watched her, and she was obviously sick.

"I'm fine." She sat down on the couch next to him, and caught her breath for a minute. She'd had food poisoning a few days before, and said she thought it had something to do with that. Her stomach was still queasy, and had been for days.

"Sit down for a few minutes. You've been running around all morning." She'd been up and down the ladder a dozen times taking ornaments off the tree, and chasing the children. The sitter was off on Sundays and holidays.

"I'm fine, honestly," she insisted a minute later, and stood up very quickly. She had a lot to do, and didn't want to waste time. And the moment she got up, he turned to look at her, as her eyes rolled slowly back in her head, and she slid to the floor at his feet. She had fainted.

He was on the floor next to her instantly, on his knees, checking her pulse, and listening to see if she was breathing. He had his face close to hers, as she opened her eyes slowly and moaned softly. She had no idea what had happened. One minute she was looking at him, and the next she was lying on the floor staring up at him. He looked frantic.

"Kate, what happened? What do you feel?" She was thirty-one years old, and suddenly looked like she was dying to him.

"I don't know," she looked scared and a little woozy. "I just got dizzy." The wife of one of Joe's pilots had just died of a brain tumor, and it was all he could think of as she got slowly to her feet.

"I'm taking you to the hospital. Now," he said, helping her back onto the couch. She didn't try to get up, she was glad to be lying down, although she was feeling a lot better.

"I'm sure it's nothing. We can't leave the kids anyway. I'll call the doctor."

"Just lie there," he told her. She did, and a little while later, she was asleep, while he watched her. He didn't want to tell her, but he was worried sick. In all the years he'd known her, she had never fainted. He was still sitting on the couch next to her when she woke up, and she looked much better. And over his protests, that night she cooked them all dinner, but he noticed that she ate very little. He made her promise that she would see the doctor in the morning, and he was already planning to call the head of Columbia-Presbyterian Hospital. He was an old friend and a flying buff, and Joe wanted to get the names of the best doctors in New York in case it turned out to be as serious as he feared it would be. But Kate seemed much more nonchalant about it than he did. He looked so upset that when they went to bed that night, she didn't have the heart to keep it from him any longer. She turned to him just as he was about to turn off the light, and kissed him. He was convinced she was dying, and he was fighting back tears as he held her close to him.

"Sweetheart, don't worry, I'm fine. . . . I didn't want you to be mad at me," particularly over the holidays. She had wanted to wait until January at least, but she knew she couldn't now. It wasn't fair to worry him.

"Why would I be mad at you? It's not your fault if you're sick, Kate," he said gently, as she lay back against the pillow.

"I'm not sick. . . . I'm pregnant." If she had hit him with a brick, it would have had less effect on him than what she just told him.

"You're *what*?" He looked dumbstruck.

"We're having a baby." She sounded very calm, and he could see easily that she was happy about it, although she'd been worried about his reaction to the news.

"How long have you known?" He felt thoroughly duped. She'd been keeping it from him.

"Since just before Christmas. The baby's due in August." It had happened before Thanksgiving.

"You tricked me!" he said, leaping out of bed in a fury. She had never seen him as angry, as she lay in bed and watched him storm around the room. He was throwing things on the floor, and slammed the door to her bathroom. It was the reaction she had feared, and not the one she had hoped for.

"I didn't trick you," she said softly.

"The hell you didn't. You said you were using something." She had used birth control for years, ever since the miscarriage at Radcliffe, except when she was married to Andy.

"I did use something, but it must have slipped. Joe, that happens."

"Why now? I told you when we talked about it a few months ago that I didn't want kids. You must have just gone right home that night and flushed your diaphragm down the toilet. Don't you care what I want?" He looked outraged and her lip was trembling. His needs were in sharp conflict with hers.

"Of course I do, it was an accident, Joe. I couldn't help it. Worse things could happen." But not in Joe's mind. She hadn't listened to him and he felt trapped suddenly.

"Not much. Dammit, Kate. Get rid of it. I don't want it."

"Joe, you don't mean that!" She looked shocked, he was having a total tantrum.

"I do. I'm not having a baby at my age. Have an abortion." He finally threw himself down on the bed, and glared at her. She was horrified by what he was saying.

"Joe, we're married . . . it's our baby . . . it's not going to change anything in our lives. I'll get a nurse and I can still travel with you."

"I don't care, I don't want it." He looked like a five-year-old running the world as he sat in bed, literally fuming at her.

"I'm not going to have an abortion," she said calmly. "I lost our baby once before. I'm not going to kill another." That had been eleven years before, but she still remembered every hideous second of it, and the grief she had felt over losing their baby. It had taken her months to recover.

"You're going to kill me, if you have this kid, Kate. And jeopardize our marriage. We have enough strain on us now, you're the one who says I'm never here. And now you're going to be whining constantly that I'm not home with our baby. Christ, if this was what you wanted, you should have married another guy, or stayed married to Andy. He seems to have a kid every time he looks at a woman." He and his wife were expecting their new baby shortly, but Kate was wounded by Joe's comment.

"I want to be married to you, Joe. I always did. This isn't fair. It wasn't my fault," and she really wanted it. But he was convinced that she had tricked him into having a baby, and nothing she could say would convince him otherwise.

He turned off the light and rolled over with his back to her a few minutes later, and he was gone when she woke up the next morning. She was feeling sick over his reaction to the news the night before, and even more so when she thought of him telling her to have an abortion. But apparently he meant it, because he brought it up again that night. He was grateful that she didn't have a terminal illness as he had feared at first when she fainted, but as far as he was concerned, this was the next worst thing to a brain tumor.

"I thought about what you said last night, Kate, about . . . you know, the pregnancy. . . ." He had trouble even calling it a baby. And he was staring at his plate when he talked to her. It was as though he didn't even want to see her. But for a minute, she thought he was going to relent and tell her he was sorry. "The more I thought about it today, the more I knew how wrong it is for us. I know it upsets you, Kate, but I really think you have to end it. It's the best thing for both of us, and the other children. It's going to be upsetting enough for them when Andy and his new wife have a kid, if we have a baby too, they're going to end up feeling like nobody loves them, and they'll wind up jealous and neurotic." It was the best argument he could come up with, and Kate almost laughed at him, except she was so upset by what he was saying. He still wanted her to have an abortion.

"Other kids seem to survive having siblings," she said sensibly. She was not going to let him sway her, but she also didn't want it to cost them their marriage. And she had never seen Joe as upset as he'd been the night before when she told him. He was calmer now, but no happier than he'd been at her announcement.

"Their parents aren't divorced, Kate."

"Joe . . . I'm not going to have an abortion." It was as clear as she could make it to him. "I won't. I love you. And I want to have our baby."

He didn't say a word to her, and he stayed in his study that night until he came to bed. And the next day he left for his four-week trip to

Europe. He didn't even say goodbye to her before he left. He just stormed out of the house.

It was a whole week this time before he called her, which was unusual for him. But he had been stewing while he was gone, and all she could do was leave him alone. He called her from Madrid, and he sounded businesslike and subdued. He asked how she was, and how the children were, and then he told her what he was doing. And after a few minutes, he told her he'd call her again sometime soon. In the end, he called her three times in four weeks. And she knew that when he came back, he was only going to be in New York for two days. After that, he was going to Hong Kong and Japan, and he wouldn't be back in New York for another three weeks. He was back in his rat race again.

He flew back to New York on the first of February, and the kids were already in bed when he got home. Kate was in the living room, watching television, and she looked up with a start when she heard him come in. It took him a few minutes to walk into the living room, and he approached her slowly when he did. He hadn't even called to tell her when he was arriving.

"How are you, Kate?" It was a cool greeting after a long four weeks and very little contact from him, and she assumed that he was still angry at her. It was beginning to remind her of the icy atmosphere between her and Andy after he had refused to give her a divorce, and she was suddenly afraid that Joe would end their marriage over the baby. It would have been a crazy thing to do, but she was beginning to wonder if he'd ever forgive her for what had happened, whether or not it was her fault.

"I'm fine. How are you?" she said cautiously, as he sat down in a chair across from her.

"Tired," he said. It had been a long flight.

"Did everything go okay?" She hadn't spoken to him in a week, and she was so happy to see him, she would have liked to throw her arms around his neck, but she didn't dare.

"More or less. What about you?" He glanced at her cryptically and she sighed. It was easy to guess what he wanted to know.

"I didn't have an abortion, if that's what you mean," she said, looking away from him. It was a battle of wills over one tiny life. It seemed a sad state of affairs to her. "I told you I wouldn't."

"I know," was all he could say, and then he walked across the room to sit next to her. He put an arm around her shoulders and pulled her close to him. "I don't know why you want this baby, Kate." He sounded exhausted and sad, but no longer angry at her, and she was relieved.

"Because I love you, you dope," she said in a choked voice, snuggling close to him. She had missed him so much, and been worried about how angry he was at her.

"I love you too. I think it's a dumb thing for us to do. But I guess if that's the way it is, I'll live with it. Just don't expect me to do diapers, or walk it around all night while it cries. I'm an old man, Kate, I need my sleep." He looked down at her with a lopsided smile, and she looked at him incredulously. She loved him so much, and even when he made a lot of noise, in the end he always did the right thing.

"You're not an old man, Joe."

"Yes, I am." He didn't tell her, but he had gone to sit in a church in Rome, to think about it. He wasn't a religious man, but when he'd come out, he had decided to let her have the baby, if it meant so much to her. "Just don't faint on me again. You damn near gave me a heart attack. Have you been feeling okay?" He looked concerned.

"I'm fine." She was so relieved that she didn't dare tell him that the doctor thought she was growing so fast that it might be twins. Joe had barely survived the idea of one baby, she couldn't bear to think what he'd say if he thought there were two.

They went to the kitchen after that, and she talked animatedly, telling him everything she'd done, who she'd seen, where she'd been.

He loved listening to her, even when he was tired. He loved her energy, the look in her eyes, and the way she looked, and most of all the way she made him feel. Somehow, even when he was tired, she brought excitement into his life. It was what had pulled him to her the first time he'd laid eyes on her, and held him ever since.

They sat at the kitchen table and talked for a long time, and when they finally went to bed, they were best friends again. He had missed her for the past month, just as she had missed him. He couldn't even begin to imagine what having a baby would be like. But if he was going to have one, he'd decided, it might as well be with her.

When they went to sleep that night, he put his arms around her. He loved feeling the silk of her skin next to him. And he was amazed, when he ran his hands lightly over her belly, he could feel a small round bump. She had her back to him so she couldn't see his face, but Joe smiled as he drifted off to sleep.

21

JOE WAS IN THE ORIENT and California for most of February, and Kate flew out to meet him in L.A. at the end of the month. He was in great spirits when he arrived, the trip had gone well and he'd accomplished great things. And when he saw Kate, he was surprised to see she'd gained weight.

"You've gotten fat," he teased.

"Thanks a lot." She was happy to see him, and all was well. Kate still didn't tell Joe that the doctor thought it might be twins.

Joe had never seen her during any of her pregnancies, and he was uneasy at times being with her. He was always worried that she'd faint again, didn't feel well, or might get hurt. He was so anxious about making love with her, that Kate laughed at him.

"It's okay, Joe, I'm fine." He didn't want her to drive, scolded her when she danced, and didn't think she should swim. "I'm not going to stay in bed for the next six months."

"You will if I tell you to." But in spite of his fears, they spent more time than usual making love. The trip to L.A. was like a honeymoon for them. In spite of the baby, or maybe because of it, he felt unusually close to her.

He spent two weeks in New York when they got back, and then he was off again. Kate was getting used to it, she kept busy with the kids and seeing friends. And the pregnancy gave her something to look forward to. She could hardly wait for the baby to come. It was due at the end of August, or possibly earlier, if it was twins. The doctor had warned her that she might have to go to bed for the last two months. But so far, despite her size, he hadn't heard two heartbeats, only one.

Andy's baby was born in March. Kate sent them a gift and a little note, congratulating them. He looked happy whenever he came to pick up the kids. It was as though the time they had spent together had never been. He just seemed like someone she had known a long time before. She remembered him best from the time they'd been friends. Their marriage was too painful to think about, for both of them.

Joe was in Paris in April when Andy called her late one Friday afternoon. He was supposed to pick Reed up and take him to their house in Connecticut for the weekend, but he was stuck at work. His wife was with the baby and they were both sick, and she couldn't come to town to pick him up.

"Maybe you could put him on the train, Kate. Julie can pick him up in Greenwich. I won't be home till late."

She didn't think it was a good idea, and Reed was disappointed not to go. He loved going to Greenwich to visit them. She called Andy back after she'd talked to their son, and offered to drive him out. It was only an hour's ride each way, the weather was warm, and with Joe gone, she had nothing else to do. She had no other plans.

"Are you sure? I hate to do that to you." She was five months pregnant, and she felt fine.

"It'll be fun. It'll give me something to do." Reed was excited when she told him. She left Stephanie with the sitter, they would be back too late for the little girl to go, and she and Reed took off for Greenwich at six o'clock. She told the sitter she'd be back by eight. It was midnight in Paris, and Joe had already called.

They hit a little traffic on the way out, but nothing unreasonable, and they arrived at Andy's house at seven-fifteen. Julie had the baby in her arms, she was colicky, and they both had colds. The baby looked just like Andy, and a little bit like Reed. She gave Reed a kiss when she left him with his stepmother. Julie offered her something to eat, but Kate wanted to get back, and they both laughed and agreed that she looked huge. She was getting more certain every day that it was twins. "Maybe it's a baby elephant," Kate laughed, and then got back in her car. She rolled down her window and put the radio on, it was a warm night, and she enjoyed the drive. She was back on the parkway at a quarter to eight. But at midnight, the sitter called the Greenwich house. Kate had never come home.

Julie answered when Kate's baby-sitter called, and she sounded concerned. The sitter thought at first that maybe Kate had decided to stop on the way and see friends. But by midnight, she had the uneasy feeling that something was wrong. And she decided to call the Scotts to see if Kate had been tired, and stayed with them. She didn't think she would, but it seemed worth a call. And Julie sounded surprised that Kate hadn't gotten home. She had no idea what Kate's plans had been. She hadn't stayed more than a few minutes after she dropped off Reed. Julie turned to Andy, who was half asleep, and asked if Kate had said anything to him, and he shook his head as he opened his eyes.

"She probably met friends for dinner in New York. She said Joe's away." And he knew she mostly went out on her own.

"She wasn't really dressed for it," Julie said. She'd been wearing a cotton skirt and a loose top, her hair was pulled back in a ponytail, and she'd had sandals on her feet.

"Maybe she went to a movie," Andy said as he went back to sleep. But Julie told the sitter to call again if Kate didn't come home. She'd always liked Kate, and had no ax to grind with her. She knew Kate had hurt Andy terribly, when she got involved with Joe again, but Andy was philosophical about it now that he had remarried. And Julie was grateful that Kate had let him go. She was blissfully happy with him.

The sitter called again the next morning at seven o'clock, and this time Andy was very concerned.

"That's not like her," he said to Julie as he hung up the phone. Reed was downstairs having breakfast, and he didn't want him to know. "I'll call the highway patrol and see if anything happened on the Merritt last night." She was a good driver, and there was no reason for her to have an accident, but you never knew.

He waited for what seemed like hours for the highway patrol to answer the phone, and he described Kate and her car. She used a Chevrolet station wagon to drive the kids around, and it was a good solid car. It seemed like forever before the patrolman came back on the line.

"We had a head-on at Norwalk last night, at eight-fifteen. A Chevrolet station wagon and a Buick sedan. The driver of the Buick was killed, the driver of the Chevy was unconscious when they got her out. Female driver, thirty-two years old, there's no description of her here. They took her to the hospital at ten o'clock. It took them two hours to get her out of the car." It was all he knew, but it was more than enough. Andy turned to Julie and told her what he'd heard. He was already dialing the number for the hospital the patrolman had given him. Andy's hands were shaking as he waited for them to answer the phone.

The nurse in the emergency room told him what she knew. Kate was there, she was unconscious, she was in critical condition. And the hospital hadn't been able to reach anyone when they called her home. They had called after midnight the night before, the sitter must have been asleep by then. Andy looked at Julie grimly when he hung up.

"She's in critical condition. She's got a head injury and a broken leg."

"What about the baby?" his wife whispered, feeling sorry for her.

"I don't know. They didn't say." He put his clothes on then, and told Julie he was going to the hospital, which seemed like a reasonable thing to do, as far as she was concerned.

"Shouldn't you call Joe?" Julie asked.

"Let's see what I find out first."

It took Andy half an hour to drive to the hospital where they'd taken her, and when he walked into her room, he was horrified by what he saw. There was a huge bandage on her head, a cast on her leg, and he saw as soon as he entered the room that the sheet across her stomach was flat. She didn't know it yet, but she'd lost the baby in the car. It brought tears to his eyes to see the condition she was in, and he walked over to her and gently took her hand. It brought back so many memories just looking at her. In their early days, there had been so many happy times. And the thought of the first year of their marriage always warmed his heart.

She was still in a coma when he left the room. And when he spoke to the doctor, he told Andy that they weren't sure yet if she'd survive. It was going to be touch and go for a while.

Andy sat in the waiting room for hours, and it reminded him of when Reed had been born and he'd been there all day, worrying about her. This was far worse, and as soon as he'd seen her, he called the baby-sitter in New York and told her she had to get hold of Joe.

"I don't know how, Mr. Scott," she said, bursting into tears. She'd been afraid that something awful had happened to Kate, and it had. She'd had a terrible feeling about it when she hadn't come home. But she hadn't heard the phone when it rang late that night. "Mrs. Allbright has the name of the hotel, I think, but I don't know where it is. He usually calls her. It's easier that way."

"Do you know what city he's in?" It was a hell of a way to live, Andy thought, with a husband who was always on the road. But he knew that Kate was willing to do anything she had to, to be married to Joe. She would have done anything and everything for him, and had.

"No, I don't," the sitter continued to cry. "Paris, I think. I think that's what she said. He called yesterday."

"Do you think he'll call today?"

"Maybe. He doesn't call every day. Sometimes he doesn't call for a few days." As Andy listened, he hated him, for what he wasn't doing for Kate. She deserved to have someone around to take care of her, not a traveling salesman running around the world, selling his airline and his planes.

Andy told the sitter what to tell Joe if he called, what condition Kate was in, and the hospital where she was. And he told her that no matter what, day or night, she was not to leave the phone. He couldn't even call Joe's office, because it was the weekend. If they didn't hear from him soon, Andy was afraid Kate would be dead by the time he called. He couldn't have done anything for her at this point, but it would have been nice for her if he'd been there, or if someone knew where he could be found.

"Is . . . is the baby all right?" the sitter asked cautiously, and there was a long pause.

"I don't know." He didn't think it was his place to tell her that it had died. He thought that Joe should know first.

And after he hung up, Andy called Kate's parents, who were frantic when they heard about the accident. Andy told them he'd keep them aware of any further developments, and they said they'd come down from Boston as soon as they could. And then he called Julie and asked her to drive into town with the kids and pick Stevie up, but to leave the sitter in the city in case Joe called.

"How is she?" Julie asked, feeling some strange bond to Kate.

"Pretty bad," Andy answered, and then went back to Kate's room again. He stayed until after six o'clock. He called New York, and Joe hadn't called.

He and Julie took turns calling the hospital through the night, and they said nothing to the kids. Reed sensed that something was going on, but he had been happy playing outside all afternoon, and his father had told him that his mother had gone away for the weekend. And the following week, he and Julie had agreed to keep him out of school and in Greenwich with them.

Kate didn't regain consciousness all through the weekend, and Joe never called. Her parents were there, looking devastated. Her situation didn't worsen, nor did it improve, she was just hanging there, in limbo, between life and death. From what Andy could see when he returned to the hospital on Sunday afternoon, she was hanging by the merest thread. And still there was no sign of Joe. Her mother cried every time someone mentioned his name.

Andy called Joe's office first thing the next day. He stayed home from work himself. Joe's secretary informed him that Mr. Allbright was en route from France to Spain, and she was sure she'd hear from him later in the day. He explained what the situation was, and Hazel was distraught. She said she would do everything she could to find him in the next few hours.

Andy didn't hear back from her until five o'clock. Joe had changed his plans and left a message in Madrid. No one had gotten hold of him, and she had missed him at the hotel in Paris when he checked out. She said she thought he was going to London, but she wasn't absolutely sure. She had left messages for him at every hotel in Europe where he stayed.

When they finally heard from Joe on Tuesday afternoon, he told Hazel that he had spent the weekend on a boat in the South of France. He had opted not to go to Spain, and taken a day off, which was rare for him. And there had been no way he could have called Kate. He had just gotten to London at midnight on Tuesday, and got Hazel's message at the hotel.

"What's wrong?" He had no idea how hard everyone had tried to locate him, and no suspicion that something had happened to Kate. He thought Hazel was frantic over some business problem that had come up, and he was in no great hurry to find out. He was relaxed and happy after the three-day sailing weekend, and he hated to spoil the mood he was in with bad news.

"It's your wife," Hazel went right to the point, and told him about Kate's accident. She explained that Kate was in critical condition in a hospital in Connecticut, and Andy Scott had called.

"What was she doing in Connecticut?" He hadn't absorbed what Hazel had told him yet. And the question he asked was absurd.

"I think she drove Reed out on Friday night. It happened on the way back and she was alone."

It was slowly dawning on him, as he listened to her. "I've got to get back," he said instantly, but they both knew that at that hour, it was too late for him to catch a plane, and he didn't have any of his own with him. He had been traveling on commercial flights, which was rare for him. "I'll do what I can. I don't think I can get back till tomorrow afternoon. Do you have the number of the hospital?" She gave it to him, and he immediately hung up and called. And after he hung up, he sat staring across the room. He couldn't believe what they had said. She was barely alive, and she'd lost the babies, the nurse explained. She told him Kate had been pregnant with twins. But all he could think of as he sat on the bed at Claridge's was what he would do if she died.

22

JOE WALKED INTO the Greenwich Hospital at six o'clock on Wednesday night. It had been five days since the accident. Kate was on a respirator, and being fed through a tube. She hadn't regained consciousness, although they thought the head injury had improved. The swelling was slightly down, and they thought it was a good sign. Her parents had gone back to their motel nearby to rest. And Andy Scott was standing next to her when Joe walked in. The two men exchanged a long look across her bed, and Joe could see in Andy's eyes everything he thought of him.

"How is she?" Joe asked, as he touched her hand. She was so pale, she looked as though she were dead to him, but Andy thought he'd seen a slight improvement in her late that afternoon. He hadn't been to work all week. He didn't feel right leaving Kate alone, and Julie had her hands full with the kids. The sitter had come out from New York to help once they'd heard from Joe.

"She's about the same," Andy said through clenched teeth.

Joe noticed her flat belly immediately, and it touched his heart, knowing what it would mean to her. He had even gotten more excited about the baby recently, or babies as it turned out, but they meant nothing to him now. All he cared about was Kate.

"Thank you for being here with her," Joe said politely to Andy, as Andy picked up his jacket and prepared to leave the room. There was a nurse sitting next to her, watching the two men. She wasn't clear about their relationship to Kate, but it was obvious that there was no love lost between them.

Andy stopped as he was about to leave the room and spoke in a low voice to Joe. "Where the hell were you, man? No one heard from you for four days." He had responsibilities and a pregnant wife, two stepchildren. Andy couldn't even conceive of disappearing for days on end like that. He wondered if he'd been cheating on her, but he didn't know Joe. That was the way he was. Kate had gotten used to it, but there were still times when it was hard on her. Joe reached out when he was ready to, and sometimes he didn't call for days. It was inconceivable to Andy that no one had known where Joe was. This was a perfect example of why he couldn't afford to disappear. Andy couldn't imagine doing anything like it to his wife and kids.

"I was on a boat," Joe said coolly. It seemed an adequate explanation to him. "I came as soon as I heard," but even he felt uncomfortable that she had been in the hospital for five days without him. He just didn't want to answer for it to Andy Scott. It was none of his business anymore, all she was to him was the mother of his kids. To Andy, that seemed enough. "Do her parents know?" Joe suddenly wondered. He hadn't even thought to ask Hazel when he called her.

"They're here," Andy explained. "They're staying in a motel."

"Thanks for your help," Joe said, dismissing him.

"Call if we can do anything," Andy said, and left the room, as Joe sat down next to her. The nurse stepped away and busied herself at the sink near the door so that Joe could have some time alone with his wife. And once Andy was gone, Joe looked at her with deeply troubled eyes. He couldn't even imagine losing Kate.

No matter how odd their relationship seemed to other people, he was deeply in love with her, and had been for fifteen years. She was his best friend, his comfort, his mentor, his laughter, his joy, his conscience sometimes, and always had been the love of his life, the only woman he had ever really loved.

"Kate, don't leave me . . . ," he whispered, as the nurse stood just outside the room. "Please, baby . . . come back. . . ." He sat there next to her for hours, holding her hand, with tears running down his cheeks.

A doctor came to check her bandages, and at midnight, they set a cot up for Joe. He had decided to spend the night. He didn't want to be at home in the city if she died. But he lay awake all night, and kept glancing at her. And miraculously, at four in the morning, she stirred. Joe had just started to drift off, but the moment he heard her moan, he sat up. The nurse was checking her eyes.

"What's happening?" he asked as the nurse took her vital signs. She had a stethoscope in her ears and couldn't hear what he'd said. And then, Kate moaned again, and with her eyes still closed, she turned her head toward him. It was as though even in the dark caverns of unconsciousness, she knew he was there. "Baby, it's me . . . I'm right here . . . open your eyes." But this time, she made no sound, and he went back to his cot. But he had a strange sense in the room, as though someone was watching him. It was as though he could feel her in his own skin, and he was terrified she would die. It made him realize how much he loved her, and he had always known how much she loved him. They just didn't always want the same things. She wanted to be with him, and he needed to roam the world with his planes. But he didn't love her any less because of it, his focus was just different than hers. And he thought she had accepted that. He didn't know why, but he felt guilty about the accident. He wouldn't have admitted it to anyone, but he thought he should have been there. He had had no sense that anything had happened to her, he had spent a wonderful three days on his friend's boat. He was British and they'd flown together in the war. He'd even thought about Kate a lot, and the baby they were going to have. In retrospect, he couldn't even imagine what it would have been like having twins. But that was beside the point.

Joe never went to sleep that night, and at six o'clock he got up and brushed his teeth and washed his face. He had just walked back to her bed to look at her, when she stirred slightly, and opened her eyes. She gazed right into his, and he could barely breathe he was so surprised.

"That's better," he smiled at her, feeling relief wash over him like a tidal wave. "Welcome back." She made a little noise that sounded like a sigh, and then closed her eyes again, and he could hardly wait for the nurse to come in so he could tell her Kate was awake. Before she ever came back into the room, Kate looked at him again, and made an enormous effort to speak to him. She didn't seem surprised to see him there.

"What happened . . ." Her voice was so faint he could hardly hear, but he bent close to her face so as not to miss the words.

"You had an accident," he whispered back, not sure why he did. He didn't want to overwhelm her by talking too loud.

"Is Reed okay?" She remembered being in the car with him, but not that it had happened on the way back.

"He's fine." He was praying that she wouldn't ask about the baby yet. He didn't want her to know it had died, or that it had been twins. "Just take it easy, sweetheart. I'm right here with you. You're going to be fine." He was praying she would.

She frowned as she looked at him, as though trying to understand what he'd said. "Why are you here? . . . You're away . . ."

"No, I'm not. I'm right here. I came back."

"Why?" She had no idea how badly injured she had been, which was just as well. And then instinctively, he saw her hand go to her middle section, he tried to stop her but she got there too soon. Her eyes opened wide and she looked at him, and before he could say anything, there were tears rolling down her cheeks.

"Kate, don't . . ." It was all he could say as he kissed her hand, and kept it to his lips. "Please, sweetheart . . ."

"Where's our baby?" She managed to choke out the words and then gave an animal sound, it was like a long keening wail, as she clung to him, and he reached down and held her in his arms. He was careful not to hurt her head. She knew instinctively what had happened, and there was nothing he could do to comfort her. He was just glad she was alive.

When the nurse came back, she brought the doctor in, and they were pleased to see she had regained consciousness, but the doctor told Joe in the hall she wasn't out of the woods yet. She had had a serious concussion and been in a coma for five days. Her leg was badly fractured, and she'd hemorrhaged when she lost the twins. He was anticipating a long recovery, and she would have to convalesce for several months. And he was concerned that she might not be able to get pregnant again. The damage in the accident had been considerable, and not just to the twins. But Joe felt that was the least of it, he was far more concerned about her. He didn't want more children anyway, particularly not if it was dangerous for Kate.

She was so upset when she realized she'd lost the twins that they sedated her, and Joe left for New York. He wanted to go to the office, and pick up some things at home, for both of them. He was back in Greenwich at five o'clock that afternoon. Her parents were just leaving her, and Elizabeth Jamison wouldn't even speak to him. There were tears in Clarke's eyes when he turned to Joe.

"You should have been here, Joe," was all he said, as they left the room, and Joe didn't argue the point. But he felt Clarke's words like a knife in his heart. He could understand how they felt. Although it all seemed a little unreasonable to him. It had been sheer bad luck that she'd gotten in an accident and lost the twins. He had a right to go on business trips, after all, although maybe not to disappear on a boat for three days, with a pregnant wife at home. But he had thought she was fine. And his being there wouldn't have changed anything, except that he might not have let her drive to Connecticut. But he couldn't protect her every hour of the day. The driver who had hit her had been drunk, the tests showed. It could have happened anywhere, anytime, even if he'd been driving the car. He was just an easy scapegoat now, he felt, because he'd been gone. But none of it had been his fault or in his control. He was her husband, not God.

By the end of the week, Joe had Kate transferred to a hospital in New York. It was easier for him to see her there, and he thought it might cheer her up to see her friends if they came to visit her, but she was so depressed, she refused to see anyone. She told him she wanted to die.

He spent the weekend at the hospital with her, and they talked to Reed on the phone, but afterward all she did was cry. She was in terrible shape. He wouldn't have admitted it to anyone, but he was relieved to fly to L.A. for three days the following week. He felt totally helpless with Kate. And this time, he called and checked in every few hours.

It was the end of April when she came home from the hospital. She was on crutches with a smaller cast, and her head was fine again. She only got headaches once in a while, and they took the cast off her leg in early May. She looked like herself again, and had lost a lot of weight. But the woman Joe came home to at night was not the one he had married. It was as though the bright light he had always seen shining from her soul had gone out. She was tired and depressed most of the time, refused to go out. And most of the time, she sat home and cried. Joe had no idea what to do for her, she hardly talked to him, seldom spoke, was completely disinterested in everything he said. Seeing her like that was driving him insane.

In June, the kids went to stay with Andy and Julie for a month, and it only made things worse when Kate heard Julie was already pregnant again. She knew by then that her babies had been twins, and all she did was mourn what she could no longer have.

"Maybe it's better this way, we're too old for more kids," Joe said awkwardly, trying to rationalize it to her. He didn't know what to say, but it only made her angry at him. "We'll have more time for each other, and you can travel with me more." But she didn't want to go anywhere with him. He offered to take her to Europe, or the West Coast. But Kate just sat around at home.

Joe tried with everything he knew for two months to cheer her up, and then he did what he knew best. He escaped. It was too hard being with her. She was constantly angry and depressed. It was as though she blamed him, just as everyone else did, for not being there, for the accident, and the lost twins. He couldn't take it anymore. The old demon guilt was nipping at his heels again. He took every trip he could, and he needed to, he'd been home with her for a long time, and his empire was starting to show signs of strain. By the time Joe hit the road again, his nerves were raw. And all they did was argue when he called home. It was like a nightmare that just wouldn't end. He didn't want it to be that way, but he no longer knew what to do, or how to find Kate. She was lost somewhere, and the woman she'd become only drove him away.

Joe traveled constantly for three months, and by the end of summer, they felt like strangers every time he came home. She went to Cape Cod with her parents and the kids, and this time he didn't come. He stayed in L.A. He was sure her mother had plenty to say about it, but he no longer cared. She'd been hateful to him for years. And he no longer felt he had to prove anything to her, or even to Kate. He'd come home, he'd been there, he'd done everything he could, and it was no longer ever enough.

He was home for two weeks in September, and hoped by then she'd be in better spirits again, but when he told her he had to go to Japan, Kate had a fit.

"Again? When are you ever here?" She was turning into a shrew, and was already more than halfway there. Joe was sorry he'd come home at all.

"I'm there when you need me, Kate. I stayed home for as long as I could. I have a business to run. You're welcome to go with me if you want." His voice sounded cold and withdrawn.

"I don't." She was restless and unhappy and argumentative, and it only made things worse between them. "When are you coming home?" she spat at him, and for the first time ever he could imagine hating her. He didn't want to, but she was giving him no other choice. Whoever she had once been seemed to be long gone. He knew she was upset about the twins, but she was killing him, and beginning to seem dead herself. And the worst part was that she wanted him desperately, needed him to make it better for her, but she was so lost in her own miseries, she didn't know how to reach out to him. Every time she wanted to, her own despair and the anger it produced only drove him away. They couldn't find each other anymore, and all she wanted was him. She had never stopped loving him, the person she really hated now was herself. She replayed it in her head a thousand times, driving the car, losing the twins, wondering why she had volunteered to drive Reed to Greenwich that night. If she hadn't, the babies would have been born by then. And now she would never have Joe's child. He had been firm with her that he didn't want to try again. She hated him for that too, and when she couldn't find the words to express her pain, she turned her fury on him. All Joe knew was he no longer had a wife. They were strangers and enemies living under the same roof. And he was rarely there.

In October, Joe was home for a total of four days. And the more he stayed away, the worse Kate got. His absences made her feel abandoned and desperate and betrayed, and only fueled her rage, and her mother goading her constantly didn't help. As far as Liz was concerned, Joe was using Kate, he just wanted her as a figurehead wife. Kate was even beginning to think he didn't love her anymore, and instead of loving him to bring him back again, all she did was slam the door in his face. After a while, he didn't approach her anymore. They hadn't made love since her accident, and by late October, it had been six months, and Joe had had enough.

"Kate, you're killing me," he tried to explain as gently as he could. He was only home for the weekend that time, and she correctly sensed that all he did now was run away. He couldn't stand the anger, the accusations, or the guilt anymore. "I can't come home to this every time. You have to get over it. I know it's painful for you, and it's terrible that you lost the twins, but I don't want to lose us." He hadn't seen the woman he loved in six months. All she had become was an angry ghost. "You have two great kids, why can't we just be happy with them? Why don't you come to L.A. with me? You haven't been out to the house in months." He was trying everything he could think of to pull her back.

"I don't want to go anywhere," she snapped at him, and this time he snapped back. He had tried to be patient with her, but it didn't get him anywhere, except angry and hurt.

"No, you don't, do you, Kate? You just want to sit here, feeling sorry for yourself. Well, for chrissake, Kate, goddamn grow up. I can't sit here holding your hand all the time. I can't bring those babies back, and who knows, maybe it was for the best, maybe we weren't meant to have more kids. It wasn't our decision, it was God's."

"That's what you wanted anyway, wasn't it? You wanted me to have an abortion so you didn't have to be bothered coming home more than ten minutes a month. Don't tell me how much you've done for me, or how lucky I am, or whose decision it was to let my babies die . . . don't tell me a goddamn thing, Joe, because you're never here anyway. It took you five goddamn days to come home when they thought I was going to die. So where the hell do you get off telling me to grow up? You're out there flying your damn planes and having a good time all over the goddamn world, while I sit here with my kids. Maybe you're the one who needs to grow up!" He looked like she had taken a blow-torch to him, and he said nothing to her. He walked out of the apartment and slammed the door, and stayed at the Plaza that night. And all she did was lie on her bed and sob. She had said everything she hadn't wanted to say to him. But she was so filled with misery and grief, and so lonely for him all the time. And all she had done was make it worse. She wanted him more than anything, wanted him to fix it for her, and she hated him because he could not. He couldn't bring her babies back, couldn't stay home with her, couldn't turn back the clock. She had wanted them so much, and still wanted him, and she knew she was do-ing everything she could to drive him away, and didn't know why. There was no one she could talk to about it. It was as though she had fallen into a black hole six months before, and couldn't find her way back up. And there was no one to rescue her. She knew she had to do it herself, but she had no idea how.

He came back to the apartment the next day, but only long enough to pack a bag and leave for L.A. And just seeing him pack panicked her. Joe seemed icy cold, and unnaturally controlled.

"I'll call you, Kate," he said quietly. He didn't know what else to say to her. He thought she hated him. And she didn't know how to tell him she hated herself. In spite of all the fire and debris she threw at him, he was still the one she loved. But it would have been hard to convince Joe of that. She had said such terrible things to him, and been so unkind to him that for the first time he was beginning to wonder if they would ever find each other again. And the guilt she had engen-dered in him only made him want to escape. Joe felt overwhelmed and he had never been as lonely or as miserable in his life.

He stayed in L.A. for a month, and ran the company from there. He even had Hazel fly out so he didn't have to go home. It was nearly Thanksgiving when he finally came back. He opened the door gingerly when he came home, and was startled when Reed flew into his arms.

"Joe! You're back!!" He was happy to see the boy. The children were one of the things he loved most about Kate, particularly these days, and he missed them when he stayed away.

"I missed you, ace," Joe said with a broad grin. And he had missed Kate too. A lot more than he'd expected to, which was why he'd come home. "Where's your mom?"

"She's out. She went to a movie with friends. She does that a lot." Reed was five, and he thought Joe was the best. He hated it when Joe was gone, and his mom cried all the time. She had for a long time. Stevie was only three, and asleep by the time Joe got home.

And when Kate came back from the movies, she was surprised to see Joe. She looked calmer than she had when he left, and he cautiously took her in his arms. He never knew when she was going to attack. They hardly ever spoke on the phone anymore when he was gone.

"I missed you," he said, and meant every word of it.

"Me too," she said as she clung to him and started to cry. She seemed better this time, as though she were slowly coming back from the terrible place she had been.

"I missed you before I left too," he said, and she knew what he meant.

"I don't know what happened to me. . . . I must have hit my head harder than I thought." She had been through a lot. The accident, losing the twins, it all seemed too much. And her mother was constantly whipping her up. He wished Kate would stop talking to her, but he knew it was something he couldn't ask.

She was much better this time, and they both finally began to relax. They agreed to stay home for the holidays, and not spend Thanksgiving with her parents in Boston this year. He thought it would be more than he could take, but he didn't say that to her. He just said he thought it would be good for them to stay home, and she agreed, which was a huge relief to him. But by sheer bad luck, three days before Thanksgiving he got a cable from Japan. Everything was in a mess there, and they insisted he had to come. It wasn't what he wanted to do, but for the sake of his future dealings with them, he knew he had to go. He hated to tell Kate.

And when he did, she looked shocked. "Can't you tell them it's Thanksgiving here? This is important, Joe." She was near tears when he explained it to her, and they were both trying not to get into a fight. Things had been better for a while.

"My business is important too, Kate," he said in a calm voice.

"I need you here this year, Joe. This is hard for me." She was still upset about the twins, although she was better than she'd been in months. "Don't leave me alone." It was the plea of an anguished child, a child who had lost her father to suicide, and a woman who had recently lost not one, but two babies that she had wanted so desperately. Joe knew he couldn't change any of that, and he expected Kate to be an adult.

"Do you want to come with me?" It was all he could think of at that point. But she shook her head.

"I can't leave the kids on Thanksgiving, Joe. What would they think?"

"That you need to take a trip with me. Send them to the Scotts'." But she didn't want to do that. She wanted to spend Thanksgiving at home with them, and with him. She tried everything she could to talk him out of going, and he kept explaining to her that he wanted to be with her, but he had to go. "I'll come home in a week. No matter what." But that didn't do it for her. She felt as though he was putting his business first again, and putting her last. She looked like a child as she sat in their bed crying the morning he left. "Kate, don't do this to me. I don't want to leave. I told you, I have no choice. It's not fair for

you to make me feel guilty over this. Make this work for both of us."
She nodded and blew her nose, and kissed him before he left. She
wanted to understand, but she was feeling abandoned anyway. Joe had
invited her to go with him, and he wanted her to, but she wouldn't.
She took the kids to Boston instead.

And in the end, he was gone for twice as long as he said. He came
home in two weeks instead of one. He didn't even stop in California on
the way home. But when he got back to New York, Kate was icy cold.
Her mother had worked hard on her in the two weeks that he'd been
gone. She seemed to have a huge investment in convincing Kate that
he was rotten to her and didn't give a damn. She had never forgiven
him for taking five days to come home when Kate had the accident
and lost the twins. And she had hated him long before that. She had
never approved of him from the first, because he hadn't married Kate,
and when he had it had cost her her marriage to Andy Scott, whom Liz
loved. It was as though she wanted to destroy what he and Kate had, at
all costs. And she was doing a good job of it. In two short weeks, she
had turned Kate around again, and they hardly spoke the night he
came home.

He didn't apologize to her, he didn't explain it again, he didn't defend himself for having been gone. He was tired of doing that, he had
been doing it for months. He played with the kids that night, and read
quietly when they went to bed. He wanted to give Kate time to calm
down and readjust. He knew that his comings and goings were hard
for her, and she needed time to warm up to him again sometimes, particularly if her mother had been talking to her a lot.

He told her about Japan when she came to bed, and acted as though
nothing was wrong. Sometimes that worked too, if he didn't react to
her. It was hard for him when he was tired after a long trip. But he tried
to be as patient as he could. He didn't want things to revert to the way
they had been for the six months before he left. Things had improved

for a while, and he wanted them to continue to head that way. But he could tell that he'd lost ground with her while he'd been gone. The holidays were a big deal to her and her family, and his not being there for Thanksgiving meant a lot, more than it did to him. To him, it meant a badly timed business trip. To her, it was a slap in the face, or worse, it meant that he didn't love her as much as she'd thought, or perhaps at all. Her mother had tried to convince her of that.

Things calmed down a little in the next few days, and he was home for more than two weeks. He and Kate went to buy a Christmas tree with Stevie and Reed, and decorated it. And for the first time, he saw Kate laugh and smile like the old days. Her spark had finally come back. It had been a tough year for them, particularly for her, but she was finally out of the woods, and he could see light up ahead. And it felt very good to him. It was about time. It had been a very hard time for him too.

Three days before Christmas, he got a call telling him he had to go to L.A. But he wasn't worried about it. He wasn't going to stay long, he only had to attend meetings for a day, and after that he'd fly home. He promised to be home on Christmas Eve. And even Kate didn't react this time. She was so used to his comings and goings. L.A. seemed like a short hop to both of them. She was relaxed and friendly when he left, and for once he didn't feel guilty about a trip. They even made love the morning he left.

Everything went fine in L.A. It was far less fine in New York. It had been snowing since he left, and one of the worst blizzards in history hit the city the morning of Christmas Eve. He was still confident they could land in it and he would be home on time, with any luck. And then they closed Idlewild, and canceled his flight minutes before they took off. The plane taxied back to the gate. There was nothing he could do. He was stuck.

He went back to the house and called Kate, and she understood.

Nothing was moving in New York. There were two feet of fresh snow in Central Park.

"It's okay, sweetheart. I understand," she said, much to his relief, and she did. Even Joe couldn't pull it off, and she didn't want him risking his life to get home. He would have had to land as far away as Chicago or Minneapolis and then take the train home. It didn't make sense. She promised to explain it to the kids. And they had a nice Christmas anyway. But when she thought about it afterward she realized that in three years of being married to him, he had missed two Christmases out of three. And when she explained to her parents on the phone on Christmas Day that Joe was stuck in L.A., her mother said, "Of course." It made it hard for Kate. She was always making excuses for him, explaining why he couldn't be there at times that were important to everyone else, and particularly to her. She wondered sometimes if he avoided their holidays intentionally, because Christmas and other holidays had been so depressing for him as a kid. But whatever the reason, she always felt hurt when he didn't make it home for some major event, no matter how good his intentions were or his efforts to be there. The only one who never seemed to mind was Reed. Joe could do no wrong in his book. Or in Kate's most of the time. But she was disappointed anyway.

And as long as Joe was stuck in L.A., he decided to stay and do some work. He came home a week later on New Year's Eve. They were supposed to go out with friends, but when she saw how tired he was, they canceled and went to bed. It didn't seem fair to make him put a tuxedo on and go out. It was just the way their life was. They lived around Joe's trips and his inability to stick to plans. He was always either coming or going or away. She didn't even complain, but somehow it took a toll nonetheless.

They celebrated their anniversary, and then it all started again. He was gone for most of January, half of February, all of March, three weeks in April, and four in May. She complained about it repeatedly and when she sat down and counted in June, they had been together three weeks in six months. And she was beginning to wonder if he was doing it to escape her. It seemed inconceivable to her that anyone had to be away as much as he was. And she said as much to Joe. All he could hear was her criticism, and all he could feel was the guilt that was a primal part of him. She was beginning to seem like a mother he had failed. It was beginning to seem impossible to run his business and meet her needs as well. And she was refusing to understand that it was just the nature of his work, and what he loved to do. He had to be in Tokyo, Hong Kong, Madrid, Paris, London, Rome, Milan, L.A. Even if she had gone with him, he never stayed in any city for more than a few days. She went on a couple of trips with him that year, but she was always sitting in a hotel room waiting for him, and eating room service alone. It made more sense for her to stay home with her kids.

She tried talking to him, but he was sick of hearing it, and being made to feel guilty, and she was tired of his being gone. She loved him more than she ever had, but the last couple of years had taken a toll on both of them. Her accident the year before had ripped them apart, and they'd found their way back to each other again, but the same spark wasn't there anymore. She was thirty-three years old, living with a man she never saw. And he was forty-five, at the height of his career. She knew she had another twenty years of it, and it would get worse, maybe even a lot worse, before it got better. He had opened up new vistas in aviation, and was adding more routes, designing even more extraordinary planes, and he seemed to have less and less time for her. She didn't want to complain about it anymore, but three weeks in six months didn't give them enough time. No matter how good his reasons were, and they were most of the time, he just wasn't there.

"I want to be with you, Joe," she said sadly when he came home for a few days in June. It was an all too familiar refrain. She wanted to find a compromise so they could be together more, but Joe had too much on his mind to discuss it with her. He was more involved in his business than ever, rather than less, and he liked it that way. He was on his way to London the next day. He didn't tell her that for the rest of the year, he would be traveling even more. The fight seemed to have gone out of both of them.

It wasn't about doing battle, but accepting what they had. And other than the feelings they'd had for each other for sixteen years, they never had enough time together anymore to enjoy each other, or build anything. He had long since stopped trying to push her into traveling with him. The kids were still small, and needed her, and she hated leaving them. Reed was six, and Stephanie was almost four, and Joe knew that for another fifteen years or so, she was going to have a hard time leaving them. From what he could see, as he looked ahead, they were going to be pulled apart a thousand ways for another fifteen or twenty years. Their lives were going separate ways, and no matter how hard she swam to keep up with him, or how much he cared, they were so far apart most of the time, they couldn't even see each other anymore.

She came to California to see him in July, and she brought the kids. She took them to Disneyland, and Joe took all of them up in a fabulous new plane that had just been built. But halfway through their trip, Joe had to leave for Hong Kong for an emergency. He flew straight to London from there, and Kate took the children to the Cape. Joe didn't come to Cape Cod at all that summer. He couldn't stand her mother anymore, and told Kate bluntly that he wasn't going there again. And they came home earlier than usual that summer, because her father got very sick.

Joe seemed to be on the go constantly, and it was mid-September before their paths crossed again, and he actually came home to spend three weeks in New York. But when she saw him this time, she knew something had changed. At first, she thought it was another woman, but after the first week he'd been home, she realized it was something far worse. Joe just couldn't do it anymore. He couldn't have the career he wanted and worry about her. In the end, he had chosen to escape. The price of loving her, or anyone, was simply too great.

He had been swept away by the tides of his career, the airplanes he had built had taken over the industry all over the world. The airline he had started eleven years before was the biggest and most successful of its kind. Joe had created a monster that had devoured both of them. He knew he had a choice at that point, the world he had created for himself, or her. And the moment she knew that, and looked in his eyes, she felt an icy chill in the air. The worst of it was that she knew he still loved her, and she still felt everything she ever had for him, but he had flown so far away from her that there was no way for her to reach him again. If he wanted her, he had to find a way to bring her with him. And he had figured out several months before that it wasn't possible. No matter how much he loved her, he just couldn't do it anymore. He felt too guilty leaving her all the time, seldom seeing her, explaining it, apologizing, and never being there for her kids. It was why, he realized, instinctively he had never wanted children of his own, and was actually relieved when she lost the twins. He couldn't have it all, he had discovered, and more than that, he couldn't give Kate what she needed or what she deserved.

He had been thinking about it all summer, and when he saw her in New York, it nearly tore his heart out, but he knew he was sure. The answer had been a long time coming because the questions were too hard. If she had asked him if he still loved her, he would have had to say he did. But her mother had called it correctly from the beginning. And so had he. In the end, Joe's first love was his planes. And what he had wanted from Kate, and to share with her, had been an impossible dream.

It took him days to say it to her, but finally he did. The night before he left for London, to acquire a small airline there, he saw Kate lying next to him in their bed, and knew he could never come back to her again. He would rather have shot her than say the words to her, but if for no other reason than that he loved her, he knew he had to free himself, and her.

"Kate." She turned to him as he said her name, and it was as though she knew before he spoke. She had seen something terrifying in his eyes for three weeks, and had done everything she could not to provoke him this time. She had tried to stay small and stay away from him, and not anger him. They hadn't had a fight in months. But it had nothing to do with fighting, or not loving her. It had to do with him. He wanted more in his life than he was willing to share with her. He had nothing left to give. In sixteen years of loving her, he had given what he had, or could. The rest of what was left he wanted for himself. And he no longer wanted to apologize or explain or have to comfort her. He knew how abandoned she felt when he was gone, but he no longer cared. Meeting her needs and his own was just too much work for him.

Kate turned to look at him without saying a word. She looked like a deer that was about to be killed.

He took a breath and plunged. It was never going to be better saying it to her some other time. It could only get worse. There would be Thanksgiving and Christmas, and their anniversary, and holidays he didn't even know or care about, and then the summer and Cape Cod again. He had been married to her for three and a half years, and as it turned out, it was all he wanted from her, and all he wanted to give. He had been right from the first, he didn't want to be married or have kids, even hers, much as he had come to love them. But he didn't love any of them enough to stay with them. All he really needed and wanted in his life were planes. It was easier and safer for him. With only planes in his life, he would never get hurt. His own fears were greater than his need for her.

"I'm leaving you, Kate," he said so softly that she didn't hear him at first. She just stared at him, thinking she had misheard the words. She had felt something coming for days, and she thought it was something like a long trip he was afraid to tell her about, but she had never expected this.

"What did you just say?" She felt crazy for a minute, as though the whole world had spun out of control. He couldn't possibly have said what she thought she just heard. But he had.

"I said I'm leaving you," he couldn't look at her as he said it, and she stared at him. "I can't do this anymore, Kate." As he said it, he looked back at her again, and he almost cringed when he saw the look in her eyes. It was the same look he had seen in the hospital in Connecticut when she discovered her babies had died. And probably the look on her face as a child when her father committed suicide. It was a look of total devastation, and the ultimate abandonment. And he felt wracked with guilt again doing that to her. But rather than making him feel closer to her, his own guilt drove them further apart.

"Why?" It was all she could say. She felt as though a scalpel had just sliced right through her heart. It was as though he had pulled it right out of her and dropped it on the floor. She could hardly catch her breath. "Why are you saying this to me? Is there someone else?" But she knew even before he answered her that it was about something much more profound than that. Something he didn't want and had never wanted to have. He had everything he had ever wanted now, just as she had the day she married him. And only one of them was going to get to keep the gift life had given them. The gift she had given him from her heart was one he no longer wanted from her. It was as simple as that. For him.

"There's no one else, Kate. There isn't even us anymore. You were right. I'm gone all the time. The truth is I can't be here. And you can't be with me." The real truth was he wanted his life to himself. He wanted work and not love. The price he had to pay for love was too high for him. He had to allow himself to feel, and he didn't want to feel anything.

"Is that what this is about? If I could be with you, would you want to stay married to me?" She was frantically thinking about sharing the kids with Andy equally. Whatever it took, even if it meant giving up time with them, she didn't want to lose Joe. But he was slowly shaking his head. He had to be honest with her. It was all they had left. He was trading honesty for love.

"It's not that, Kate. It's about me, and who I want to be when I grow up. Your mother was right. And I guess I was too. The planes come first. Maybe that's why she always hated me so much, or distrusted me, because she knew that this was who I really am. I've been hiding it from both of us, mostly from myself. I can't be what you need, and you're young enough to find someone else. I can't do this anymore."

"Are you serious? Just like that? Go out and find someone else? I love you, Joe. I have since I was seventeen years old. You don't just walk away from that." She started to cry as she said it to him, but he didn't reach out for her. It would only have made things worse, or so he thought.

"Sometimes you do walk away, Kate. Sometimes you have to take a good look at who you are, and what you want, and what you don't have. I don't have what it takes to be married to you, or anyone else, and I'm tired of feeling guilty about it." He was sure, as he sat in bed with her, that he would never marry again. In marrying her, he had made a huge mistake. She was so loving and so giving, and she wanted so much from him. And all he really wanted was to build and fly his planes. It sounded childish when he said it out loud, and incredibly selfish, but it was enough for him.

"I don't care how much you're gone," she said reasonably, "I can keep myself busy with the kids. Joe, you can't just throw us away. I love you . . . the kids love you. . . . I don't care how little we see each other, I'd rather be married to you than anyone else." But he couldn't say the same. He knew he wanted freedom more than anything. The freedom to continue building his empire, and design extraordinary planes, the freedom not to love her anymore. He had given all he had to give. He had realized that summer that he'd been faking it for the last year. He didn't want to do that to her, or to himself. He had nothing left. He'd been running on fumes. He hated calling her, hated being there, hated getting home for holidays, making excuses when he couldn't get back for things that were important to her. He had given her nearly four years. It had been enough for him.

She sat in bed looking shell-shocked, and when he was through, she started to cry again. She could sense with everything she'd ever felt for him that she had already lost him, perhaps had years before. He had slipped away quietly one day, and she had never seen him go. And now all he was doing was picking up his things. The one thing he didn't want to take with him was her. She had no idea what she was going to do with the rest of her life. Die, she hoped. After being married to him, and seeing her dreams come true, no matter how hard it was sometimes, she couldn't imagine living without him. But she knew she had to now. It was as though someone had come to tell her he had died. In a way, he had. He had opted for work and success, and not love. It seemed a poor choice to her.

"You and the kids can stay in the apartment for as long as you like. I'm going to stay in California for the rest of the year." He had asked Hazel that morning if she would move out to L.A. till the end of the year. She had grandchildren in New York, but she had thought it would be a fun thing to do. She'd had no idea he was planning to leave Kate behind permanently.

Kate looked horrified. "You've already decided all that? When did you make up your mind?"

"Probably a long time ago. I think I knew this summer. And when I came back to New York, I thought it was the right time. There's no point hanging on anymore. I think I've been gone for a long time." What had happened? What had she done? How had she failed him? It was impossible to believe that she hadn't done something terrible to him. But the truth was she hadn't, other than marry him. It was the one thing he didn't want, and thought he had. But he'd been wrong. She fascinated him, she intrigued him, she excited him, but that was all it had ever been for him. He had been drawn to her like moth to flame, but he wanted the sky rather than her warmth, and he had flown away.

She lay beside him and cried quietly all night. She stroked his hair, and looked at him as he slept. If he had been anyone else, she would have thought he was insane. But there was something very cold and calculating about what he had said. It was the only way he knew to save himself, and it reminded her of their ending in New Jersey years before. Not knowing what else to do, Joe shut down emotionally and ran away. She had been dispensed with, dismissed, as she understood it, he didn't want her anymore. It was the cruelest thing anyone had ever done to her. In some ways, even crueler than her father's suicide. In Kate's eyes, the reasons Joe had offered weren't adequate to justify his leaving her, although they were to him. Gouging her out of his heart, no matter how painful to him or her, was all he knew how to do.

She never slept all night, and at first light she got up, washed her face, and then went back to bed. He lay close to her, as he always did, when he woke up. But this time, he said nothing, he simply rolled over and got out of bed.

And when he left the apartment for his flight to London, he said goodbye to her very carefully. He didn't want to raise any false hopes that he'd change his mind. He was leaving her forever, and she knew it to her very soul.

"I love you, Joe," she said, and for an instant he saw the girl he had once met, in her pale blue satin evening gown, with the dark auburn hair. He remembered her eyes that night, and they were the same ones he saw now. But as he looked into them he saw immeasurable pain. But she looked scarcely different than she had sixteen years before. "I'll always love you," she whispered, as she realized she was seeing him for the last time. They would never be together this way again. He had purposely not made love to her during his entire stay in New York. He hadn't wanted to mislead her and he didn't want to now. He was sending her back to her own life, so he could reclaim his.

"Take care of yourself," he said softly, taking one last long look at her. It was hard to let her go, in his own way he had loved her as best he could. Not the way she had loved him, but in the best ways he knew how. It would have been enough for her, but not for him. The funny thing was, he wanted less and not more. "I was right, you know," he said, as she stood looking up at him, engraving him in her memory, the face she loved so much, the eyes, the cheekbones, the cleft chin. "It was an impossible dream. It always was."

"It didn't have to be," she said, her blue eyes blazing at him. Even now, in so much pain, she was more beautiful than he wanted to see. More beautiful than he needed her to be. "We could still have this, Joe. We could have it all." What she said was true, he knew, but he didn't want it anymore. He told himself he had enough without her.

"I don't want it, Kate," he said cruelly, but he wanted her to understand, he couldn't hurt her anymore. He couldn't stand the guilt or the pain.

She watched him without saying another word as he walked out and closed the door.

23

AFTER LEAVING KATE, Joe went to California for six months, and moved to London for five months after that. He offered her a huge settlement, which she gracefully declined. She had her own money, and she didn't want anything from him. All she had ever wanted for sixteen years was to be his wife. She had been that for four, which was all Joe Allbright had to give, or so he believed when he left.

Kate had caused him so much pain, and inflicted such intense guilt on him, that all Joe wanted was to flee. He had wanted her more than anything, loved her more than he had ever dared, given more than he had known he was capable of. And in spite of everything, it hadn't been enough for her. For all the years of their marriage, he felt she had wanted more and more and more of him. It had terrified him, and brought up all of his old wounds. Every time he listened to her, he could hear his cousin's voice telling him what a rotten kid he was, and how disappointed she was in him. Just seeing Kate, whenever he came home, reminded him of how inadequate he had felt as a child, and what a failure he believed he was as a human being and a man. It was a demon he'd been fleeing all his life. And even the vast empire he had built couldn't protect him from it. The pain he saw in Kate's eyes catapulted him back to the worst of his boyhood again and conjured up all his guilts. In the end, it was easier for him to be alone than to be tormented by her, or cause her pain. Every time he knew he hurt or disappointed her, it was agony for him. And there was a selfish side to him as well. He didn't want to meet anyone's needs but his own.

It took Kate months to understand what had happened to them. The divorce had been filed by then, and they had been separated for nearly a year. He had refused to see her during that time, but called occasionally to check on her and the kids. For months, Kate had wandered around the house they'd rented, in a daze. The hardest part was learning to live without him again. It was like learning to live without air.

She thought constantly about what had happened to them, trying to understand her part in it. And through the months of her despair, the light began to dawn, slowly at first, and in time she could see how her reaching out and wanting more time with him had panicked him. Without meaning to, she had terrified him. Not knowing how else to deal with her, or stop the deadly dance, he could think of nothing else but to run away. He had never wanted to do that to her, but in the end, he knew that he would hurt her more, and himself, if he stayed.

At first, all Kate could think about was what she had lost when he left, and for months her own panic grew worse. She thought about losing her father years before. And she endured another blow when Clarke died in the spring. And just as she had years before, Kate's mother retreated into her own world, and all but disappeared. Kate cried herself to sleep at night, and the loneliness she felt was overpowering. But as the months drifted by, she slowly found her feet again.

Joe had suggested she go to Reno to speed up the divorce, but she had filed it in New York instead, knowing it would take longer. It was her final act of clinging to him. She was still holding on to him by a single rapidly fraying thread. And in fact she had nothing left of him but his name.

It would have been hard to say when the change happened in her. It didn't come suddenly. It wasn't a sudden awakening. It was a slow, arduous winding path up a mountainside toward maturity and growth. And as she climbed the mountain day by day, she grew strong. The things that had once so desperately frightened her seemed less ominous. She had lost so much of what mattered most to her that abandonment was finally a monster she had faced and conquered on her own. Of all the things that terrified her, losing him had been her worst fear. But she had, and lived.

Her children were the first to see the change in her, long before Kate was even aware of it herself. She laughed more often, and cried less easily. She went on a trip to Paris with them. And this time, when Joe called when she came home, to see how they were, he heard something different in her voice. It was ephemeral and intangible, and he would have been hard put to explain what it was. But Kate no longer sounded terrified or desperate about being alone. She had gone on endless walks in Paris, down backstreets and on boulevards, thinking about him. She hadn't seen him in nearly a year by then. He had stayed well away from her, and had every intention of never seeing her again, although he had moved back to an apartment in New York.

"You sound happy, Kate," Joe said quietly. He couldn't help wondering, in spite of himself, if there was a new man in her life. He wanted that for her, and yet at the same time, he hoped not. He had avoided all the available women he had met for the past year. He didn't want to get tangled up with anyone. Perhaps ever again, he told himself. As always, for Joe, it was easier to be alone. But he had missed Kate, and the warmth she brought to his life, for many months. What kept him away from her was that the price of being with her and loving her was too high for him. He was certain that to approach, or even see her again, would only sear his wings again.

"I think I am happy," Kate laughed. "God knows why. My mother is driving me crazy, she's so lonely without Clarke. Stevie cut most of her hair off last week. And Reed knocked out both of his front teeth playing baseball with a friend."

"That sounds about right," Joe laughed. He had forgotten what it was like living with them. But at the same time, he had not.

As Kate did every morning when she woke up, he remembered only too well what it was like waking up next to her. He had not touched a woman for an entire year. Kate had begun seeing other men for dinner from time to time, but she could not bring herself to do more than that. They all paled in comparison to him. She couldn't imagine being with anyone else. And when she came home at night, she was relieved to climb into her bed alone. In truth, being alone no longer seemed menacing to her. It had grown comfortable, she had the children and friends. She had looked loss in the eye and she had not died of it. And slowly, she realized that nothing would ever frighten her in just that way again. She could see it all so much more clearly now. She could see how frightening being married had been for him. She wanted to tell him how sorry she was. But she knew from everything he had said to her that it was too late to make any difference to him.

It was a month later, when she was writing quietly one day, in a journal she kept, that Joe called about some detail of the divorce. She had continued to refuse to take money from him. Clarke had left half his fortune to her, and she had never wanted to take anything from Joe. He suggested his lawyer send some documents to her. It was about a piece of property he had just sold, and he wanted her to sign a quit-claim deed. She agreed, but for a moment on the phone, her voice sounded odd.

"Am I ever going to see you again?" she asked, sounding forlorn. She still missed seeing him and touching him, the smell of him, the feel of him, but she accepted now that he was gone forever from her life. She knew she would not die of it, but it still felt like losing an essential part

of her, like a leg or an arm, or her heart. But she was entirely prepared
to go on without him. She had no other choice, and she had made her
peace with it at last.

"Do you suppose we should see each other, Kate?" he asked, hesitating. For more than a year, he had thought of her as dangerous. It wasn't
that she meant to be, but he was afraid that if he even saw her he
would fall in love with her all over again, and the deadly dance would
begin again. It was a risk he was no longer willing to take. And he was
far too cognizant of her charms. "It probably isn't a good idea," he said
quietly before she could answer him.

"Probably not," she agreed. And for once she didn't sound devastated, or distraught. There was no desperation in her voice. No subtle
reproach to cause him guilt. She sounded peaceful, and sensible, and
calm. She went on talking to him about a new subdivision he had
formed, and a new plane he had designed. And after he hung up, it
gnawed at him. He had never heard her sound quite like that. She
sounded suddenly grown up. And he realized that, even more than he
had, she had moved on. She had found freedom finally. And in losing
him, she had found peace. She had faced the worst of her fears, looked
the monsters squarely in the eye, and had somehow managed to make
peace not only with herself, but with him, and go on with her life. She
knew there was no chance he would ever come back. She had given up
the dream.

He lay awake long into the night, thinking about her, and in the
morning he told himself how unkind it had been of him not to at least
see the kids. It wasn't their fault that his marriage to their mother
hadn't worked out. He realized then that she had never reproached him
for it. She had begrudged him nothing in the past year. She had asked
nothing of him. She had fallen down the abyss she had always feared,
and instead of hanging on to him to survive, and strangling him, she
had let go. The thought of it mystified him, and all he could ask

himself as he went to work that day was why. He couldn't help thinking that it had to be because she was clinging to another man. There had to be. He had felt devoured by her needs. But late that afternoon, he called her again. The same document was still sitting on his desk. He had forgotten to give it to his secretary the day before to send to Kate.

When he called her, Kate answered the phone. He always felt some trepidation when he called. He knew that one day it would be answered by a man. But Kate sounded distracted and relaxed when she picked up the phone.

"Oh . . . hi . . . sorry . . . I was in the tub." Her words instantly conjured up images he had been repressing for months. He no longer wanted to think of her that way. There was no reason to. As far as Joe was concerned, she was gone. It had to be that way. There had been no other choice, for either of them. He knew he had done the right thing. He had saved himself. If he hadn't, she would have destroyed his life, and driven him insane. The guilt and complaints she had constantly hurled at him had been worse than bullets or knives to Joe. In the end, he knew they would have cost him everything he was. But she sounded so innocent. It was hard to believe that she had presented such a dire threat little more than a year before. His memory of the pain and guilt he had felt was finally growing dim.

"I forgot to send you that paper to sign yesterday," he said apologetically, trying not to think of her standing naked at the phone. He wondered if she was wrapped in a towel, or wearing a robe. He stared out the window, and all he could see was Kate as he held the phone. "I'll drop it by." He could have sent it by messenger, or mailed it to her. They both knew that. But Kate sounded casual as she smiled at her end.

"Do you want to come up when you drop it off?" There was a long empty pause, as Joe thought about it, and her. His instincts told him to hang up on her, and run away, to resist all of her unspoken and long since unseen charms. He didn't want her in his life again, and yet she still was. He was still married to her, and she was his wife.

"I . . . uh . . . is that a good idea? Seeing each other, I mean." A little voice in Joe's head was telling him to run.

"I don't see why not. I think I can handle it. What about you?" She might as well have said "I'm over you," and Joe had no way of knowing it, but she was not, and thought she'd never be. But there was no point saying that to him.

"I suppose it would be all right," he said, sounding distant again. But Kate didn't seem to mind. He no longer frightened her. He couldn't leave her now. He already had. All the worst possible things had happened to her, all the things she used to have nightmares about, and she had survived.

More important, even from the distance, she had finally understood who Joe was. And even if she never saw him again, there was no question in her mind. She knew she would always love him, he would always be the standard against which she would measure other men. He was the biggest and the best, the only man she had ever truly loved, and the one she had accepted that she couldn't have. Knowing that, and that it was in part her fault that she had lost him, had been hard blows to recover from, but nonetheless she had. And she had come out of it, not broken but strong. He had never heard her sound quite like that before. Even over the phone, he knew there was something different about her. She no longer sounded like the wife he had left, but a much loved old friend. It made him long for her suddenly as he hadn't in months.

"When do you want to come by?" Kate asked hospitably.

"When will the kids be home?" he asked, feeling lonelier than he had in months. Suddenly it was Joe who felt the full impact of the loss, and he wasn't even sure why. Why now? Until then, he had protected himself so well.

"They're at Andy's this week," Kate said apologetically about Stevie and Reed. "Maybe, if we don't throw things at each other, you could come by and see them another time." He could hear in her voice that she was laughing at him.

"I'd like that," he said happily. He felt young and foolish suddenly, and then reminded himself instantly of how dangerous she was. For a moment, he thought of sending her the papers by messenger after all. But Kate continued to sound calm, because she was.

"How about five?" she asked.

"Five what?" He was panicking. He was afraid to see her again. What if she blamed him for everything that had gone wrong? What if she told him what a bastard he had been? What if she accused him of abandoning her? But there was none of that in Kate's voice as she laughed.

"Five o'clock, silly. You sound a little distracted. Are you all right?"

"I'm fine. And five o'clock will be fine. I won't stay long."

"I'll leave the door open," she teased, "you don't even have to sit down." She knew he was panicking, but not why. It never occurred to her that he might be nervous about seeing her. She loved him anyway. His vulnerability and fears only made him more lovable. She had learned so much. Her only regret was not being able to share it with him. She knew she would never get that chance, and doubted if, after that afternoon, she would ever see him again. Once his quitclaim deed was signed, he had no reason to see her again.

"See you at five," he said, sounding businesslike, and Kate smiled as she hung up the phone. She knew it was ridiculous to still love a man who was divorcing her. It made no sense, but nothing in their lives ever had. She was thirty-four years old, and she had finally grown up, it saddened her to realize that the woman she had brought to their marriage had been a frightened child. It had been unfair to both of them. She had wanted him to make up for all the pain she'd had as a little girl. There was no way he could do that for her, and no way she could soothe his wounds, while she was crying out herself. They had been two children, frightened in the night, and all Joe had known how to do was run away. She loved him in spite of it, and the soul searching she had done had served her well.

Joe arrived promptly at five o'clock, with his documents in hand. He seemed awkward at first, but all it did was remind her of the first time they'd met. She kept a safe distance from him, and made no attempt to approach. They sat and talked quietly, about the children, his work, and a new plane he wanted to design. It had been a longtime dream for him. Her dreams had all been of him. She was surprised herself to find how easy it was to love him as he was, just sitting there, a little stiff at first, and gradually he warmed up. He had been there for nearly an hour when she offered him a drink, and he smiled. Just seeing him touched her heart. She would have loved to put her arms around him and tell him she would always love him, but she wouldn't have dared. She sat across the room from him, admiring him, and loving him, like a beautiful bird she could see but never touch. If she did, she knew he would fly away. He had given her that chance, more than once, and she had wounded him. She knew that chance would never come her away again. All she could do now was love him silently, and wish him well. It was enough, and all she had left to give. It was all Joe would accept from her ever again.

It was nearly eight o'clock when Joe left. She signed the papers for him, and was surprised when he called her back the next day. He sounded awkward again, but this time he relaxed more rapidly, and then nearly strangled on the words when he invited her to lunch. She was amazed. Kate had no way of knowing it, but she had haunted him all night. She was everything he had always loved in her, and she hadn't frightened him. He wasn't sure if her newfound independence was a trick, or something he wanted to see in her. But he could sense that something had changed profoundly in her, and the aura he sensed around her was no longer hunger or guilt or pain or need, but warmth and peace with him and herself. He remembered now what he had loved in her, and was wondering if they could be friends.

"Lunch?" She sounded more than a little stunned. But after they talked for a while, it sounded feasible to her as well. She was only slightly afraid of falling more deeply in love with him again, but she was still in love with him anyway. She had nothing to lose. All she had at risk was more pain. But she trusted him now, more than she had before, and Kate realized it was because she trusted herself. She could cope with whatever life would bring. That was new, too, and Joe sensed it in her.

They had lunch at the Plaza two days after he called. And went for a walk in the park the following weekend. They talked about the mess they'd made and what might have been, what couldn't be. And she finally had a chance to apologize to him. She had wanted to for months, and was grateful for the opportunity to tell him how deeply she regretted the pain she had caused him. It pained her almost as much as it had him to know how she had frightened him, and wounded him. She had punished herself a thousand times in the past year for all she hadn't understood about him. And she had finally begun to forgive herself for her stupidity, and Joe for his.

"I know. I was so stupid, Joe. I didn't understand. I kept grabbing at you, and the more I did, the more you wanted to run away. I don't know why I didn't see it then. It took me a long time to figure it out. I wish I'd been smarter." Knowing how terrified he was of guilt and entanglement, it was a miracle that he had stayed as long as he had.

"I made some mistakes too," he said honestly. "And I was in love with you." Kate felt a quiver in her heart as she noticed the past tense, but that was fair too. It came as no surprise. It was an aberration of some kind, she knew, that she was still in love with him, and suspected she might always be. She felt that after all that had happened, she no longer deserved another chance with him.

They went back to the house afterward, and he saw Stevie and Reed for the first time since he'd left. And they squealed in delight the moment they saw him. It was a happy afternoon. And she was quiet for a long time after he left. She wanted to believe they could be friends. She had no right to anything more from him, and she told herself it would be enough for her. On his way home, he was trying to convince himself of the same thing. It had to be. He knew they could not try again. It was still too dangerous, and potentially, too painful for him, and always would be.

Their friendship continued for the next two months. They went to dinner occasionally, and lunch on Saturdays. She made dinner on Sunday nights for him and the kids. And when he went away, she thought of him, but it was no longer the drama it had once been. In fact, it was no drama at all. She was no longer sure what they shared, but whatever it was, they hid it behind the mask of friendship for two months. It was comfortable for them.

It was a rainy Saturday afternoon when the children were with Andy in Connecticut, when Joe came by unexpectedly to lend her a book they had talked about the week before. She thanked him, and offered him a cup of tea. It wasn't all he wanted from her, but he had no idea how to walk across the bridge from friendship to something new. They both knew that they could no longer go back to where they once had been. If they ventured forth at all, it had to be to a different place. And Joe was stumped as to how to proceed.

It all happened surprisingly naturally. She had just poured the tea into a cup, when she looked up and saw Joe standing very close to her.

He said nothing as she set the teapot down, and then he gently pulled her close to him.

"How crazy would it be, Kate, if I told you I'm still in love with you?" She held her breath as she heard the words.

"Very," she said quietly, nestling close to him, trying not to remember the things they could no longer share, the parts of him she could no longer see. "I was terrible to you," she said remorsefully.

"I was a fool. I acted like a kid. I was scared, Kate."

"Me too," she confessed in a whisper, as her arms went around him. "We were so stupid, I wish we hadn't been . . . I wish I could have known then all that I do now. I always loved you," she said softly, feeling closer to him than she had in a year.

"I always loved you." He could feel the silk of her hair on his cheek as he held her close. "I just didn't know how to handle it. I felt so guilty all the time. It made me want to run away from you." He paused for a moment and then went on. "Do you really think we've learned something, Kate?" But they both knew they had. He could see it in her and feel it in himself. They were no longer afraid.

"You're wonderful just the way you are, and I can love you just like this," she said with a smile, "whether you're here or not. Your being gone doesn't scare me anymore. I wish I'd done it differently," Kate said mournfully.

He didn't answer her, but kissed her instead. He felt safe with her, probably for the first time since they'd met. He'd always been in love with her, but he had never felt safe with her, not like this. They stood in the kitchen, kissing for a long time, and then without saying more to her, he put an arm around her and they walked to her bedroom, and then he looked at her, hesitating. It brought back so many memories, just kissing her.

"I'm not sure what I'm doing here . . . we're probably both crazy . . .

and I'm not sure I'll survive it if we mess this up again . . . but I have this crazy feeling . . . I don't think we will this time," Joe said.

"I never thought you'd trust me again." Kate's eyes were enormous as she looked at him.

"Neither did I," he said, and kissed her again. But he did trust her now. She knew him better than she ever had during their entire marriage. He was safe with her finally and she with him. And they both knew it. They had never stopped loving each other. The only frightening thought, to both of them, was how close they had come to losing each other. They had gone right to the edge of the precipice, and then stopped. The hand of Providence had been kind to them.

He spent the weekend with her, and when the kids came home, they were happy to find him there. The rest slid quietly into place again, as though he had never left. He had sold their apartment in New York months before, and he moved into her house for a while, and eventually they bought a house together, and moved in. He went on his trips, and was sometimes gone for weeks at a time. But Kate didn't mind. They talked on the phone, and she was happy, just as she had known she would be. And so was he. This time, it worked, and felt like a miracle to them. And when they had arguments, they were roaring ones, but like fireworks they lit up the sky and were forgotten quickly afterward. They were happy together, happier than they had ever been. They had quietly canceled the divorce as soon as he moved back in.

It had been a good life, for both of them, and it was nearly seventeen years since the time they'd spent apart. They had been right to trust each other one last time. The years they had spent together since had proven them right.

When the children left for their own lives, they had more time alone. Kate traveled with him, but she was always comfortable at home. There were no more demons in her life. They had slain their dragons long before, but not without considerable grief for both of them. The early years had taken a toll on them for a time, but in the end it made them both grateful for what they had learned. She had learned not to pull on him, not to entangle him, not to bring up the ghosts of his past, rattle the sabers of guilt at him. And proud bird that he was, he flew down from his skies and came as close as he could to Kate. In their later years, it was close enough for her, and all she wanted or needed from him. The wounds had been healed at last.

They had been blessed with a great gift, a rare love, a bond so powerful that even they, in their foolishness, had been unable to sever it. The storm had raged, and the house they had built stood strong. Joe and Kate understood each other, as few people did. It was ultimately the pearl of great price that people search a lifetime for. They had found each other and lost each other, and found each other again, in a dozen ways, a dozen times. The miracle was that they had been given one last chance. One final, final chance, and there was no doubt in either of their minds, right to the end, that they had won, or how lucky they had been. They had come so close to losing everything, and their last chance had been the right one finally. For both of them. They had found not only love, but peace. This time, the miracle was theirs to keep.

EPILOGUE

JOE'S FUNERAL HAD all the pomp and circumstance that was due to him. Kate had put it together in every detail. It was her final gift to him. And as she left the house with Stephanie and Reed in the limousine, Kate stared out the window at the snow, thinking about him, and all he had been to her. She found herself thinking back to Cape Cod, and the war, the time they'd spent in New Jersey, building his company. She had still understood so little about him then. She could have painted a portrait of him now in rainbow hues. She knew him better than she had known anyone. It was inconceivable to her that he was gone.

As she stepped out of the car with Reed and Stephanie, she felt panic begin to clutch her soul. What would she do now with the rest of her life? How would she survive without him? They had been given a reprieve seventeen years before, halfway through the time they'd shared. She had almost lost him then. And if she had, her life would have been so different for all these years. Two lives forever changed. Even Joe had acknowledged more than once that it would have been a terrible loss to them.

The church was filled with dignitaries and important men. The governor was delivering the eulogy, and the President had said he would try to come, but in the end had sent the Vice President instead. The President was traveling in the Middle East, and even for Joe, it was too far to come. But he had sent a telegram to Kate.

Kate and her children sat in the front pew, with a sea of people filling the church. And she knew that Andy and Julie were there somewhere. Her mother had died four years before. And Kate had caught a glimpse of Lindbergh's widow Anne, as she walked in, wearing a black suit and a hat, still in deep mourning herself. Joe had spoken at Charles's funeral only four months before. It seemed a strange irony that the two greatest pilots of all time had died within months of each other. It was a grievous loss to the world, but far more so to Kate.

Joe's office had helped her to arrange some of the details, and the service was beautiful, the words spoken about him powerful. Tears rolled slowly down Kate's cheeks, as she clutched her children's hands. It made her think of her father's funeral when she had been a little girl, when her mother had been devastated and remote. It had been Joe who healed her heart finally. Joe who had opened her eyes and taught her so much about herself and the world. She had conquered Everest with him. And the life they had shared had been extraordinary in a thousand ways.

The people who had come to pay their respects to him hung back silently, as Kate followed the casket slowly down the main aisle of the church, and watched them put it in the hearse. The smell of roses hung heavy in the air. She was silent and her head was bowed as she stepped back into the limousine for the drive to the cemetery, and a thousand people filed quietly out of the church. They had heard things about him from the eulogies that most of them had already known, his flying feats, his war record, his many accomplishments, his genius, the way he had changed the face of aviation. They said all the things Joe would have wanted said about him. But Kate was the only one in his life who had ever truly known Joe. He was the only man she had ever really loved. And for all the pain they'd caused each other in the early years, they had shared a life finally that had brought them both immeasurable joy. She had learned everything she had to know. And he had been happy with her. She had loved him well. Knowing that brought her some sense of comfort now. But she still could not imagine the rest of her life without Joe.

Stephanie and Reed spoke quietly in the car on the way to the cemetery, and left their mother alone. Kate sat lost in thought, watching the wintry countryside slide by, thinking of all the memories they'd shared. The tapestry of their life had been rich beyond compare.

Only Kate and her children had gone to the cemetery. Kate had wanted to be there with them alone, and with her memories of Joe. Because of the explosion, they were burying an empty casket. It was a final gesture of respect, as a minister said a brief blessing and then left. And in kindness to her, Stephanie and Reed walked back to the limousine and left her alone.

"How am I going to do this, Joe?" she whispered as she stood looking at the casket. Where would she go? How would she live without seeing him again? It was like being a child again when they had buried her father, and she could feel ancient wounds coming to life again. She stood there for a long time, thinking about Joe, and then it was as though she could sense him standing next to her. He was the man she had always dreamed of, the hero she had fallen in love with when she was barely more than a girl, the man she had waited to come home from the war, the man she had nearly lost and then found again, by miracle, seventeen years before. There had been a lot of miracles in their life together, and he had been the best of them. And she knew, as she stood there, that he had taken her heart with him. There would never be anyone in her life like Joe. He had taught her all of life's important lessons, healed all her wounds, as she had healed his. He had touched deep into her soul. He had taught her not only about love, but about freedom. He had taught her about letting go. When she loved him most, she had set him free, and eventually he had always come home.

She knew as she stood there that this was his final freedom, his last flight away from her. She had to let him go again. And in doing so, he would never leave her, just as he really hadn't left her before. He had come home to her, flown away, and come back again. And even when he was gone, he loved her, just as he loved her now, and she loved him. It had become a love that was strong and sure, and needed no promises or words. It just was.

She had learned the dance steps almost to perfection finally. She had learned just how to do it for him. How to stand back. How to let him be. How to love him. How to let him come and go, and appreciate him for all he was. She was so grateful for all that she had learned from him.

"Fly, my darling," she whispered. . . . "Fly. . . . I love you . . . ," she said as she took a single white rose and laid it on the casket they would bury in his name. And as she did, she felt her fears disappear. She knew he would never be far from her. He would fly, as he always had, in his own skies, whether or not she could see him next to her. But wherever she went, he would always be there with her. She would remember everything he had taught her, all of life's most valuable lessons. He had given her all she needed now to live on without him. And he had taught her well.

They had learned each other to perfection, loved each other in just the way that worked for them. What she'd had of him, she took with her. Just as he had taken the best of her with him. She knew without question that he would always love her, just as she would always love him. The dance was over, but it would never end.